D0051203

RACHEL LEE

wrote her first play in the third grade for a school assembly, and by the age of twelve she was hooked on writing. She's lived all over the United States, on both the East and West coasts, and now resides in Florida.

Having held jobs as a security officer, real estate agent and optician, she uses these experiences, as well as her natural flair for creativity, to write stories that are undeniably romantic. "After all, life is the biggest romantic adventure of all—and if you're open and aware, the most marvelous things are just waiting to be discovered."

A CONARD COUNTY Homecoming

RACHEL LEE

Silhouette Books

Published by Silhouette Books

America's Publisher of Contemporary Romance

SILHOUETTE BOOKS

ISBN 0-373-48394-5

by Request

A CONARD COUNTY HOMECOMING

Copyright © 1999 by Harlequin Books S.A.

The publisher acknowledges the copyright holders of the individual works as follows:

MISS EMMALINE AND THE ARCHANGEL
Copyright © 1993 by Susan Civil

IRONHEART
Copyright © 1993 by Susan Civil

Visit us at www.romance.net

Printed in U.S.A.

CONTENTS

Dear Reader,

I always think of the two books in this volume as a pair. Writing *Miss Emmaline and the Archangel* affected the writing of *Ironheart* in a most unexpected way, and I can honestly say *Ironheart* wouldn't have been the same book if *Miss Emmaline* hadn't come first.

It's not that the stories depend on each other, because they really don't. Rather, when I finished *Miss Emmaline* I was emotionally exhausted from all the deep, dark feelings I'd dealt with, so that when I turned to write *Ironheart,* I needed to write something emotionally very different.

To me, *Miss Emmaline* will always be a dark book. I never think of it without seeing the nighttime. But when I think of *Ironheart,* I think of sunshine—not because the characters didn't have any problems, but because their problems didn't take them to the darkest places of the heart, the way the ones in *Miss Emmaline* did. Emma and Gage start without any hope at all. Sara and Gideon both have a lot of hope, but life has knocked them down.

In both books the characters use their problems as a starting point for growth, though, and in both books they find the healing balm of love.

Love doesn't conquer all, but love gives us the strength to face life. That's what Emma, Gage, Sara and Gideon discover here.

Enjoy!

Rachel Lee

MISS EMMALINE
AND THE ARCHANGEL

For Dad

Chapter 1

Pain clawed at Gage Dalton with fiery talons, driving him from the stark emptiness of his apartment above the bar out into the dark emptiness of the misty night. The staircase from his door slanted down the outside of the two-story brick building, and his boot heels thudded heavily on the wood steps as he descended. The snowy alley was dark, deserted. Not even a cat prowled in the shadows.

At the foot of the stairs, he hesitated. The Friday night ruckus from the bar came clearly from around the corner, louder than it was even in his rooms, which were directly above it. Mahoney must have opened the double front doors to let in some of the refreshing, chilly night air. It wouldn't be long before a Conard County deputy would show up to quiet things down.

He stood there a little longer, listening to the noise, not wanting to be part of it, but drawn to the promise that a couple of shots of whiskey could dull his senses, numb his nerves, ease the pain. He seldom accepted that promise. Usually, he walked. There were times when it got so bad that he paced off every street in town, up one side and down the other. Conard City wasn't very large, but it was large enough that he could spend three or four hours that way without retracing a single step.

Tonight he decided to allow himself the whiskey. It would take the edge off the razor-sharp pain, would ease the chill of the night air. Turning the corner onto the sidewalk, he stepped into Mahoney's.

Silence spread around him in a slow, ever-widening wave as he walked unevenly to the bar. Gage Dalton was that kind of man. When he walked into a room, any room, other men instinctively gave him space. They sensed that he hadn't a damn thing left to lose, that he had forgotten the meaning of fear. That made him both dangerous and unpredictable. With a man like that, it was safer to leave him alone in a bubble of silence and space.

Mahoney saw him coming, and filled two shot glasses with good Scotch. Gage threw a few bills on the bar and downed the shots one after the other, like medicine. Then he turned and limped back toward the door, a tall, rangy man with a disfigured face and silver hair. Mystery hung around him like a pall.

Behind him, the silence slowly filled in with talk, but little laughter.

"Damn!" Emmaline Conard never swore, but she swore now, for the third time in as many minutes. Her car wouldn't start, it was late, and it was cold and she really didn't want to walk the five blocks to her house alone.

Which was silly, really, she told herself as she tried yet again to get the engine to turn over. The starter ground and groaned sluggishly, warning her that she was killing her battery.

"Damn!" she said again, and let her head drop against the steering wheel. She would have to walk. It wasn't as if she weren't properly dressed for the damp, cold night. Having lived in Wyoming all her life, she knew better than to go anywhere in December without adequate clothing because any unforeseen problem could become life-threatening in a climate this cold.

She was wearing boots and a parka, and warm wool slacks, sufficient for the short distance and a temperature that was only slightly below freezing. She could easily and safely walk home.

Except that she quite simply couldn't do it. She reminded herself that this was Conard City, that she knew each and every one of the five thousand souls who inhabited the county, and that she was as safe on the streets in this town as she was in her own bed. It didn't help. She had a fear of walking darkened streets alone that went far beyond reason and bordered on phobia.

So, she told herself, trying to be brisk and positive, she would just go back into the library and spend the night in her office. Or she could call the sheriff's office and ask for a deputy to drive her home. Nate Tate and his deputies were always wonderful about things like that, always ready to help a neighbor out. They wouldn't even think it odd that she didn't just walk.

Unfortunately, she also had a thing that bordered on phobia about being alone in a car with a man, even men as gallant as most of the Conard County deputies.

Nor did she want to call one of her friends, who would be bound to find it curious that Emma didn't just walk a distance that, by local standards, was insignificant.

She shuddered and tried one last time to turn the engine over. Just one more time before she gave up and faced the inevitable: an uncomfortable night on the floor in her office.

The fear was so deeply rooted in her that she had long since given up arguing with it. To this day she had no idea exactly what had happened to her, only that during her senior year at college she had awakened in the hospital to discover she had been so badly assaulted and beaten that she had been comatose for weeks. She had no memory of the days immediately preceding the assault, and only fragmented memories of the first few weeks after awakening. What she *did* have was an unreasoning fear of darkened streets and of being alone in a car with a man.

But until this very moment, neither of those fears had seemed particularly inconvenient. Now they closed around her like an iron cage.

Swearing again, she pounded on the steering wheel and gave the ignition one more try. This time the starter sounded like a windup Victrola that had completely wound down.

"Oh, damn." She sighed, sagging back against the seat. Suddenly she felt closer to tears than anger. Now she would have to cross the dark parking lot again. Admittedly, years of practice had made it easier. These days she was even able to cross it at a brisk walk rather than a dead run. But it was still a gauntlet she had to run, and once a day was enough. More than enough.

Suddenly, like a vision from her worst nightmare, a shadowy figure appeared around the corner of the library building. Emma drew a sharp breath, and her grip on the steering wheel tightened until her knuckles were white. Oh, God!

The figure stood there a moment, legs spread, backlit by a streetlight so that he was nothing but the pitch-black silhouette of a man in a cowboy hat. Then, with an uneven gait, he began to walk toward Emma's car.

Panic exploded in her head like a blinding light and she clawed desperately at the door handle. *Run!*

"Miss Emma?" The shadowy figure paused halfway across the parking lot. "Miss Emma, it's Gage Dalton. Are you having car trouble?"

Relief hit her as hard as the panic had. Gage Dalton. She knew who he was. Everybody knew who he was. The old biddies at church gossiped and speculated about him without a kernel of fact to go on beyond his disfigured face and limp. They said he looked like hell's own archangel. But everyone also knew that he worked part-time for Nate Tate at the sheriff's office, so he couldn't be a bad guy. Not a really bad guy. And at the moment, he was as good as a uniformed deputy, as far as Emma was concerned.

But relief had left her weak and shaking, and she couldn't

seem to move or talk. All she could do was sit there with the car door half-open, and tremble and try to cope with the conviction that she had somehow just escaped the reenactment of a nightmare she couldn't remember.

"Miss Emma?" He stepped a little closer.

Everyone in the county called her Miss Emma. She didn't know how it had started—probably with the children who came to the library—but after nearly a decade as the Conard County librarian, she was addressed that way by nearly everyone.

"Mis-mister Dalton," she finally managed to gasp.

Her acknowledgement gave him permission to approach. He did so slowly, unthreateningly, hands safely tucked into the pockets of his leather bomber jacket. When he got to within a yard, he squatted facing her, his movement hesitant, betraying his pain. "Sounded like you ran your battery to death."

She nodded, still trying to get control of her breathing. "It wouldn't start, and I just kept trying, like an idiot."

"I've done that a time or two myself. Come on, I'll walk you home."

With those simple words he solved her entire problem. Emma rose on shaky legs and reached for her briefcase and purse. Gage took the briefcase from her with a polite "Let me," and waited while she locked the car.

As they turned the corner from the parking lot onto the sidewalk, the streetlight illuminated the disfigured side of Gage Dalton's face. His cheek looked as if it had been badly burned, and a jagged scar ran from his temple to his jaw. Emma snatched her gaze away, not wanting him to catch her staring. His limp concerned her far more than his disfigurement, anyway. It surely couldn't be comfortable for him to walk this distance.

The silence between them didn't seem to bother him, but it disturbed Emma. Having grown up in this county, she was accustomed to friendly conversation with everyone she met and unaccustomed to silence. Worse, it felt churlish and unneighborly not to be friendly when he was going out of his way to escort her home safely.

He was an…intimidating man, though. Not frightening, though she imagined he could easily be terrifying. At the moment, however, he was simply…intimidating. Tall, whipcord lean, limping, disfigured. Dressed in black from head to toe as was his custom—a custom well remarked on by nearly everyone in Conard County. Hell's own archangel, indeed.

Well, hell's own archangel was walking her home, ensuring her safety as if such gallantry came naturally to him. The least she could do was be civil to him. She spoke.

"I appreciate your escort, Mr. Dalton. I know it sounds silly, especially here in this quiet little town, but I don't care to be alone on dark streets." Which was as close as she ever came to admitting her terror.

"My pleasure, Miss Emma," he replied in that whispery rasp that sounded more ruined than natural. "Small town or not, it's an unfortunate fact that women aren't safe in this country."

"That's a rather broad statement," Emma protested, though she quite frankly felt that way herself.

"A true statement," Gage remarked. "It has been projected that three out of four will eventually become the victims of sexual assault, and statistics on other types of crime are just as shocking. No, ma'am, this country isn't safe for women."

My word! Emma thought, startled. "I had no idea!"

"Few people do." He paused at a corner, his stormy eyes sweeping the intersection with automatic caution as they waited for a car full of laughing teenagers to speed by. Then he gently clasped her elbow and stepped into the street with her. "The picture it paints of our society, of men in particular, isn't something we want to look at."

Emma stole a glance up at him, and he suddenly looked down at her. Their gazes locked for a strangely intense moment. When she at last tore her eyes from his, she felt oddly disturbed. Subtly irritated.

"I'm sorry, Miss Emma," Gage said after a moment. "I guess that wasn't a good topic to bring up when you're walking down a dark street with a man you don't know."

"Well, it's not exactly as if I don't know you, Mr. Dalton," Emma protested. "I mean…well, I know *of* you. That you work for Nathan Tate. And I consider Sheriff Tate to be an impeccable judge of men." As had her father, Judge Conard, before her. For the moment she chose to ignore the fact that no one was infallible, not even Nate Tate.

For the moment it was simply miraculous that she was actually walking down this street. She might not know Gage Dalton, but his presence was amazingly like a magic shield, holding the darkness at bay, holding back the crushing weight of the night, making it possible for her to walk and talk and breathe as if she were a perfectly normal person.

Years ago, before whatever it was had happened to her, she had loved the darkness, loved the night. In the summers she had often been found on her back in the grass, looking up at the brilliant stars, dreaming of distant shores and alien worlds, wondering if in some backyard light-years away another girl was staring up at the infinite cosmos and dreaming, too.

Impulsively, she confided the memory to the man beside her, then bit her lip, wondering if she sounded like a ridiculously naive country bumpkin. Gage Dalton had lived his life elsewhere, and Conard County must seem like an incredible backwater to him.

"I liked to do that, too," he said, astonishing her. "My other favorite thing was watching the clouds on a summer afternoon. I can't remember exactly when it was I grew up too much, or got too busy…." His voice trailed off.

"I can't, either," Emma said when the silence became too marked. This man, she felt, was not accustomed to sharing memories, feelings, or any other part of himself. "Perhaps I'll try it again this summer. Only I think I'll lie on the chaise in my backyard, rather than the grass."

He glanced down at her. "Why? The grass feels better."

Emma wrinkled her nose. "Insects. The grass is crawling with them. That's what an education does for you, Mr. Dalton. All those precious books I love so well have made me conscious of the insects in the grass and the parasites in the beef I used to eat rare."

He astonished her again with a short, husky laugh. "Where's your sense of adventure, Miss Emma?"

She frowned thoughtfully a moment, then said, "I honestly don't believe I have one. Not these days, at any rate." She glanced up at him again and dared a question. "What made you decide to move to Conard City? It must seem like the end of the earth to most people."

They walked nearly another half block before he answered. The wind nipped coldly at her cheeks, and she pulled her collar up, wondering how her innocent question could have offended him. And it must have offended him, or he would have answered readily.

But he did answer, finally. Slowly. Sounding thoughtful. "It *does* seem like the end of the earth," he agreed. "That's why I'm here."

Which told her exactly nothing at all.

Emmaline Conard, while she suffered from a couple of phobias and some occasional squeamishness, was not, and never had been, a coward. Life had taught her a few lessons, lessons learned the same way a child learns to avoid a hot stove, but cowardice—timidity—was not her nature. Until given cause to feel otherwise, she feared very little. Consequently, she plunged right ahead and asked another question.

"Did you know Sheriff Tate before you moved here?"

Again Gage looked down at her. "Looking for some grist for the gossip mill?" he asked softly. Too softly.

Emma shivered at the silky note in that too-husky, ruined voice. The warning was unmistakable. "No." Her tone was sharp, the same one she used on the troublesome children in the library. "I don't gossip, Mr. Dalton. I was simply trying to make pleasant conversation with a new neighbor. It's rather hard to find something to discuss with a stranger!''

His grasp on her elbow remained gentle, but Emma battled a desire to pull away from his touch. The urge was childish, of course. The fact that the man was difficult didn't give her an excuse to act like a two-year-old. Besides, she thought, casting an uneasy look around, she didn't want to make him stalk off, not before they reached her house.

A half block later, the sound of his voice startled her into renewed awareness.

''I knew Nate before I moved here,'' he said.

As an olive branch, it left a great deal to be desired, but Emma readily accepted it. In a place as sparsely populated as Conard County, where everyone had need to rely on his neighbors from time to time, allowances were made for nearly every kind of eccentricity or quirk.

''I suspect,'' she said pleasantly, ''that Sheriff Tate would make a wonderful ambassador. At least a half-dozen people have moved here because of him.''

''He loves this place,'' Gage agreed.

Had Emma been less stubborn, she probably would have thrown up her hands right then. Trying to converse with this man was like throwing pebbles into a pool that refused to make ripples. Like throwing stones into a well and never hearing the impact. Ridiculous! Stubbornly, she made one more attempt. ''Will you be at Deputy Parish's wedding tomorrow afternoon?''

''Won't everyone?''

Emma almost laughed at that. It was true. Micah Parish and Faith Williams had tried to arrange a quiet ceremony in Good Shepherd Church, but Reverend Fromberg had let the news slip to some of the Bible Study Group, and the next thing the couple knew, the whole county was in on the planning. The wedding ceremony would take place at Good Shepherd, but the reception, originally planned to be punch and cake at Nathan Tate's home, had turned into a covered-dish dinner in the high school gymnasium, with cases of champagne donated by several civic organizations. "Does Deputy Parish mind?" she asked Gage, knowing he worked with Parish.

"No." After a moment, he added to the unvarnished word, "Actually, I think both he and Faith are touched by it."

"Deputy Parish has earned a lot of respect in this county." Emma glanced up at Gage. "I hope he realizes that."

"I don't think that's something a man ever truly realizes."

That said a great deal about Gage Dalton, Emma thought. She wondered if he even suspected how much he had betrayed about himself with that simple remark. Probably not. She had the distinct feeling that he wasn't a man who ever consciously exposed himself.

And once again they had reached a conversational dead end. Emma wondered if this man was as maddening to talk to when you knew him well. If anyone ever even knew him well.

Well, it wasn't her problem. If he was simply going to respond to her gambits and make none of his own, then she might as well conduct the conversation with herself.

"I need to do something about a Christmas tree," she said. The thought had been plaguing her all day. "Ever since my great-grandfather, Eugene, built the house on Front Street, it's been traditional to have a large tree in the bay window. Lance Severn usually gets one for me and keeps it at the nursery, but he was sick this fall, and I never thought to make other arrangements."

"How big a tree?"

"Usually twelve feet. They built ceilings high in the old days, and anything shorter looks dwarfed." She sighed. "I guess I'll just have to put up a dwarf this year."

"Will Conard City be appalled?"

Startled by his teasing question, she darted a look up at him and found him smiling faintly down at her. Lord, it *was* possible for this cold, hard man to look friendly. Just a little. "Probably," she said, when she remembered the question. "It's a tradition. People come in from all over the county to see the decorations and trees on Front Street. On the Sunday evening before Christmas, the choirs from all the churches get together and go up and down the street caroling, and the homes are opened to offer hot cider and cookies to everyone who comes. It's one of the most beautiful events of the year.''

And there was her house, thank goodness. She was hardly conscious of quickening her step in her eagerness to be indoors and safe, and away from this disturbing man.

They had only gone another dozen steps, not quite reaching the end of her shoveled driveway, when Gage gave a muffled curse. Startled, Emma looked up at him and then came to an abrupt halt.

The man was in agony, she realized. His entire face had turned into a rigid mask, and his lips had compressed into a thin, tight line. When she halted, he stopped immediately and closed his eyes. She longed to know what was wrong, but felt she had no right to ask. Instead she reacted with a woman's natural instincts, taking her elbow from his grasp and slipping her arm through his.

''Do you think,'' she asked quietly, ''that you can make it a little farther? I'm sure I have some brandy.''

His eyes snapped open and stared straight down into hers. His eyes burned, she thought uneasily, but couldn't look away. Their touch was like hot phosphorous. Hell's own archangel.

''Come,'' she said, instinct overriding conscious worries, and natural inclinations drowning caution. As spontaneously as she breathed, she slipped her arm around his waist and urged him forward. ''Lean on me if it helps.''

For an instant he stood rigid, resisting as if he had been carved on the spot from native stone, but then he stepped forward with her. His arm came to rest around her slender shoulders, and he leaned, just a very little, on her.

His limp had grown considerably more pronounced, Emma realized, biting her lip in distress. Lord, how could she have been so inconsiderate as to hurry the man the way she had? His pace had been slow from the outset, and if she had thought about it, she would have known that was because of his limp, not a gallant attempt to measure his step to hers.

And now, as he leaned a little on her and they moved so closely that her hip brushed his, she smelled the faint odor of whiskey on him. He must have been hurting fiercely, she thought, because Gage Dalton had lived long enough in Conard County that if he was inclined to drink heavily, or even frequently, every soul would have long since heard about it. Therefore, he'd been drinking for medicinal purposes.

"Can you manage the steps?" she asked him as she guided him around back to the kitchen door. During the days, the rest of the house grew cold because she turned the heat way down, but the kitchen stayed warmer because of the water heater. Right now it was probably the only comfortable room in the house.

"Yeah." The word was clipped. He took his arm from her shoulders. "But I—"

"Oh, stuff it," Emma said impatiently. "You men are all such stubborn little boys at heart. You're hurting, Gage Dalton, and you may as well have a glass of brandy for the pain and warm yourself up a little in my kitchen. Then you can go back to being a macho idiot in a much more comfortable condition."

Silence greeted her speech, which was probably just as well, Emma thought as she fumbled her key from her purse and unlocked the door. She definitely needed to put a leash on her tongue. She was beginning to sound like her great-aunt Isabel, another Conard family spinster. Lord, what a horrifying thought!

Embarrassed by her own behavior, she hardly dared look at Gage as she waved him to a chair at the big round oak table and rushed about turning up the heat, starting coffee and stretching to reach the dusty bottle of brandy on the top shelf.

Without warning, a long, powerful arm reached past her and snagged the bottle.

And suddenly, for Emma, time froze as she found herself trapped between a large, hard, male body and the counter.

Panic exploded blindingly in her head, and instinct caused her to twist away. The next thing she knew, she and Gage were on opposite sides of her kitchen, he frowning at her as he held the brandy bottle by its neck and watched her warily, she gasping as if someone had leeched all the air from the room.

After a moment Gage turned and reached for two of the snifters that had been on the same shelf. While Emma watched in disbelief and tried to regain control of her breathing and her hammering heart, he washed the two glasses at her sink and filled them with brandy. Then he sat at the table, placing one glass across from him for her.

"Claustrophobia's a terrible thing," he said, keeping his attention on his glass. "Sorry I crowded you." He lifted his snifter and sipped. "Great brandy."

Claustrophobia. That was all he thought it was. Relief that he had provided his own explanation and wouldn't question her weakened her. For nearly a minute she didn't move, simply stood and collected herself, more embarrassed than she had felt in years. First she had treated the man like one of the recalcitrant children she often dealt with at the library, and then she had turned crazy on him when he had simply tried to help her. Oh, Lord, Lord.

"It was kind of you to ask me in," Gage said presently, still not looking at her as she cowered in her corner. He stretched his left leg out and began to dig his knuckles into his powerful thigh muscles as if he could gouge out the ache. "The cold seems to make it worse."

Emma drew a deep, shuddery breath and tried to appear composed. "Do you hurt often?"

"All the time."

All the time? She couldn't imagine how awful that must be. Regaining control of her body, she moved to the table and sat across from him. The statement had been unvarnished, offering no further information, spoken matter-of-factly in a way that said he wanted no pity. An offering, she realized, to balance his discovery of her "claustrophobia." She wouldn't have expected such sensitivity from him. From any man, come to that. Emmaline Conard didn't have the world's highest opinion of men as a group.

She also owed him some kind of apology. "I'm sorry I lectured you the way I did about coming inside."

He looked up and met her gaze. His eyes, she noticed for the first time, were a stormy gray-green, like the sky before a bad squall. It was an unusual, beautiful color.

"That's okay," he said, and the corners of his mouth lifted in a faint, lopsided smile. "I'm used to it. When I was a kid, I don't think I ever got out of the library without at least one lecture from the librarian."

Emma was surprised to feel herself smiling back at him. "Was she such a dragon?"

"I always thought so, but in retrospect, I think I was a hell-raiser."

"I'm surprised you spent any time at all there, then."

Gage gave a small shake of his head. "I always loved books. Still do. All the lectures in the world couldn't keep me away from them."

Emma suddenly had a poignant vision of Gage Dalton as a small boy. There were a few young hell-raisers who came to her own library regularly, and they were all poor, defiant and wild, and starved for attention, affection and ideas. Once again, she didn't think Gage knew how much he had betrayed about himself.

"The coffee's ready," she said after a moment. "Would you like some?"

"Please. Black."

He looked at her then, but she forced herself to turn away and get the cups. He made her uneasy. Not the kind of uneasiness she felt in the dark, but something else altogether. His gaze was hypnotic, somehow. Fiery. Sulfurous. Brimstone. A startled laugh almost escaped her. Lord, how her imagination took off sometimes!

She was like a candle flame, Gage thought. Her red hair was

caught back tightly into a clip at her nape, but he suspected that hair was untamable. Judging by the cloud of it below her barrette, it would, if freed, instantly become a springy mass of tight, wild curls, a halo of fire. She had probably hated that hair all her life long.

She was a little taller than average, sturdily built, not a fragile porcelain doll, but a strong woman. The kind of woman who would have pioneered the West and survived. No one would ever call her delicate, but the delicacy was there nonetheless. It was there in the fine grain of her pale skin, in the faint blue veins apparent through it. It was there in those smoky, soft green eyes when they darted his way.

Something long dormant stirred deep inside Gage. He wanted to step on it, squash it ruthlessly as if it were a snake. Instead, he faced it dead on. For the first time since—since *then,* he was seeing a woman as a woman, reacting to a woman as a woman. He wouldn't have minded it half so much if he had reacted this way to Molly Garrity, the waitress at Mahoney's. Molly was an uncomplicated woman who was ever ready to ease a man's physical needs.

Gage didn't particularly care whether he ever felt desire again, but if he had to start feeling it again, he wished to hell it could be directed at someone besides Emma Conard. She was apparently, by all reports, a dyed-in-the-wool spinster who took strips out of the hide of any man foolish enough to approach her as a woman. And even if that wasn't true, she wasn't the kind of woman who was meant for casual affairs, and he would never again be in the market for anything else.

He kept his gaze on the coffee cup as she carried it over to him and tried not to notice that her slacks and bulky sweater didn't entirely conceal a well-proportioned shape. "Thanks."

"You're welcome. Will you excuse me for a second? I want to get the mail from out front."

"Sure."

He allowed his eyes to stray for a moment, to watch her derriere sway gently as she passed through the door into a

darkened room beyond. Then, in the brief privacy, he closed
his eyes and tensed, inwardly battering down the wolves of
emotional and physical pain that never stopped howling at the
walls of ice behind which he confined them. His constant com-
panions, they had long since ceased to frighten him, but they
still tormented him, some times more than others.

The sound of Emma's returning footsteps alerted him. When
she reentered the kitchen, she found Gage sipping his coffee.
She tossed a small stack of mail on the table and sat across
from him.

"I wonder what this could be," she said, pointing at a large
brown envelope. "I don't get anything at this address except
bills and junk mail." She gave him a small smile. "The good
stuff all comes to the library."

He glanced at the envelope. It sure didn't look like junk mail.
A stamp for the exact amount of postage sat crookedly in the
corner, and the addressing had been done sloppily on a type-
writer. "Don't mind me," he said. "Satisfy your curiosity."

She took him at his word. He felt a rare twinge of amusement when he saw her remove a letter opener from the drawer
behind her to neatly slit the flap. He should have guessed she
wouldn't be the tear-it-open type.

"The postmark is Laramie," she remarked. "I used to know
some people..."

Her voice trailed off as she drew a large, glossy, black-and-
white photograph from the envelope. As Gage watched, her
expression changed from perplexity to consternation, and then
to something very like shock. Her hand trembled until the
photo shook like a leaf in the wind. Suddenly, she flung it from
her. Closing her eyes, she covered her mouth with her hand.

"Miss Emma?" Gage immediately swung around in his
chair and leaned across the table. A glance at the photograph
told him it showed nothing but a hammered-metal dagger,
probably an archaeological artifact. Nothing to cause such distress. "Miss Emma? What's wrong?"

"I...don't know." She gave a shaky laugh and opened her

eyes. Gage noted that she was careful to avoid glancing at the photograph. "When I looked at that thing it was as if...I don't know. A chill hit me without warning."

He reached for the picture. "Do you mind?"

She shook her head and wrapped her arms around herself as if she was freezing. "Be my guest. I must be coming down with something."

The last was more a comment to herself, and Gage treated it as such as he studied the dagger. It was a simple instrument, crudely shaped at hilt and pommel, and scored with cross-hatching for decoration and grip. The blade appeared to be manufactured of the same beaten metal, but the edge had been honed on a whetting stone; fine polishing marks were visible. In the very top of the pommel, a stone of some kind had been set. It might have been glass or a gemstone of high quality. Impossible to tell in the gray tones of the photo.

"It looks like some kind of archaeological artifact," he remarked after a moment. "An old one, I'd think. It's crude." He glanced up quickly to take stock of her reaction and found her staring at the photo as if it were a live snake that might at any moment strike. "Miss Emma?"

She blinked. Slowly her hazy green eyes lifted to his stormy ones. "Sorry. That thing...that thing is hideous!"

Her reaction was extreme, but Gage didn't argue with it. "Was there a letter in the envelope? Somebody looking for contributions for a museum or something?" Her reaction was rousing his investigative instincts, he realized. There was something else going on here.

She reached for the envelope immediately. "Of course. Why didn't I...? Nothing." She dropped the envelope. "Of course. That's what it is. The letter just got left out. Why didn't I think of that?" She gave a brittle, short laugh. "Well, I'll just throw it out."

As she reached for it, Gage drew it back. "If you don't want it, would you mind if I kept it?"

She settled back on her seat, her eyes wide as they studied

him. "Well, I...certainly not. You're welcome to it. But why?"

He shrugged. "It looks familiar somehow. I'd like to place the period. It's just an old hobby of mine."

"Please. Keep it."

"Thanks." He reached for the envelope, slipped the photo back into it and tucked the whole inside his half-unzipped leather jacket. "Great coffee, Miss Emma. We need you to come over to the sheriff's office and show us how to do it."

The color began to return to her cheeks, and while she didn't seem quite as relaxed as before, neither was she as uptight as she had been when she saw the photograph. A puzzle, Gage thought. A real puzzle. He was going to find out everything possible about that dagger and see if he could get to the bottom of it. He had never been able to resist a puzzle.

He would have liked to question her about her reaction, find out more about how the picture had made her feel, what connections she had made when she saw it, but he guessed she wasn't about to become a passive interrogation subject. No, most likely Miss Emma would throw him out on his butt.

And out on his butt was where he ought to be, he thought, tossing down the last of his brandy. Emma Conard had done a rare, neighborly thing when she invited him in, but she hadn't asked him to take up residence. A polite guest would take his leave now that he was a little warmer.

He gathered his muscles a little at a time, getting ready to stand. His slowness was partly reluctance, but partly the fact that, since the explosion that had turned his life into a living hell, the simple things were no longer quite so easy to do. These days, getting out of bed was an achievement.

Finally, feeling that he could rise without groaning or losing his balance, he shoved himself up from the chair. The redistribution of his weight always caused a sharp pain in his hip and leg, but he was prepared for that and hardly noticed it.

"My thanks for the brandy and coffee, Miss Emma. I'll say good night now."

She didn't argue; he hadn't expected her to. She thanked him for escorting her home and then watched him through the storm door as he limped down her driveway toward the street.

Once there, he turned away from the center of town, planning to walk until the demons subsided.

In her front yard, though, he saw a small, discreet sign sticking up from a snowbank, lettered in black on white: Room Available. He paused and looked up at her house, a rambling two-story frame structure with a wide porch. It sure would be nicer than the rooms above Mahoney's, he thought. Quieter. And it wouldn't stink like fry cooking and stale beer all the time.

Miss Emma would never rent a room to a man, he thought. Never.

But he turned anyway and limped back around to her kitchen door to ask. As he came back up the driveway, he could see her through the row of three windows beside the door. She was clearing the coffee cups and snifters from the table and carrying them toward the sink, but as she came back to the table with a dishcloth, she suddenly paused. For a moment she stared fixedly into space, and then she shuddered, closed her eyes and wrapped her arms tightly around herself.

Gage halted and hesitated, unsure whether to disturb her. Could she still be upset by that photograph? It seemed such a crazy thing for her to get bent out of shape over. But she *had* gotten bent out of shape. Seriously so. Something about that photo had first perplexed her and then frightened her. He wished he knew what connection her mind had made that had caused her to consider the picture such a threat.

As he watched, she shook herself visibly and then bent over the table to wipe it clean. Hesitating no longer, Gage strode up to her door. She jumped when he knocked, then showed utter relief when she recognized him. She hurried to open the door.

"Mr. Dalton! Is something wrong?"

"No, ma'am. I just saw your sign out front." He shifted his

stance, wondering why the words were suddenly so difficult to speak. "I might be interested in the room."

"Oh!" She bit her lower lip and studied him. He was standing on the second step, so they were at eye level with one another, and waiting impassively for her answer. "Mr. Dalton," she said finally, "please don't take this personally, but I really don't think it would be wise for me to rent the room to a gentleman. This is a small town...." She trailed off, obviously at a loss.

Gage nodded and gave her a faint, crooked half smile. "Thought so. Never hurts to ask, though. Good night, Miss Emma."

As he walked down the dark driveway, snow began to fall gently. He heard the door close behind him, as so many doors had closed behind him in life.

Just another closed door, he told himself. That was all. Just another closed door.

Chapter 2

Emma watched Gage walk away and felt like a world-class heel. But really, she couldn't take a man as a roomer. The whole of Conard County would become convinced that the starchy Miss Emmaline Conard had suddenly developed a case of round heels. Some of them would probably even demand that she be removed from her job so that their dear little children wouldn't be corrupted by her influence.

Not that Emma cared about such narrow-minded people. She really didn't. The judge had raised her to set her own course and live up to her own standards; he had taught her that you couldn't please all of the people all of the time. But the judge had also taught her that appearances were everything. A man could be hanged for appearances, quite literally, and a murderer could walk away a free man for the same reason.

If Emma really had an affair, she wouldn't be ashamed if everyone knew about it, would hardly care what they thought. But she wasn't going to be hanged for a sheep when she was a mere lamb. No way.

Still... She bit her lip and watched Gage disappear into the dark. A few gently falling snowflakes caught the light from the kitchen and sparkled.

It was almost Christmas, and he looked so alone. Where would he go, what would he do, for the holidays? Did he have family somewhere he could join? Or would he spend the holiday treeless, cheerless, alone, going to Maude's diner for Christmas dinner?

Well, it wasn't her problem, she told herself as she finished straightening the kitchen. Not her problem at all. Gage Dalton was a mature adult, and if he was alone it was by choice. Just as she was alone by choice.

Snapping the light switch off, she headed for her bedroom at the rear of the house. As long as she didn't have a roomer, she kept the upstairs closed off to conserve on heat. Even after five years, it felt odd to be using her father's bedroom, but she really couldn't afford not to. Heating all of this old house all winter without a roomer to help with the expense would devour her savings in no time at all.

As a small child, she had come into this room to spend an occasional night with her widowed grandmother. Her father and mother had slept upstairs in a room right across the hall from her own, and her brother Gene had been right next door.

An invitation to spend the night with Grandma had been exciting, special. Magic. Even now, closing her eyes, she could remember lying in the big old bed with the blanket drawn up to her chin, watching as Grandma let down her astonishing hair. All day long she kept it neatly tucked into a roll under a net, but at night she brushed it out to her hips and then braided it for sleeping. To four-year-old Emma, that hair had seemed to come from nowhere, a surprising magician's trick.

When Emma had been six, Grandma had died. By the time she was eight, her mother and brother Gene were both gone, killed in an accident on a snowy road in the mountains. The old house, once so full, had become incredibly empty, and it was years before Emma grew used to having the upstairs to herself, used to Judge Conard sleeping in Grandma's room.

Nothing had changed. The walls were still covered in dark green silk wallpaper; the curtains were yellowing sheers that covered even yellower shades. The huge walnut armoire still covered most of one wall, the tall walnut highboy graced the other. The master bath boasted a black linoleum floor and a claw-footed tub that was probably worth a great deal of money.

And now Emma slept in the same bed that had served all her forebears since Grandfather Eustace came back from the trenches in France and announced he was leaving the ranch to his brother Ralph and going to law school. Ralph had lost the ranch during the Great Depression, but Eustace had prospered, eventually bringing his son, Eugene, Emma's father, into the law firm of Conard and Conard.

Emma's brother Gene had been destined to be the next Conard lawyer until he had died on that snowy mountain road. Emma had tried to fill his place, and the judge had encouraged her, but after she was assaulted she just plain couldn't do it. The judge never said anything, never criticized or bemoaned fate, but Emma had never been able to believe he wasn't disappointed in her. He had wanted a lawyer and gotten a librarian, and when he died, the law firm died with him.

Now she slept in a bed she had always felt too small for and rattled around in this big old house like the seeds in a dried up old gourd, and she was trapped, because she had no alternatives left. The world outside Conard County had proved itself evil and cruel. The mere thought of stepping outside the safety of this county petrified her. She told herself it didn't matter, that she didn't want to leave anyway, but occasionally she admitted there was a huge difference between staying because she wanted to and staying because she couldn't leave.

Gage Dalton wouldn't be the only person in Conard County spending Christmas alone, Emma thought wearily as she at last climbed between cool sheets. Nor would he be the only one doing so by choice. After a couple of miserable holidays as the fifth wheel at friends' celebrations, she had taken to turning down every one of the well-meant invitations she received. It was easier by far to be alone than to be an onlooker.

She was tired tonight, she realized as sleep swiftly sucked her into a lazy whirlpool. So sleepy.

The golden dagger hovered above her, hammered metal, gleaming evilly, the ruby on its pommel twinkling like a teardrop of blood. Suddenly it lifted and flashed downward.

Emma screamed and sat bolt upright in the dark. She was alone. The house was empty, silent save for the familiar rattle from the heating ducts as hot air rushed through them. Gasping, she fell back against her pillows and waited for her heart to stop galloping.

That awful photograph must have set off a nightmare. But what a nightmare! It had been years since she'd had even a moderately bad dream. Years, in fact, since she had even been aware of dreaming.

And it was silly, so silly, to have gotten so upset over that photo. Certainly Gage had been right when he said it was probably a fund-raiser for some museum. What else on earth could it possibly be?

But her heart continued to pound in a painful rhythm, and in the dark she kept seeing the flash of gold, now from the corner of her eye, as if she couldn't quite bring it into view. What was wrong with her? It was just an old artifact of some kind or another, nothing threatening at all. But how did she know it was golden? Why was she so convinced that the stone on the pommel was bloodred? Why had a simple photograph invaded her dreams?

Disturbed, she finally gave in and turned on the lamp beside her bed. The Tiffany shade, a treasure of her grandmother's, cast spangles of brilliant color around the room. Just then the regulator clock in the dining room sounded the hour with three deep chimes.

Surrounded by familiar and beloved sounds and sights, Emma snuggled back under her blankets and waited for sleep to return. It wouldn't be the first time in her adult life that she had slept with the light on. What a bundle of fears and nerves she was, and she couldn't even remember why she had become this way.

But that was a blessing, she reminded herself. She never wanted to remember what had been done to her. Never. Traumatic amnesia was a heaven-sent blessing, and not even to be relieved of her present fears did she want to remember what had caused them.

It was shortly after three when Gage realized he was once again standing outside Emmaline Conard's house. The hours of walking had finally battered down the grinding pain in his leg and worn out the wolves that gnawed at his soul. He had intended to return to his rooms above Mahoney's to rest up for Micah's wedding, but somehow he had strayed this way.

Why?

Something was wrong. Something was mortally wrong. God, he hated this feeling! Every time he got it, something awful happened, and most of the time there wasn't a damn thing he could do to prevent it.

Smothering a curse, he turned sharply away from the Conard home and headed toward Mahoney's as fast as his limp would permit. Never again, by God. Never again. Involvement carried a price he wasn't prepared to pay. Not again.

Emma thought Gage Dalton resembled a black hole amidst the swirl of wedding festivities. Nearly five hundred people crowded the high school gym, snacking from the smorgasbord of covered dishes everyone had brought and dancing to the amplified sounds of the school principal's pop-music collection. Gage, however, sat in splendid solitude in a dimly lit corner far from the hub of the excitement.

He had shed his customary black jeans and shirt for a charcoal gray suit in honor of the occasion, but the change did little to alleviate the sense of darkness and gloom that traveled with him. For a wild instant Emma actually wondered if, like a black hole, he swallowed all the sound and light around him. Perhaps if she stepped close enough, she would enter the bubble of silence that seemed to shield him from the world around him.

For all that, she continued to ease her way through the crowd in his general direction, taking care to avoid Don Fenster as she did so. Childish as it was, she and Don hadn't spoken for nearly twenty years, ever since Emma had popped him in the nose. It wasn't that she was still mad at him, but every time he saw her, his lip curled in a way that killed any desire on her part to speak to him. He'd been a brat as a child, she thought now, and as a grown man he was still a brat. *She* would have been perfectly content to let bygones be bygones, but not Don. No, he wanted to turn a childhood argument into the Hatfields and McCoys.

Sniffing in unconscious disapproval, she returned her attention to Gage Dalton. Everyone else here was laughing and talking and having a wonderful time, and it seemed terribly wrong to Emma that he should be sitting alone in that dark corner.

Just as she approached the table, Jeff Cumberland, one of the county's most prominent ranchers, settled into a folding chair across from Gage. Emma reached them just in time to hear Jeff say, "Have you and Micah learned anything new about my cattle?"

Everyone in Conard County had heard that Jeff had lost three of his best cattle, two heifers and a prize bull, to the mutilations that were an on-again, off-again mystery from Kentucky to Montana. Periodically livestock were found with their genitals and tongues missing. Experts contended that the apparent surgical precision of the always bloodless wounds was due to shrinkage of the flesh, and that however strange the mutilations might appear, they were in fact normal predator activity. Farmers and ranchers were not so easily convinced that any predator would take only the tongue and genitals and leave everything else intact. Since nothing could be proved one way or the other, most people had come to an uneasy acceptance of the mutilations.

Last month, however, Jeff Cumberland had had three cattle mutilated in one short week. The Sheriff's Department evidently tried to keep things quiet but had failed. Ever since then, Emma had sensed a restless anger among the ranchers, a frustrated need to do something to defend their herds and catch the culprits.

When she pulled out a chair and joined Jeff and Gage at the table, the two men acknowledged her with distracted nods.

"Not one damn thing," Gage said in answer to Jeff's question.

Jeff's jaw tightened. "When the experts at the lab don't even agree—" He bit off the sentence, leaving it incomplete.

"The experts don't agree?" Emma repeated. She hadn't heard this before. "What do you mean, they don't agree? I thought they always said it was normal predation."

Both men stared at her as if they had just realized she was there. She hadn't been meant to hear this, Emma understood. Gage looked a little perturbed, and Jeff looked dismayed.

"They do," Gage said shortly. "That's what they always say."

Emma looked at Jeff, who nodded. "That's what they say, Emma."

"Then why did you say…?" Her voice trailed off and she looked sternly at Jeff. "I don't like being lied to, Jeffrey Cumberland, and I'm certainly no gossip you need to hide things from!"

Jeff threw up his hands. "Enough!" he said. "I've got enough on my mind, and I'm not going to be lectured to like a schoolboy by you or anybody else. You've turned into a scold, Emmaline Conard. Your daddy would shake his head!"

Emma watched Jeff snatch his hat up from the table and stalk away. Something inside her hurt, she realized. Jeff's angry words had wounded her. Had she really turned into a scold?

Oh, Lord, what if she *was* turning into another Great-aunt Isabel?

Gage's voice pierced her thoughts. "It sounds as if you two go back a long way."

"Jeff is my cousin," Emma admitted, trying to stifle the hurt and appear unconcerned. "He's older, and when I was really little, he often used to look after me. But what about his cattle, Mr. Dalton?" She searched his impassive face, trying to find any clue. "I know as well as anyone how much Jeff has invested in his breeding stock, and it's a lot more than money. If someone is deliberately trying to destroy them—"

Gage silenced her in an instant by suddenly reaching out and catching her chin in his hard, warm palm. He turned her face up to him, and suddenly their eyes were only inches apart, their mouths every bit as close. Emma forgot what she had been saying, what she had been thinking. For the first time in a decade, she was close to a man, aware of a man, and feeling like a woman. Like a whole woman.

"Miss Emma," he murmured in that husky, ruined, *sexy* voice, "do you think we could discuss this someplace less public?"

Before she could find her voice, let alone an appropriate word in response to that utterly suggestive question, a mocking voice intruded.

"Better look out, Dalton. She'll take a strip out of a man's hide for a lot less than what you're doing right now."

The remark sounded teasing, but Emma knew better. She wrenched her chin free of Gage's grip and glared up at Earl Newton. Earl had been the person responsible for starting the rumor that Emma had succumbed to the blandishments of a traveling man while she was away at college, had even hinted that she had born this nonexistent man a child and given it up for adoption. Emma presumed Earl had started the nastiness because she had repeatedly refused to go out with him. At least, she could think of no other reason for starting such a vicious rumor. All that was a decade in the past, of course, but Emma still heard references to her "traveling man."

Oh, how she wished there were something she could say that would wipe the smirk off Earl's face forever! But she had learned, painfully, that the only way to handle Earl and others like him was to pretend they had no effect on her at all.

She averted her face, intending to ignore Earl as if he had suddenly fallen through the floor and vanished. Much to her amazement, Gage shoved his chair back from the table and rose stiffly to face the other man.

"Maybe," Gage said to Earl, "you'd like to try picking on somebody your own size, Newton. We could go talk this over *outside*."

The words were softly spoken, but menacing nonetheless. Emma wasn't at all surprised when Earl suddenly shifted uneasily and claimed he'd just been teasing.

"Sure," said Gage. "Me, too. I don't think Miss Emma much appreciates it, though, and I can understand why."

Earl stole a quick look at Emma. "Sorry, Miss Emma. Just joking."

Emma watched Earl scuttle off and tried to control the urge to just run and hide in the nearest dark corner. No doubt Gage had heard about her "traveling man," and he'd been in town only a few months. No doubt he, too, had heard how she chewed up any man who asked her out.

"It's not true," she heard herself say. "It's really not true. I just...don't date." She couldn't even look at him.

"That's your prerogative, ma'am. None of my business. Or anybody else's." He shifted his weight and bent a little, as if he was trying to ease stiff muscles. "I need to get out of here. I need to walk."

The words were said in a forceful, blunt tone that deprived them of casualness. Emma looked up swiftly and understood that Gage was getting claustrophobic from pain. She had felt like that when she was in the hospital, as if the only way to cope with the agony was to move and keep moving. She rose.

"Would you like some company?" she asked. "I'm ready to go home, and my car's still in the shop. I'd like to walk, but if you—"

He cut her off with an abrupt wave of his hand. "Sure. Let's go."

They waited just long enough to see the bride and groom make good their escape, and then they escaped themselves into the cold late afternoon. The sun was nearing the horizon, ready to plunge Conard County into another long winter night. Last night's dusting of fresh snow crunched beneath their boots, and their breath puffed in white clouds.

"It's colder," Emma remarked. Colder than yesterday. What she really wanted to do was tell him that none of what he had heard about her was true. For years she had lived with the shadows of those rumors, had accepted her father's assurance that the people who really counted, the ones who knew her and cared, wouldn't believe any such trash. Gage Dalton, however, didn't know her. He was new to the county, and if he heard the rumors, he would probably believe them. For some reason, she couldn't stand the thought.

She sighed and told herself it was stupid to worry about such things at this late date. It was such an old story, and Gage wouldn't even care if it were true. Why should he? And why was she making such a mountain out of an old, old molehill?

"I apologize for the way I hushed you in there," Gage said abruptly. "Nate wants this business with Jeff's cattle kept as much under wraps as possible, and I think it's wise. Upsetting half the people in the county won't help anyone, least of all those of us who are investigating the matter."

Remembering the *way* he had hushed her, Emma felt momentarily breathless. Just because she was dedicated to spinsterhood didn't mean she didn't have a woman's normal drives. Gage had reminded her forcibly of that fact, though she was sure it had been the farthest thing from his mind. No, he had simply seized the quickest way of silencing her in such a public place, a way that would put an entirely different color on their conversation, should anyone wonder what they had been discussing. A brilliant move on his part, she thought. Brilliant. It had sure fooled Earl, whose approach had probably precipitated Gage's action.

"I guess I can understand why Sheriff Tate doesn't want everybody seeing aliens behind every bush and snowdrift," Emma said. The sky was taking on that deep, deep blue cast to the east, the dark brightness of evening. "But there *was* something unusual about what happened to Jeff's cattle. Everyone knows that, Mr. Dalton."

With automatic gallantry, he gripped her elbow as they stepped from the curb into a snowy street. There was surprisingly little traffic, Emma thought. Probably because almost everyone was partying at the gym. She stuffed her hands deeper into the pockets of her parka and tucked her chin down closer to her chest, trying to retain every bit of warmth she could.

They walked nearly two more blocks before Gage answered her. "Everyone *believes* that, Miss Emma. Nobody *knows* it."

"What did the lab say?"

He glanced down at her and then changed the subject with a ruthlessness that left her breathless. "Did you ever figure out why that photograph of the dagger scared you spitless last night?"

They passed Maude's diner and Good Shepherd Church, and were walking past the courthouse when Emma found enough breath to speak. "No," she said.

"I wondered."

And then, before good sense could overrule her, she blurted out the rest of it. "I had nightmares about it last night. Awful nightmares. I kept seeing it swing down at me, as if it was going to stab me." Oh, Lord, that sounded completely and totally neurotic! *Why* had she ever confided that?

"That's awful," Gage said after a moment. "I've had nightmares like that."

Startled, she looked up at him. "About knives?"

"About bombs."

Bombs. Oh, God. Bombs. She didn't need him to explain why he had nightmares about bombs. His scarred face was explanation enough. "But I've never seen that dagger before," she argued. "Never."

Gage remained silent as they walked by the library. "Maybe not," he said presently. "Maybe it reminded you of something else. Who knows? I just meant that I know about those kinds of nightmares, is all. No fun."

"No," she agreed. She stole another upward glance at him, her gaze skimming the shiny burned tissue, the jagged scar that slashed his cheek. A bomb. She looked quickly away, not wanting him to catch her staring. He didn't seem to be self-conscious about it, but he might just be good at hiding the fact that he was. She was good at that herself. Most people never guessed just how thin Emma Conard's skin really was.

A bomb. Good grief. Had it been directed at him? Or had it been some kind of accident? What had he done during all those years before he came to Conard County? What had driven him to come to the "ends of the earth"? She wished she had the nerve to ask him, even though she knew perfectly well that he would never answer her. In fact, now that she thought about it, it was astonishing that he had even mentioned the bomb. She seriously doubted that Gage Dalton ever let anything just *slip*. So why had he told her?

He was silent so long that when he at last spoke, Emma was nearly startled.

"Is the dream still bothering you now?" he asked.

"A little," she admitted. "It's like I can't quite shake it. I'll be doing something else and suddenly see the dagger in my mind's eye." She gave a deprecating laugh. "It'll wear off, I'm sure."

"I'm sure," he agreed noncommittally.

When her house came within sight, still a block up the street, Emma saw her discreet black-and-white sign advertising for a roomer and thought of Gage's interest in it. It seemed odd, when she thought about it, that a bachelor man would have any desire to live under a spinster's roof. Surely it would crimp his life-style?

"Where do you live now?" she heard herself asking him.

"Above Mahoney's."

"Oh." How unpleasant. "I imagine it's noisy?"

"Until closing," he agreed. "It always smells like stale beer and fried food."

"How macho."

He glanced sharply down at her and caught the teasing twinkle in her hazy green eyes. Slowly, like the reluctant opening of a rusty door, he smiled. It spread from the corners of his mouth, where it drew a crooked, curved line, pulled off center by his scars. It crept up to the corners of his eyes, creasing them attractively, and then eased the bleakness of his gray-green eyes.

Emma caught her breath. It was like watching a glorious sunrise to see Gage Dalton genuinely smile. Night vanished, replaced by a warm glow.

"Are you a teaser, Miss Emma?" he asked softly.

"I'm afraid so," she admitted, giving him a smile in return. "You need to understand that I was raised here, but in a different way than most women. Men are men in Conard County, Mr. Dalton, but most of it is pure pretense."

"And you see through it."

She shrugged. "I never thought it made a man less of a man if he scraped the manure off his boots at the door."

"Your father never needed to scrape his boots, did he?"

"No, he was a judge. But he did all those other manly things, from hunting every fall to bending his elbow at Mahoney's. It's expected hereabouts. The difference between my father and many of the other men around here is that he was aware of what he was doing. It was politic, and he did it politically."

"Is that why you don't date? Because you think you see through them?"

"No." Her lips compressed tightly, and she quickened her pace, not caring if she caused him another spasm in his leg.

His question had been mocking, when she had only been joking with him. "I have a very high respect for quite a number of the men in this county, Mr. Dalton. Sheriff Tate. Jeff Cumberland. Tom Preston. Shall I make you a list?"

He caught her elbow and stopped her. "I can't walk this fast, Miss Emma," he told her quietly. Frankly.

She felt like a complete and total jerk. She had been teasing, but she had come off sounding like an utter snob. Then, with an unforgivable lack of courtesy, she had hurried her pace, knowing full well she would cause him pain.

Slowly, ashamed of herself, she faced him and raised her eyes to his. "I'm sorry. I'm really not a snob, and I was only joking." She didn't say anything about walking too fast. He might mistake anything she said as pity, and she was far from feeling any pity for this dark, dangerous man.

He studied her a moment and then gave her a faint smile. "And I don't mind scraping the manure from my boots."

She didn't want to go home, she realized as they walked steadily closer to her house. Suddenly she didn't want to be alone there, didn't want to rattle around listening to the endless ticking of the old clocks, waiting for the regulator to chime six so she could start preparing her solitary dinner.

Just then her foot hit a patch of ice hidden beneath the fresh, undisturbed powder of last night's new snow. She gasped and tensed, expecting to land on her bottom, but strong hands caught her halfway down, catching her beneath her arms.

"Damn!" Gage whispered the word, a short sharp exclamation, and then sucked a hissing breath of air through his teeth as the pain swamped him. From his spine, it rolled through him in tidal waves of agony, until cold sweat beaded his face and even his teeth seemed to hurt. For an endless span of time that felt like an eternity but could only be a few seconds, he held Emma suspended as he was frozen in the grip of a pain so fierce it completely shut him down.

Then, gently, he lowered her to the ground.

Emma scrambled immediately to her feet, concerned because

of the way he had sworn and then caught his breath. One look at him as he stood there white lipped and half doubled over, with sweat beading his face, told her just how much he hurt. She didn't bother scolding him for catching her, didn't bother asking what she could do. People in severe pain tended to get very impatient at that kind of thing.

So she simply waited for the worst to pass. When he started to straighten, she stepped to his side and slipped her arm around his waist just as she had last night.

"I still have that brandy," she commented. "And with the holidays coming, I went out this morning and bought a few bottles of good Scotch and bourbon."

Gage released a long sigh and let his arm come to rest around her shoulders as they continued toward her house. "I could do with a stiff Scotch," he said after a moment.

"I thought you might. But don't you have something stronger you could take? Some kind of pain pill?"

He shook his head.

"Why not?" She felt indignant. "Surely—"

He interrupted without apology. "I refuse to turn myself into an addict, Miss Emma. Any kind of addict."

She could respect that, but it didn't make her feel any better to think of this man hurting and unable to escape the pain for even a brief while. "Will it always be like this?" she asked.

"I don't know."

She hadn't turned the heat down earlier when she left for the reception, so she took Gage into the house through the front door this time. He settled into the Kennedy rocker with obvious relief, as her father often had when his back troubled him.

Emma hurried to fix him a Scotch, a double, though he didn't ask for it, and told him she would be back as soon as she started a pot of coffee.

He probably wouldn't mind being alone for a few minutes, she told herself. A few minutes to grimace and groan and shift around until he got reasonably comfortable would be welcome, she was sure. Maybe he would like to use the heating pad. And maybe he would be offended if she offered. Men could be so asinine about things like that.

Standing in the kitchen, waiting for the coffee to finish brewing, Emma suddenly had the feeling that she was looking through some kind of distorted glass. The familiar room looked different somehow, and the familiar sounds of the house seemed…threatening.

Uneasy, she rubbed her arms and looked around the room. It was as if…as if the house had been invaded somehow. Nothing appeared to be out of place, everything looked just as it always had, but the sense of invasion refused to dissipate.

Out of the corner of her eye, she thought she saw something move. Whirling around, her heart hammering, she looked toward the windows but saw nothing. Nothing. That didn't keep her from hurrying over and drawing all the café curtains against the night.

What was wrong with her? she wondered edgily as she hurried to prepare a tray with mugs and some leftover chocolate-chip cookies she had baked for the children's story hour. Nightmares, that ridiculous reaction to the photograph of what was surely some kind of historical artifact, and now this sense of… of…

Unseen watchers.

A shudder rippled through her even as she scolded herself for silliness. She didn't believe in ghosts or things that went bump in the night. Even as a child such things had never troubled her, except for that brief time when, at four, she had become convinced there was an alligator under her bed. She had lived alone in this house for five years now, and never once had she felt uneasy.

Shaking herself, she thrust her anxiousness aside and filled two mugs with hot, rich coffee. It was a blend she ordered specially, the one small indulgence she allowed herself on her tight budget. She hoped Gage liked it.

He was sitting in the rocker with his eyes closed, the empty highball glass in his hand. As soon as she stepped into the room, even though she tried to be quiet, his eyes snapped open. He didn't move, just watched her set the tray on the coffee table and settle herself on the couch.

He didn't want to move, she realized. He must have found a good position. Leaning over, she took the glass from his hand. "More?"

"No, thanks. That was plenty."

"Coffee, then?"

"Please."

She leaned over again to pass the mug to him, so he didn't have to reach.

"You're a kind woman, Emma Conard," he said, surprising her.

She glanced up from her own mug and found he had once again closed his eyes. "Not really. It's just that I know what it's like to hurt, and what it's like to find the one position on earth where it almost doesn't hurt. There were a couple of times when I might have killed a nurse if I'd had a gun."

A short, husky laugh escaped him. "I know all about that."

"I thought you might. Would you care for a cookie?"

What he really wanted, she thought a few minutes later, was to sleep. His eyes kept closing when the conversation lagged, and his head rested against the back of the rocker.

Well, this was ridiculous, Emma decided. Rising, she told Gage she would be back in a few minutes. Only she didn't come back. Instead, she went to her bedroom at the back of the house and changed into jeans, warm socks and a favorite green sweatshirt. She took her time brushing her stubborn hair into a relatively neat ponytail, scrubbing off the makeup she hated to wear and applied only for special occasions. And when at last she crept back to the living room, she found Gage sleeping soundly in the rocker.

Satisfied, she went to the kitchen and started preparing a considerably larger meal than she would have cooked for herself alone. It distracted her from the deepening winter night and the persistent uncomfortable feeling that she was being watched. That something terrible was about to happen.

When Gage awoke, it was to the golden glow of lamplight and the mouth-watering aroma of baking chicken. For an instant he wondered where he was, but then he remembered Emma Conard telling him she would be back in a minute. Judging by the enticing smells wafting his way, he'd been asleep for some time. Turning his head a little, he saw her. Looking all of eighteen, she was curled up in a corner of the couch, her feet tucked beneath her. Absently, she played with a corkscrew of her red hair while she read a paperback book.

He watched her turn a page and wondered why she had let him sleep like this and why she seemed to be so unperturbed by his rudeness. He must have been snoozing for a couple of hours. Most hostesses surely would have found some way to wake him. He certainly wouldn't have blamed anyone for shaking him awake and sending him on his way.

Now that he was awake, though, he should say something, apologize, take his leave. Instead, comfortable in the rocker as he was seldom comfortable, he sat perfectly still and watched her read.

That hair of hers was beautiful, he thought, and wished again that he could see it unbound. Her skin was creamy, like living satin, and he imagined that if he touched it, she would feel warm and smooth. Her mouth was generous, the kind of mouth that made men fantasize a million and one things, all of them erotic. Why didn't she date? Had she been mistreated by some boyfriend?

Suddenly, as if she felt his gaze on her, Emma looked up. When she saw he was awake, she smiled.

"Good nap?" she asked.

"You should have tossed me out, Miss Emma. That was incredibly rude of me."

She shook her head. "You needed it, and I didn't mind at

all. Dinner will be ready in another half hour. If you don't want to move, I can bring you a tray in here.''

Damn it, he couldn't believe this. The woman didn't even know him. Why should she go to so much trouble?

He was a hard man, she thought, and he didn't know what to make of her. So she told him. "Look, Mr. Dalton, you've been kind enough to escort me home on two occasions. Apart from that, you're a neighbor. You needed to sleep, you obviously found the rocker comfortable enough to sleep in, and I'd have to be some kind of twisted, heartless beast to wake you up and throw you out. Besides, I lived with a great deal of pain after my—after my accident years ago, and I know how difficult it can be to get any sleep at all. As for dinner, I was going to cook anyway, and it didn't take one bit of additional effort to throw an extra potato into the oven.'' She suddenly smiled with exaggerated sweetness. "Can you handle that?''

"Do I have any choice?''

She studied him a moment, doubtfully, and then realized he was teasing. Her smile broadened. "I guess I didn't give you one.''

"And I'm glad you didn't.'' He allowed a smile to show. "I appreciate it, Miss Emma. I really do. And I think I'm going to get one of these rockers for myself. I had no idea how comfortable one would be.''

She nodded. "They don't look all that great, but my father was partial to it because of his back. You didn't hurt yourself when you caught me, did you?''

The last words came out in a rush, telling him just how much she had worried about that.

"No. It's an old injury, and nothing that I don't feel a dozen times a day. Don't worry about it.''

He must have been a truly charming man before he was hurt, Emma thought a short while later as she thickened the gravy. Flashes of that charm still broke through the abrupt, harsh, dark envelope that pain had wrapped around him. And he must have been sinfully handsome before his injury. The vestiges of it were still there in his bone structure, in the chiseled line of his jaw. The premature gray of his hair, a silvery color, merely added an additional dash of mystery to him.

Turning from the stove to add some more water to the thickener she was using in the gravy, Emma glanced toward the kitchen window.

And screamed.

Chapter 3

When he heard the scream and a crash, Gage hit the floor running. Automatically, his hand dived beneath his suit jacket, searching for the gun he used to always carry, and when he found nothing, he swore fiercely. No gun. No weapon at all, except himself. These days, that was no bargain.

Before the sound of Emma's scream had fully died, he kicked open the kitchen door and peered around the doorjamb to assess the situation.

Emma stood alone, pressed back against the counter, her terrified gaze leaping from the door he had just kicked open to the windows beyond which the world had turned dark. At her feet lay a mess of white paste and shattered ceramic.

"Emma?" Seeing no one else, Gage eased into the room. "Emma, what happened?"

Her eyes were huge as they sought him. She shuddered once, wildly, and then wrapped her arms around herself. "Someone was staring in the window."

Gage reached the door in two long strides and threw it open. Standing on the back stoop, he scanned the driveway, what he could see of the street and the snow beneath the kitchen windows.

"Do you see anything?"

Emma stood behind him in the open door, and he spared her a glance. "Not much. Have you got a flashlight?"

"I'll get it."

To see over the café curtains into the kitchen while standing on the ground, a man would have to be better than eight feet tall, Gage figured. Either that, or he'd need a ladder, and it was moot anyway, because the snow below the windows was undisturbed—except for some snow that had fallen off the roof....

He snapped his head up and peered at the roof, just as Emma returned.

"Here," she said, and gave him the light.

The snow was disturbed along the eaves, Gage saw. Taking the flashlight, he descended the steps and backed his way across the driveway while shining the light at the roof over the kitchen. The snow was stirred up, but cats could have done that, and surely, if a man had been up there, he and Emma would have heard him scramble away to safety.

The Conard house had two stories, but the second story had been a late addition, Gage judged, and had been erected over only part of the house. The kitchen roof was at the single story level, not as steep as the peaked gables of the second floor, and easy for a man to get onto. Still, a fast dash across the roof would have made enough noise to tell the tale.

"Gage?"

Emma was waiting in the doorway, Gage saw, shivering from the cold and frowning. He limped back toward her.

"Nothing," he said. "Whoever it was is gone now. What exactly did you see?"

He closed the door behind himself, shutting out the night.

"It all happened so fast— Oh! The gravy!" She turned quickly to the stove and reached for the wire whisk. Another half minute and it would have been scorched.

"Did you recognize the face?" Gage asked

"No." She turned off the gas under the gravy. "Dinner is just about ready."

Gage was habitually short on patience these days. Constant pain did devastating things to a man's temper. "Emma, will you just look at me and answer my questions?"

She spun around to face him, anger bringing color to her cheeks. "I *am* answering you, Mr. Dalton! I am also trying to keep dinner from being ruined. Furthermore, I don't believe I gave you permission to address me so familiarly!"

"Familiarly? You don't know the meaning of the word. *Honey* would be familiar! Damn it, woman—"

"And don't you swear at me, either!"

The pain was building up again, thanks to his careless dash from the living room. A hot poker was jamming into his lower back and sending rivers of burning lava down his left leg. He wanted to ignore it. He tried to ignore it, hating the weakness, but accepting the agony as his due. He couldn't ignore it, however, when fiery talons gripped his thigh and dug in deeply. He drew a sharp breath and squeezed his eyes shut. He would be damned if he would let this woman see how much he was hurting.

But Emma saw. Suddenly she was beside him, slipping her arm around him, talking in the sweetest, gentlest voice, a voice that made him think of cool spring water bubbling over mossy rocks. He clung to the soothing sound as if it were a lifeline thrown down into hell.

"Let's get you back in the rocker," she said, gently urging him toward the living room. "You were comfortable there—oh, I just know you hurt yourself when you caught me. You should just have let me fall!"

"No." He scowled fiercely down at her, but it was a wasted effort, because all he could see was the top of her head. "I didn't hurt myself. I'm just having a bad day. Will you stop mothering me?"

The next thing he knew, he was back in the Kennedy rocker with two fingers of Scotch in his highball glass.

"I'll be right back with a tray," Emma said briskly. "Then you can question me to your heart's content while we eat."

It *was* just a bad day. Though he was never entirely free of pain, most of the time, with the aid of aspirin, he could ignore it. Periodically, though, his damaged nerves howled and all but crippled him. Usually he walked himself into exhaustion, but tonight he tossed off the Scotch Emma had poured. Damn, the woman was a human bulldozer. And it galled him that she was seeing him this way. When this spell passed off in a few days or a week, nobody would be able to tell that he hurt. It was only when it got this bad that he couldn't always hide it.

Emma opened up a pair of TV tables, setting one before Gage so he wouldn't have to move more than his hands to dine. He watched her over the rim of his glass, noting the way her full breasts swayed when she moved, liking the way the lamplight caught the gold highlights in her hair. She was, he thought, a striking woman. Neither pretty nor beautiful, she would always be memorable.

For the first time in many, many months, he wanted to touch a woman's breasts and bury his flesh deep in hers. He wanted to feel a woman's cool, smooth palms on his back and buttocks, wanted to feel the sting of her nails as she tried to get closer and closer. He wanted her twisting and writhing and sweaty and hungry beneath him. All female animal.

Damn!

He looked away as Emma bent toward him to set a heaping plate of chicken, potatoes and asparagus before him. Not now. Not now. Not ever. Giving himself a giant mental yank, he turned his attention back to the Peeping Tom.

"Just what exactly did you see out that window?" he demanded.

Emma bristled a little, but she understood his irritation. She *was* trying to avoid the subject. She really didn't want to think about it, but whether she wanted to or not, she knew perfectly well that, come midnight, she would be lying in her bed remembering it. Forcing herself to remain outwardly calm, she offered him the gravy boat and smiled when he scowled at it but took it anyway.

"I saw a face," she said. "A face. I didn't recognize it, but it was distorted somehow. I wonder if the person might have been wearing a stocking? No, it didn't look like that. It wasn't a squashing kind of distortion. No, it was...pulled somehow."

"Pulled?" He simply stared at her, trying to follow her line of thought.

"Well, that isn't a very good word, but I don't know how else... Yes! That's it. It looked distorted, as if it were on the other side of a fish-eye lens! Like looking through a peephole in a door. I don't think I would recognize my closest friend through one of those things."

Gage set down the gravy boat and slipped his hand into the inside breast pocket of his suit jacket to pull out a pen and small pad. He scribbled down a few key words. "What about colors? Hair, eyes, anything."

"What about eating your dinner before it turns stone cold? I think maybe there was dark hair, but it could have been a stocking cap. I don't know. It was all so fast...."

She sounded so calm about the thing that he wanted to shake her. *She* had been the one who had screamed, after all, and brought him tearing into the kitchen as if he was still able to deal with such situations. And now she sat here acting as if she were the queen serving tea, and he was an importunate subject. Yes, he wanted to shake her.

That was when he noticed that her hands were trembling.

Something tight and angry in him relaxed as he realized that Emma Conard was all bluff. Mirrors and smoke. And she was so damn good at it that she must have had a lot of practice at hiding her fear.

Why? Fear of what? Intrigued, Gage settled back in the rocker, tucked his notebook away and picked up his fork. First he had to deal with the Peeping Tom. Then he would look into the mystery of Emmaline Conard.

"This is really good," he told her after he had tasted everything. "Was the face in the window upside-down?"

"Thank you. No. Right side up. Why?"

"Kind of hard to hang down from the eaves and look into the window right side up."

"Oh!" She looked up from her own plate and watched him slice another mouthful of chicken. She wondered if any other man in the county would have used a knife and fork on chicken. Probably not. Around here, chicken was finger food. "Well, it was definitely right side up. I just assumed someone was standing out there."

"He'd have had to be eight feet tall or able to fly, and considering there aren't any footprints under the window, he must have been flying."

Emma's hand tightened on her linen napkin. "Are you being sarcastic?"

"Not at all. I'm serious. When I didn't see any disturbance in the snow beneath the windows, I assumed the peeper must have been hanging over the edge of the roof, but then he would have had to be upside-down, and you're sure he wasn't. Of course, maybe he was wearing a mask upside down. That would definitely explain that part of it. Now we only need to figure out why you didn't hear anybody on the roof. Unless you did?"

Emma shook her head. "No. Not a thing." Inwardly she quailed. This was awful. Who would have done such a thing, and why? She thought she knew everyone in Conard County so well that if any of them had a propensity for this sort of thing, she would know. And that was utterly ridiculous, wasn't it? Nobody ever knew his neighbors well enough to be sure of something like that.

Gage had been watching her more closely than she knew, and he read far more in the slight flickers in her face than she would have dreamed. At that moment he changed tack. "I'm sure," he said, "it was just a kid playing a prank. Who did you scold at the library in the last few days?"

Emma's relief was palpable, so palpable that it told Gage just how much fear she had been hiding. That, too, was another mystery to add to his list of mysteries about this woman. Why had she reacted so strongly to that photo of the dagger last night? Why did she find it necessary to hide her fear about the Peeping Tom?

"I'm going to call the department," he told her when he finished eating. "A deputy will keep an eye on your house tonight."

"But you said—"

He refused to look at her. This woman was beginning to get under his skin, and he couldn't allow that. "It probably was some juvenile playing a prank. That's the most likely explanation, given that we haven't had any other incidents reported. But in case he decides to come back and try tó give you another scare, there'll be someone outside."

She rose with him, following him as he headed for the kitchen to use the phone. "But isn't that a little extreme?" Oh, Lord, she could just imagine the gossip. Miss Emma, starchy spinster, was starting to imagine lurking rapists behind every bush. She would be the laughingstock of Mahoney's. "Mr. Dalton…"

"Call me Gage." He had just reached the phone, but he turned abruptly to face her. "Look, Emma, I have a personal thing about cruds who pick on women and children. I won't stand for it. Not for one damn minute."

She looked up at him. A tall woman, she was accustomed to meeting most men at eye level. Gage was five or six inches taller, and the difference made her feel small. Delicate. Feminine. It made her notice that the dark stubble of the day's growth of beard had begun to appear on his uninjured cheek. It made her notice the broad-shouldered, slim-hipped way he filled out his suit. It made her notice his hands, dark, lean and large.

She caught her breath and backed up. For long years she had schooled herself not to notice such things, had taught her body to pretend it had no needs and never felt empty. Her walls and barriers suddenly felt weak and shaky. Abruptly she turned. "Fine," she said, and headed back to the living room to clean up from dinner.

Twenty minutes later a deputy arrived. Sara Yates was Conard County's only female deputy, and probably Emma's closest woman friend in the county. Sara took one look at Gage, and another at Emma, and grinned in a way Emma didn't at all like.

"What's this about a Peeping Tom, Gage?" Sara asked, turning away from Emma before the latter could say anything.

Gage explained the sequence of events rapidly, clearly, concisely, in a way that told Emma he had long experience of making such reports. Rumor in the county had it that Gage Dalton had been a lawman somewhere before he came here to work part-time for Nathan Tate, and it appeared rumor was right. Emma couldn't have explained things so well or clearly if she'd had hours to prepare.

Sara trained her spotlight on the eaves, and she and Gage together began a close examination of the scene. Feeling useless, Emma went back inside to wash the dishes.

She was just wiping the counters down when Gage and Sara came back inside. Gage looked cold, Emma thought. He should at least have put on his jacket.

"Well," he said, "we found out how it was done."

Sara held up a long piece of twine from which hung the shred of a balloon. "Just a prank, Emma," she said. "Gage and I figure that the hoaxster shot it with a BB gun when you screamed. Makes it spookier that way."

Gage and Sara had stayed to have coffee and pie with Emma, and then Sara had driven Gage back to his place.

Alone in the big, empty old house, Emma felt uneasy. Just a prank, she told herself, and forced herself through her nightly routine of checking locks and windows. While she showered, she tried to repress images out of *Psycho*—surely a movie no solitary woman should ever watch—and then she proved she could conquer her nerves by lingering to dust herself with talcum powder.

Finally, edgy beyond belief, she dived into her bed and pulled the covers up to her eyes just like a little kid who was scared of the dark.

And she *was* afraid of the dark, she admitted. Thirty years old, and petrified of the night, of shadows, of empty streets. Petrified of being wounded again the way Joe Murphy had wounded her all those years ago.

She and Joe had become engaged halfway through her senior year in college. Just two weeks before the assault that had changed her life forever. When she had come out of her coma and learned what had happened to her, she had naturally turned to Joe for understanding and comfort.

Instead, he had broken their engagement. "The whole point of getting married is having children," he'd told her. "You can't have kids anymore, Emma. What's the point?"

What's the point?

Tucked under her blankets now, with the light beside the bed blazing brightly to hold back all the terrors that had no names, Emma squeezed her eyes shut against an old pain that still felt like a spear in her heart. Over the years, she had come to understand that Joe had been the smallest of the losses she had suffered. Her real loss had been the loss of her womanhood. The thing that Emma believed most made a woman a woman, the thing that gave her meaning and purpose, that made her desirable as a mate, was gone forever, never to be recovered. And never again would she risk even the remote possibility that a man might reject her because she was barren.

Lying alone in her empty bed, she listened to mocking whispers that seemed to come from just beyond the range of her hearing. The feeling of invasion returned. There was something evil out there, something waiting. Something looking. For her.

* * *

Gage drooped over his coffeepot the following morning. Wearing nothing but his black jeans, zipped but not buttoned, he cursed the strangely wild mood that had led him to stop in Mahoney's last night after Sara dropped him off. Seeing him, Mahoney had poured the usual two shots, but Gage had lingered for another two, and then another. He had only a vague memory of eventually climbing the stairs and falling onto his bed.

Hell, he *never* did that. The last time he had tied one on had been just after... He squashed the thought before it could be born. Some things didn't bear remembering. Some things had to be buried before they drove you mad.

He swore at the coffeepot and wondered why it was so damn sluggish this morning. He swore at himself for getting hung over, though it was only a small hangover. He swore at his back for hurting, then swore at life in general. And when he got done with that, he swore at Emma Conard for being so sexy when she was so damn uptight. At this moment he would have bet a year's pay she was a virgin. He swore again. She must surely be the last virgin on earth over the age of eighteen. Why the hell did she have to cross his path?

Someone knocked timidly on the door. Gage glared at it over his shoulder. Probably Mahoney coming to find out why he was swearing so viciously. Mahoney lived downstairs, behind the bar.

The knock came again, stronger. What the hell?

"Door's open," he growled. "Come on in, Mahoney."

When he heard the soft gasp behind him, he knew it wasn't Mahoney. Hell's bells, he didn't even have a shirt on, and he knew what Emma could see. And knew it was Emma. Somehow he just knew, though why the devil she would look him up on a Sunday morning...

He turned slowly, certain he would find shock and horror. Burn scars sure as hell weren't pretty. He found the shock and horror, all right. And tears sparkling on the dark fringe of lashes that framed her misty green eyes.

"Oh, Gage," she whispered. "Oh, Gage."

"I'll get a shirt." He headed toward the bedroom, trying to keep his front toward her. His chest wasn't bad at all, hardly marked. He'd been heading away from the car, going back to get the forgotten diaper bag when... He choked that thought off, too.

"It's...all right," she said. "You don't have to. I know it's early and..." She blinked, and a tear ran down her cheek. "I'm sorry I barged in on you but...I need your help."

She turned her back to him and folded her arms around herself, and he knew in that instant how much it had cost her to come here and ask for his help. Emma Conard was a proud, independent woman who hated to admit any fear.

He hesitated momentarily, torn by an unexpected urge to go to her and comfort her. Instead, he dashed into his bedroom and grabbed a sweatshirt that was hanging over the foot of the bed. Tugging it swiftly on, he returned to Emma.

"What happened?"

She didn't turn to face him, but stared out the uncurtained window at the brick wall on the other side of the alley. "I went out to get my paper from the porch this morning and found...a decapitated rabbit."

Something inside him froze. "On your porch?"

"On my porch. Anyway, what with that and last night and...everything, I thought that if you were still interested in renting a room from me, I'd be awfully grateful not to be alone in that house."

He didn't answer immediately. "Did you call the sheriff?"

She nodded. "They came out and took the carcass, and Dave Winters suggested that maybe I could have a friend stay with me while they try to figure out if this is serious or just kids."

Now she turned and looked at him. "I can understand that you might not want the room anymore, but it really wasn't anything personal when I turned you down before."

"No, I understood that. It'll take me a couple of hours to box up my stuff, but I'll come."

"Thank you. I'm on my way to church, but I'll be back home in about an hour and a half. Come whenever you feel like it."

He reached out and touched her arm. "Let me drive you to church."

Her faced blanched. Damn it, he wondered, what the hell was it with this woman? Why should the offer of a lift drain all the color from her face?

"No, really, it's just a short walk," she said, backing up and giving him a fragile, forced smile. "I'll see you later."

He followed her to the door and watched her descend the wooden staircase, thinking that perhaps she shouldn't go anywhere alone until this thing was settled. Damn, what had happened to the deputy who was supposed to be watching her house? A decapitated rabbit went far beyond a funny face painted on a balloon, but, disgusting as it was, it still didn't exceed the realm of possible teenage pranks. Given that, he could hardly stick to her side like a watchdog.

But he could make certain she was safe when she was at home, he thought, as she disappeared around the corner of the building. He could make certain that if she didn't turn up where she was supposed to be, someone would notice it.

Turning his back on the cold, clear day, Gage shut the door. Forgetting his hangover, he poured himself some coffee and then went to dig out the boxes he had saved in the storage closet.

Damn, he hated this feeling that something terrible was about to happen. It clung to his neck and shoulders like chilly, wet leaves, ominous and foreboding.

Emma hadn't told Gage the half of it, mostly because she was sure she would look and feel like a fool if she did. The rabbit was a tangible thing, proof that she hadn't utterly lost her mind. She could call the sheriff to deal with something like that.

But she couldn't call the sheriff to deal with her nightmares.

There wasn't anyone she could tell that she had dreamed of the dagger again last night. She couldn't tell anyone that its image had begun to haunt the edges of her mind, like a memory she couldn't quite grasp. She couldn't tell anyone about the other nightmare she had had last night, when the balloon face had become a real face, a face she seemed to know but not know. A stranger she remembered. A man who terrified her.

The man who had hurt her?

Dawn had taken a terribly long time coming this morning. Lights had blazed at Emma's house for hours, holding the night at bay, but only with the arrival of the sun did she feel she was again safe.

It was crazy, it was creepy, and it was something she couldn't tell anyone else about. She walked into the church that morning looking for a comfort that no one on earth could give her, because there was no one on earth she could tell.

Gage pulled his black Suburban into Emma's driveway shortly after noon. She heard his engine as he pulled up and hurried out to the kitchen to meet him. During the time since she had gotten back from church, her nerves had stretched tighter and tighter, and even the old regulator's ticking had become ominous. Nor did it do a darn bit of good to remind herself how many years she had lived quite happily in this house. It just didn't feel safe any longer.

She reached the door as Gage was climbing out of the Suburban. Inexplicably, her breath locked in her throat, and she froze in astonishment as the most unexpected yearning squeezed her heart.

He was dressed, as usual, in head-to-toe black: black jeans, black Stetson, black boots, black leather jacket. On the surface, at least, he was everything she had always avoided. He looked like a brewing storm, like trouble distilled.

That didn't keep her from wishing she could know what it felt like to be held by him. Every cell in her body suddenly ached just to feel his arms around her.

But that was ridiculous. Absurd. Unthinkable. Ignoring the ache, she opened the door just as Gage pulled the first of his boxes from the back end of the truck.

"Hi," she called, and felt her breath catch again as he looked up at her and smiled back. "What can I do to help?"

"Keep the rocker warm," he replied, climbing the steps. "My back's going to kill me after this."

"Let me—"

"No." The word was flat, unequivocal.

Emma stepped back to let him pass. "I can ask the boys next door—"

"No." He halted and turned to look at her. "I may hurt like hell, Emma, but don't ever mistake me for being helpless or an invalid."

She watched his narrow flanks as he walked away and wondered why she had never before noticed just how sexy a man's bottom could be in a pair of jeans. Suddenly she charged after him.

"Doing a job like this when you know it's going to hurt you is just plain foolhardy, Gage Dalton!"

He was already climbing the stairs. "So I'm a macho idiot. But once you start giving ground, lady, it's hell to get it back."

Emma stood watching him climb the rest of the stairs, thinking that he was probably right.

"Which room?" he asked.

"Take your pick. The front bedroom has the hardest mattress, though, if that's important to your back."

"Thanks."

Nice buns, she thought again, and almost giggled at her own foolishness. It was such a relief to have another person in the house that she was a little giddy.

Gage did it all himself, every last damn box and book. And he had a lot of books. They constituted the major part of his possessions.

"Emma?" he called down the stairs. "Would it be a problem if I took a bookcase out of one of the other rooms?"

She appeared at the foot of the stairs, wiping her hands on an apron. Delicious aromas were filling the house again. "Help yourself." The bookcases had been empty since she had donated the books—mostly very old novels—to Sweetwater Nursing Home. Her own books, and the handed-down ones that she treasured, filled the floor-to-ceiling bookcases in her study. "Do you need any help?"

"No, but thanks."

Well, that was the most gracious refusal he'd yet given her, Emma thought as she headed back into the kitchen to finish peeling potatoes. It had been a while since she had cooked a big Sunday dinner for anyone but herself, and she was enjoying it. She was enjoying, too, the noise from upstairs as Gage moved around and unpacked.

The house had been empty and silent for too long, Emma thought now. Her last roomer had been a middle-aged French teacher who had spent her time quietly and unobtrusively upstairs reading or grading papers. Emma had hardly known the woman was in the house. Somehow she didn't think she would be unaware of Gage.

Even the runner in the upstairs hallway didn't entirely silence his booted feet, and floorboards creaked under his every step. The sounds made the house feel alive once again.

He came down the stairs again for another load and sniffed appreciatively as he passed through the kitchen.

"It sure smells a lot better than Mahoney's," he told her.

"You're invited to join me," she said—casually, she hoped, because she suddenly didn't feel at all casual about asking this man to dine with her. "Roast beef, oven-browned potatoes, candied carrots…"

"Say no more. I'll be there with bells on."

He managed to get the last box upstairs without knuckling under to the pain that flayed him, but when he reached the room that final time, he knew he couldn't have made one more trip.

Leaving the last boxes untouched for now, he grabbed a couple of his towels and headed for the bathroom. What he needed was a long, hot soak, and that claw-footed tub looked big enough to hold him, unlike most modern tubs.

A twenty-minute soak eased the worst of the spasms. Back in his room, he stretched out on the bed, facedown, and groaned with sheer relief. God, he almost didn't hurt at all. Almost. Let it last, just a little while. Just a little while.

Emma hesitated at the foot of the stairs, wondering if she should call Gage down to dinner or go upstairs to get him. Things had been so quiet since he finished his bath that she thought he might have fallen asleep. If that was so, she didn't want to wake him. The poor man probably needed whatever sleep he could manage to get, and while he was asleep he wouldn't feel the pain.

After a few more moments of indecision, she decided to go up and peek in on him. If he was sleeping, she could save his dinner to reheat later.

The door to his room stood wide open, and she saw him lying facedown on the bed. Jeans and a black T-shirt covered him decently, but his feet were bare, and there was something about them that made him seem oddly vulnerable.

Emma hesitated on the threshold. "Gage?" She said his name softly, hoping not to disturb him if he wasn't awake.

"I'm awake, Emma," he said, his voice muffled, "but I think I'm paralyzed. Maybe you'd better eat without me."

"Paralyzed?" She stepped into the room, closer to him, and battled an urge to hurry over and touch him somehow. "Did you hurt yourself?"

"Naw. Actually, I don't hurt at all. Not at all. And I just discovered I'm a coward."

"Why?"

"I'm afraid to move."

She gave a small laugh. "I can sure see why. Okay, I'll save your dinner for you."

"You don't have to—"

"I want to," she interrupted. "I'd offer to bring it up here, but I don't see how you can eat in that position."

"Me, neither. Well, I'll be surprised if this lasts even another few minutes. Just don't wait on me."

Turning away was somehow difficult, but she did it, descending the stairs with her mind full of the look of him lying sprawled on the bed, her hands wishing they could have touched him.

Lord, Lord, Emma, what's gotten into you? Yes, he's a virile-looking man, an attractive man for all he's aloof and difficult at times, but he's not the first attractive man you've ever seen. Why are you reacting to *him?*

And why *shouldn't* she react? some other part of her wondered. Gage Dalton was no more interested in any kind of involvement than she was. Reacting to him was about as safe as such a thing could be. He would never notice her as a woman, not in a million years. And if he should, just maybe, make a pass at her, maybe she could succumb. After all, she would go into it with her eyes open, knowing from the first that that was all it would ever be.

There had been a time in her life when moral strictures would have prevented her from even considering such a thing. Even with Joe, she had never permitted any more than a few kisses, because she hadn't wanted to be a tease and she knew she wouldn't go all the way.

But now she was past thirty, facing middle age as a perennial spinster, and some part of her resented the hell out of that. Why shouldn't she taste the forbidden apple a few times? She would have the rest of her life to aspire to sainthood. But now, right now, Emma Conard felt a crying need for human warmth, a human touch, human contact.

She felt, she admitted, a crying need for a man's heat and desire. She wanted to know what it felt like to be swept away by the dizzying feelings she had read about, wanted to know what real passion was, what real desire meant, and how it felt to be wanted like that.

And then she wanted to be able to walk away with a whole heart.

She could have laughed at her own foolishness just then, except that it hurt too much. She felt as if she were drying up and blowing away. Someday little children would scurry out of her way and whisper behind her back the way they had with Great-aunt Isabel.

It was enough to make her want to smash something. There were just no answers for why life could be so unfair. No answers at all. She had done nothing to deserve the assault that had ruined her life. Nothing.

But then, Gage had probably done nothing to deserve what had happened to him, either.

There was just no explaining it. No explaining it at all.

Muffled by distance, she heard Gage swear suddenly. Well, he would probably be coming down for dinner, she thought, as she heard him swear again. His vacation from pain was over.

Chapter 4

"**I** need to go out on a case," Gage said.

Emma immediately glanced toward the window and the night beyond. In a few short days she had grown accustomed to Gage's presence in the house, to the comfort it gave her. He had offered to pay more to have his meals included in the rent, and she had accepted, but that hadn't kept him from going out and stocking the pantry on Monday. Since then he had helped with the cooking and washed the dishes every night. Then, as the evening deepened, he would settle into the Kennedy rocker in the living room and read.

Tonight a phone call had come just as they were finishing dinner, and now he had to leave.

Emma's insides knotted, and her heart sped up. This evening she would be alone. Alone with the strange, disturbing images that flickered around the edges of her mind, unrecognizable glimpses of faces, sounds not quite heard. All she knew was that these flickers, these glimpses of what might be distorted memories, frightened her. For the last several days she had kept herself continuously busy, trying to squelch what seemed to be a growing pressure just beneath the level of her waking thoughts.

And now Gage had to go out. Maybe she could persuade Sara to come over until he got back. Or maybe she could go over to Sara's. Or maybe, she told herself sternly, she could just stay home by herself as she had been doing these many years without any trouble at all. What ever was the matter with her?

"Want to go with me?" Gage asked.

"Hmm?" Emma looked up from the plates she was carrying to the sink. "I'm sorry, what did you say?"

"Would you like to go with me? It's a clear night, and a quarter moon is rising. It'd make a pretty drive out to the Bar C."

The Bar C was her cousin Jeff's ranch, and that was the first part of his speech that penetrated. "Oh, no! Not another mutilation!"

"Afraid so. Would you like to come with me?"

"Come?" And suddenly she understood. Alone in the car with him. With a man. Her hands started to shake violently, and she hurried to the counter to set the plates down. "I...I can't. Thanks anyway."

"Why not?" He hadn't missed the way her hands had started to tremble, or the way she had paled. "Emma?"

"I...just can't."

He ought to leave right now, he thought with a kind of aching desperation. He didn't need any more problems in his life, a life already so burdened with painful problems that he sometimes felt as if he were wearing a lead overcoat. It was a selfish thought, though, and it shamed him even as he had it.

"Emma," he said, "is it me? Or is it the car?"

"Just go take care of your case, Gage. I'll be fine."

"I don't want to leave you here alone."

She faced him then, attempting a smile. "I'll give Sara a call. I think she's off duty tonight. You don't need to worry about me."

"She's on duty. She's the one who called me." Frowning, Gage stepped closer. "Emma, tell me."

And somehow it just came blurting out. Nobody in Conard County knew what had happened to her, because her father had protected her secret. He hadn't wanted her to suffer the curious looks and the endless speculation, not to mention the callous or careless questions. So no one here knew a thing about the assault. Emma had been happy to leave it that way, so why was she now telling this man her deepest, darkest secret?

"When...when I was a senior in college, I was assaulted. I don't remember anything about it but...I was in a coma for weeks, and after I woke I needed all kinds of rehabilitation."

"My God." Gage barely breathed the words.

Emma closed her eyes, not wanting to see his pity. She shrugged, as if these were matters of no concern. "I still don't know what happened, and no one was ever charged with it, but I have a few silly fears I can't seem to shake." Again she shrugged. "I can't get into a car with a man. I just...can't...do it."

She expected him to say, "Well, all right, then," or something else equally dismissive, then leave. Instead, his ruined voice took on an incredibly gentle tone.

"That's all right, Emma," he said. "That's all right. Perfectly understandable. I'll get someone over here to keep an eye on things while I'm gone."

Her eyes popped open. "Oh, no! Oh, Gage, really... everyone will hear about it, and they'll start wondering if I've gone off the deep end. Don't bother. I'll be fine, really. It'll only be a couple of hours, right? And nothing else has happened since the rabbit." And why was she trying to talk him out of giving her exactly the comfort she needed? Lord, Emma, you really *are* losing your mind!

Gage hesitated, but finally he said, "Okay. I'll get back just as soon as I can."

At the door, though, he suddenly turned around and came back. But he didn't stop a polite distance away. No, he came right up to her, to within a foot, and took her gently by the shoulders, moving her away from the counter.

"I don't want you to get claustrophobic because you're caught between me and the counter," he said gruffly in answer to the questioning but incredibly trusting look on her face. He couldn't imagine why this woman should trust him at all. He couldn't imagine why he hadn't been able to get out that door without coming back to touch her. To kiss her. And for the moment he was past wondering about it.

When Gage's stormy gaze moved from her eyes to her lips, Emma caught her breath in agonizing hope. The last time she had felt like this, she had been sixteen, and Lefty Sjodgren, the school's star quarterback, had taken her to a movie. She had felt like this then, too, standing on her porch as they said goodnight, hoping against hope that Lefty would give her her first kiss. That kiss had been a huge disappointment. Somehow she didn't think Gage's would be a disappointment at all.

His head bowed a fraction, then hesitated. He wasn't sure he should do this. Not sure at all. Nor was she, but she didn't want to miss it. There might never again be a chance to feel this man's lips on hers, and she was going out of her mind wanting to know. She lifted her mouth, just a fraction. Just enough.

A soft, husky whisper of sound escaped him, causing her insides to clench sharply. Pleasurably. A sensation she hadn't felt in years.

"I shouldn't do this," he muttered, and then his mouth covered hers with hungry heat. Not too much, he warned himself. Not too much. This woman was inexperienced and fearful of men. Just a little kiss, just a sop to the aching need to hold her tightly and bury himself in her slick, silky heat. Living with her was rapidly turning into a new kind of hell for him, a hell he had no desire to run from. Not yet, anyway.

Her hands fluttered uncertainly and then came to rest on his hips, holding him gently. He nearly groaned with sheer pleasure at the touch. It wasn't a sexy touch, or even a hungry one, but it wasn't rejecting him, either. It had been so long since he had been touched. So damn long.

He meant to break away, meant the kiss to be gentle and noninflammatory, but somehow it didn't stop there. His tongue slipped past his guard and ran slowly, tenderly, along Emma's lips, tasting the coffee they had just drunk, coaxing her to give him more. Stop. He had to stop. But, oh, God, it had been so long, and he needed the gentleness, the softness, the heat. The longing rolled over him, overwhelming him, sweeping him up in aching waves.

Emma felt the coaxing, enticing sweep of his tongue across her lips all the way to the soles of her feet. Long-untested instincts took over before she even knew it. Her hands tightened on his hard, narrow hips as she leaned even closer, seeking deeper pressure, and opened her mouth to take him into her. At the first hot thrust of his tongue, her entire body took flame. Hungers long denied, long buried, sprang to immediate life. When his hands slipped from her shoulders to enfold her in a tight embrace, she wanted to sob for sheer joy. Nothing had ever felt so good, so right.

Suddenly Gage tore his mouth from hers and pressed his cheek to hers. For long moments he continued to hold her snugly, and then his embrace gentled. "That got a little out of hand," he said softly. Slowly, gently, soothingly, he stroked her back from shoulder to waist.

Emma could feel him withdrawing, rebuilding his internal barriers brick by brick. She recognized the wisdom of it and knew she should step back now. But for a few seconds she remained within his embrace, paralyzed by an urgent need to burrow into him, to never again know the loneliness that lurked just beyond the magic circle of his arms.

Ridiculous, she told herself and, with a sigh, eased backward. Gage released her instantly. He didn't immediately leave, however. Instead, he reached out and touched her cheek with gentle fingertips. "I'll get back just as soon as I can, Emma."

She smiled. "I'll be fine, Gage, really. There's no reason to think there's any real danger from these pranks. I guess my nerves just ran away with me on Sunday.''

He hesitated a moment longer, then nodded and left, grabbing his Stetson from the peg as he passed out the door.

Once he was out in his Suburban, however, he radioed the department and told them to keep a sharp eye on Emma's house. She might have grown sanguine, but he hadn't. For three days now he'd been trying to connect the decapitated rabbit with the cattle mutilations, then trying not to connect them, telling himself that the rabbit was just inspired by the cattle. Somehow that didn't feel right, though. Nothing felt right, and his gut kept insisting these were no ordinary pranks.

His hands tightened on the steering wheel as he thought of Emma alone in that big old house, and even knowing a deputy would keep an eye on the place didn't make him feel a whole lot better. There were plenty of ways to get around such surveillance. He himself was a master of them.

And then there was Emma herself. The outline she had stammered out for him tonight was ghastly even in its bare-bones form. It twisted something inside him, something that had been dead ever since...before. And, unfortunately, he'd seen enough of that kind of violence in his life to be able to fill in Emma's outline with gruesome images.

He shifted on the seat, seeking to ease the tension in his lower back before it became uncomfortable. Such adjustments of his posture had grown so automatic that he was hardly aware of them. The movements made him appear restless, though, even when he wasn't. Like a caged wolf.

He was a man accustomed to accepting the way things were, like them or not, but right now he experienced a vain wish that he hadn't kissed Emma Conard. He didn't like the feelings that had goaded him back across the kitchen and driven him to taste her mouth. He didn't like having feelings at all anymore. Feelings were a dangerous roller coaster with as many lows as there were highs. And some of the lows twisted a man inside out and left him smashed for good.

Having a personal and intimate acquaintance with the depths of hell, Gage had no desire to experience any new tortures. But Miss Emma's mouth had been sweet and warm, water to a man in a desert. Her inexperienced response had been instant and generous, and her hands on his hips had been a touch of heaven. Just remembering it made his loins clench sharply. Part of him, at least, was coming back to life in a headlong rush.

A wise man would probably bail out right now. When it came to some things, though, Gage had never been a wise man. For the time being, Miss Emmaline Conard needed his protection and the security his presence in her house gave her. Never in his life, not once, had he been able to walk away from that kind of need.

Emma sat in the middle of the living room surrounded by boxes of decorations she had dragged down from an upstairs closet. Traditional Christmas carols played loudly from the stereo, and every light blazed. The curtains were drawn tightly, letting not so much as a wedge of the night into the room.

She'd completely forgotten the tree in all the uproar this week, but tomorrow, she promised herself, she would find a large one. In the meantime she could put up the garlands and wreaths, and replace blue candles with red and green ones in all the brass sconces.

The rhythm of the familiar tasks soothed her, bringing back memories that alternately brought a smile to her lips or tightened her throat. So many Christmases past, so many memories, etched in the brilliance of the holiday season. Somehow those memories took on a brightness and a golden warmth that her other memories lacked.

Except for the last several years. Oh, she thoroughly enjoyed the festivities before Christmas, looked forward to the annual open house, when Front Street filled with carolers and good cheer. But, since her father's death, that was the extent of it. On Christmas Eve she still went to the candlelight ceremony at the church, but that had become a time when she mourned her father's absence. And Christmas Day always dawned gray for her, even if the sun shone brilliantly.

A lousy commentary, she told herself, and tried to shrug away the morbid thoughts. And still, glittering at the edge of her mind like shards of sharp glass, were the images and sounds she couldn't quite grasp. Feeling their pressure suddenly, like a volcano trying to erupt into her conscious world, she stood abruptly and went to get herself another cup of coffee.

Moving around would help. Maybe she would bake a pie, get her mind off memories of Christmas past and onto something productive, something pleasant. Like the way Gage had dug into the blueberry pie she had served on Sunday.

Like the way he had kissed her tonight. A shiver ran through her, a pleasant river of remembered sensation. She couldn't imagine why he had done that. It had seemed to come out of nowhere, without warning or provocation.

Absently, she began to cut shortening into flour to make a pie crust, intending to use the canned cherry filling she had in the pantry. It had been a while since she had made a cherry pie.

The entire front of her body had been imprinted with every hard line of Gage's, she thought. The zipper of his jacket had pressed against her left breast when he had hugged her, and she could still remember the way his hips had felt beneath her hands. What if she had tightened her hold? What if she had drawn those hips closer, had pressed herself to them? Would he have answered her questions and initiated her into the mysteries of lovemaking?

Another shiver passed through her, a shiver of longing. Oh, Lord, Emma, this is dangerous! Do you really think you're capable of having an affair without getting involved emotionally? If you give your body, you'll give your soul and your heart, and it'll be worse by far than what Joe Murphy did to you. Because he'll leave, Emma. You know he'll leave. He's not a man who gives much of himself, and even if he were, what would he want with *you?*

It was ironic, she sometimes thought, that with all the injuries and damage she had suffered from her unknown attacker and Joe Murphy, she hadn't developed a complete distaste for men. That her sexuality hadn't died, but instead had needed to be continually smothered over the years. Given that no man would want her, why couldn't she have learned to want no man?

An unladylike word escaped her beneath her breath. At the same moment, the tape playing in the living room came to an end and the house was plunged into utter silence.

The unexpected ring of the phone was a jarring note. Emma started and then wiped her hands on her apron. Not for the first time she swore she was going to replace that wall phone with one that chirped rather than rang. Her phone at work had spoiled her with its quiet buzzing, and she had gotten so she hated the way this one jangled.

Tucking the receiver between her ear and shoulder, she said, "Hello?"

The line was open, an echoing silence that told her someone was on the other end, listening. Then there was a click, followed by a dial tone.

Emma stood stock-still for a moment, listening to the hum of the empty line, and then slowly she placed the receiver back in the cradle.

A wrong number, she told herself. Someone without the basic manners to apologize, that was all. Just a social cretin.

She started shivering then, with a cold that seemed to come from deep within her. Inescapably, inexplicably, she felt *watched.*

Snow that had been crusted earlier in the day by the sun's warmth crunched under Gage's boots as he walked away from the brightly lit mutilation scene. Beside him walked Sheriff Nathan Tate, a burly, ruddy-complected man with a deep, gravelly voice.

"The skinning of the skull is a new one," Nate remarked.

"I've heard of it with mutilations in other places," Gage replied. "The bone is still pink, so it's pretty recent. We need to have the lab find out if there are any marks on the bone from whatever tool was used to do the butchering."

Nate nodded. "I wish Micah was here. I swear that Injun reads the vibes in the air around things."

Gage chuckled almost in spite of himself. "You're sounding like a product of the sixties."

"I *am* a product of the sixties."

"Well, Micah will be back next week," Gage said. "In the meantime, we'll have to rely on modern science."

"I haven't been real pleased with the lab lately. They can't even agree with each other about this."

"They sure as hell ought to be able to tell a tooth mark from a knife mark on that skull, though." Gage paused beside his Suburban and looked back toward the floodlit site. "It's beginning to feel like a vendetta against Cumberland and the Bar C."

Nate made a grunt of acknowledgement.

"They sure aren't being killed where they're found," Gage said presently. "There'd have to be at least *some* sign of struggle, and there never is. Where does all the blood go? Why aren't there ever any tracks going in or out from the site? Damn it, Nate, I'm beginning to believe in little green men."

Nate made another grunt. "Except that there's no sign of tissue cautery. The cases blamed on the little green men almost always include heat damage to the tissue, as if from laser surgery."

"That's right." Gage was becoming something of an expert on the subject as his investigation progressed. "My guy at the lab said that was the core of contention on the last carcasses we sent up. Without any heat damage, the argument over whether the flesh was torn or cut evidently got pretty hot. I'm pretty much settled in my own mind on this, though."

Nate poked a toothpick into his mouth. "Little green men?"

"More like ordinary human beings. I'm willing to bet the lab finds knife marks on that skull, not tooth marks."

"What if they don't find anything at all?"

Gage shook his head. "Then it's little green men. But there's still tissue on that skull, Nate. Mark my words, our culprit is human."

A short, rueful laugh escaped Nate. "Damn, I hope so. I don't relish Jeff's reaction if I have to tell him it'll take Buck Rogers to put a stop to this."

"I'd settle for Superman," Sara Yates remarked as she joined them. "Nate, Ed Dewhurst and I are going to keep the carcass company until we can get it loaded on a truck. You have any special instructions?"

Nate shook his head. "Just the usual."

"Wrap the head," Gage said. "Wrap it in something to keep it from getting banged up."

"Good thought," Nate agreed. He looked at Gage. "You get back to Miss Emma. I don't like the smell of that mess, either. Damned if I know what this county is coming to." Shaking his head, he walked back to the carcass with Sara.

Gage looked after him a moment, understanding Nate's frustration. Lately it had been one damn thing after another. It seemed not so very long ago that Nate had been urging him to come out this way, promising him all the peace and healing he could ever hope for.

Well, it wasn't as peaceful as Nate had promised, that was for sure. But it wasn't as taxing, agonizing and frustrating as working undercover, either. Given his choice, he would still take Conard County and cattle mutilations over his old job.

Heading back into town, he stepped on the gas a little, knowing he wouldn't get stopped, because his Suburban was familiar to all the lawmen in the county. That was new for him, that feeling of being known, of being part of the group. Working undercover, he'd taken his chances with the law like everybody else, and a couple of times he'd gotten batted around a little by cops who thought he was just another addict or pusher.

Getting knocked around with a nightstick had done wonders for his credibility on the streets, but it had sure made him feel alone. And angry. He'd been born with a burr under his saddle, but working the streets had made him furious to the deepest corner of his soul.

It was a refreshing, wonderful relief to look out the windows of the Suburban and see miles and miles of pristine countryside gleaming beneath a blanket of sparkling snow. It was breathtaking to see deer and buffalo and cattle everywhere he went outside town, and to be able to walk the streets of Conard City at three in the morning and see nothing more unsavory than a drunk cowpoke sleeping at the wheel of his pickup.

Whatever was happening with Jeff's cattle didn't fit the Conard County he'd come to know in his several months here, nor did the rabbit on Emma's porch. He knew the scent of evil. He'd smelled it on too many filthy streets and in too many sleazy hallways. Something evil had come to Conard County.

Emma was removing the cherry pie from the oven when Gage pulled up in the driveway. She turned, holding the pie in her oven-mitt-covered hands as he came in the house.

He paused, leaning back against the door he had just closed, and astonished her with a sudden, unexpected grin, a crooked expression because of his scarred cheek. "My, my," he said. "Donna Reed, move over."

The teasing remark surprised a laugh out of her. She never would have imagined Gage Dalton to be a tease. He sure didn't look like one as he leaned against the door in his habitual black: leather jacket, boots, hat, jeans. He looked like a promise of trouble.

Still smiling, she set the pie on the cooling rack in the center of the table. "You're welcome to a piece when it cools a little."

"I like my cherries hot."

Emma froze for just an instant, wondering if that had been a double entendre, or if her imagination was running wild because the man had given her one little kiss—a kiss that she now assured herself had been meant to comfort, not to arouse.

"Not this hot," she retorted in her best librarian's voice. "What did you find at the Bar C?"

"A dead cow with a skinned skull."

Emma grimaced. "Grotesque."

"Yeah. And not very illuminating." Still leaning against the door, he watched Emma strip off her oven mitts and tuck them into a drawer. "Everything okay with you?"

She looked toward him and suddenly caught her breath. She had looked at him before, had noticed before how masculine he was, how very attractive despite his scarred face. But now she saw those same things while knowing how his mouth had felt on hers, how his strong arms had felt around her. Now she looked at him with eyes that knew just how easily he could spark her to flame.

Deep inside, down low, she felt a hollow ache, felt the weight of emptiness, and wondered how a lack could feel so heavy. Quickly she forced herself to look away, reminding herself that even if he wanted her, he would never want to keep her, because she was not a whole woman. He might make love to her, but he would never love her, and she would be a damn fool to set herself up for that kind of heartache.

"Emma? Are you all right?"

"I'm fine." Realizing she had frozen in place, just staring off into space, she flushed faintly. "Just preoccupied, I guess."

He gave her a brief nod and levered himself away from the door, wincing a little as he did so. "I've got some good news for you."

"You do?" Unable to imagine what that could possibly be, she faced him expectantly and tried not to notice again just how narrow his hips were. What was it about narrow hips on a man?

"I stopped at the Quick Shop for gas and ran into Lance Severn. I asked him where we could get you a twelve-foot tree on short notice, and he said he had one waiting for you and wondered when you were coming to get it. I said I'd be there in the morning.''

"Oh, my! He remembered!" Emma felt herself getting all misty eyed. "He's been so ill, I never wanted to say a word. It never occurred to me he'd remember all on his own. He's had so much on his mind."

"Well, he remembered." He hung his hat on the peg and leaned over the table, sniffing appreciatively. "How long do I have to wait?"

Feeling suddenly happy, and touched by Gage's almost boyishly wistful look at the pie, Emma gave a little laugh. "Ten minutes. It'll take that long to make the coffee."

"For that, I can wait. It's cold out there and getting colder." He tugged at his jacket and winced a little as he shrugged it off. "You've been okay while I was gone?"

"Of course. I started putting up Christmas decorations. Go see the living room." The phone call was forgotten, and the uneasiness she had felt was too embarrassing to talk about. For a moment, just a moment, she *felt* like Donna Reed welcoming her husband home at the end of a long day. She'd never felt that way before and was sure she never would again, so she surrendered to the feeling with a kind of melancholy eagerness. As soon as she had started the coffee, she followed Gage.

"Damn," she heard him say softly as she came up behind him. He stood in the arched doorway of the living room, surveying the changes. Garlands of evergreen decorated with bright red and green bows graced the mantelpiece, and the Nativity scene her great-grandfather had carved and painted with painstaking care filled an entire corner beside the bow window where the tree would be placed. On every table red or green candles filled polished brass holders, and here and there were sprigs of holly. Even without the tree, the room had become very Christmasy.

When he realized she had come up beside him, he looked down at her with a crooked smile. "You've been busy. It's nice. Real nice." He looked back at the room.

Something was wrong, Emma realized. Something was terribly, terribly wrong. The tension in him was palpable. "Gage?"

"I...um...think I'd better pass on that pie and coffee." He glanced at her again with a faint smile that never made it past his lips. He looked like a man in mortal pain who was trying to hide it. "I'm, uh, tired and my back's killing me. I'll see you in the morning."

Perplexed, she watched him climb the stairs, wishing she could somehow help him, knowing there was no possible way. Something had happened, she thought again, and turned to look at the living room. Something in here had wounded him. Frowning, she stood there for a long time, trying without success to see what it had been.

He just hadn't been prepared for it, Gage told himself in the morning as he shaved his uninjured cheek and chin. Now he knew how it was going to hit him, and he would deal with it better. He would be braced for the blow now.

Two Christmases ago he'd been in the hospital, out of his mind on painkillers, half-crazed by his losses, past being reached by anything at all except a desperate agony nothing could help. Looking back, he had a vague recollection of a few friends, a few colleagues, showing up with a specially prepared dinner for him, but he was pretty sure he hadn't eaten it. Last Christmas...last Christmas he'd been holed up in Clint Maddox's cabin in the Catoctin Mountains and had missed the entire holiday season.

He just hadn't been prepared for the flood of rushing feelings, the sudden upsurge of memories. He hadn't been ready to face his ghosts. Maybe he still wasn't, but at least he would be ready to withstand the soul-ripping agony if they suddenly showed up again, summoned by the sight or sound of Christmas.

Downstairs in the kitchen, he was surprised to find the coffee ready and the pie in the center of the table with a yellow sticky note on the clear plastic cover. Emma's very precise hand-writing informed him that she had an early meeting with the library governing committee. A second sticky note suggested he have the pie for breakfast, and if he really liked hot cherries, a minute in the microwave would do it.

A woman who suggested pie for breakfast? She must be unique, Gage thought in amusement. His mother would have been horrified. His wife would have—

Ruthlessly, he broke off that thought and turned his attention to the present. He slipped a large wedge of the pie into the microwave and kept an eye on it while he sipped a mug of coffee.

An early meeting. Emma was in for a long day, then, because she never finished up at the library before seven. Usually, she went in to open at ten, but here it was just seven-thirty.

Well, he could help her out a little, he supposed, by getting that damn tree from Severn's place and setting it up in the living room. The task would also give him a chance to face all the decorations without a concerned audience, a chance to test the memories and his own emotional soreness until he was sure he could cope in public.

He would do that right after he finished up with some things at the sheriff's office. And while he was thinking about it, maybe he would call Brian Webster to find out if he had received the photo of the dagger yet. Emma's dismay over that picture still pricked at him, like a jigsaw piece he couldn't quite place. He'd mailed the photo back East to Webster, who was an expert in such matters, and if that dagger wasn't some kind of Halloween joke, Webster would have it placed in no time. And placing it might put the mystery to rest.

Downtown, across from the courthouse square, Gage pulled his Suburban into a slot marked Official Vehicles Only and waved at Deputy Charlie Huskins, who was just backing out one of the department's Blazers.

Charlie rolled down his window and leaned out, grinning hugely. "That Suburban isn't an official vehicle, Gage."

"Nate probably wouldn't agree. He pays most of my mileage."

Inside the storefront offices, Ed Dewhurst was manning the desk and phone, and Velma Jansen, the dispatcher, was leaning back in her chair, blowing a cloud of cigarette smoke into the air. Velma was one of Gage's favorite characters in Conard County, a scrawny, leathery, sixtyish woman with a big mouth and a bigger heart. She stuck her nose into the business of all the department's employees, and nobody ever really seemed to mind it.

"'Morning, Velma, Ed."

"'Morning to you, too, Casanova," Velma said.

Gage paused midstep on his way to the private office Nate had given him and faced Velma. "What's that crack mean?"

Velma blew another cloud of smoke. "Rumor has it you thawed the ice princess."

Slowly Gage turned and limped back to Velma. "I'm renting a room from Miss Emma, Velma." He spoke the words quietly, but they held enough threat to cause Ed to stiffen when he heard them.

"Of course you are, Gage," Velma said. "That's what I tell any idiot stupid enough to pass the gossip on. Just thought you ought to know what's being said."

"I can't do a damn thing about what people are saying."

"Did I say you should? I just thought you should know. I hate the way the person being talked about is the last to know. If you start feeling like people are staring or whispering, you have a right to know you're not imagining it."

Gage looked down into Velma's face, a road map of lines and creases, and a sudden laugh escaped him. "Yeah, you're right. It feels weird to have conversations halt when you come into a room."

"Well, if it's any consolation, most of the speculation is friendly, not nasty."

Some consolation, Gage thought, heading again for his office. He doubted very much that Emma would see it that way.

Stalwartly ignoring the wreath somebody had hung on the closed door of his office at the back of the building, Gage left the door open and dropped into the battered leather chair behind the even more battered wood desk.

So Miss Emma had been right about people talking, he mused. He'd spent most of his life on the streets of big cities, where people were apt to be deaf, dumb and blind if you were murdered right before their eyes.

When you lived in the combat zone called the inner city, you didn't give a damn about anything as inconsequential as who was living together. You worried about whether the guy next door was a pusher, and if he was, you worried about how you could avoid seeing something that might get you killed. At least, when you were a kid you did. When you grew up, you either became a pusher or joined the army to get out.

And then, maybe, if you were a big enough fool, you learned to be tough and got yourself an education, and then you went back and tried to clean up the streets so some other kid wouldn't have to grow up like that. Yeah, if you were a big enough fool, you did something dumb like that. And found yourself living on the streets without even your own name to comfort you for months at a time, running the very risks you'd tried to get away from by staying on the right side of the law. Yeah, it took a big fool to do that.

So he was a big fool, and he'd paid a price for foolishness that was higher than he had ever imagined possible.

Sighing, he rubbed irritably at his temples with his fingertips. There was tension there, and it had been growing since he got up this morning. He had the unpleasant feeling that things were closing in, that he was going to have to deal with matters that were beyond dealing with. He was used to keeping himself compartmentalized, to dividing himself into two people with separate lives. Once before, his separate lives had crashed together in a cataclysm that had cost him everything. Now he felt that things he had deliberately buried were going to surface in another cataclysm, this one purely emotional.

"Hell." With one muttered word, he slammed the lid back down on the grave of his past and forced his attention to the present. First, he needed to call the state lab and tell Herm Abbott about the new cattle carcass they were shipping up to him. Herm, unfortunately, wouldn't perform the necropsy, but as a lab assistant he would have access to whatever the pathologist found. It was Herm who had told Gage that the two veterinary pathologists disagreed about the earlier mutilations of Jeff's cattle, and Herm who had promised to see that Gage was told everything, not just what one person or another considered to be reasonable or politic.

Fifteen minutes later, with Herm's assurances still ringing in his ears, Gage picked up the phone once again and this time punched in a number on the East Coast.

"Professor Webster's office," a musical female voice answered.

"Hi, Sally. This is Gage Dalton."

"Gage! My word, it's been a dog's age! Where are you? Are you in town?"

"No, I'm all the way out in the wilds of Wyoming."

There was the briefest pause, then Sally said, "Can I ask? Or should I just keep my mouth shut?"

"It's a change of scenery, Sally. A good change, I think. I'm working for the sheriff out here. I haven't seen a drug pusher since I got here. Or an addict, for that matter. There must be one somewhere, but I sure as hell haven't seen him. Is Brian around?"

"He's in class right now, and he's got a seminar directly after. Do you want him to call?"

"I sent him a large envelope last Saturday, and I was just wondering if he'd gotten it, and if he had any ideas about the picture I sent."

"I haven't seen it yet. I sure would have noticed a letter

from Wyoming. Why don't you give me your number so he can call you later?''

Gage gave her both the office number and Emma's number, asked a few questions about her husband and the Airedale terriers they raised, and then hung up.

His hand was shaking and his palm was damp. He studied his reaction with a kind of detachment, recognizing that he had crossed one of the invisible boundaries he had laid between himself and the past. The voices of old friends brought back memories and erased some of the distance of time.

And once again he ruthlessly stepped on the rising tide of feeling. Picking up the phone, he called Lance Severn to find out if he would need to bring someone to help load the twelve-foot tree onto his Suburban. Lance said his son would help.

Now, Gage thought, pushing back his chair and reaching for his jacket and hat, now he would go face the ghosts of Christmas past.

Chapter 5

Lance Severn's son, Walt, was a strapping college football player who was home on semester break. He handled the twelve-foot tree as carelessly as if it weighed nothing, leaving Gage with little to do except help tie it to the tailgate.

"I'm not sure I'll go back to Laramie for the spring semester," Walt told Gage. "Spring's a busy time for the nursery, and Dad'll worry constantly about the things he's not up to doing. Like this tree. He fretted and fretted about it. I kept telling him Bill Hascome could handle it, but Dad was convinced nobody but him could pick out a tree good enough for Miss Emma. Finally I came home two weeks ago and took care of it myself."

"It's a beautiful tree, all right," Gage acknowledged as he helped tie it down. "Miss Emma will love it."

"I went out to the Fenster ranch to get it. The old man planted a stand of trees to make some extra money. Up until he died three years past, he did it all himself. Now his widow has the grandson staying with her, and he keeps after it somewhat. Trees are getting a little ragged, though. Not what they used to be.''

"They don't just grow this way naturally?"

"Nope. Need pruning and trimming to get 'em full like most folks want. And around here, they need a lot more water than nature provides. Don Fenster, the grandson, isn't regular enough about it. Guess he's caught up with those friends he's got staying with him. Bunch of creeps, if you ask me.''

A faint smile of amusement came to Gage's mouth. Walt Severn sounded exactly like his father, a man who was nearly forty years older. And probably half of Conard County was talking about Emma and himself in the same casual way. The realization damped Gage's amusement and made him feel honor-bound to press Walt about Fenster's "creeps," and maybe get him to admit he was exaggerating.

"What makes you so sure they're creeps?" he asked Walt.

Walt shrugged as he tied another knot in the jute rope. "They've been living off that old woman for months now, and that just isn't right. They didn't even act neighborly when I came out to get the tree, just sort of stared and smirked." He gave the knot a final yank. "Creeps, that's all. We don't need that kind in Conard County."

Gage had a sudden vision of Walt twenty years down the road, helping tie Miss Emma's tree to some vehicle or other and talking just the same way. Ten years ago, even five, Gage would have thought such a life was wasted. Now, he looked at Walt Severn and envied him.

"I'll follow along in my truck," Walt said. "We'll have this tree set up before Miss Emma comes home for lunch."

Gage hesitated. "I'm not sure where she wants it, Walt."

"I am." The husky young man flashed a huge grin. "The Conards have been putting their tree in exactly the same place at least since I was born, and probably longer."

Later Gage sat cross-legged on the floor before the undec-orated tree and stared blindly up into its branches. With Walt's help, it really hadn't taken long to position and brace the tree. Walt must have helped his father with this job in the past, because he had even known that the tree stand was out in the detached garage.

Emma had brought out all the decorations last night, and Gage had forced himself to look through the boxes for the light strings so he could test the bulbs, a task that had traditionally been his at home. Somewhere in the process, though, he had fallen into the past. The strands of lights lay around him, winking gaily, completely forgotten.

A band was tightening around his chest, making breathing difficult, and his throat nearly closed as the tide of memory poured over him. Good memories. Happy memories. Lost memories. The ones that cut him to the quick with their simplicity and their hopefulness. Their blind innocence. The little things. The touch of a child's hand and the sound of a child's laugh. The warmth of a woman's arms closing around him as she laughed and wept at the same time. The joy of bringing joy to another.

Lost. Gone. Buried.

Ah, God! He drew a ragged breath, trying to expand his chest until the band of tightness would snap and set him free. It was in vain. Nothing, nothing, could set him free of loss.

"Gage?"

The sound of Emma's voice reached him but failed to penetrate the walls of grief that confined him. He drew another painful breath, struggling to break loose.

The sight of Gage's face struck Emma to her core. Wet trails of tears marked his cheeks, but he appeared oblivious of them, of her, of everything but whatever pain racked him.

She reacted instinctively, dropping to her knees beside him, putting her arms around him, pressing her soft cheek to his injured one. "Oh, Gage," she whispered. "Oh, Gage, tell me what I can do."

"Nothing…nothing…" His words were little more than a rusty, cracked whisper, but even as he refused her, his arms closed around her, squeezing until her ribs ached. She didn't care. Tightening her own arms around him until she couldn't hold him any harder, she pressed her face into the warm flesh of his neck and gave him what comfort closeness could.

"I'll be all right," he whispered roughly. "I'll be all right."

But she felt the shudders rip through him, shudders that would have turned into wrenching sobs if they had been hers. His grief became a palpable thing for her, so real she could feel it. This was not the pain, the agony that afflicted him physically. This was emotional and spoke of terrible losses. Just so had her father shuddered when he stood beside the graves of his wife and son.

"I'll be all right," he said again, but he didn't loosen his hold on her. When he lay back on the rug, Emma let him take her with him, let him hold her tightly against him and press his wet face into the softness of her shoulder. She forgot she needed to get back to work, forgot she had come home only to grab a sandwich and freshen up a little. She forgot everything except the man she held, the man who held her as if she was a lifeline.

Her fingers found their way into his silvery hair and caressed him soothingly, telling him with their touch that she was there, that she cared. It was little enough to do.

How many minutes passed, neither of them could have said. One last shudder passed through Gage, and then his arms slackened. Emma immediately loosened her own hold but found herself hoping against hope that he wouldn't pull away from her. Not yet. It felt so good to lie like this, to be held like this, to be so close to the warmth of another human being. She might never again be this close to another person, to a man, and she wasn't ready to relinquish the comfort.

Gage stirred. She kept her eyes closed when he shifted against her and bit back the protest when she thought he would leave her. But he didn't leave. A sigh escaped him, a heavy sound, and his arms moved, changing the way he held her against him, but not releasing her. Content that he wouldn't go just yet, she unconsciously snuggled closer.

Gage shifted again, abruptly, rolling onto his back and carrying her with him so that she lay on top of him. Suddenly the whole character of the embrace had changed. Emma's eyes snapped open, and she found herself staring down into eyes the color of a summer squall that were set in a face suddenly as hard as iron.

He didn't say anything. Not a word. She felt his hands at the nape of her neck, pulling at the barrette that bound her hair. Suddenly the clasp opened and her hair was free, springing up with a life of its own until it made a sparkling halo of fire around her face.

It was every bit as curly, kinky and wild as he had thought it would be, and every bit as soft and silky. He reached up and burrowed his fingers into it, luxuriating in it, finding her scalp with fingertips that seemed to have grown excruciatingly sensitive. She was warm, and she was alive, and he needed her vitality desperately.

The touch of his fingers on her scalp sent wild shivers trickling through Emma, running down her back to the base of her spine and then settling in her center like an uncertain edginess. She should stop this now, she thought. Whatever was happening, she should call a halt before she got in any deeper.

But her body was busy noting every hard angle of Gage's frame beneath her. She had never before been pressed this intimately against a man, and her nerves were taking a pleasurable inventory, awakening senses she hadn't known she had. Her breasts felt the hardness of his chest beneath them and began to ache in a way that made her want to rub herself against him to find ease. Her softer stomach fitted perfectly within the hard hollow of his, and his hard, narrow hips wedged against hers as if they were custom-fit.

And there, way down low, right against her most secret place, she felt the equally secret bulge of his manhood. Awareness sent an exquisite sizzle along her nerve endings, springing from the meeting of their thighs to every other point in her body.

Common sense dictated she should get out of this dangerous position right now, but common sense fled before the lava flow of desire that began to pour through her. Passion, never before experienced, made her a prisoner to her senses and paralyzed her will. Pinned by need, she stayed.

"Beautiful," Gage whispered hoarsely. "Why do you pull it back when it's so beautiful?" He fluffed her hair even more around her face and watched how it seemed to cling to his fingers.

She could have told him that she'd spent her life trying to get that hair to behave like hair instead of some wild thing with a mind all its own, but the words wouldn't come. The stroking of his fingers, the intensity of his gray-green gaze, deprived her of speech. The only sound she wanted to make, or was even capable of, was a whimper of pure pleasure. She retained enough sense to swallow it.

But then he pulled her startled face down to his and covered her mouth with a soft, wet kiss. "Let me in, Emma," he whispered roughly. "Let me in. God, I need to—"

He never completed the thought, because her lips parted, opening to receive him as if his will was hers. She knew, in some deep, aware corner of her heart, that he was using passion to exorcise his demons, that he was subduing pain with pleasure. Even this understanding failed to restore her good sense. She needed to give what he was taking. Her naturally generous nature wanted to give him any kind of surcease, and her long-denied femininity felt it was taking as much as it was giving.

She needed to know what a man's hunger felt like, needed to know what it meant to be desired, and he needed to replace his pain with that same hunger. For a little while they could each take what they needed. There could be no harm in that.

His kiss deepened, his tongue roughly stroking hers as if maybe, just maybe, he could find complete satisfaction in this if only he just thrust hard enough, deep enough, rhythmically enough. Never in her life had Emma dreamed that a kiss could be so passionate, so intimate, so arousing, or that something so near violence could be this erotic. A whimper escaped her as she opened her mouth wider and gave him back thrust for thrust. In her innocence she had no notion of the symbolism of her response. She knew only that she wanted to make him feel all that he was making her feel.

She was sure as hell making him feel. Gage had felt nothing but pain of one kind or another for so long now that he was nearly stunned by the sudden upsurging of desire. He had forgotten what it was to want something besides escape.

Some gentlemanly instinct tried to rear its head, reminding him of Emma's inexperience and his obligation to keep matters from getting out of hand, but he stepped ruthlessly on it. He was no gentleman. He was a street fighter from the slums, no white knight to protect a lady from herself. When she whimpered and pressed closer, the internal battle ended completely. She wanted him, too. It was enough.

"God, Emma," he whispered roughly in his ruined voice, breaking the kiss but holding her head close so that he could suck and nip at her lips. They were swollen and wet, and very, very sweet. She would be like that everywhere, he thought. Fresh and clean and sweet....

Her hands curled on his chest as he kissed her, kneading him until he thought he would lose his mind from wanting deeper, harder touches. *Slow down,* he told himself. *Slow down*. The last thing on earth he wanted was to frighten Emma.

But her fingers suddenly dug into him as he thrust his tongue roughly into her mouth once more, and then words spilled from him. Demands. Needs.

"Open my shirt, Emma."

She lifted her head a little and blinked sleepily down at him, her soft green eyes almost dazed looking. "Your shirt?" she repeated huskily. The mere thought made everything inside her clench pleasurably.

"I need your hands on my skin."

She drew a sharp breath and lowered her gaze to his chest. "Oh, yes…" she breathed. Without further hesitation she grabbed the front and ripped the snaps open with an eagerness that reached out and touched him somewhere deep inside.

And when her palms spread out on his chest, he unleashed a deep sound of pleasure. He'd forgotten how good it felt to be touched, to feel skin on skin. "Now your blouse, Emma. Open it."

The husky, hoarse command sent a jolt of excitement racing through her that turned her legs numb. It was followed immediately by a rushing tide of modesty that paralyzed her.

"Emma?" Gage looked up at her, and what he saw pierced his sensual preoccupation. The tart Miss Emma, who was reputed to strip the hide from any man who treated her like a woman, was trembling and blushing and making him wonder yet again if she was indeed a virgin. And he was treating her like a…like a…oh, hell.

He rolled suddenly, causing Emma to gasp in surprise, as she found their positions were reversed. Emma lay on her back on the rug, looking up at Gage, who propped himself on one elbow and held her in place by the simple expedient of resting his powerful thigh across both of hers.

Looking down into her confused and embarrassed face, he felt like the crud he probably was. Gently, he touched her cheek, brushed the wild, beautiful mane of hair back from her face. "I'm sorry, Emma," he said softly.

"F-for what?"

What a hell of a question, he thought with an unexpected burst of amusement that erased the last of his tension. He would have thought that was self-explanatory, given the circumstances. "I'm sorry I embarrassed you," he said. "Sorry I shocked you." But not, damn it, sorry he had touched her or discovered the passion she kept so well hidden. It was going to increase his misery while he shared her roof, but he couldn't regret it. Couldn't regret, either, that he had just discovered he was capable of feeling again. Not at this moment, anyhow. Later he would probably regret it like hell.

Emma's blush deepened, and her gaze lowered, only to dart quickly away from the bare expanse of his chest. Soft, dark hair covered his pectorals, and now she knew how that hair felt. Wanted to feel it again. "I...wasn't shocked," she admitted, her honesty springing from innocence. She never dreamed the electric effect that truthfulness was having on the man who hovered over her. "I liked touching you."

"You looked like a frightened rabbit," he said gently, ignoring the demands of his body in favor of treating this woman the way she deserved. Street fighter or not, he loathed anyone who preyed on women. He felt self-disgust that he had even for an instant forgotten himself enough to take advantage of Emma.

"I was...I never..." Her blush heightened painfully, and she averted her face.

That was when he stopped suspecting and knew for sure that Emma had never been with a man before. The surety filled him with a tide of tenderness. "I know," he said softly. Catching her chin in his hand, he turned her face back to him and waited until she opened her eyes. "That's why I'm apologizing. I got carried away. I wanted to feel your hands on me, and I wanted to touch you the same way. Anyway, I was moving too fast and I asked for too much, and I embarrassed you. I'm sorry."

And her chance to find out what it was all about was slipping away, Emma thought ruefully, because she was too inexperienced to know how to take advantage of it. What irony! If only there was some way to tell him that she wanted more but didn't want to go too far. That she wanted to experience these wonderful, new things but not get into any trouble with it. Oh, Emma, wish for the moon, why don't you!

But Gage was incredibly alert to the least little signal, and Emma was practically broadcasting. Her eyes strayed again to his chest, and she licked her upper lip with a slow sensuality that threw him almost instantly into overdrive.

"Emma?" His voice was a husky whisper, and he felt almost as he had at sixteen when he tried to talk a girl into making out a little. Eager, impatient, terrified that the edgy longing in him would go unanswered.

"Hmm?" Slowly, reluctantly, her eyes drifted upward from his chest to his face. She didn't feel at all afraid, and embarrassment was beginning to fade as the air around her seemed to thicken again. All her awareness seemed to be flowing from her brain into the rest of her body, making her conscious of a growing heaviness, a strange, nervous anticipation.

"Want to…play a little?" he asked hoarsely.

"Play?" Understanding speared downward through her, causing a deep clenching inside her, followed by a heavy pulsing.

He saw her comprehension, and something in him knotted hungrily. "Just…explore a little."

Explore. She licked her lips. Hell's own archangel was seducing her in tiny little steps, and she didn't think she gave a damn. *Explore.* In childhood that word had somehow become associated in her mind with forbidden pleasures. Somebody at some time must have said something…. *Explore.* The word alone was enough to make her tingle from head to toe.

"Emma?" He bent his head, ignoring the ache in his lower back as he responded to the one in his loins. "Yes or no, Emma, but you have to say something."

She drew a shaky breath. "I don't want to go too far." It sounded stupid, and even in her agitated state she thought she sounded like a child, but it was a line she felt she had to draw while she could still draw one.

"I know." He barely breathed the words as he found her mouth with his and brushed a gentle, persuasive kiss there. "I know. I swear I won't hurt you, but damn it, lady, we both need some touching and holding."

Yes, she thought. Yes. That was exactly what she needed. Touching and holding. Closeness and comfort. He needed to forget his pain, and she needed to feel wanted. Surely they could give each other that much.

"Yes," she murmured shakily. "Just a little."

"Then touch me, Emma. Any way you want to."

Before she could do more than register his command, his mouth took hers again in a deep kiss, making her feel that he simply couldn't get enough of the taste of her. In, out, his tongue moved surely, strongly, and she never knew exactly when her hips picked up the rhythm and began to rock ever so slightly in response. It wasn't much of a movement, but it drew a groan from Gage.

He lifted his head and looked down at her from a face gone hard with passion. His eyes, though, those stormy eyes, were sleepy, gentle, reassuring. "Ah, Emma," he sighed, "you're a witch."

"And you're hell's own archangel," she heard herself say. She regretted the words almost as soon as they escaped her, but he surprised her by laughing softly.

"So I've heard," he murmured. "So I've heard." His hand slipped away from her shoulder swiftly and captured her breast through the silk of her blouse before she realized what he was doing. Her reaction was instantaneous, sharp, exquisite. She arched and whimpered softly.

"Yes," Gage whispered near her ear, causing another shiver to run through her. "Like that, Emma. Just like that."

He made her feel as if she was doing something wonderful for him when, in fact, he was the one giving her pleasure. No one had ever trespassed so far with her, and she had never imagined such a touch could feel so good. Even through the layers of her blouse and bra, the hardening point of her nipple could be felt, and Gage's fingers zeroed in on it, stroking back and forth until she bucked almost wildly beneath him.

"That's good, Emma. That's good. Just feel."

But she wanted more than to just feel what he was doing. She wanted to do a little exploring of her own. To that end she reached up and tunneled her fingers into his chest hair, reveling in the softness of the hair, the warmth and smoothness of the skin beneath. With every movement of her hands, she tested him and found iron-hard strength.

When her fingers accidentally grazed the hard peak of his small nipple, he caught his breath, telling her that in that way, at least, he was no different than she.

Gage's fingers froze on Emma's breast when he felt the heat of her breath on the aching point of his own nipple. "Yesss..." he hissed and instinctively leaned closer, encouraging her. The touch of her lips and tongue sent a zap of electricity straight from his nipple to his groin and was followed by a convulsive shudder of pleasure.

The sound of his groan, the tightening of his hand on her breast, thrilled Emma. Never had she imagined herself having such an effect on a man. It gave her an incredible sense of power to realize that she could imprison him in the same exciting web that he was weaving around her. It made her feel vital and alive to be able to evoke such pleasure. It made her feel incredibly generous and giving to know that she was making him feel so good.

And it loosened some deep-rooted inhibition within her. She was not alone in what she was experiencing and doing, and so she was no longer afraid or embarrassed. Trust blossomed for the man who was sharing himself as intimately as he was asking her to share herself. She forgot, for the moment, that no man could want her for long. She forgot she was crippled in an essential way. Forgot that her woman's purpose had been torn from her, and that her worthlessness had been thrown up into her face by a man she had loved.

She forgot how a man could wound her.

"Damn it, Emma..." The sound was one of sheer sexual enjoyment, torn from deep within Gage. His breath was ragged in her ear, and hers was ragged in his. "So sweet," he whispered, his breath catching. "So sweet...."

She wound her arms around him, wanting him closer, wanting to feel him with every cell of her being. She wanted his hands on her breasts, then his mouth, and when she felt him at last—at long last!—fumbling at the buttons of her blouse, excitement exploded like white heat within her.

And then the phone rang.

Reality washed over Emma in an icy, embarrassing tide. She snatched her arms away from Gage as if he burned her and squeezed her eyes shut. Oh, Emma! Lord, Lord, how could you have?

She wanted to sink through the floor, to die, to disappear, to do almost anything but face the man she had moments ago been kissing and holding and exploring. How could she have forgotten herself like this? It wasn't as if she even knew him, because she didn't, not really. She had behaved like a shameless wanton.

"I'll get it," Gage growled as the phone rang yet again, then again. "You stay right here. Don't you dare run. We need to talk."

Talking was the last thing she could imagine herself doing right now, and certainly not with the man she had forgotten herself with. He couldn't actually mean to discuss their intimacy, could he? Or to resume it?

As soon as Gage reached the kitchen, she scrambled to her feet, determined to somehow escape. She had an extra parka, an old one, in her bedroom, and a spare set of car keys. She could slip out the front door while he was in the kitchen....

"Emma, it's for you. It's Linda."

Her assistant at the library. No doubt wondering where she had disappeared to.

She slipped past Gage into the kitchen, miserably aware of the disheveled state of her hair and clothing. She must look like a trollop, and by now Gage must certainly think she was one. He probably had her figured for a desperate old maid who would do anything at all to snare a man. Humiliation burned her cheeks and thickened her voice when she answered the phone.

"I hate bothering you," Linda said briskly, "but you said you'd be back in a half hour, and I was getting worried."

"I'm sorry, Linda. I...had a little problem. I'll be there shortly."

"No rush," Linda said warmly. "There's only me and Mr. Craig here, and I can handle things. I was just worried." She hesitated almost audibly. "Emma, really...is everything okay? You sound funny."

"I'm fine. Maybe just getting a cold." Emma said goodbye and hung up the phone, wishing she could crawl under a rock and hide. Anything but turn around and face Gage, who was standing behind her. She could feel him, as if his presence changed the very atmosphere. Hell's own archangel. Maybe that was brimstone she smelled, because she'd sure come close to succumbing to temptation.

"Emma."

That husky, ruined voice felt like black velvet on all her nerve endings, sending shivers through her that she now recognized as being purely sexual. She didn't want to turn, yet she did, facing him with downcast eyes. What was it about this man that overrode her good sense and caused her to do things she ordinarily wouldn't do?

"Emma, don't."

He was suddenly standing right before her, and he placed a finger beneath her chin, urging her to look up. Emma stubbornly refused.

Gage sighed. "I'm sorry," he said harshly. "I apologize. That should never have happened. It won't happen again. You don't have the experience to handle a man like me, and I damn well know it. I took advantage of you."

That wasn't entirely true, and Emma knew it. She might be utterly lacking in experience, but what had happened between them had happened with her complete cooperation. She couldn't understand why he was shouldering the whole blame himself.

Slowly she raised her green eyes and met him look for look. "There's enough blame to go around," she said stubbornly.

Her remark surprised him. He stared at her a moment, and then a slow smile creased his cheeks. "Guess so, Miss Emma. But right now you look good enough to eat, and I'm feeling like hell's own archangel on a weekend pass. Maybe you better freshen up while I make you a quick sandwich so you can get back to work."

Good enough to eat! My word, Emma thought as she hurried back to her bedroom. My word!

A look in the mirror brought her embarrassed blush back full strength, though. Her hair was tousled and wild around her face, and her blouse was wrinkled beyond hope. She would have to change. Well, that was all right. It would make a good excuse for her tardiness in returning to work. She could tell Linda she had spilled something on herself.

Good enough to eat. My word!

And what had he meant, *a man like him?*

It was snowing again, lightly, when Emma locked up the library for the day. She glanced out the tall, mullioned windows as she switched off the lights and saw the familiar sparkle of falling flakes. Downstairs, when she stepped out into the back parking lot, she found that nearly an inch of fresh powder had accumulated. A nearby streetlight turned some of the falling flakes into whirling glitter.

For a long moment Emma just stood there, watching the snow fall, reaching into herself for some of the Christmas spirit she seemed to be sadly lacking this year. Trying not to remember that she had to go home and that Gage would be waiting. How was she ever to face him again? How did two people ever look one another in the eye when they had actually…gone all the way? The question was undoubtedly indicative of her naïveté.

Sighing, she drew up the collar of her coat and took the

plunge she always dreaded, the step into the dark, empty parking lot.

The instant she moved away from the building, the back of her neck began to prickle. It always did. She always had the uneasy, uncomfortable feeling that someone was about to seize her from behind. Unconsciously, she quickened her step.

It had been terrible today, she thought. The library had felt like a huge, echoing cavern, especially after Linda had departed at three, leaving Emma by herself. Even Mr. Craig, an elderly gentleman who spent most of his days in the reading room, had abandoned her, saying he had things to do for Christmas. She should be used to this by now, she told herself. December was her quietest month. Except for the children's story hour, which was always especially well attended at this time of year, she could have closed up shop entirely. People had no time for reading just now.

Except for Emma herself. She had scads of time for reading. And she might well have lost herself in the latest horror novel if her life hadn't begun to feel as if she were caught in one. Perhaps she needed to speak with Dr. MacArdle or Dr. Randall. Maybe one of them could reassure her about the feeling of pressure that kept growing in her mind. Maybe they could explain the flashes of glittering gold she kept glimpsing from the corners of her eyes, the voices that sounded like distant mumbling on a poorly tuned radio.

She was beginning to feel as if she was haunted, and the feeling quickened her steps even more. Glancing over her shoulder, she scanned the lot hastily, making sure she was still alone. The snow would have to be wiped from the windshield. She hated that. It made her feel so exposed to the night, to anyone who might come upon her.

It had been snowing just like this the night she was attacked. She had been walking down the street toward her dorm, hurrying because of the way the wind cut—

When had she remembered that?

Emma froze in place, blinking into the dark and the swirling snowflakes, cast back in time to a night she hadn't been able to remember since it happened. The memory was there as if it had never been gone. Vivid. Cold. Not yet terrifying, except that now she knew that the most terrifying events of her life had been about to happen.

Oh, God, what if she remembered the rest of it? She didn't want to...didn't want to, didn't want to didn't want to didn't want—

"Miss Emma?"

Whirling, she saw a man emerge from the shadows and the falling snow.

"Emma?"

Gage. It was Gage. He drew closer, and she could see the white flakes on his shoulders, on his black Stetson. Closer yet he came, and she could see his scarred cheek and the dark pools of his eyes beneath the shadowing brim of his hat.

"Emma?"

She closed the last two steps between them as if he was the only shelter from the Furies. All her embarrassment was forgotten. Gage promised protection. How she knew that, she couldn't have said. She just knew that she could count on him.

"What's wrong?" he asked as she flew to him. There was no hesitation in the way he wrapped his arms around her and hugged her close, no reluctance in the way he bent his head to look down at her. "Emma?" And then, as if he understood, he pressed her head to his shoulder and held her snugly. "Shh...shh...shh."

"I remembered. I remembered. Gage, I don't want to remember any more. I don't want to remember what happened. I don't! I don't, I don't, I don't...."

"Shh...hush, baby. Hush. Let's get you home. We'll get you warmed up and get you a shot of brandy, and then you can tell me what's happening. Come on, honey. Come on...."

Little by little, he urged her toward her car, and finally he got her in the passenger seat, the seat belt buckled around her.

With a couple sweeps of his arm, he wiped the fresh snow from the windshield.

When he came around to the driver's side and started to slide in behind the wheel, she screamed. "No!"

He froze, half in and half out of the car. "Emma?" Damn it, he'd forgotten that she couldn't stand to be in a car with a man. Now how the hell were they going to deal with this? He didn't think she was in any way fit to drive at this moment. She was, unless he missed his guess, very near hysteria.

He backed out of the car and squatted, looking in at her as she pressed back against the car door and watched him warily.

"Emma, you know I won't hurt you. Not intentionally."

"I...know," she whispered. "I know. But when you...I just...something happens, Gage! I don't know why."

"Well, then, I'll just walk back."

"No!"

He sighed and pushed his hat back on his head. "Emma, I don't think this is the time or place for a course of desensitization therapy. It's cold out here, and the longer we hold still, the more we'll feel it. I'll just walk back to the house." He started to straighten, but Emma called his name. Slowly, ignoring the protest of his back and leg, he squatted again.

"I think...I think I can control it for the length of time it'll take us to get back to the house."

"You screamed the last time I tried to get into this car. If you don't mind, I'd rather not have to explain to half of the Conard County Sheriff's Department that I wasn't trying to assault you."

Emma blinked rapidly, battling an urge to weep. "Gage, please!"

"Aw, hell." He sighed and wondered if he would ever in his life learn to resist the plea of a sad or frightened woman. "Okay. I'll try to get in once more, but, Emma, if you can't handle it, that's it. I'll walk."

"I can handle it," she said raggedly, already growing tense at just the prospect. "I can handle it."

To Gage it sounded as if she was trying to convince herself more than him. He waited a moment, then straightened and once again attempted to slide into the car.

Her tension was enough to make the air crackle, he thought as he settled onto the seat. She gulped air as if she had just run a marathon, she hugged the car door as if she might slip far enough away to feel safe, and her hands were knotted into white-knuckled fists. Wonderful. It sure made a man feel good to make a woman feel like that. Sort of like Attila the Hun, or Bluebeard.

Before he closed the door, he accepted the keys from Emma's trembling hand and started the engine. He looked at Emma once more. "All right?"

She gave a short, jerky nod. Gage reached out and closed the door. Only Emma's sharply drawn breath testified to her increased tension when she was closed up with him. Releasing the brake, Gage edged them out of the lot, taking care on the slick, fresh snow.

Emma spoke breathlessly. "However did you manage to be right there when I needed you?" As soon as the words were out, she wished she could snatch them back. They placed unnecessary significance on Gage's appearance in the parking lot and revealed too much of how relieved she had been to see him.

"I walk a lot," he said. "It distracts me."

From his pain, Emma thought, and tried to loosen her grip on the door handle.

"I saw the lights at the library go out, and I came around the rear to make sure you reached your car safely," Gage continued. "I'm glad I did."

Emma was, too. She wondered how much longer she was going to be able to endure the impossible tension that gripped her from being closed in the car with a man like this, and thought that she could endure it at all only because it was Gage.

"Almost there, Em," Gage said a few moments later.

"This is humiliating!" The words burst from her as she battled back yet another impulse to fling the door open and jump out.

"Why humiliating? You can't help it."

"But it's such a small thing, and it's so stupid!" She drew a deep, shaky breath, battling to appear in control of herself when everything inside her was shrieking at her to run. "I hate to be stupid."

"I don't think you're being stupid at all."

Stupid or not, the minute he pulled the car to a halt beside his Suburban at the rear of the house, Emma bolted. She couldn't stand another minute in the car, not another ten seconds, and she scrambled out as if the demons of hell were after her. Then, utterly embarrassed, she hurried into the house with every intention of hiding in her bedroom, away from this disturbing man who had seen parts of her soul that had never before been exposed to anyone.

But Gage caught up with her halfway across the kitchen and swung her around, catching her to him and holding her as she struggled.

"Stop it, Emma. Stop it," he said sharply. "We have to talk, and you damn well know it. If you're remembering, I need to know what might be coming so I can help."

"Help? What kind of help...?" She pushed at him, trying to get away.

"What if you remember in the dead of night, Emma? Who's going to be there for you if you remember what that man did?"

She froze, and then slowly, unhappily, lifted her wide, frightened green eyes to his. "I don't want to remember, Gage. I don't!"

"How are you going to prevent it, Emma?"

She shuddered. "I don't know."

"You can't prevent it. You can't. It'll happen. You're sitting on a time bomb, and if you've started remembering any of it, then the fuse is a short one."

She turned from him slowly, and he let go of her. "I'm

going to change,'' she said tonelessly. "I need to make dinner.''

Damn, Gage thought. He never would have pegged her for an ostrich. Did she really think that if she pretended it didn't exist, it would just go away? The lady was riding for one hell of a fall. One *hell* of a fall.

At the kitchen door she turned to look at him. "Who was there for you, when *you* remembered?''

When he didn't answer, she turned away and left him alone in the echoing silence of the kitchen.

Chapter 6

Gage, too, had experienced traumatic amnesia, though probably not for as long or to as great a degree as she had, Emma thought as she changed into her jeans with shaky hands. How else could he be so sure that she was about to remember all of it? How else could he be so sure that she was going to need someone when it broke? How else could he believe that she had really forgotten what had happened to her?

In retrospect, she realized how odd it was that he never questioned or doubted her when she had told him she couldn't remember. On the several occasions years ago, when she had tried to discuss it with a few college friends, she had met first with disbelief and then with all kinds of questions about what it felt like not to remember.

Gage hadn't questioned her, which meant he knew, and the fact that he knew meant he was probably right that she was verging on complete recovery of her memory. Oh, Lord!

She found Gage in the kitchen, reheating the soup she had made last night and slicing a loaf of bakery bread.

"Sit," he said quietly. "I'm taking care of dinner."

They ate in silence, neither one of them too terribly hungry, and then Gage poured them both mugs of coffee. When he settled into the chair facing her, pain flashed across his face, twisting his once-handsome features. Emma resisted an urge to reach out to him. The last time she had reached out, she'd wound up rolling around on her living room rug in a very improper fashion. There was, however, a burning question she couldn't smother.

"What did *you* forget?" she asked him.

Gage's head jerked, almost as if she had slapped him. A long, tense moment passed before he looked at her. "Sounds. I forgot the sounds. I never did see—" He cut himself off and looked away. He dragged in a deep breath before he continued. "I assumed—everyone assumed—that I'd been immediately knocked unconscious by the blast. When I started to remember…I thought I was losing my mind." *There was never a chance. Never.*

"Sounds? You mean the explosion?"

His gray-green eyes suddenly bored into her. "Screams. I mean the screams."

Emma's hand flew to her mouth, and she suddenly felt as if she would be sick. She should never have asked. She should never have disturbed this man's ghosts.

Gage sighed and looked down at his mug. Let it go, he told himself. Just let it go.

"What were you before you came here?"

He looked up again, tempted to tell her to drop it. He didn't want to discuss his past. His past was a closed book as far as he was concerned, and the more tightly closed he kept it, the better. When he walked the streets and traveled the roads of Conard County, people might stare at his disfigured face and wonder, but they didn't look at him with pity. They didn't whisper about him, because he gave them nothing to whisper about. He was as anonymous as a man could be when he stayed in one place.

But he was going to ask this woman to tell him things nobody in the county knew about her. As far as he had been able to determine, nobody in Conard County—with the possible exception of Nate Tate, who wouldn't betray a secret even at gunpoint—had any idea that Emmaline Conard had anything darker in her past than the assumed traveling man.

He needed to know more than she had already told him, though, because if her memory returned, somebody in this damn county would need to know what was happening. Somebody was going to have to hold her and listen to her and reassure her, and the lot would probably fall to him simply because he was sharing her roof.

Besides, he thought with grim resignation, she was going to need someone who would understand what was happening, and he was probably the only person around here who could.

"Okay," he said. "Okay. I worked for the Drug Enforcement Administration. DEA. I operated undercover in several major cities against drug kingpins."

"And one of them tried to kill you with a bomb?"

Such a simple, bald statement, he found himself thinking. It couldn't begin to convey what had actually happened. "Yeah."

"But if you were undercover—"

"My cover was blown. It happens." God, he wanted to get away from this now, before they edged any closer to the abyss of pain that was always just a single misstep away. "I'd appreciate it if you wouldn't tell anyone what I've just told you."

Emma nodded. "You have my word. I suppose you still have enemies?"

"A few." He would let her think that was the reason he wanted his secrets kept. Personally, he didn't care a bucket of hog swill if one of those guys came looking for him. It would be a swift way out of hell.

Except that hell didn't feel quite so empty and quite so cold with Emmaline Conard sitting across the table from him, her tightly bound hair like a candle flame in the dark. "Let your hair down, Emma."

She blinked. "I don't think that would be wise."

"Damn it, woman, are you always wise? Always cautious and careful and proper?"

Her lower lip quivered, just a little. "No. I certainly wasn't being proper or wise or cautious when I...when you...when we..." Oh, Lord, Emma, how could you bring that up? But her chest ached beneath a great weight, a weight compounded of unmet desires and loneliness. Of a feeling that even this man who had swept her halfway to the stars could see only an uptight old maid. Of a feeling that life had conspired to deprive her of everything that mattered, that this man scorned the walls she had needed to build to protect herself.

"Oh, hell." Gage looked quickly away and then moved so swiftly that she nearly jumped. Reaching out, he captured both her hands and held them tightly. "I'm sorry, Emma. Really. Talking about the past turns me into a bastard. Besides, I don't know how to deal with a woman like you."

"Like me?" Her lip quivered even more perceptibly. "What's so unusual about me? I'm just a woman like any other."

"No, you're not. Damn it, lady, I was raised on the streets like a wild dog. My mother was hooked on heroin by the time I was five, and my dad was knifed to death in a fight when I was six. Nobody ever taught me a damn thing, and all I ever learned I got out of books, once I could read. The army taught me table manners and how to keep clean, how to fight back with something besides a knife and a broken bottle. They sent me to school and taught me I could be something besides a punk. Then I joined the DEA and went back on the streets. I know about hookers and runaways and junkies, and about the hopeless ones who keep trying to avoid the muck, but I don't know a damn thing about satin and lace and churchgoing ladies."

"So because I haven't lived on the streets, I'm a different species?"

Her eyes were sparking angrily at him, and he was almost relieved to see it. It was a vast improvement over the quivering lip. "I didn't say that. I just mean I don't know exactly how to talk to a lady like you. I'm rough and blunt, and sometimes I'm coarse."

"You've done just fine so far, Gage Dalton."

"Good. Then maybe you'll get around to telling me what it was you remembered today. And what exactly it is that you're so afraid of remembering."

Emma's hands tightened in his. "You really think I'm going to remember it all?"

"That's what usually happens, they tell me."

"I don't want to." Her voice was thin, uncertain, totally unlike the Miss Emma who had most of the males in the county terrorized. "I don't see why I need to remember it. It was years ago, and apart from a few small fears, it doesn't affect me at all any longer." Except for one small but essential biological lack. What would Gage think of that? she wondered, and then told herself it didn't matter in the least, because it would never become an issue.

"Maybe you don't need to remember it, but if you remembered something today, then you're probably going to remember everything."

Emma tugged her hands from his, telling herself that, yes, his skin was warm and dry and callused from hard work, and that she would probably cheerfully fling her virtue away if he wanted to put those hands on her flesh, but that she really didn't need anyone to hold her hand. She had coped this far, and she could continue to cope. She had her pride, after all.

"What did you remember, Emma?"

"Nothing, really." She looked down at her mug. "It was— I was walking back to the dorm from the campus library. It was late at night, cold, snowing like it was tonight. I'm not sure how I know it was right before...it happened. I just know."

Gage nodded. "You just know, Emma. The rest of the memories are there, but you can't reach them. It's all in context, though. Your unconscious mind knows exactly what comes next.''

Emma nodded and lifted her gaze to his. "I knew. You're right. Standing out there in that parking lot tonight, I knew exactly what would come next.''

She wrapped her arms around herself, feeling cold and wishing she were a small child who could crawl into a parent's lap and find all the comfort she needed in a hug. That kind of comfort had vanished from her life when her mother died. Besides, she told herself sternly, adult problems couldn't be handled so simply. All the hugs in the world couldn't comfort her now.

"Talk to me, Emma," Gage said softly. "What do you know about what happened to you?''

The weight in her chest grew crushing. She drew a ragged breath, and then another, and wondered if she could even make herself say the words.

"Th-they told me he grabbed me when I was walking back to the dorm. They f-found a lead pipe with my blood and hair on it beside the sidewalk, so they think he must have stunned me by hitting me over the head once or twice.''

Gage muttered an oath. "No prints?''

Emma inhaled deeply, slowly, battling for calm and control. "No. It was winter. He was wearing gloves.''

Gage froze, struck by the way she had said that. "You remember that, don't you?'' he asked softly.

Emma looked startled. "I-I guess I do. I see leather gloves. Black leather. Big hands. I don't know how I know that.''

"It's all right, don't worry about it. What else do you know?''

"That he was—that he—oh, God, Gage, I *can't!*''

He reached out, capturing her hands again, squeezing them reassuringly. "It's all right, Emma. It's okay. You're safe now.''

"I've never told anyone about it! Never. Even if I can't

remember it, it's awful to even say it, to talk about it…. I don't think—''

''Did he rape you?'' He didn't really want to be so blunt, but he had to know what she would be facing when the time came, and if he let Emma back off now, he would never find out. If she couldn't tell him, he'd ask outright.

Emma gasped. ''No!'' She tried to jerk her hands free, but he wouldn't let go. His expression was fixed, hard, not at all reassuring.

''Did he torture you?''

Emma stiffened and grew utterly still. Expression vanished from her face, leaving her to look as if she had been carved from palest marble. ''Yes.'' It was a mere breath of sound.

Gage recognized what was happening, because it had happened to him countless times. Something in her had drawn back from all the uncomfortable, painful feelings. She had distanced herself.

''How badly did he injure you, apart from the coma?''

''Badly enough,'' Emma said tonelessly. ''He left me for dead in one of those large trash bins. Somebody saw something and was suspicious and called the police. They found me before I froze or bled to death.''

Gage muttered a string of curses, one after another, quietly but emphatically. Rising, he limped around the table and drew Emma up from her chair and into his arms. There was more here, he thought, as he held her close and offered what little comfort he could. Something had happened that she hadn't told him, something that was keeping this fresher in her mind than it should be when she couldn't even remember what had been done to her. Something was keeping her raw.

He thought of taking her into the living room because it was a cozier environment than the kitchen and might help soothe her, but then he remembered the undecorated Christmas tree. It wouldn't soothe *him* to sit in there. That left the library or study or whatever the hell Emma called it, with its ceiling-to-floor books, big old desk and leather sofa. Emma would probably feel comfortable there, and as long as he didn't have to deal with Christmas, too, Gage didn't give a damn.

"Go on into the study," he told Emma as he released her. "I'll bring the brandy."

Numbly, Emma obeyed. The calm that filled her was not natural, and in some detached fashion, she knew it. It was the calm of muffling barriers slammed into place to prevent emotional overload. Even the urge to run, to somehow escape, was silenced.

Gage joined her on the sofa with the brandy bottle and two snifters. "Here," he said, thrusting a filled snifter toward her. "Take it like medicine. You can sip the next one."

She tilted her head, studying him dispassionately. "I never get drunk."

"Tonight you're getting sloshed."

"Why?"

"Because if we're both lucky, you'll go to sleep and stay that way until morning. Frankly, Emma m'dear, I've had enough emotional turmoil for one day. If I can postpone the next round for a little while, I will."

She studied him solemnly and opened her mouth to ask what had made him weep earlier, but bit back the words before they escaped. Instead she tossed off the brandy and then held her glass out for more. He was right, she thought. They would both be better off if she could just knock herself out. Neither one of them wanted to handle any more.

"Slowly now," he cautioned her when he had refilled the snifter. "I don't want to give you a hangover."

"What the hell difference does it make?" Emma asked, and then clapped a horrified hand over her mouth. She *never* talked like that!

Gage astonished her by laughing. Honestly, truly laughing. "You're cute when you forget yourself, Emma. You ought to do it more often."

She said nothing, afraid she would only dig a deeper hole for herself. Waiting for the embarrassed blush to fade from her cheeks, she watched Gage ease himself into a more comfortable position on the couch. His every movement spoke of caution, as if the slightest wrong move could cause him severe pain.

"I can bring the Kennedy rocker in here, if you like," she offered. Comprehension was a little late in coming, but she suddenly understood that Gage had a problem with Christmas. Nothing else could explain his reaction to the living room last night, his tears before the tree this morning, and his desire to sit in here this evening.

"No, it's all right," he assured her. "It just takes me a little time to settle, that's all."

Emma leaned her head back against the couch and watched him without a thought for how rude it was to stare. He didn't seem to notice, anyway. His eyes roamed the bookshelves, and from time to time he shifted restlessly, as if he couldn't quite get comfortable.

So he had been raised on the streets. Like a wild dog, he had said. She couldn't imagine it. She could, however, imagine how defiant and angry he must have been. What had happened, she wondered, to turn him into this mature, contained man? If he had ever been a punk, no sign of it remained, except possibly in his preference for black leather.

"What's it like, working undercover?" she heard herself ask.

Slowly, Gage turned his head and looked at her. "Terrifying. Exciting. Boring. And sometimes it's the biggest ego trip on earth."

"What exactly did you do? Make buys on street corners?"

Gage shook his head. "Sometimes. The last few years, I infiltrated the bigger drug organizations. I wasn't interested in the street pushers then."

"How did you do that? I mean, I wouldn't know where to begin to look for a street pusher, let alone one of the big guys."

"It's easy when DEA backs you up. I'd just move into an area and start my own drug operation. I'd start really small and grow just fast enough to be noticed. After a while, I'd appear to be infringing on the big guy's territory, and his thugs would pay me a little visit. I'd be cooperative enough to let them know I'd be willing to discuss business, but that I wasn't going to be frightened away.'' A simple, clear explanation of what was, in reality, a complex, dangerous game of emotional and psychological chess. A game that in an instant could turn violent and bloody.

Emma shook her head. ''I can't imagine doing anything that nerve-racking. How did you ever stand the tension?''

Gage sighed. This woman was going to pry every one of his most personal secrets from him, but somehow he couldn't bring himself to lie. He'd lived in the shadows of half-truths for too damn long. ''I'd think about my brother. He OD'd a couple of weeks after our father died. Cort was eight.''

''Eight? Your brother was only eight?'' Emma was appalled beyond words. She was aware such things happened, of course, but they happened elsewhere, to people she didn't know. Until this very instant, such things had seemed distant, like a war in another country.

''You're very fortunate here in Conard County,'' Gage remarked. He took another sip of brandy and shifted yet again as the hot poker in his back took another jab at him. ''Drugs are becoming a problem in even the smallest towns.''

''I've heard. I think we need to thank Sheriff Tate that it isn't a big problem here. He started that drug-education program in the schools ten years ago, even at the kindergarten level. May I have some more brandy?''

Gage glanced at her empty glass, and one corner of his mouth lifted. ''Lady, it's your bottle. You can have as much as you want.'' He poured a generous amount into her glass.

''It's relaxing me,'' she admitted.

Right to sleep, Gage hoped. All afternoon he'd cursed his carelessness with Emma. She was about as sexually innocent as a woman could be, and there was no getting around the fact that he'd taken advantage of her innocence. Carried away on new feelings, she hadn't even begun to realize her danger or

how much at his mercy she had been. Gage had enough experience to know, though. He hadn't even unbuttoned her
blouse, yet she'd been within moments of giving him any damn
thing he wanted.

That unexpected responsiveness had haunted him all afternoon, making him feel both guilty and hungry. He didn't like
to think of himself as a seducer of innocent women. All his
experience had been with women who knew the score and how
to handle both their emotions and their bodies. Even his wife…

He cut that thought off before it could blossom into pain. It
wasn't to the point, anyway. The point was, he had no business
taking advantage of Emmaline Conard.

But, he admitted, he sure would like to. The woman was like
tinder, ready to burst into flame. She made him eager and nervous and horny as hell just by walking into the room. Now he
was plagued with the knowledge of her responsiveness, the way
she arched toward him and begged with her body for more.
Now he knew that kissing her was incendiary, that her breast
was made to fit his hand, and that in a mere five minutes he
could probably have her naked and writhing beneath him.

Damn!

Slowly he turned to look at her again and found her snuggled
into her corner of the leather couch, her head lolling back, eyes
closed, stockinged feet tucked beneath her. Something in him
ached, and he wished he *could* reach out. Just to hold her, he
told himself. Just to hold her.

How the hell had a woman like her escaped marriage? Why
did such a passionate woman avoid men? He couldn't believe
all the cowboys around here were dead blind, so Miss Emma
herself had to be the sole cause of her unattached state. And
there had to be a damn good reason for that.

"I'm scared," Emma said abruptly. She set her empty snifter
down sharply.

Enough booze for now, Gage thought. "Scared of what?"

"Of remembering. Of going to sleep."

"Sleep? Why sleep?"

"I keep having nightmares. Terrible, terrible dreams."

Gage could have told her that was part of it, but he forgot what he meant to say when Emma suddenly crawled down the couch and curled up against his side, trying to burrow into him. Without a thought for the consequences, he wound his arm around her slender shoulders and pulled her as close as he could get her.

"There's a dagger," Emma said shakily. "Like the one in the picture I got in the mail. You remember?"

"I remember." He tensed, sensing importance in this.

"I keep seeing it in my dreams, only it's golden, and there's a big, bloodred ruby in the pommel." She gave an unhappy little laugh. "I even see it when I'm awake, out of the corner of my eye. I keep jumping, expecting it to stab me. I'm losing my mind!"

"No...no...you're perfectly sane, Emma, I swear." And tomorrow morning, first thing, he was going to call Brian about that damn photo. He was beginning to think that there was more to it than mere fund-raising. "Does it hurt you in your dreams?"

"No..." She sighed. "I always wake up before it hits me. Sometimes I wake up screaming. I've been afraid that you heard me."

"No, I never heard you. Maybe you only think you scream."

"Maybe. I hate it, Gage. It's happening every night, and I just wish it would stop! I sleep with the lights on, and it's getting harder and harder to fall asleep, because I know it will happen again."

He hugged her and brushed a comforting kiss on the top of her head. Then, damning himself for a fool, he brought his other arm up and released her barrette. Time to distract her, he told himself.

"I love your hair, Red," he said gruffly. "It's almost alive."

She sighed. "I hate it. I've never been able to style it or make it behave."

"It's beautiful just the way it is." Slowly, gently, he fluffed it. "It looks like living fire, and it feels so soft." Gently he stroked it, and from time to time his fingers brushed the delicate, satiny skin of her neck. When they did, she sighed, and his groin tightened.

Playing with fire, he thought, and kept right on doing it. Hell's own archangel was accustomed to flying close to the flame, he thought wryly. He'd certainly done it often enough.

Emma was completely lost in the pleasure of being held by Gage. At the moment she didn't care that tomorrow she would be embarrassed by the way she had crawled into his arms. Just now, all that mattered was that he held her and stroked her and made her feel safe and welcome.

Beneath her cheek, his chest was hard and his heart beat strongly. He was warm, and he smelled wonderful, of soap and of something deeper, darker. Something exotic and erotic. Something that made her want to turn her face into him and nuzzle him, something that made her want to climb into his lap and press herself to him in ways she could barely imagine.

And, quite naturally, her embarrassment dulled by brandy, her thoughts drifted back to what had happened at lunch. How silly, she thought now, that she'd wasted the entire afternoon wishing it hadn't happened. Truth was, she had loved every minute of it and wished she knew how to ask for more.

"You're playing a dangerous game, Miss Emma." Gage's voice was little more than a rough, low whisper.

Emma suddenly realized that her fingers had slipped between the snaps on his black shirt and were absently stroking the skin beneath. Instantly she grew still. Her wits were muddled by the brandy, but not so muddled that she didn't know what he meant. She had, however, lost her usual sense of caution.

"I'm sorry," she said. "I was thinking about…earlier." She shouldn't have admitted that, she thought hazily, and tomorrow she was going to be upset that she had, but now, at this moment, it felt like the right thing to do. *This* was right, she thought a little dizzily. Being close to Gage like this was the most natural thing she had ever felt.

"Damn it, Emma, why don't you try a little prevarication once in a while?"

"Why?" She raised her hazy green eyes to his darker gaze.

But Gage was beginning to feel as addled as she was—from her closeness, though, not the brandy. He had hardly touched the stuff, but now he wished he had drunk enough to dull his senses. "Did you like what we did earlier?"

"Oh, yesss…" The words escaped her on a tremulous sigh.

Oh, no. Gage looked into her upturned face, into her sleepy eyes, and felt everything inside him tense with an urge to pounce. Slowly his gaze drifted downward to her soft, sweet lips, lips that were already slightly parted, lips she now moistened with a maddeningly sensual sweep of the tip of her tongue.

The worst of it was, he thought, that she didn't have the faintest idea what she was doing to him. In her utter innocence she was absorbed by what she was feeling and totally oblivious to the havoc she was wreaking. It was the sexiest damn thing he'd ever seen in his life.

His whole body was pulsing in time to his arousal, and a devil whispered rationalizations into his inner ear. Just a kiss or two, the demon whispered. What harm was that? A couple of kisses, maybe a feel or two. She would enjoy it every bit as much as he would. He could make them both throb a little, ache a little, yearn a little, and then he could send her safely to bed, because he would be damned if he'd take advantage of a drunken virgin. He'd committed a lot of sins in his misspent life, but that was one he never wanted on his conscience.

But a kiss or two? She was asking and he was willing, and if he didn't let it go any further, what harm could there be?

So easy, he thought, to sell his soul. Bending, he touched his lips to hers, felt the warm rush of her breath as she sighed her pleasure. That sigh nudged him even closer to the edge. Even the ever-present pain in his back and leg faded away before the uprush of aching passion. He wanted this woman.

He could never have her, had no right to ever take her, but he wanted her like hell on fire.

"Emma...oh, damn, woman..." She felt so good in his arms, seemed to fit every angle and plane of his body as if she had been made for him. She filled a hole, made him feel like a man, made him feel like he had thought he would never feel again. Briefly, he rejoiced in life.

"Oh, Gage," she sighed shakily between kisses. "Oh, Gage..."

He ran his tongue along the smooth edges of her teeth, along the satiny, sensitive insides of her cheeks and lips. He felt her restless stirrings against him and suddenly lifted her so that she straddled his lap.

"Oh!" Startled, she opened her drowsy eyes and looked straight into his.

"It's okay, Emma," he whispered roughly. "We're just playing a little, remember?"

She nodded, hardly caring whether they were playing or deadly serious. Her knees were on either side of his narrow hips, making her acutely aware of how exposed her most private place was. And she was made even more restless by the growing ache that found nothing to answer it, and by the need to clamp her thighs together, a need he had completely stymied.

"Come closer, Red," he whispered, hell's own archangel seducing her with coaxing words. "Come closer." His hands closed on her hips, pulling her down until her femininity rested squarely against his engorged manhood. "That's it," he whispered. "Closer, Em. Closer."

She came closer, needing it as much as he, and when his hands slipped behind her to cup the roundness of her bottom and press her into him, she could do nothing but moan in utter relief.

"That's good, isn't it?" he whispered right into her ear, causing a sinuous shiver to run all the way to her toes. Gently, he pressed her into him again. "So good... What a temptress you are, lady. That's it. Just press against me whenever you feel like it…. Ahh…''

Dimly, he realized he had gone far past the couple of kisses he had intended. And then he wondered what the hell difference it made; he was already damned anyway. One more sin could hardly matter. When Emma rocked her hips against him again, slowly, deeply, catching her breath as she did so, he stopped thinking at all.

''Sit up, baby…sit up for me.''

When she straightened, she pressed herself even more tightly to him. The sensation caused her to draw a sharp breath of pleasure that almost distracted her from the popping sound as Gage ripped his shirt open. She recognized the sound, though, and opened her eyes just a little so she could look at him through her lashes. He was beautiful, she thought, so beautiful, like a dark angel. Archangel.

He took her hands from his shoulders and laid them on his naked chest. ''Touch me, Emma,'' he demanded. ''Touch me.''

Without the least hesitation she began to knead his powerful chest muscles with gentle movements. ''I like the way you feel,'' she murmured unsteadily. ''Smooth and rough all at once….''

Her blouse was open almost before she realized what he was doing, and when she felt the warm brush of his fingers against the soft skin of her midriff, she merely sighed and looked down. Dark hands reached for the front fastening of her simple white bra, and the sight was so erotic that everything within her clenched sharply. ''Gage…''

He heard the way her breath caught, and his own caught in response. ''Has anyone ever touched your breasts, Emma? Or kissed them?''

She gave a jerky negative shake of her head and then, as the bra clasp released, closed her eyes against a shaft of feeling so strong she didn't think she could bear it. She knew people did such things, but for years she had refused to even think of them, because such thoughts always made her feel so achy and empty, so lonely and alone.

"Oh, Emma," Gage breathed huskily as he stared hungrily at the satiny globes he had just revealed. She was small but full, and her nipples were rosy and already erect. Gently, knowing the sensation would startle her, he reached up and touched her with a careful fingertip.

"Oh!" She jerked as feeling speared through her, and her eyes flew open. "Oh, Gage!"

"It's fantastic, isn't it?" Leaning forward, he wrapped his arms around her hips and ran his tongue slowly, enticingly, in a circle around her knotted nipple. "Mmm," he growled deeply as he felt shivers ripple through her. "It just gets better and better, Em. Better and better.... Ahh, that's it. Rock against me, sweet. Just like that...."

Emma had long ago decided that lovemaking must feel good, but she had never dreamed it would feel like another plateau of existence altogether. She had never imagined that embarrassment would vanish, and shame along with it. That she could actually clutch a man's head to her breast as she whimpered and rubbed against him.

Gently, with exquisite care, Gage drew her nipple into his mouth and sucked. Her response was instantaneous, a soft moan escaped her as she drew taut against him. God, he loved the way she responded. There was something to be said for inexperience, something to be said for the joy of wakening a woman who had no preconceptions or misconceptions.

His own body felt as if it were about to explode. The need was stronger in him than he could remember ever feeling, the urge to bury himself deeply in her welcoming heat almost enough to override his last scruple.

But not quite enough to override the last scrap of his sense. He had no way to protect her from pregnancy. He had thought about going out that afternoon and buying some condoms, but he had talked himself out of it. As long as he couldn't risk impregnating her, he would retain some self-control. For her sake, far more than his own, he had resisted temptation.

Now, knowing he could not go any further than this without taking an unconscionable risk, he was able to batter down his desires just enough to maintain control. He would give her what she needed because he had aroused the passion in her, but he would take nothing for himself but her pleasure. Damn, Dalton, he thought sarcastically, aren't we the noble one? Because he was enjoying this at least as much as Emma, even knowing how he was going to ache later, when he put her aside. He was enjoying every single little bit of this, reveling in sensations he had believed he would never feel again—feeling every one of them more intensely than he had ever dreamed possible.

He moved his mouth to Emma's other breast, teasing and tormenting her there with exquisite care until she was sobbing for breath and pressing herself against him in a relentless search for release.

"That's it, Em," he whispered encouragingly. Gripping her hips, he encouraged her movements against him. "Oh, that's good, Em. That's great. It feels so damn good!"

"Gage?" His name was a frightened question, and she stiffened.

"Easy, babe. Easy. Let it happen…oh, honey, it'll feel so good…." He moved her hips, forcing her to climb the last few terrifying steps to the pinnacle. "Come on, Em," he said roughly. "Come on…just let it happen…."

"Gage!" It was a short, sharp cry as she arched one final time against him, then collapsed on his chest.

He held her, stroking her from head to hip, murmuring gently to her as he took an incredible, simple pleasure from holding her like this. It was even possible to ignore his own aching loins and the shaft of pain in his lower back in favor of the warm comfort of her skin against his. Such a precious feeling, he thought, the touch of skin on skin, her chest to his. So damn precious.

"You're beautiful, Emma. Beautiful, warm and passionate," he whispered as he held her. "I wouldn't have missed that for the world. Not for the world."

For a long, long time Emma lay drowsily in his arms, more replete than she had ever felt. His stroking hands on her back assured her of her welcome on his lap, and the contact of their bare chests was a warm intimacy that made her feel even more satisfied. But gradually she began to think again.

"Gage?"

"Hmm?" His hands never paused as he enjoyed the smooth line of her back and the warmth of her against his palms.

"That was the Big O, wasn't it?"

A soft, amused sound escaped him. "It sure looked like it."

"I don't think it could have been anything else. I never imagined it was like that."

"It's not the kind of thing anyone can really imagine." Wrapping his arms around her, he squeezed her. "Fantastic, isn't it?" He was feeling warm and generous and very saintly at the moment, he realized. Kind of a high for hell's own archangel to be so selfless. He almost laughed aloud at himself.

"Mmm." She stirred a little and looked up at him. "But what about you?"

That was one question he'd been hoping she wouldn't ask. Damn Miss Emma and her honesty. "Don't worry about it, Red."

"But—"

He cut her off by placing his fingers against her lips. "Emma, don't. I don't have any way to protect you." As an excuse, it was one of the best. He somehow thought that if he tried to take the high moral ground on this one and claim he didn't want to take a virgin, she would try to talk him out of it. The pregnancy argument was one she couldn't counter.

"Protect me?" It didn't connect in her muzzy mind. "From what?"

"Pregnancy," he said, beginning to feel the early twinges

of desperation. She was innocent, he reminded himself. Unaccustomed to thinking in such terms.

But suddenly she stiffened against him, and all the warm relaxation he had felt and enjoyed in her was gone.

"Emma? Emma, what's wrong? You can't honestly think I'd take a chance like that with you. You don't want to get pregnant—"

"I wish I could!" she said with sudden fierceness. Her hands turned into fists on his shoulders, and she sat up, struggling to escape from his lap.

"Emma?" He caught her by the waist and ignored her struggles to get away. "Emma, what do you mean?"

Tell him, commanded a voice in her head. *Tell him now.* He would go away then. He would go away before she started to care any more than she already did. Before it was too late for her heart and soul. And just as suddenly as she had gone wild, she grew utterly calm.

"I can't get pregnant," she said tonelessly. "The attack damaged me so badly that...I'm barren."

His hands relaxed at her waist as shock ripped through him. Before he could absorb what she had said, before he could do anything at all, she twisted from his hold and fled.

Chapter 7

Several times Gage came to her bedroom door and knocked. "Emma, talk to me. Call me names, tell me what a slug I am, but for God's sake, talk to me."

Each time Emma listened to him but felt no desire to answer. She lay on her back in the middle of the bed, staring up at the jewel-like colors the Tiffany lamp cast on the ceiling. Some pains ran so deep that they made you numb, she thought distantly. She felt numb right now. Numb to everything.

"Emma, come on. Open the door. I'll bring you some of that Earl Grey tea I found in the pantry. Emma?"

She ignored him, and after a while he went away again. She didn't think he'd given up, though. No, he would come back later and knock on the door. Maybe she should shout something at him, tell him to drop dead or get lost or something. He'd opened the wound. He'd awakened all the feelings she had learned to suppress. He had turned her into an aching, wanting, needing woman when she wasn't a woman at all anymore.

She wondered if she could stand it.

* * *

Gage stood staring at the closed door of Emma's bedroom and wondered why it always seemed to turn out this way. Karma. It had to be karma. There had to be some reason why everything he touched turned to ashes, why pain dogged his every step. He'd tried to make the woman feel good, truly good, and instead he'd managed to rip open her deepest wounds.

The door had a solid core, he realized as he stared at the dark, varnished surface. It was the good old-fashioned kind of door, not the thin, modern kind that he could put his fist through.

So he would just have to do something. No way was he going to leave Emma alone to sink into despair. Damned if he could understand this hang-up women had with babies, anyway. He loved kids, sure. Had loved his—scratch that. Nothing wrong with kids, but he couldn't understand this insane passion to have them. How could you love a kid you had never even held yet? How could you be so sure you'd want the little bugger before you knew whether he would even be tolerable? Women were in love with the *idea* of having kids, but as a man, he couldn't begin to understand it.

But he *could* understand that women felt that way, and he could understand that he had just stumbled on the reason why Emma avoided men. Now she was lying in there as raw as a gaping wound, and he'd done that to her. It didn't matter that he hadn't meant to. He'd done it. Now he had to figure out how to fix it.

No, not fix it. There was no fixing this one. But he couldn't leave her alone with it. Nobody should be alone with that kind of pain.

But the solid oak door stood between them.

So he'd pick the damn lock.

Turning, he limped toward the stairway and then climbed the steps slowly, glad there was no one to see him. His back was kicking up pretty bad right now. Why the hell hadn't he stayed in the apartment above Mahoney's? Then he could have limped down the stairs, had a couple of shots and gone for a long walk into oblivion. Instead, he was limping up these damn stairs to get his case of lock picks and worrying about a woman who wouldn't even talk to him.

Yeah, it had to be karma. He must have sold his soul in another lifetime, too.

Forget the long walk, he thought when he reached the top of the stairs. Sweat beaded his brow, the cold sweat of pain. A long, hot bath would be the ticket right now. But no. He was going to climb down those stairs, paying for at least half his sins in the process, and then he was going to shake Miss Emmaline Conard until her teeth rattled.

And probably work up another twenty years of bad karma as a result.

He swore loudly, succinctly, and turned into his bedroom. The picks were in the bottom drawer of the dresser, of course. Under the jock strap he figured would cause any blushing old maid to slam the drawer shut before she looked any further. Not that Emma had pried, but when he'd first moved over here, he hadn't known her at all. She might have been inclined to snoop. Now he knew the thought would never even enter her head.

Unfortunately, now he had to bend to get to them. Holding his breath against the inevitable agony, he bent down to retrieve the small leather wallet. On the way back up, he groaned. He couldn't help it.

He must be out of his mind, he thought. Absolutely, positively out of his ever-loving mind. Why was he getting involved with this woman's problems? Sure, it was nice not to have to live with the noise and stale-beer smell above Mahoney's, but he'd come here for quiet, not an emotional marathon. He'd come here, too, because a woman had looked at him with frightened green eyes and told him that she would feel safer if he shared her house with her.

He'd almost lost sight of that. But maybe all her fears were related to her returning memories and not to anything real at all. The balloon thing was a typical juvenile stunt, and even the decapitated rabbit didn't go far beyond the pale. He could just imagine some smart-aleck sixteen-year-old boy bagging the rabbit with his shotgun and then getting the idea of scaring the old-maid librarian. It wasn't necessarily anything threatening at all.

But his instincts pricked uneasily, and that business about the dagger in her dreams being like the one in the photograph…well, it was too soon to dismiss Miss Emma's fears. He couldn't imagine any reason on earth why anyone should want to harm her, though. But then, a sicko never needed a reason.

Gritting his teeth, he limped back down the stairs. Maybe later he would break down and take one of his pain pills. He almost never took them, because he had a healthy fear of addiction, but it had been months since the last one. Maybe tonight he would give in.

Her bedroom lock was as old-fashioned as the door, with a big keyhole and a simple double-tumbler arrangement. He picked it without any difficulty at all—other than straightening from his squat. He groaned as he did so and shoved the door open.

"Get out of here, Gage," Emma said flatly. There was no expression in her voice at all, not even irritation.

"Don't think so, Miss Emma," he said just as flatly. He closed the door behind him and limped over to the bed. She was lying in the middle of it, staring at the ceiling, and she hadn't even bothered to fasten her clothing. Now, with him staring down at her, she seemed to be unaware that a tempting strip of satiny skin and the soft curve of one breast were visible. That troubled him. She should have clutched the edges of fabric together and glared at him.

He sighed and yanked open the snaps of his shirt. The sound of popping snaps drew her wary gaze to him. "Just don't want you to feel underdressed, ma'am," he said and threw his shirt aside.

Turning, he reached for the comforter at the foot of her bed and unfolded it, snapping it once sharply as he spread it over her. Then, pretending to ignore her, he sat on the edge of her bed and yanked at his boots. That drew another unwilling groan from him.

And then he nearly jumped out of his skin, because he felt the soft touch of warm fingers on his back.

"Your poor back," Emma whispered. "Your poor back."

"Everybody's got scars of one kind or another, Emma. You ought to know that by now."

"How it must have hurt."

"Actually, it didn't hurt at all until a week later." He got his boot off, then turned and slipped under the comforter beside her. Without a by-your-leave, he tugged her into his arms and held her close, chest to chest, thigh to thigh.

"I'm sorry, Red," he said gruffly. "I sure as hell didn't mean to hurt you."

"I know that," she admitted. "You aren't the one who hurt me. It's just…sometimes…"

"I know. Sometimes it hurts too much to bear."

She nodded and allowed herself to relax against him.

"I've got a great idea, Em," he said a few minutes later.

"Hmm?"

"Why don't you just go to sleep? If you have any nightmares, I'll be right here. And tomorrow things will look better. Or so they keep telling me."

"But what about you?" She *was* feeling drowsy, drained by the day's events and all the emotional turmoil.

"Red, I'll be a happy man if I just don't have to move again until dawn. Especially if I don't have to climb the stairs."

"I'm sorry you hurt," she said sleepily.

"I'm sorry you hurt, too, Emma. Now go to sleep."

During the night, Gage awoke in a state of flaming arousal to find himself and Emma tucked together like spoons. Her bottom nestled warmly against his aching loins, and his arm was wrapped snugly around her as his hand cradled her bare breast. In fact, he thought sourly, the only part of him that wasn't aching and throbbing was his back, for once.

The light was on. He had left it on in case Emma awoke, because he didn't want her to come awake from a nightmare in the dark with a strange man holding her. It illuminated her hair, catching the gold highlights and setting them on fire. Such beautiful hair, as soft as silk. It brushed his chin and chest like wisps of dreams that could never be.

He sighed and tried to relax his internal tensions. The nights were always the deadliest hours for him. Things had a way of creeping past the strongest guard and pouncing without warning. On the nights when sleep eluded him, he walked hard and fast, just as hard and fast as he walked when pain flogged him.

But tonight he didn't want to leave Emma alone. He knew what it was like to be afraid to sleep because of the nightmares, and he knew what it was like to awaken alone and have to struggle your way back to reality without the anchor of a familiar voice. Tonight, at least, Emma wasn't going to have to face that.

He owed her one, he thought. Maybe he even owed her a couple. For the last several days he had avoided thinking about Miss Emmaline Conard and his response to her, but here, alone in the night, with her close and warm in his arms, he could scarcely avoid it.

Her generosity of nature wasn't something he was used to. If Miss Emma hadn't dragged him into her house for brandy the night he walked her home, he could have kept her safely pigeonholed as one of the local characters—odd, amusing, but not someone he would have gone out of his way to become acquainted with. Since coming to Conard County he'd gone out of his way to become acquainted with very few people. Micah Parish, Ransom Laird, Jeff Cumberland…just a very few men who knew what it was to face the abyss.

And now Miss Emma. Miss Emma, who hadn't known him from Adam but had dragged him into her warm kitchen and offered him brandy because he hurt. Miss Emma, who had let him fall asleep in her living room and then served him the best dinner he had eaten in years. Emma, who forgot all her caution and wisdom every time she thought he might be hurting.

Like earlier this evening. Even in her own pain she had reached out in response to his. Surely that made her more unusual than rubies and diamonds? More precious than gold? Even his oldest and closest friends got uneasy and eager to get away when they were reminded of what had happened to him. It was one of the reasons he'd packed up and accepted Nate's invitation to come to Wyoming. He couldn't stand the way gazes slid away from him and conversations suddenly became brittle whenever somebody said the ''wrong'' thing. People had been tiptoeing around him as if he were some kind of time bomb. Or some kind of unpredictable invalid.

Out here, he pretty much got left alone. Mahoney would pour him a couple of shots without trying to analyze him. Nate gave him enough interesting cases to keep him busy and never hinted that maybe Gage wasn't up to doing something. Folks on the street nodded politely when he limped by, and they'd even gotten used to his disfigured face finally, so they didn't notice it one way or the other. The good ladies in the Good Shepherd Bible Study Group tittered that he looked like hell's own archangel, but even that seemed purely amusing to him— especially since they giggled and blushed like young girls whenever he spoke to any of them. And Maude, who owned the diner, always made sure there was a fresh wedge of pie for him when he stopped in.

It was as close to normal as he had come in a long time. As close as he could ever get, he supposed. A man who had spent fourteen years of his life working almost continuously undercover eventually forgot how to really be part of anything. Survival demanded that you appear involved without actually getting involved, that you participate while always remaining an observer. It meant changing personalities like a chameleon changed colors. In the end, maybe it meant losing yourself.

Sighing again, he pressed his face to Emma's neck. Her scent was hypnotic, fresh and womanly, totally natural and utterly erotic. The comforter that cocooned them caught the aroma and surrounded him in it. Her breast was warm and satiny beneath his palm, and he had the worst time convincing himself not to take advantage of the fact. Emma was sleeping, a sign of trust he couldn't betray.

Cautiously he moved his hand to safer ground, on her tummy, and then he closed his eyes, willing himself to sleep. The gripping, clenching, burning pain had for the moment let him go, and now would be a great time to sleep.

Except that he couldn't seem to sleep. He didn't feel especially drowsy, but he didn't feel especially like getting up, either. Instead his mind drifted, for once, into safe channels, carrying him back to his youth, when his refuge had been the city library. He could stay warm there on the coldest winter day, get cool there on the hottest days, and escape entirely on the worst ones.

In retrospect, the librarian hadn't been a dragon at all. Mrs. Scott had insisted on quiet, common courtesy and respect for the books, and on a couple of occasions she had spoken sharply to him for forgetting where he was. Overall, though, she had encouraged his love of reading. Looking back, he could see that when he had finished one book, she had been ready to hand him another. She had started him on the Hardy Boys, led him on to Monte Cristo and the Three Musketeers, and helped him to wade through Walter Scott. Even Captain Blood and the Scarlet Pimpernel—whom he held responsible for making him think undercover work was romantic—even they had been introduced to him by Mrs. Scott.

Mrs. Scott, he sometimes thought wryly, was therefore ultimately responsible for Gage Dalton and his funny notions of honor and duty and loyalty. Responsible for his even crazier notion about making the world a better place. Boy, he'd lost that one the hard way. There was a real war out there, and a few DEA operatives sure as hell weren't going to win more than a couple of skirmishes. Battling drugs was like battling Medusa. Every time you lopped off one snake head, there was another one right there. And in the process something inside you turned to stone, because there was just so much ugliness a man could stand.

And the fact that he could even make that comparison he owed entirely to Mrs. Scott of the vast bosom, the overwhelming perfume and the orthopedic shoes. In retrospect Gage even allowed she might not really have hated him after all, despite her frequent frowns and sharp reprimands.

But never in a million years would he have envisioned himself with the hots for a librarian. Or have imagined lying in bed holding one like this. In his mind librarians had been pigeonholed with nuns and Attila the Hun.

Well, that was just so much hogwash, anyway. Most of the preconceptions he had developed in his youth had blown away with time and experience. This was just another one. Emma had a few dragonish, stereotyped librarian characteristics, but beneath all the defenses he had found a shy, generous, warm, loving and very passionate young woman. One who deserved something a hell of a lot better than hell's own archangel.

Besides, he wasn't ever again going to sign on for that rollercoaster ride. Once was enough. No man in his right mind would take risks like that a second time. No way. Hell's own archangel had safely locked up his heart and thrown away the key.

Another sigh escaped him, a heavier one this time. He opened his eyes to fill them once more with the enticing flame of Emma's hair and the pale satin of her cheek, and then he gave himself up to sleep.

The knife glittered evilly, coldly gold, threatening, the blood-drop ruby like a malevolent eye. Voices whispered, laughing, fractured, a steady background to a lost, frightened whimper. Slowly, so slowly, the dagger lifted. Higher and higher it rose, then plunged downward in a swift, destroying arc.

"Emma!"

The scream rose from so deep in her that it left her insides raw, then erupted from her throat with shattering force.

"Emma!"

She sat bolt upright. Her eyes snapped open and stared uncomprehendingly at the familiar sights of her own bedroom. Grandma's room. The judge's room.

"Emma?"

That ruined voice was now as familiar to her as her own, and it was a lifeline in the darkness of her soul and mind. She turned and threw herself into Gage's waiting arms.

"It's okay," he whispered achingly. "It's okay, Emma."

If she had been alone, eventually she would have calmed herself and restored her self-control. But she was not alone. Now, right now, someone was there to take care of her, and it was like permission to give up the struggle. For just a few minutes she could lean on someone else.

And she did. Before she could gather her wits or her resources, she was clinging to Gage, and huge, silent tears were running down her cheeks. "I can't stand any more of this," she whispered brokenly. "I can't."

There wasn't a damn thing to say to that, Gage thought. He'd been at just that point more than once himself, the point where one little thing more would shatter you like glass.

"I know the feeling," he said rustily. "Come on. Let's get out of here."

Slowly, she leaned back a little and looked up at him from big, wet eyes. "Get out of here?"

"Take a walk. Walking is great therapy, Red. Works out all the kinks, tires you out good, and gets you back on an even keel. I promise."

"It's cold out there," she said in faint protest.

"So bundle up. Don't tell me you don't have the clothes, Emma. You've lived here all your life."

Not waiting for an answer, he turned away and lowered his feet to the floor. He had to bite back a groan when his back filed a protest, but he had a lot of practice at it.

"Ten minutes, Red. If you're real good, maybe we'll drive down to the creek and walk there."

Emma glanced at the digital display on her clock radio. Three in the morning and he wanted to go for a walk along the creek bank? She glanced around the room once more as he disappeared through the door and decided that maybe walking in the dark was a more inviting prospect than staying here any longer.

She started to crawl out of the bed, and that was when she realized her blouse was still open and her bra unfastened. Oh, Lord! Emma, Emma, what's come over you? How could you have…?

And then, like a burst of light in the night, memories came to her, reminding her of how Gage had made her feel last night, how intimately he had kissed her and how tenderly he had held her. How he had insisted on coming to her despite her locked door, and had held her through the night. She remembered waking once or twice to feel him pressed so warmly to her, remembered that once his hand had been cradling her breast.

He had given her care and tenderness and the most exciting and sensual experience of her life, and she was reacting like a prude. Like an old maid. Like Great-aunt Isabel, who had told her to carry a book with her everywhere, to sit on in case she should ever be obliged to sit on a man's lap in a crowded bus. Considering there were no buses other than school buses in Conard County, the advice had been singularly useless. Emma had crowed with laughter for weeks every time she thought of it. A book, for crying out loud.

Good grief, was she actually beginning to *think* like Great-aunt Isabel?

The thought brought her scurrying off the bed toward her closet, where she definitely had adequate clothing for the cold night air. She promised herself not to have another prudish thought, to be honest about how much she had enjoyed everything Gage had showed her.

And to be honest with herself, at least, about how much she wanted to experience it again.

The temperature had fallen into the teens, and their steps crunched crisply on the undisturbed snow along the bank of Conard Creek. Emma's initial chill, which had come as much from the early hour as the cold, had worn off as they walked, and she began to enjoy the unearthly beauty of the night. The light from the waxing moon was strong, silvering the sparkling snow and frost.

There had been a time when she had loved to walk at night, summer or winter. The attack had changed all that. Drawing a deep breath, she forced her thoughts away from that direction.

"Feeling better?" Gage asked presently.

"Much. This was a good idea." In fact, his suggestion of a walk had yanked her out of the dregs of her nightmare faster than anything else she could think of could have. From the moment he had suggested it, the miasma of horror had faded rapidly.

"You know," Emma said a little while later, "I often wonder about my ancestor, the one who first came here to homestead."

"Why?"

"I wonder about his ego. I mean, look at it—Conard County, Conard Creek, Conard City. Do you have any idea how embarrassing it was at times to grow up as a Conard?"

"Nope." He glanced down at her, a crooked smile drawing up one side of his mouth. "Where I come from, they didn't even have Dalton Street."

"There's a Conard Street on the east side of town," Emma reminded him.

"I noticed it."

"Maybe I can talk the city council into changing it to Dalton Street. Would you like that?"

"No. I like my low profile."

"I'd like to know what a low profile feels like. Anyhow, I

figure Edgar Conard must have been an egomaniac. If I'd been the first person to settle out here, I think I would have given everything Indian names."

"Some of those unpronounceable words that are sixteen syllables long?"

Emma gave a small, quiet laugh. "Maybe. Anything but Conard."

"I don't think you ought to be embarrassed about it, Em. It took a special kind of person to be a pioneer. Maybe a little ego was a necessary trait for survival."

"Maybe."

"You could use a little ego yourself."

The remark sounded casual, but it didn't strike Emma that way. At the implied criticism, she grew defensive. "What's that supposed to mean?"

He stopped walking, obliging her to do the same. His hat shadowed his face from the revealing moonlight, but her upturned face was mercilessly exposed. "It means that you're not worthless, whatever you keep telling yourself," he said quietly.

"Oh, now we get amateur psychology?"

He considered turning away right then. If he just walked into the night, Emma's problems need never trouble him again. And he sure as hell didn't want to get involved. But he couldn't walk way, he realized, because no one else in Conard County knew what Emma's problem was, and no one but him would have the gumption to confront her about it, anyway. She pretty much had all the rest of them cowed, except for a few sleazeballs who didn't have the sense to know better.

"No amateur psychology," he said quietly. "I never read a psychology book in my life, Red."

"Then what the devil are you babbling about?"

He almost smiled. Emma, he knew, wasn't one to speak so bluntly or discourteously under most circumstances. He had her on the defensive but good.

"Working undercover," he said, resuming their walk, "requires a pretty good understanding of human nature."

"Really."

"Yes, really. My life depended on being able to size up an opponent with only a little bit to go on—the way he stood, the way he talked, a couple of things he said. I was pretty good at it."

"Indeed."

He couldn't suppress an amused smile. "Indeed," he mimicked. "The fact that I'm still alive proves it."

This time she didn't make any smart comment at all.

"It's not book knowledge I'm talking about," Gage continued presently. "It's a gut instinct for what the other person will say or do because of the kinds of hang-ups he's got. It's a knack for knowing what buttons to push—or not to push."

"So you're pushing my buttons?" Rage began to simmer in her. She didn't like this at all.

"Nope. I don't manipulate people I consider to be my friends. I'm just trying to tell you that your self-opinion is about a hundred percent too low."

"What makes you such an authority?" she asked waspishly. He was treading in sensitive territory, and she didn't at all like it.

"The fact that I'm not you," he said easily. "The fact that I can evidently see all the good things you can't. Lady, you've got a lot of sterling qualities. Quit underestimating yourself. End of discussion."

Sterling qualities, she thought as she traipsed along beside Gage. It sounded like something her father would have said. She had a lot of sterling qualities, did she? Well, what about the not-so-sterling ones? The slightly tarnished or downright damaged qualities? So what if she had a few sterling qualities, or even a lot of them?

"Sterling qualities" sounded like something you would say to a homely girl who had once again been passed over for a date. It was the kind of reassurance a parent spouted when a child was convinced no one in the world loved her. It was not the kind of thing a man said to a woman he was interested in. It was, in short, a consolation prize.

The understanding at once relieved her and disappointed her. On the one hand, she had tasted temptation and found it sweet. On the other, she was scared to death that if Gage held her close too many more times, he would walk away with her heart in his pocket. And he *would* walk away. He might be perfectly kind and understanding about her sterility, but when it came to an enduring relationship, he would be looking for a whole woman. What man wouldn't?

Therefore, she told herself, it was far better that he think of her sterling qualities rather than her other ones.

"Emma?"

She looked up from the snowy ground she had been fiercely studying as they walked and realized that she had left Gage behind. She turned immediately. "Are you all right?"

"Every time you get perturbed you go into double-time," he said wryly. "Unfortunately, since I broke my back, I haven't been able to move that fast for long."

"You broke your back?" Forgetting her own problems for a moment, she hurried back to his side. "In the explosion?"

He gave a short nod.

"Lean on me if you need to," she offered as she reached his side. "I suppose it's a miracle you can walk at all, then."

"Maybe." He didn't like leaning on anyone, and he couldn't quite swallow the idea that anything in his miserable, hellacious life might ever have been a miracle.

"What causes the pain?"

"Nerve damage, old muscle damage. Sometimes I think it's pure orneriness."

If that was meant to be humorous, Emma couldn't see it that way. When he didn't drape his arm around her shoulder, she began walking at a slower pace. He moved right beside her.

Emma wondered sourly if Great-aunt Isabel had been complimented on her sterling qualities.

Probably.

* * *

Emma stood before the Christmas tree, staring up into its unadorned branches as early-morning sun poured like warm honey over it. She was dressed for work but had a few minutes yet before she needed to go. Gage had been gone for hours, but she had half expected that. He wasn't a man who wanted to get close to anyone. His desire to keep his distance would protect them both.

But the distance, while it was protective, didn't answer questions, and she had at least a couple to ask this morning.

What had happened to make Christmas such a time of grief for him? Why had he gone to so much trouble to make sure she had her tree, then sat here surrounded by light strings and wept the horrible, silent tears that in a man like him must spring from the deepest well in his soul? And then, she saw now, after she had gone back to work, he had forced himself to come in here and string the lights on the tree.

Once you start giving ground, lady, it's hell to get it back. Her memory of him saying that was vivid, and it probably explained the tree and the lights. He was trying not to give any ground. Or possibly trying to regain some he had lost.

For a moment Emma seriously considered getting rid of the tree. Instead, she moved the Kennedy rocker into the study and put away the box of decorations that had been intended to grace the mantelpiece in there. Gage would have this haven until the holidays were past.

Turning to leave the room, she found herself staring at the black leather couch. Lord! The brandy had certainly loosened her inhibitions, but, unfortunately, it hadn't dulled her memory any. Vividly, in embarrassing detail, she could remember everything she had done. Everything Gage had done. Every luscious touch and kiss and sensation.... Oh, Lord!

Quite apart from her sense of horror over her conduct, her body experienced an exquisite, clenching thrill at the very memory of what had occurred. Yes, she told herself tartly, it was a very good thing that Gage wanted to reestablish some kind of space between them. Apparently she was quite capable of succumbing to temptation. In fact, she was more than eager to succumb. It must come from too many years alone, she told herself. It was merely a reaction to…to sensory deprivation. Yes. That was it.

Oh, Emma, she thought gloomily moments later, you know better than to lie to yourself. What had happened with Gage had happened because he turned her on. Didn't she practically drool over the sight of his buns in his jeans? Never in her life had she noticed a man's physical attributes that way. Never. What was this? Some kind of delayed adolescence?

Still shaking her head over her own behavior, she slipped on her parka and reached for her purse. Maybe, instead of checking out the latest thriller for the weekend, she should check out a romance. There was a lot she didn't know about such things, and it occurred to her that a better understanding might do her some good.

The phone rang just as she was opening the door. Sighing, she dropped her purse on the counter and reached for the receiver.

"Hello?"

Silence answered her. The silence of someone on the other end, listening. Perhaps they hadn't heard her.

"Hello?" she repeated, louder. "Is anyone there?"

Again no answer. Well, Emma thought, there must be something wrong with the line.

"I can't hear you," she said into the phone. "The line must be bad. Goodbye."

She felt a little foolish talking to an empty line like that, but it could have been any of her friends, and she didn't want to be rude. Although in all likelihood, she admitted as she climbed into her car, it was probably one of those horrible telephone sales people who were nice until you told them you weren't interested.

She backed out of the driveway, but just as she was about

to wheel into the street, she looked back at her house and gasped.

There, in hideous, brilliant color, on the fresh snow between her car's tire tracks, where she had parked overnight, was a huge patch of scarlet that looked exactly like fresh blood.

Chapter 8

Gage had gone out to Jeff Cumberland's place first thing, because the rancher had spotted some marks in the snow on a remote section of his ranch. Together, with Jeff in the pilot's seat, the two of them had flown out to take a look.

"Looks like helicopter skid marks to me," Gage said as they circled slowly. "Lots of them. Have you had any cattle out here in the last couple months?"

"You bet."

The two men exchanged significant looks.

"Any out here now?" Gage asked.

"Nope. We rounded 'em up and brought 'em in closer last week. Getting a herd through the winter takes some logistic planning, let me tell you. And this looks like it'll be a bad one."

"What makes you say that?"

"We've had more than half our annual snowfall, and it isn't even Christmas yet."

"Maybe we'll be lucky."

"Lucky don't feed cows," Jeff said dryly.

"How close are the herds now?" Gage asked him. "Would you hear a chopper if it came in to swipe another of your head?"

"I might, if the wind was blowing the right direction. It's sure as hell a sound I'd recognize anywhere."

"Micah's getting back from his honeymoon tomorrow," Gage observed. "I'll see if I can't get him out here on Sunday. He'll be able to read a story in those tracks."

Jeff nodded.

"In the meantime, don't let anybody go out there. We don't want to lose any evidence."

"Damn straight," Jeff said tautly. "Wasn't so long ago we hanged rustlers."

"At least now we know for sure it's rustlers."

Jeff glanced at him and grinned unexpectedly. "Yeah. I was starting to look out for little green men."

"Don't laugh. There're plenty of these mutilations that aren't so easy to explain."

"I know, but I'm happier than a pig in mud that mine *are.* At least there's hope we can put a stop to it. Hot damn!"

After they landed and drove back to Jeff's ranch house, Gage declined the offer of breakfast. He needed to get back to the sheriff's office and find out if Brian Webster had called about the photograph yet. Sally had promised that she would have Brian call just as soon as he received the photograph, and since it was now late morning on the East Coast, he must have gotten his mail for the day.

It was 10:30 when he pulled up before the sheriff's office. Emma, he thought, was probably deep in her work at the library. Placing books on shelves, perhaps. Or making new entries for the card catalogue. There must be a dozen things a librarian did that he had no idea of.

He was trying to imagine them as he stepped into the offices, and also trying not to get too impatient about whether Brian had called. He might have a class, of course, or some meeting to keep him from calling Gage right away.

"Gage?" Velma snagged his attention from the dispatcher's desk. "Gage, you better get up to Miss Emma's. She hollered for Sara a little while ago, and now Sara's hollering for the crime-scene team. And that includes you."

Gage froze. "Emma?"

"She's all right, boy, except for her nerves. As I understand it, there's blood all over her driveway, though. Not hers," Velma added swiftly when she saw the look on Gage's face. "It's not *her* blood. Nate has already headed over there."

Her last few words trailed after him as he headed out the door.

Emma was standing with Sara, the sheriff and another deputy at the edge of her driveway. The convergence of three sheriff's Blazers with flashing lights had drawn some of her neighbors out of their houses to watch from a distance, but no one came too close when they saw that Emma was all right. Later they would undoubtedly all take a moment to drop by and speak with her.

Gage's black Suburban growled to a slushy halt behind Nate's Blazer, and that was when Emma felt the last of her terror seep away. Gage was here. She didn't even try to argue with the irrational feeling of safety that swept through her in a warm tide. Gage meant safety, and that was a gut instinct that knew no logic.

He met her eyes from across the twenty feet of snow that separated them. The contact was almost electric, and it hurried his limping steps toward her and the cluster of lawmen. She was pale, he thought, but not afraid. No, her hazy green eyes were sparking with anger.

"Will you look at that?" she demanded angrily of him when he reached her. She pointed at her driveway. "Will you just look at that?"

Reluctantly he tore his attention from her small, delicate features and looked to where she pointed. Blood stayed crimson on snow, and this blood was a ghastly crimson. Bright. Jarring. Threatening.

Someone had used blood to draw a five-pointed star inside a circle on the snow between the tire ruts in Emma's driveway. Gage recognized it instantly, then recognized the tightening in his gut as honest-to-God dread.

"It's a pentagram," he said. And in each of the five star points had been written a letter: E-M-M-A-C.

Emma C, Gage thought, as the fist in his belly tightened its grip even more. Someone was threatening her. Someone was deliberately trying to terrify her. There was no question in his mind now that this went past an ordinary teenage prank. He glanced up at Nate. The sheriff's face was like carved granite.

"We need samples of the blood," Gage said. "What about footprints?" Suddenly he faced Emma. "You were parked right there last night, weren't you?"

She nodded. "I saw it when I backed out of the driveway. I don't understand how somebody could have drawn something so intricate under my car, though."

Gage shook his head. "That little car of yours could be picked up and moved by a few average-size people. I've done it." He scanned the ground, seeing instantly that everything was too trampled to yield any useful footprints. "I wonder when it happened, whether we were even here...."

Nate arched an enquiring brow, and Sara glanced at Emma, a suspicious curve to her mouth.

Nate spoke into the tense silence. "Where might you have been?"

"We went for a walk down by the creek early this morning," Gage said. "I guess we were gone more than an hour. It doesn't matter. They had plenty of time to pull this stunt, regardless."

"It wouldn't take a whole lot of time, or even make much noise," Nate agreed. "I guess somebody's a little mad at you, Miss Emma."

"It certainly looks that way," Emma said sharply. "Whoever it is must be about fourteen years old. This is ridiculous, Sheriff. Juvenile. How can they possibly think they'll scare me with a stupid pentagram in the snow?''

Gage squatted, ignoring a sudden, shearing pain, and studied the symbol. ''I wonder if that's cow blood.''

''Hell,'' said Nate. ''I didn't even think of that.''

Sara spoke. ''I don't see why there should be any connection between the mutilations and Emma, though.''

''Why not?'' Nate growled. ''Damn near everything seems to happen around this county lately. Why not rustlers who get their jollies by scaring maiden ladies?''

''Rustlers?'' Emma repeated, refusing to let Nate's reference to maiden ladies disturb her. ''You've decided Jeff's cattle are being hurt by rustlers?''

''A strange kind of rustler,'' Sara remarked. She looked at Gage. ''What did you find at the Bar C this morning?''

''Helicopter skid tracks. Our villains are human for sure.''

''Well, at least that's settled,'' Nate said sourly.

''Did you ever doubt it would be?'' Gage asked.

''Not really. But at least I have concrete reassurance now for all the worried ranchers. I'm not equipped for space wars, son. That much is obvious.''

Still squatting beside the pentagram, Gage glanced up and surprised them all with a grin. ''What, no laser guns and particle beams?''

''Nope. Just a couple of automatic weapons.''

''I'm glad you all find this so amusing,'' Emma said tartly. ''Well, if everyone's satisfied, *I* have to get to work. No one else will open the library!''

She would have loved to stalk over to her car and drive away in high dudgeon, but two of the sheriff's vehicles blocked her car in the driveway, so she had to content herself with stomping into the kitchen. Her reaction was a little silly, she supposed once she was inside and warming up with a fresh cup of coffee, but she honestly didn't think any of them were taking this seriously enough.

Yes, it was juvenile, just as the rabbit and the balloon had been juvenile, but the combination of the three things gave her the uneasy feeling of being stalked. Nor was the thought that someone really wanted to terrify her exactly an easy one to live with.

The idea that someone in the county might actually want to do more than frighten her or annoy her was unthinkable, but Emma knew the unthinkable happened. For her, such possibilities were far from remote. She had been the victim of violence once before in her life, and that made it all the harder for her to dismiss the possibility of it now.

Irritated, annoyed, frightened, she paced the kitchen with her mug in her hands and listened to the rustle of voices at the edge of her consciousness, felt the internal pressure of memories she wanted to keep buried, glimpsed the flashes of gold from the corners of her eyes.

She wasn't going to open the library today, she decided abruptly. To heck with it. Nobody would come today, anyway, except possibly Mr. Craig, and she could call him and tell him not to. There was no story hour to worry about, no scheduled event, and today she wouldn't even have had an assistant. Friday was the quietest day of the week.

Giving herself no opportunity to change her mind, she phoned Mr. Craig and told him she had a touch of stomach virus and wouldn't be opening. He was sympathetic and told her that he hadn't planned to come in, anyway.

"There's snow in the forecast again, Miss Emma," the elderly gentleman told her. "Can you believe it? I don't think I recall this much snow so early in a winter in at least fifty years. It's a good day to stay indoors and off the roads."

"I believe that's exactly what I'll do, Mr. Craig."

She changed from her gray wool slacks and blouse into jeans and a navy blue flannel shirt, then went into the living room to decorate the tree. It took some doing, but she refused to look out the kitchen window to find out what the sheriff and Gage were up to. If they wanted to treat this cavalierly, she didn't want to know about it. When she had first seen that pentagram, something deep within her had turned cold. Anger had briefly squelched her fear, but now she felt afraid again.

What was it? she wondered as she knelt before the twinkling tree and adjusted the red velvet skirt. Most people lived ordinary, pleasant and relatively uneventful lives, didn't they? Of course, she reminded herself before she could sink into the quicksand of self-pity, that was precisely what she had been doing for years now—leading a quiet, uneventful life.

Sighing, she climbed to her feet and began to open the boxes of cherished ornaments. Some were as old as her family's history in Conard County. Some were as new as last Christmas. Each year Emma continued the family tradition of purchasing one or two new ornaments for the tree. Last year's brass angel would join all the memories from Christmases past and, eventually, all the soon-to-be-created memories of future Christmases.

One of the first ornaments she lifted from the box was a ceramic angel garbed in a white-and-gold gown that had been handsewn by her grandmother. As she turned with it in her hands, she saw Gage hovering in the doorway.

"My grandmother made this," she said impulsively, holding it up for him to see. "She was ten at the time. It still amazes me when I look at these tiny little stitches. I never would have had the patience."

Gage stepped reluctantly into the room, his gaze moving from her face to the angel and back again. "It's beautiful," he said rustily. "Aren't you going to work?"

"I've decided to take a sick day. It'll be the first one in three years. I'm entitled, don't you think?" Turning toward the tree, she looked for a good branch for the angel.

"I don't want you here alone."

Emma shrugged one shoulder, pretending an indifference she didn't feel. "I'll be fine. Nobody's going to bother me in broad daylight."

Gage sighed and stepped closer. "Broad daylight doesn't

cover the inside of this house. If someone got in here, no one would know you were in trouble.''

''I'm still not sure why you think anyone wants to get in here. We've had a few juvenile pranks, that's all.''

''So far.'' He came another step closer. ''Listen, I sent that photo of the dagger to a friend of mine back East. He's a college professor, and he's a recognized expert in weaponry. I'm expecting him to call today and identify that knife for me. I need to get back to the office to find out if he's called yet. If he hasn't, I'm going to call him.''

Emma turned slowly to face him, the angel still in her hands. ''You sent him the photograph?'' she repeated, her breath catching painfully. ''I thought...I thought...''

''You thought I'd dismissed it,'' he said heavily. ''I couldn't, Emma. Not when it upset you like that.''

She looked down at the angel and realized that her fingers were crushing the white satin and gold braid. ''You think it's part of this other stuff.''

''It may have been the opening move. I don't know. I just know it bothered you, and I'm not going to rest until I find out why.''

If Emma thought hard—very, very hard—she could almost remember a time when someone had taken any of her feelings that seriously. When someone had made her feel that she mattered enough. When someone had cared enough. Her throat tightened painfully as she stood there looking down at the angel. Funny that a total stranger made her feel cherished in a way she hadn't felt since childhood.

''Emma, why don't you come with me to the office? I'll help you with the tree when we get back. It won't take long.''

It would nearly kill him to help decorate the tree, she thought, raising her head so she could look at him. She had learned a lot of things about Gage Dalton in one short week, but this was the first time she realized he was noble. He would ignore his own anguish to take care of her. He might be an archangel, she thought now, but he sure as heck didn't belong to hell. He was battered and nearly broken from trying to make things right. Battered, nearly broken—and completely unbowed, because here he was taking up his sword again, determined to make things right, this time for her.

He stood now, hips canted to one side, minute movements betraying his pain-induced restlessness as he waited for her to agree with what he thought best.

He was a hero, she thought, swallowing hard. A genuine, real-life hero. The kind that nobody noticed, because they did the hard, dirty jobs quietly. She swallowed again. "You can call from here, if you want. I don't mind."

"I need to make a couple of calls, not just one."

She shrugged a shoulder again. "Whatever you think best."

Unexpectedly, he held out a hand to her. Emma hesitated only an instant. Carefully setting the angel down on the box, she closed the space between them and gave Gage her hand. Leather creaked as he pulled her to him and then wrapped her in powerful arms, in leather and the male hardness of him.

"Come on, Em," he said huskily. "We'll get it all straightened out, I swear."

She could have stayed there forever, she thought longingly, just filling her senses with him. The leather beneath her cheek was still cold from the outdoors, and the scent of the winter day clung to him. But beneath that smell of cold and snow there was the aroma of Gage, a mixture of man and soap that was heady and somehow satisfying.

"Come to the office with me, Em."

She sighed. "Okay."

He held her a moment longer, as if he, too, was reluctant to break away, and then he let her go.

"Just grab your jacket," he said. "The Suburban's already warm."

Emma looked up at him. "You're so sure I'll be able to get into it with you?"

He gave her a small, crooked smile, a smile that conveyed

a surprising warmth. "Sure. We got you into it last night, didn't we?"

Emma closed her eyes, remembering the ride to and from the creek. She was sure she had taken five years off the life expectancy of her cardiovascular system. Surely a heart wasn't meant to beat two hundred times a minute? And her fingers still ached a little from the way she had hung on to the door handle. Frankly, she didn't *want* to do it again.

"Okay," she said. "Okay." Maybe this time it would be easier. And it was Gage, after all.

Getting into the Suburban with him *was* easier this morning. The instinctive panic eased after the first jolt, not entirely letting go, but making the ride a far sight easier on her. Gage was good, too, doing nothing to prolong their time together in the cab and talking all the way, trying to distract her. And this time, when they parked, Emma didn't scramble out as if demons were chasing her. She didn't exactly linger, but she climbed out with some dignity.

Velma Jansen greeted her pleasantly, but with a speculative look that made Emma think she might be in for some quizzing from the ladies of the Bible Study Group come Sunday morning. Velma was nothing if not a ringleader among those women, Emma thought.

Velma spoke to Gage. "Ed is driving the samples up to the lab. They'll get them today."

"Thanks, Velma." Gage touched Emma's elbow. "My office is back here."

"Why is Ed driving the samples to the lab?" She saw the wreath on Gage's door and wondered at it as he ushered her to a chair.

"Because it's Friday. Everything will get hung up for another two days if the samples don't get there until Monday. This way we should at least know what kind of blood it was—if it was blood."

Emma stared at him. "It sure didn't look like anything else."

"Smelled like blood, too," Gage agreed. He reached for the phone and punched in the lab's number while he watched Emma survey his office. "Herm Abbott, please," he said into the receiver. "Gage Dalton, Conard County Sheriff's Department."

Books, Emma thought. He had so many books. These had official-sounding titles, all of them related to law enforcement and investigations. She'd never really thought about it, but it appeared that law enforcement required a great deal of study.

"Hey, Herm," Gage said, "Gage Dalton here. No, I realize you haven't received that last carcass yet. I was calling because one of our deputies is hand-carrying some blood samples up to you. I'd like to know as soon as you figure out whether it's human or animal, and if it's animal, what kind."

Emma watched him shift in his chair as he sought a comfortable position for his back and wondered how he could stand it. She would probably cut her throat if she hurt all the time.

"I'll be at home for the rest of the day," Gage said, winding up his conversation. "Let me give you the number." He recited Emma's home phone number. "Thanks, Herm. Talk to you later."

He hung up and paused with his hand on the receiver. "Now to call about your dagger."

"It's not *my* dagger," Emma reminded him.

He started punching in another phone number. "Em, darlin', if that dagger didn't have something to do with you, I wouldn't give a damn about it. I sure as hell wouldn't have bothered Brian Webster with it. He's got more important— Hi, Sally. Gage. I got a note that Brian called?"

There was, Emma found herself thinking as she watched him, a whole world out there that knew more about Gage Dalton than she did. The woman he was talking to now, for example. He spoke as if they were very old friends, asking about her husband and her dogs, and then giving her Emma's number for Brian Webster to call him back in a couple of hours.

When he hung up, Gage swiveled his chair toward Emma,

catching a pensive, possibly sad, expression on her face. "Brian'll call me as soon as he gets out of his meeting, maybe a couple of hours. Let's you and me go get some lunch at Maude's."

He didn't want to go back and face that Christmas tree, Emma thought. Initially he'd used the phone calls as an excuse to get her out of the house, and now lunch would be another excuse to stay away for awhile longer. She opened her mouth to tell him that he really didn't have to help with the tree, that if it bothered him so much she would gladly throw the darn thing away, but something about his expression silenced her. It wasn't exactly pain that caused the tension around his eyes, or anything else she could really name. Whatever it was, it made her feel strange. Edgy. Impatient.

"If we go to Maude's for lunch," she said finally, in a smothered voice, "we'll wind up being an item."

"We're already an item, Red. Velma warned me yesterday. People are talking. Are you going to be hanged for a sheep or a lamb?"

The question was vaguely challenging, almost daring her to leap into his arms, but the tension around his eyes had eased, and in their stormy gray-green depths she saw a sparkle of amusement—an amusement that echoed her own over the fact that she had used the same comparison herself only a few days ago.

"You mean I'm still a lamb?" she asked, and then wished she could die as soon as the incautious words escaped. What *was* it about this man that kept shattering all her prudence?

Gage had risen to his feet, and now he leaned across his desk toward her, giving a melodramatic leer. "You, m'dear, are most definitely still a lamb. Take my word for it."

He watched the color bloom in Emma's cheeks and felt a smile grow on his own face. He couldn't remember the last time he had seen a woman blush, and certainly not one Emma's age. She was priceless. Absolutely priceless.

He drove them to Maude's. It was only two blocks, an easy

walk, but he wanted to give her more time in the car with him.
She had come a long way already, and he figured that each and
every time she climbed in with him, she took another step away
from the fear.

If Maude had heard of saturated fats, she hadn't allowed it
to change her cooking habits. She still served all the old stand-
bys, from fried eggs to fried potatoes, and every item on her
menu exploded with equal amounts of grease and flavor.
Maude's cooking was a sin meant to be enjoyed, and Emma
had long since learned to treat it that way. On the rare occasions when she ate here, she banished all thoughts of her waist-
line and her bathroom scale.

"I'll have the steak sandwich and fries," she told the waitress. "And coffee."

Gage ordered the same, and then, as the girl walked off, he
shifted uncomfortably, trying to find a better position on the
bench in the booth.

"Doesn't anything help?" Emma asked him.

He looked at her and slowly, ever so slowly, the corners of
his mouth lifted. "Yeah. One or two things make me forget it
for awhile."

Emma felt her color rising again. "Don't."

"Okay." He shouldn't be teasing her, he warned himself,
and not just because it embarrassed her. He'd gotten too close
to her last night, and he owed it to them both to back off before
things went any further. It wasn't as if he had anything to offer
her. And it wasn't as if she would want it, even if he had. Nor
was she experienced enough to keep her emotions from getting
tangled up if she had an affair.

So many excellent reasons to keep clear, every one of them
inarguable—except that every cell in his body wanted to love
this woman. Every inch of him ached to hold her and know
her. She was warm, passionate, unspoiled. Loving her would
be a fantastic, mind-blowing experience, he was sure. It would
be unlike any experience in his life. He had only to remember

how she had responded to him yesterday to know she would be as potent as any drug, and just as addicting.

But he didn't deserve her. And she sure as hell didn't deserve him.

And he felt guilty as hell for even thinking of such things.

He eased around again on the bench, trying to find that elusive point of balance that minimized the pain. He wouldn't find it, of course, because it didn't exist. It only felt as if it *ought* to.

"You don't have to help me decorate the tree this afternoon," Emma said after they had been served. "I know it... bothers you."

Gage's head lifted sharply, and he studied her, wondering how much else he had betrayed without realizing it. Of course, he had been sitting in front of the tree crying like a two-year-old yesterday when she came home for lunch. Not that he was ashamed of crying, because he wasn't. Some things sure as hell deserved tears. Some things deserved every tear a man could shed.

"I'll help," he said flatly, meaning to close the subject. Some things deserved tears, and other things simply had to be faced.

"You're impossible, Gage Dalton," Emma said tartly. "You won't cut yourself any slack at all, will you? And you don't care in the least how it makes the rest of us feel to be unable to spare you the least little thing!"

"I don't deserve to be spared."

The stark words caused Emma's breath to lock in her throat. His face gave away nothing, but it didn't need to. He didn't deserve to be spared? Oh, my word...

Aching for him as she had never before ached for anyone, Emma would have given the sun, the moon, the stars and the rest of her life to vanquish Gage's demons. She couldn't imagine that a man like Gage, a man so clearly upright and honorable, should have any real justification to feel that way, and it appalled her to realize that he believed he did.

"Years and years ago," Gage said presently, "I got stationed in a backwater Florida town. I grew up in Chicago, and in the army I stayed pretty much on post except when I went to classes at the university. You can't imagine what a shock it was to me, Em. Conard City is big-time compared to this place the DEA sent me. There were about a hundred people and not even a single stop sign. I'd had no idea there were places like that."

"Why did they send you there?"

"Some drug operation was flying cocaine in from South America, and we suspected they were landing near this town. My job was to be sufficiently disreputable to get a job of some kind in the organization."

He looked up from his steak suddenly and surprised her with a rueful smile. "Talk about getting your eyes opened. I was a hotshot street fighter from the big time, and suddenly I was in another world. Another planet. Another race. A twelve-year-old kid who lived up the road used to bring me squirrels for my supper. He hardly went to school at all, but he kept his mother and ten kids in meat by shooting squirrels and snaring rabbits. For me it was like stepping back centuries in time. I quit being cocky real fast. Those people knew how to survive in ways I'd never imagined."

Emma nodded encouragingly, wanting to hear more about him and not caring whether there was a point to it.

"It took about eighteen months to infiltrate the smuggling operation, but in the meantime I learned a lot. I learned that the world didn't have to be dog-eat-dog, and that a man has an obligation to his neighbors. I learned that even when it's tough, it's possible to survive without giving up the high moral ground. Without becoming an animal."

He sighed and pushed his plate aside. "A man has to accept responsibility for his life, Emma, no matter how hard it gets. That's what sets him apart from animals. Would you like some pie?"

A man has to accept responsibility for his life. Emma pondered that enigmatic statement all the way home, wondering just what Gage felt responsible for.

The fully decorated tree sparkled and twinkled in the living room like a fairy-tale vision. Gage stood beside Emma and wondered how he'd gotten through it. He had, though. Every time he had thought of turning tail, he'd reminded himself of Emma getting into the car with him. If she could do it, so could he.

And he was still here. His throat ached with grief, and his heart hammered on the edge of panic, but he was still here.

"It's beautiful," Emma said, then sighed, wondering why she kept bothering. Since her father had died, Christmas tended to remind her of all she had lost and all she lacked. Right now, looking at that beautiful tree, she wanted to cry her eyes out.

The phone rang, and Gage stiffened. "Brian. At last."

"Take it in the study," Emma suggested swiftly. "There's paper there for taking notes if you need to."

"Thanks." He was already headed that way.

Emma hesitated, longing to follow him but feeling he was entitled to his privacy on the phone. Finally her upbringing won. She headed for the kitchen to get some coffee.

It was now shortly past four, and the afternoon was darkening into evening. Snow had begun to fall earlier, but now, for the first time, she noticed they were in the midst of a blizzard.

Pulling back the café curtains, she flipped on the back porch light and looked out at her driveway. Her car was already vanishing under four inches of fresh powder, and all traces of this morning's events had been buried beneath a pristine blanket. Wind whipped the icy crystals around in a chaotic whirl and drifted the snow against the garage door. A sudden gust rattled the kitchen windows and doors, and she heard the house groan before the onslaught.

Mr. Craig was right. It was turning into a very unusual winter. A bad winter. Having lived all her life here, her thoughts turned immediately to the ranchers who would have to cope with this. Freezing winds and heavy snow meant all kinds of deadly problems for many of her neighbors.

She kept a weather radio on her counter, and she turned it on now, listening to the winter storm warning, the stockmen's advisory, the forecast for six to eight inches of fresh fall by midnight.

"Sounds bad."

Gage's voice startled her, and she whirled around to face him. "It's going to be awful for the ranchers."

"For the cops, too."

Emma nodded. "Was it your friend?"

"Yeah. Is that coffee any good?"

"I just made it."

He pulled a mug from the cabinet and poured himself some. "I'm not sure what kind of help we just got, Em, but I guess we know more than we did."

"What do you mean?" Unconsciously, her hands knotted together.

He leaned back against the counter and crossed his legs at the ankle. Lifting the mug, he took a deep swallow and sighed with pleasure. "Damn, lady, you make the best coffee."

"I buy the best beans. Gage, what did he say?"

"He said the dagger in the photo is a very poor copy of a dagger once used by Turkish *hashshashin.*"

"What's a *hash*—whatever."

"*Hashshashin.* The word is Arabic, I believe. We derive the word assassin from it, and the word hashish, which pretty much tells the story. Brian said that back during the Crusades these *hashshashin* were some kind of secret sect. Anyway, the dagger is just a very poor copy, so it sure wasn't sent as part of a fund-raising drive."

Emma pulled a chair out from the table and sat. "I don't think I like the sound of this."

"Me either, if you want the truth." He took another swig of coffee.

"A pentagram and a copy of a knife once used by a secret sect of drug-crazed killers," Emma said after a moment. "Gage, this isn't a very funny joke."

"If it's all linked." But his gut was telling him it was. "You've seen that dagger before, Emma. Haven't you?" It sounded more like a reminder than a question.

She drew a sharp breath and looked slowly up at him. "I think so," she said. "I think so, but I can't remember for sure. When—when I first saw the picture I felt as if I'd just been punched. But, honestly, I can't place it."

She wrapped her arms around herself as if she felt suddenly chilled. "Why would anybody...? Wasn't once enough?"

The anguish of her question cut him to the quick. The truth of it, though, was that he now believed she was being stalked. Nobody made a copy of a centuries-old dagger for a joke. Uppermost in his mind when he had hung up the phone had been the question: who on earth would want to stalk Emmaline Conard? It wasn't even as if she had a disgruntled former boyfriend.

And then he had realized. Her reaction to the dagger had been the answer.

Emmaline Conard was being stalked by the man who had nearly killed her ten years ago in Laramie.

Chapter 9

The storm continued to build as the evening deepened. Windows rattled ceaselessly, and the old house became noticeably draughty. Blowing snow nearly obscured the lights of the houses across the street and next door.

Emma pulled the curtains closed across the bow window behind the Christmas tree, then curled up on the couch with a book. Gage had vanished into the study directly after dinner, explaining that he needed to make some phone calls. Nearly two hours had passed, and now calls were beginning to come in for him. She wished she didn't think it had something to do with what he had learned about the dagger.

In fact, she wished she could just concentrate on the book until she was too tired to do anything but sleep. Instead, she kept feeling that something was about to pounce on her from the dark. Instead, her mind kept drifting back to what had happened between her and Gage yesterday. Caught between fright and yearning, she was too restless to read, and almost too restless to sit.

The things Gage had made her feel were too wondrous for

words, and she was honest enough to admit she wanted to feel them again. She would give almost anything if he would just walk into the room right now and take her into his arms. She wanted his kisses and touches, wanted to feel again all those marvelous, dizzying feelings. And surely, after last night, he must realize she was willing.

But he was no longer interested, and the realization cut her to the quick. Her inability to have children had turned him off, too. She could place no other interpretation on the brotherly way he had been treating her since. After all, now that he knew she couldn't get pregnant, what else could be holding him back from taking advantage of her obvious willingness? Only the fact that now that he knew she wasn't a whole woman, he no longer found her to be attractive.

The understanding made her ache, but she forced herself to face it. She prided herself on her honesty, and it would do her no good to build castles in the air, anyway. In the long run, she told herself, it was far better this way. If he made love to her because she was "safe," or avoided her because of it, it made no difference in the long term. Either way he would move on. And either way Emma would continue to be alone.

So maybe it was infinitely better if she didn't get a clearer idea than she already had of all that she was missing. Yes, of course it was.

Just remember, she reminded herself, the fable of the shoemaker and his daughter who were perfectly happy until the rich man invited them to live as he did for a day. As it stood now, Emma had an idea of what she was missing, but she didn't *know*. If she and Gage ever made love, she would know beyond any shadow of a doubt. And the knowledge could blight the rest of her life.

Gage hung up the phone once again and reached up to knead a knot out of his neck. He'd set the ball rolling, and now he could only wait to see what started coming back. Friday night, especially right before Christmas, was not the best time in the world to start bugging law-enforcement agencies for vague bits of information. The law might never sleep, but on a typical Friday night it was too busy handling trouble to want to handle routine requests for information.

Laramie PD had been cooperative enough, he guessed—after he had managed to work his way up the chain of command. They had promised to pull the file on Emma's case and express it to him in the morning. He could have asked them to fax it, but he was afraid somebody at the office might see Emma's name and let her secret out of the bag. Better to wait for express mail.

He'd also managed to persuade a friend at the drug agency to pull a wild-card search on the national crime computer. If a Turkish dagger or references to the *hashshashin* had turned up in any crime reports in the past fifteen years, he ought to know by tomorrow night.

And by tomorrow night he should have a pretty good idea who in Conard County had a criminal record. Then he could start *really* investigating.

Sighing, he leaned back in the chair and closed his eyes a moment, waiting for the clenching pain in his lower back to ease up a little. He guessed he'd better call Nate at home and tell him what he was up to. Nate would be justifiably annoyed if he thought Gage was circumventing him, but he would also understand Gage's reluctance to do all this at the office, where someone might overhear. Nate would recognize the need to protect Miss Emma's privacy. And Nate, unlike some of his deputies, could be trusted not to gossip.

He sure didn't want Emma to hear about any of this. She was already edgy enough without knowing what Gage suspected, and edgy was good enough to keep her cautious.

And last night. He swore and shifted in the chair, trying again to ease his back. The woman was as sweetly tempting as a frosted cupcake, totally vulnerable to the new feelings she had discovered, eager enough to make him hard just thinking about her.

He never should have touched her. Yesterday, when she had comforted him, he had succumbed to the closeness and his own long-unsatisfied needs, but last night, after pumping brandy into her, he should have been able to withstand the temptation. He hadn't been weakened by grief then. There was no excuse for the way he had lifted her onto his lap—except that he had wanted her. Except that he hadn't been that turned on in years, if ever. Except that Emma Conard was enough to tempt a saint, never mind hell's own archangel.

His crooked smile was self-mocking. From the moment he had set eyes on the woman, starchy and bristly as she was, he had wanted to sink his flesh into hers. He kept having the most incredibly arousing vision of her stretched out on white sheets beneath him, a sheen of perspiration glistening on her creamy skin. He could imagine holding her hands above her head while he licked...

"Damn!" He sat bolt upright and forced that fantasy back into a dark dungeon at the bottom of his brain. Thinking that way was only going to get both him and Emma into trouble. Time to call Nate and get his mind back on business. Reaching out, he lifted the receiver from the cradle.

"Gage!"

Emma's cry brought him instantly to his feet. He dashed for the study door and flung it open just in time to catch her as she came barreling through.

"Emma? Emma, what's wrong?" He could feel her shudder wildly as he held her, and she clutched at his sweater as if she wanted to climb right into him. "Emma?"

"Oh, Gage, he was wearing a mask. A horrible, hideous mask!"

Gage stiffened. "Who was wearing a mask? Who did you see, Emma? Was someone at the window?"

She shook her head jerkily. "No...no...I remembered... Oh, God, I can't stand this! I can't stand it!"

He drew her more snugly into his embrace and cradled her head against his shoulder. "You remembered something else?"

She nodded. "I could see him," she whispered shakily. "Just his head, and that horrible mask. And I knew I was... hurt...and I couldn't move. I was scared. So scared!"

The wise thing, he thought, would be to take her into the kitchen, fix her a stiff drink and keep the table firmly between them while he encouraged her to talk it out. Instead, he began backing her toward her bedroom. What this woman needed now had nothing to do with common sense and caution.

"Get yourself tucked in, Emma," he said, releasing her slowly when he had her standing beside her bed. "I'll be back in five minutes with the brandy."

"But—" She lifted frightened, doubtful eyes.

"Trust me, Red. Just do it. I'll be right back."

With shaking hands, feeling weak and sick as if she were ill, Emma changed into a flannel nightgown and crawled into the bed that had been a haven since childhood. With the covers drawn to her chin, she watched wide-eyed as Gage returned and perched beside her.

"Here," he said. "Take a stiff belt."

"Didn't we do this last night?" she asked shakily, not certain she could survive a rerun.

"Just drink the damn brandy, Emma." Scowling, he shoved it into her hand and urged her hand to her mouth. "I've traveled this road, lady. Take the brandy. Then you're going to talk until you lose your voice or you fall asleep."

She coughed as the brandy burned her throat, but she drank the full shot before she handed him the glass. "Why talk?" she asked a little hoarsely. Her eyes grew even wider when he stood and yanked his belt off his black jeans.

"Because you're not going to be able to think about anything else until you've worn this to death." He knew that for a fact. Some things honestly had to be talked to death. He eased down beside her on the bed, on top of the blankets, fully clothed except for boots and belt. "Light on or off?"

"On," she said. "Please."

"Okay." Reaching out, he tugged her, blankets and all, into

his arms. "Close your eyes and talk, Em. Tell me what you remembered. Tell me how you felt. Tell me how you feel about it right now."

For a little while she didn't say anything at all, but he understood her hesitation. The things that hurt the worst, the deepest wounds and scars, were the hardest to talk about. They were also the ones a person most needed to put into words.

He stroked her back through the blankets from shoulder to hip, and once or twice he pressed a reassuring kiss on her temple. To think he'd been a grown man before he had understood just how important it was to hold somebody close when they hurt. Before he had understood that a kiss and a hug could really heal some hurts.

"I'm mad," Emma said quietly.

"I should certainly think so," he rumbled soothingly.

"I'm furious."

"Maybe mad enough to kill." He felt her hand tighten into a fist on his chest.

"Maybe," she agreed hoarsely. "Oh, Gage, how could anyone do such things? How could anyone...?"

"How could anyone hurt *you* like that?" he completed. "Beats the hell out of me, Emma. It always has and always will. Sometimes people are careless, and I can understand that, but deliberate violence—hell, I don't understand it, either."

"He must have been sick."

"Probably."

She fell silent again, and except for the small movements her hands made against him, he would have thought she slept. He wondered if she had any idea that she was practically petting him, and thought not. She was locked in her memory. He remembered how obsessive it was possible to get with each piece as it surfaced, how you twisted it and turned it and tried to fit it into the jigsaw pattern that was beginning to emerge. How you tried to remember the missing pieces around that one recovered memory. How you feared what else might surface.

"He was wearing a mask," Emma said again, a long time

later. She sounded calmer now. Felt calmer. Gage made her feel safe, and the brandy had taken the edge off her anxiety. "Why do you think he wore a mask?"

"I don't know. A precaution, maybe, in case someone saw him." *Or maybe he didn't want Emma to recognize him?* "What kind of mask was it?"

"One of those translucent Halloween things that looks almost like a real face." She shuddered and wiggled a little closer to him. "I could almost see him inside it. Almost. It's like if I could just focus a little more clearly, I'd be able to see him."

He ran his hand down her back again, soothingly, and then took the clip from her hair so he could burrow his fingers into it and massage the tension from her scalp. "Don't push it, Emma. Believe me, it'll come in its own good time."

"I wish it would just go away."

"I know. I know." Yeah, he knew. He ached for her, ached for what she was going to face. And he found himself hoping that the blows to her head had concussed her enough that her memories of that night would always be incomplete. Some things should never be remembered. He knew all about those things, too. Emma stirred and started speaking again, her voice little more than a whisper.

"When…when I woke up in the hospital, it was—I don't know how to describe it. It was as if—"

"As if you woke up in somebody else's body in the middle of somebody else's life," he supplied.

Slowly she turned her face up, and after a moment he looked down at her, meeting her concerned green eyes. "You *do* understand," she said with relief. "The last thing I remembered was being in class, and suddenly I was in the hospital with my arms and legs in casts, and bandages… What about you?"

His hold on her tightened. It was something he tried not to remember, tried not to think about, but he felt he owed it to her. "I was pretty much out of it for a couple of days, I guess. I didn't remember the explosion. The last thing I remembered was…well, right before it happened. It wasn't until a couple of weeks later that I started to recall. It was something I didn't want to do, either.''

''Do you…do you think there's any reason to remember? I mean, is there any point at all in remembering? Or is it all pointless?''

He'd wondered that himself and wasn't sure he'd ever gotten an answer. ''I don't know, Em,'' he said finally. ''Honest to God, I don't know. Maybe it's healing of some kind. I just don't know.''

Compared to what she had forgotten, he had forgotten very little. Just a few minutes of time that he'd been able to paint with horrifying clarity in imagination. He hadn't needed to remember those moments, least of all the enraged, sick feeling when he had found he couldn't move and had lain there face-down, helplessly listening to his own screams and smelling his own flesh burn. Or the moment when a neighbor had come running and kicked snow on his back to put out the flames. Or the moment when they had lifted him onto the stretcher and he had seen the burned-out hulk of the car. The burned-out hulk of his life. Remembering those minutes had seemed so utterly pointless, except possibly to give reality to the loss. To engrave forever in stark clarity the moments when his life had ended.

''They told me about it when I woke up,'' Emma said. ''They said I'd been attacked and beaten very badly. Both my arms and legs were broken, and I had a fractured skull. It wasn't until later that they told me he had stabbed me, too. He…um…carved some kind of symbol into my stomach.''

''My God!''

''My father had it removed by a plastic surgeon before I even came out of the coma. You can hardly tell it was there now. It was…um…a…a…'' Suddenly she was gasping for air and clinging to him so hard that her nails dug into his skin even through the thick layer of his sweater. ''A—a penta-gram!''

Shock nearly froze Gage's blood. "My God, Emma, why didn't you tell me this morning?"

"B-because I forgot. I g-guess I'm good at forgetting. I just remembered that...."

He crushed her to him and gave up any hope of remaining detached or uninvolved with Emmaline Conard. He was involved already. Involved so deeply that his gut was burning with a hunger for revenge and his soul was aching with an impossible need to comfort.

There was no doubt now, he thought grimly. No doubt at all. She was being stalked.

And now Emma knew it, too.

The storm howled savagely outside, and the old house groaned and creaked before its onslaught. Emma had been asleep for hours now, and Gage sat up slowly, moving cautiously as he always did after staying in one position for very long.

"Don't go."

Emma's sleepy voice caused him to turn and look down at her. Her eyes were drowsy but open.

"I just need to go to the bathroom," he told her. "I'll be right back. Need anything?"

"Water, please."

"Coming right up."

What she needed, he thought as he left the bathroom and headed for the kitchen, was something to laugh about. Something to make her forget all the dark things for a little while. Trying to think of something, he took a minute to check all the locks and peek outside. Snow was drifting deeply against the cars in the driveway. Sure as shootin' nobody would be going anywhere in a hurry.

He filled a glass with ice water and took it back to Emma. She was sitting up, propped against the pillow, wide-awake now.

"Thank you," she said when he handed her the glass.

He sat on the edge of the bed, facing her, wishing he could remember a lousy joke or two, wondering, What now?

"You'll probably think I'm a great big chicken," she said shyly after a moment, "but I really don't want to be alone. Not since I remembered that...pentagram."

"I don't think you're a chicken, Red. In fact, I was wondering how to tell you that I don't think you ought to be alone." She needed an archangel now, the real thing, one of the ones who were immortal and invincible and who couldn't succumb to temptation. Because she was a delectable sight right now, and he was in mortal danger of succumbing.

That beautiful red hair of hers spilled all over the pillow and gleamed in the lamplight. The nightgown, for all its thick flannel, framed her breasts in a way that left deliciously little to the imagination, and he didn't need to imagine anyway. Just last night he'd touched and kissed those breasts, had sucked on those raspberry nipples until she had groaned and clutched him close. No, he didn't need to imagine when reality was so much better than pretend.

He also didn't want to take advantage of her, so when she finished the water, he set the glass on the night table and returned to his position beside her—on top of the blankets. He was touched more than he wanted to admit when she immediately snuggled close, expressing her trust in the most convincing way possible. It played havoc with his willpower and made his body feel like one great big throbbing ache—and reminded him that he didn't want to betray her trust.

"I'm sorry," she said a little while later.

"Sorry? For what?"

"You need your sleep. It isn't fair to ask you to stay with me like this."

"Fair?" He repeated the word, tasting its bitterness. "Babe, *fair* is an invention of children and wishful fools."

The harsh way he spoke caused her to tense. He had terrible things in his past, too, she reminded herself. She hadn't thought about it before, but it must have been very difficult for him to listen to her tonight. After all, he, too, had painful memories, and everything she had said must have reawakened all that for him.

In fact, she told herself sternly, for much of this entire week she had been too absorbed in herself and her own inchoate ghosts to remember that this man was dealing with some pretty powerful ghosts of his own. Still vivid in her mind was the sight of the tear streaks on his face yesterday when she had found him, and equally vivid was the horrible twisting sensation she had felt in her belly when she had witnessed so starkly and unexpectedly his pain and grief.

There were things he hadn't told her, terrible things. She sensed them roiling in his mind, sensed them in the way he tried to wall himself off. It was awful to think that she might have stirred all those things up and made them fresh for him.

"No," she said presently, "life isn't fair, is it? But that doesn't mean we shouldn't do what we can to *be* fair."

"One small candle flame in the dark, huh?"

He sounded so cynical, so hard, and maybe in some ways he was, but Emmaline Conard knew there was more to him than that. Much more. Hadn't he been there for her each and every time she'd needed someone this week? Hadn't he readily hugged her and comforted her and listened to her? Wasn't he here right now, holding her through a long, dark night?

He said he'd been raised on the streets like a wild dog, but she found him to be one of the most humane people she had ever met. One of the most caring. Because it took caring to take the risks he had taken as an undercover agent in memory of a long-dead brother. To take those risks to make the world a safer place for people you didn't even know. It took caring to feel the kind of grief she had seen in his eyes yesterday.

And you didn't need walls when you didn't have anything to protect.

Slowly she tipped her face up and leaned backward, trying to see his face. After a moment he looked down at her and their eyes locked, hers green and soft, his dark and stormy.

Ever so slowly, feeling as if she were mired in molasses, she reached up and pressed her soft palm to his scarred cheek.

She spoke quietly, achingly, a catch in her voice. "You've been hurt so badly."

"So have you." He tried to sound indifferent. He tried to *feel* indifferent. Somehow he couldn't. This woman's caring was shining sadly in her eyes, and the touch of her palm on his hideously disfigured cheek was a blessing he hadn't understood he wanted until this very moment. He tried to pull away, but somehow he couldn't do that, either. He couldn't even move the couple of inches that would take his cheek from her hand.

She held him captive with a single, simple touch.

Emma saw the tension come to his eyes, felt it creep into his muscles as he lay still beside her. He continued to hold her, but something was happening. Something was making him look wary, like a dog that's been kicked once too often, then shies away from the very touch it wants.

She felt that look in the very depths of her being, felt that wary yearning as a reflection of her own deepest fears and needs. All these years she'd been avoiding what she most wanted for fear she might get kicked again. All these years she had been alone because she didn't dare not to be.

Wasn't that incredibly stupid?

Gently, with all the empty, lonely feelings and needs rising in her, she moved her fingers on his scarred cheek. Tenderly she caressed him, trying to tell him that maybe, for just this little while, they didn't have to be lonesome.

Gage's breath locked in his throat. She didn't know what she was doing to him. She didn't have the faintest notion; she was too damn innocent to have any idea. Emma thought she was comforting him, when in fact she was pushing him right over the edge.

And it was going to take only the tiniest push, he realized with angry resignation. Yesterday, between them, they'd built the fire, and nothing had yet happened to throw water on the flames. They were licking at his loins right now, fueled by her soft touch, by her feminine scent, by the sight and feel of her in his arms.

He didn't want to do this, he thought furiously. He was going to hate himself later. He was going to curse his weakness and damn his loss of control. He was going to feel like the lowest slime and the cruddiest sleaze.

But he wasn't going to be able to stop himself.

He looked so angry, Emma thought. She might have been frightened, except that the hands holding her remained gentle as they stroked her back through the covers. Had she made him angry by touching his scarred cheek? Had it bothered him to be reminded of it? Concerned, she started to take her hand away, but just as she moved, he turned his head and pressed a kiss into the palm of her hand.

Emma caught her breath and stared wide-eyed up at him. And suddenly she was free. He didn't move, he just let go of her. Not an inch of him touched an inch of her any longer. Her hand hovered over his cheek, as if frozen there by his kiss.

"Emma," he said softly, in his husky, ruined voice, "if I touch you again, I won't be able to stop." That much conscience and control he had left, just enough to give her a chance to escape.

She didn't move, didn't flinch. She simply stopped breathing and continued to stare up at him with eyes that grew bigger and darker with each passing second.

"Tell me to go," he said, not knowing how to make it any plainer. If she didn't seize her chance to escape, he wasn't going to let her go. He was no gentleman. To the bone he was a rough, ruthless street fighter, and he wore the outward trappings of civilization for convenience. His soul had been meant for a Viking or a cossack, not for a world where men needed to confine their appetites, needs and inclinations in a social straitjacket. He had accepted the constraints as a necessity, but now they were slipping from his grasp, ripped away in a whirlwind of rising passion.

She didn't tell him to go. The pulse in her throat fluttered wildly, and she drew a deep ragged breath. And then…and then her hand settled once again on his cheek, like featherdown, so light and soft and warm. The touch made him shudder, and he felt the impact of it all the way to his frozen soul.

She had no idea. She couldn't have any idea. She was innocent, too innocent to see the violence and raging hunger in him. Too innocent to know what he might be capable of. Too innocent to realize that it wasn't wise to want to give herself to a man who was capable only of taking.

But he was no saint to turn from what was so generously offered. He had given her a chance to back away. Now it was too late—for both of them.

He reached for the blankets and stripped them away from her, flinging them to the foot of the bed with one swift movement of his arm. Only the nightgown shielded her now, and it was no barrier against the hand that suddenly cupped her breast, or the powerful thigh that was suddenly thrown across hers.

"God, I want you," he breathed raggedly against her ear. "Damn it, Em…"

Why did he have to sound so angry? she wondered hazily. Somehow, even with all the layers of cloth yet between them, he made her feel as if he was wrapping her in his body and absorbing her into himself. As if she was being inexorably drawn into the darkness he seemed to carry with him. And dimly, as she felt him tremble and press his hips achingly against her, she sensed the pure white heat that was at the core of the night that surrounded Gage Dalton.

He didn't want to feel. He didn't want to need. He didn't want to lust or hunger or yearn. He had fought his way up to the dark, icy edge of the abyss called despair, had found a precarious ledge where he could feel almost nothing at all, and now…and now…

Oh, God, she was making him *feel!*

Emotions exploded in him with all the devastating force of

a volcanic eruption. Rage scalded all the frozen places, melting ice that held the wolves at bay. Pain poured through the cracks, agonizing and fresh, making a joke out of all his denials and defenses. He had admitted he grieved. He had faced that, accepted it, and from time to time even indulged it. But he had never faced any of the other feelings about what had happened, and right here and now they burst from confinement in a maelstrom of torment.

And Emma suddenly looked like a lifeline.

Gage's face told Emma she wasn't about to enjoy the gentle seduction she had once childishly imagined for her first time. She wasn't even to enjoy the tenderness he had showed her last night when he had guided her through her first real taste of passion and fulfillment. No, she thought weakly, it wasn't going to be like that at all.

He looked so furious as he stood beside the bed and pulled his sweater over his head. He looked so…hurt. He was in mortal pain, and she didn't think it was his back this time. No, not his back.

He reached for the snap of his jeans, and some little voice in Emma's mind, some last little voice of reason, told her to get out of here now. And then, before she could consider things logically, some floodgate in her heart opened, pouring the golden warmth of understanding through her.

In an instant she left behind the last romantic notions of her youth. She understood suddenly that a woman's body could do more than give pleasure and then children to the man she loved. It could give him forgetfulness. Or reassurance. Or welcome. It could help mend hurts he couldn't speak of. It could tell him that someone in the world cared for him, cared deeply enough to take him inside her. It could, for awhile, wrap him in security and shelter him from life's cruelties. It could give him all those things men never asked for and seldom admitted they needed.

What Gage needed from her tonight, she realized as he yanked down his zipper, had little to do with pleasure. And whatever it was, she longed to give it to him.

She gasped softly when he thrust his jeans and briefs down, letting her see for the first time in her life a man in the full grip of desire. He was so…big, she thought weakly. It simply couldn't work.

Gage kicked his jeans aside and then suddenly threw his head back, standing rigid, his hands locked into fists, his expression a tortured grimace. *First time*… whispered the cool voice of reason, barely heard through the gale in his head. *Her first time*… He shuddered, clawing inwardly for some remnant of self-control, some last decent impulse to cling to.

"Emma." His ruined voice was grittier than usual, forced past the tight knot in his throat. He made himself look down at her, some corner of his mind noting that she looked like a virginal sacrifice in that damned white flannel. "Emma, I don't think I can—" His throat closed, shut down by a hunger that just kept growing despite everything.

He was beautiful, she thought, losing her fear in her own rising heat and need. So beautiful, like a dark angel. Unlike the hair on his head, his body hair wasn't silver but a dark chestnut brown. It decorated his chest in a masculine swirl and then arrowed straight downward to the most potent part of him. And there… Emma caught her breath and looked up into his anguished face.

"It's all right, Gage," she heard herself say gently, as she held out a hand. "It's all right." At that moment she felt like the earth mother, all bountiful, all understanding, all giving. He was welcome to whatever he needed from her.

Gage made a strangled sound and was suddenly beside her, suddenly hauling her into his arms and then into the curve of his naked body. "Em…oh, God, Em…" He shuddered violently when he felt her soft warm palms on the naked, scarred skin of his back, on the naked, scarred skin of his buttocks.

"It's all right," Emma murmured. "It's all right." And somehow she believed it would be, whatever happened now. The next few minutes might be unpleasant for her, but they hardly mattered next to Gage's need.

Her first time... The words rolled around in his head, and he tried, he really *tried*, to bring her with him. Grasping at the straws of restraint, he lifted her gown over her head, taking care not to pull or tear it from her. When she at last lay completely bare before him, he saw the incredible shyness in her green eyes, in the warm rush of blood to her throat and cheeks.

"Beautiful," he said hoarsely. "Beautiful." He trailed his gaze over her from head to toe, feeling his body harden and throb even more urgently as he traced each graceful curve. The breasts he had touched and kissed last night were full without being large and crowned in strawberry pink. Her nipples were already knotted and hard for him, beckoning to him. Not yet.

He trailed his gaze lower, to the incredibly narrow nip of her waist—damn, how could she be so slender, so fragile?—and lower to the thatch of fiery curls that drew his entire body like a powerful magnet.

Damn! *Her first time!* Another time he might have appreciated that. Now he could only see it as a potential hazard.

He turned his head back up and found her watching him, shyness warring with eagerness on her face. Holding on to a last, rapidly charring thread of control, he bent his head to kiss her.

The instant his hot, rough tongue touched hers, Emma was caught up in a whirlwind of escalating sensation. She became exquisitely aware of each place her bare skin touched his, and each touch fueled the yearning in her and made her press closer and closer to his heat, his strength, his hardness. Oh, yes, suddenly she needed that, too.

His hands were impatient, almost rough, as they swept over her, but she didn't mind. Oh, no. His impatience fed hers, made her feel wanted, made her feel wonderful that he wanted her enough to be impatient, to be rough. She didn't mind at all that he needed her as fast as he could get her, that he was driving toward his goal with little tenderness and only a modicum of consideration for her. She didn't mind at all, because there was nothing, absolutely nothing, as heady or as satisfying as being wanted this badly.

For the first time in a decade she felt like a woman. He had given her that, and it didn't matter a tinker's damn whether he gave her anything else. For him, for these brief minutes, she was woman enough.

Then his fingers slipped within her slick folds. She gasped, electrified by the unexpected sensation. He didn't say anything, just kept rubbing her there in a way that soon had her arching toward his touch and clinging to his hair like a lifeline.

A low growl of laughter escaped him, and he closed his mouth over her breast as his fingers continued to stroke, to delve, to test both her readiness and her inexperience.

Emma groaned, forgetting all her fantasies about being a bountiful earth mother, forgetting what it was she was understanding, and became hostage to the feelings he was giving her. Pleasure splintered again and again within her, and she wondered why the nerve that was directly connected from her nipple to her womb had never showed up in any anatomy book. Because each and every time he sucked on her breast, her insides tightened in a wild, delightful spasm. And his fingers…oh, his fingers were wicked, teaching her hungers and needs and sensations beyond imagining.

When he parted her legs and knelt between them, she had long since forgotten that she didn't think this could work. All she knew was that it *had* to work. Somehow. Anyhow. Any way.

She felt him probe where no one but he had ever touched her, and then she felt him entering…oh, my word, how he stretched her….

A sharp, searing pain jerked her out of her haze of arousal. She drew a sharp breath but swallowed the instinctive cry and stared up into Gage's grimacing face.

It didn't feel very good, she found herself thinking, wondering if he was just going to keep pushing deeper and deeper.

She wanted him out, now, before this feeling got any worse. Oh, my word, surely something was going tear?

She had known it would hurt the first time, but she hadn't been quite prepared for this feeling of uncomfortable fullness, this feeling of being stretched too far, of being sundered in two. Did women really learn to like this?

He stopped pushing inward, and she released a relieved sigh when he started to pull out. But then he plunged again, and again, and again, and she could tell he was totally absorbed by something happening inside him, so all she could do was endure....

A hot tear fell on her cheek. And then another. And another. While he climaxed, Gage Dalton wept.

Chapter 10

Nothing looked any different, Emma thought as she stared past Gage's head at the spangles of color on the ceiling. The storm still howled outside, the Tiffany lamp still cast its colors around the room, the floor hadn't cracked open to swallow her, and the ceiling hadn't caved in.

Except now a man's heavy weight lay limply on her, his body still joined to hers. Except now she knew the sights and sounds and smells of sex. Except now she was free of some invisible barrier that only at this moment did she realize had been a burden. She was no longer a virgin, and she was fiercely glad of that fact, even if she hadn't found the pot of gold at the end of the rainbow. Some women never did. She had read enough to know that much.

Her shoulder was wet where Gage's tears had fallen. It had been a brief, silent storm, over almost as soon as it happened. She hoped that his hurt had eased a little.

And she was afraid, mortally afraid, that he would get up now and leave her. Never had she felt so exposed, so vulnerable, so utterly defenseless. And she suspected he felt the same.

He had exposed himself, his anguish, his need, his loss of control. Right about now he was probably wishing he could vanish into thin air.

Regrets, Gage thought, were the manure of life, littering every damn byway and walkway. She was probably feeling them, he was *certainly* feeling them, and right now he felt as raw as if he'd been skinned.

What he regretted was that he had not given her a better experience. What he regretted was that his knapsack full of guilt and remorse was going to keep him from giving her what she really needed for the long run. He couldn't give Miss Emma love, but he sure as hell could have given her good sex, and he hadn't even done that.

He had felt those moments when she had wished he would pull away from her. He had sensed her discomfort, but he had been too far gone to stop. He'd been afraid of that, and it had happened. Now, what the hell could he do about it?

He sighed heavily and raised himself on his elbows so he could look down at Emma. At once she closed her eyes, and color rushed rosily into her cheeks.

"Look at me, Red," he said huskily, catching her face between his large hands. "Come on, look at me."

Her eyes fluttered reluctantly open, and the color staining her cheeks darkened. Gage gave her a lopsided smile.

"It doesn't get much more intimate than this, Em."

Impossibly, she felt the tug of a smile at the corners of her mouth, even as she wanted to hide her face in his shoulder. It couldn't get much more intimate, she thought. She was so completely, exquisitely aware of everywhere their bodies touched, of how he fit even now between her legs, part of him still possessing her. She was aware of textures, of smells, of pressures, of sounds. Nothing was as intimate as this.

"I'm sorry it wasn't any good for you, Emma."

"I didn't say—"

He cut her off with a quick, soft kiss. "You didn't have to say. All I did was hurt you."

"Just a little," she protested. "Besides, at first…" Her voice trailed off, and her blush heightened again.

"At first I got you really turned on," he murmured huskily. "I know. You're fire in a man's arms, Emma. You can't have any idea how good it makes a man feel when a woman responds to him like you do."

Oh, but she could, she thought, remembering the heady moments when Gage's hunger had thrilled her so. She knew exactly what he meant, and just thinking about how he had trembled for want of her was enough to make her feel hot and weak all over again.

He saw the flash of comprehension in her expression, heard it in her suddenly quickened breathing. Good, he thought. Good. He hadn't killed her desire. She was still halfway there and hoping.

He brushed another kiss against her lips, and one against her collarbone. Then he moved his hips against her, lightly, as if by accident, and smiled when he heard her swiftly drawn breath.

"That's it, Em," he whispered roughly in her ear. "Now that more pressing matters are out of the way, let's take care of unfinished business."

He rocked his pelvis against her again, slowly, and then again. Emma was amazed to feel herself rapidly spiraling back up to the heights she had just crashed from so disappointingly.

"It'll be good this time, Red. Just relax and let it happen." He shifted, covering one of her breasts with his hand and gently brushing his thumb back and forth across the nipple as he continued to rock against her. And amazingly, he felt himself harden as if he were fifteen again and not an ancient thirty-eight. "Put your hands on my butt, Emma," he ground out. "Hold me like you did before."

She did, loving the feel of those powerful muscles flexing beneath her palms as he moved against her. He was still inside her, filling her more and more with each movement, but this time it didn't feel quite so frightening. No, it was beginning to feel good.

"Does it hurt?" he asked breathlessly.

"No...no..."

"Good...?"

"Mmm..." She was lifting now, rising to meet his thrusts instead of passively accepting them as she had before. Her head began to roll restlessly, and her hands tightened on his buttocks until he felt the sting of her nails. That zapped through him like electricity and dragged a groan from his depths.

"Gage!"

He recognized that sound. It had become engraved on his soul the night before when he had brought her to the peak the first time. He slipped his hand down between them and touched her, drawing another cry from her. "Oh, Em, it's good, isn't it? Just let it happen in its own sweet time. Just...let it..." He was gasping like a marathoner on his last mile, doubtful he could hold out much longer. She turned him on like he'd never been turned on in his whole life. He wouldn't have thought he could...

He felt it happen. She came apart beneath him with a wild upward surge and a cry that pierced his heart. Her arms tightened around him, her legs wrapped around him and Miss Emmaline Conard held hell's own archangel in a timeless moment wrested from heaven.

At two in the morning Emma sat chin deep in the big, clawfooted bathtub, surrounded by scented bubbles and rising steam. Opening one eye lazily, she benefited from the sight of Gage's backside, buck naked, as he leaned into the mirror and tried to scrape stubble from his cheek with her razor. He didn't appear to be self-conscious about his scars, once he realized they didn't repel her, and she was glad. She hated to think of the pain he had endured, but those scars in no way diminished him.

"Damn," Gage muttered. "What is it with women's razors?

How the hell can you use them when they're so dull? How do they *get* so dull?''

''There's a fresh one under the sink,'' Emma said lazily. She decided that she absolutely loved being a fallen woman. It was wonderful to laze around here in her bubbles and listen to a stark-naked man gripe about razors. Yes, she could easily grow addicted to this kind of intimacy.

Gage turned, razor in hand, and looked down at her. ''Are you laughing at me?'' He pretended to scowl. ''I'm only shaving for you, you know.''

''I know.'' Her cheeks felt raw, another sensation she really didn't mind. She wondered if women stopped getting beard burn with time, or if that was always a problem. She gave him a beatific smile. ''And I told you where to find a fresh razor.''

He tossed the razor down and wiped his face with a towel. ''I'm done anyway, Red.'' A moment later he was kneeling beside the tub, catching her chin with a finger to turn her face up to him. ''How do you feel?'' he asked huskily. ''Really.''

''High as a kite,'' she admitted honestly.

Something in his face, some kind of tension, let go. ''Yeah?'' he said softly, then leaned toward her to brush a light, gentle kiss against her lips.

Her hand rose from the soapy, scented water to touch his cheek, and she thought how wonderful it was to be able to touch him so freely. How absolutely marvelous it was to have left pretense behind and to be able to honestly express desire. How phenomenally liberating it was to be desired in return. The euphoria would fade, she was sure, but she wouldn't trade these moments in time for anything in the whole world.

Gage's voice was huskier than usual. ''You about done, Emma?''

''You could join me.''

He flashed an unexpected grin. ''I might if that water didn't smell like roses. Of course, the scent will probably get all over me anyway.''

Emma's breath locked in her throat, and she felt as if she were drowning in his stormy eyes. "Will it?" she whispered.

"You bet," he whispered back. "All over every damn inch of me. This night isn't over yet, lady. Not by a long sight."

She wanted it never to be over. Never, ever. It would end, of course. Beneath her euphoria an honest part of her accepted the end as inevitable. But for now, for tonight, she wanted to live in a fool's paradise where a man could love her despite her infertility, where dreams could come true and morning never came.

"We're snowed in," Gage murmured as he brushed kisses against each of her eyelids, against her cheek and chin. "Nobody's going anywhere come morning. You don't have to open the library."

"That's right." Her agreement was breathless, the merest whisper as spiraling desire began to coalesce like a warm weight at her center. Instinctively she brought her knees together beneath the water.

"And I wouldn't want to leave you wondering," he murmured against her ear.

"Wondering...what?"

"Whether the second time was a fluke."

She gasped as his tongue speared into her ear. A shiver raced down her spine to join the growing heaviness between her legs. He'd said something, hadn't he? Was she supposed to answer?

"No, Miss Emma." His voice was little more than a rough growl. "I want you to know for sure that sex is just about the best thing a man and a woman can do together. I don't want you ever to doubt it."

Emma gasped and arched instinctively as his hand closed around her breast beneath the water. The bath salts made the water slick, and his fingers slipped silkily over her skin as he sought her nipple. She gasped again when he found it, then tilted her head to the side so he was able to nibble his way down to an exquisitely sensitive place on her neck.

"You should wear your hair down, Emma," he said huskily,

his lips leaving a hot trail from her ear to her shoulder. "It's like something out of a fairy tale, all gold and red like fire." Catching her swollen nipple between thumb and forefinger, he tugged gently on it and listened with satisfaction to the soft whimper that escaped her.

He could hardly believe it, but he was throbbing again, nowhere near critical, but definitely hungry enough that he didn't want to stop. How did she do this to him? How had she dragged him out of the frozen wastes where he'd been hiding and made him once again a man?

Hell's own archangel had been a particularly apt appellation, he thought now, as he savored each moment of Emma's growing response. People who thought of fire and brimstone didn't know. Hell was a cold place. Colder than the arctic wastes. Emptier.

Her flame was warming him, and damned if he could pull away now. Not yet. Later, but not now. Like a wolf drawn by fire, he just kept circling closer and closer to the warmth, hungry for light, for laughter, for...

He choked the thought down and focused on Emma. Lovely Emma with her wild mane of hair caught up in a gaudy clasp, her neck as pale as dairy cream rising above the slowly evaporating bubbles. Now he could see the breast he was fondling, and he felt his loins tighten even more in reaction.

"So sweet," he heard himself say roughly as another soft whimper escaped her. "God, Emma, you're the sweetest thing...."

Leaning forward, ignoring the viselike pain in his back, he pressed a deep, wet kiss on her mouth as he sent his hand foraging lower beneath suds and water. When he found her soft silky curls she arched upward, tight as a bowstring.

Gage broke off the kiss, breathing heavily now himself. "Isn't it time to get out of there, Red? Before I get in there with you and prove that an old man with a crippled back ought to know better?"

She drew a sharp breath, and her sleepy-looking eyes opened slowly. "Would you?"

"I'm getting damn close to it."

She smiled slumberously. "That makes me feel good, to hear you say that."

Suddenly smiling himself, he leaned closer and nipped her earlobe. "So it makes you feel good to bring a man to his knees, does it?"

"Just you, Gage. Only you."

The words sounded a warning in the back of his mind, but he ignored it. He figured he was earning enough bad karma tonight to turn him into a snake for at least five lifetimes to come. That being the case, he was damned well going to enjoy it.

Standing, oblivious to his own nudity or its impact on her, he grabbed a towel from the rack and then held a hand out to her.

"Come on, Venus," he said. "Time to rise from the sea foam."

All of a sudden Emma felt shy again. Somehow it suddenly seemed impossible to stand up, leaving the concealing bubbles behind, while this man watched her.

"Come on, Em," Gage said, lowering his voice to a deep, coaxing tone. "Promise I'll close my eyes."

Her gaze flew to his face and found him grinning almost wickedly. He looked so young, suddenly, she thought with a pang. Young and carefree.

"Your bubbles are almost gone, Red. There isn't a whole lot I can't see right now. Come on."

Blushing profusely, unable to look at him, she rose from the tub and kept her face averted as the water sluiced from her.

"Damn," Gage said softly. "Damn, you're gorgeous." And somehow, he was going to make Miss Emma believe that, he thought as he studied her blushing face and the way she refused to look at him. He needed to make her believe that.

Stepping forward, he wrapped the towel snugly around her

and helped her out of the tub. Then, taking the devil's own time about it, he began to rub and stroke her dry. It wasn't long before Emma forgot her momentary shyness and succumbed to the incredible pleasure of being treated as if she was precious and desirable. And beautiful. He made her feel so beautiful, which she surely was not.

"I'd carry you," he murmured huskily in her ear as he dropped the towel and drew her full, bare length against his. "I'd sweep you off your feet and carry you to bed like Rhett Butler, if I could."

He was referring to his back, and Emma hastened to reassure him. She leaned even more into him and pressed a kiss on the smooth skin of his shoulder. "I always figured I'd be terrified of falling. Not good for the mood."

He chuckled quietly and began backing toward the door. "This is nice. Oh, have I got plans for you, Miss Emma." He whispered a suggestion in her ear and felt the tremor of response ripple through her. "Ah, you like the sound of that...."

His voice was doing as much to her as any of his touches, she realized. There was something incredibly sexy about a man talking quietly in your ear, whispering of the things he'd like to do. Making suggestions that would have caused Great-aunt Isabel to swoon. Poor, dear Aunt Isabel, Emma thought dreamily as she and Gage tangled together on cool sheets. The poor woman had missed so much.

Emma didn't want to miss a bit of it. Not even the tiniest little thing. Spurred suddenly by appetites she had only just begun to discover, she pressed Gage back on the bed and straddled him on her hands and knees.

He looked up at her, a crooked smile on his face. "What's this?"

She leaned down and kissed him lightly on the lips. "I want to find out what turns you on."

A soft laugh escaped him. "Lady, *you* turn me on. The way you walk, the way you smile, the way your breasts bounce when you laugh...I don't think there's one thing about you that doesn't turn me on. If there is, I've been too turned on all week to notice it.''

He captured her breasts in his hands and rubbed his thumbs over her nipples, drawing a long, low sound from her. "That turns me on, too," he murmured. "The way you respond. The way you sound."

"But I want to please you," she said when she could find breath.

"You do, Emma. Oh, baby, you do." But he understood. She wanted to be active, not just passive. She wanted to participate. She wanted to draw from him the same sounds he drew from her. So he told her what he liked. And then endured the exquisite torture of having her try it all out.

And, oh, how it excited her to excite him. When she licked his small nipple to a hard point and sucked on it, drawing a deep moan from him, she felt a tug of pleasure in her own center every bit as strong as if he had been sucking her breast. When he guided her hands to his arousal and taught her how to stroke his silky length, her insides clenched again and again in a deep, wrenching throb of pleasure.

Somehow, at some point, it had become impossible to tell who was giving and who was receiving, who was touching and who was touched.

When Gage eased her onto her back and scooted down to bury his face in her musky, dewy core, she was prepared to give him anything he wanted, because each new experience only sent her higher and higher in the excruciatingly wonderful spiral of passion.

The touch of his tongue electrified her, a sensation so powerful that it bordered on pain. She tried instinctively to pull away, but he caught her hips in his powerful hands and held her still.

"Let me, Emma," he said roughly. "Let me taste you."

Oh, my word! she thought hazily. His touch, his voice, his demand, they all added fuel to the fire. She had never dreamed that simple, ordinary words could be so erotic.

"Yes," she said hoarsely, totally unable to say no. "But it hurts...."

"Not for long. It's just so new...Emma, sweet...so sweet..."

The sensations were so new, so sharp, so exquisite, that she reached the brink swiftly and then stalled there, unable to find her way over. Writhing, she clawed the sheets, and then, in a moment so intense it seemed to halt time in its course, she tumbled over.

She would never forget, she thought dazedly. She would never forget the way her thighs had clamped around his head, holding him to her. Never forget the low sound of triumph he had made when he knew she had reached the apex. Would never, ever forget the instant when he slid up over her and slipped into her, causing a deep, clenching thrill to spear through her. Would never forget the way he lifted her hips to him and made her climb the peak one more time, this time with him.

She would never forget the way he felt when he collapsed on her and lay tiredly against her, his muscles quivering, his breath gasping. She would surely never forget the sound of his name on her lips or the sound of hers on his as they slowly slipped back into reality.

And most definitely, most assuredly, she would never forget the moment she realized she loved him.

Lying on his side, Gage watched Emma sleep. Her silky, curly hair cascaded like wildfire over the pillow; her golden eyelashes shadowed her pale cheeks. In repose she looked remarkably fragile and delicate, in marked contrast to her waking manner of strength and competence. From the outside, no man would ever guess how soft, how warm, how utterly vulnerable, was Emmaline Conard.

He'd been lying there for what seemed ages, just watching her. The throb of pain in his back was persistent, but it seemed unimportant beside the tightness in his chest, a tightness born of unaccustomed emotions. Miss Emma had opened old wounds simply by giving herself to him. He shouldn't have allowed her to do that. He couldn't allow her to keep on doing it. He couldn't ever again be responsible for anyone else's well-being. No way. And he couldn't allow his own internal walls to be torn down, his defenses to be breached. They were the only things that stood between him and madness. Or so he sometimes thought.

If he had half a brain, he would get out of this bed now and make it clear that this night would never happen again. Let her know that nothing would come of this. Make it clear that she wasn't to count on him for anything. Show her that he could only give her pain.

But he stayed, and in the soft light from the Tiffany lamp, he watched her sleep. *Titania,* he thought, a crazy thought but one that seemed suddenly apt. A fairy princess with flaming hair and incredibly delicate features slumbered trustingly beside him, and for this little while he allowed himself to forget that he didn't deserve her trust.

Tomorrow, he thought with a shudder, tomorrow would be soon enough to return to hell.

Reaching out, he touched a soft curl. He never lost control, but he had lost control tonight. Emma and a couple of nurses from long ago were the only people on the planet who had seen Gage Dalton completely stripped to raw feeling. He should feel uneasy, threatened, embarrassed, that she had seen him shaking with need and almost out of his mind with hunger, but he didn't. Somehow he felt his vulnerability was in safe hands with Emma.

He felt *he* was in safe hands with Emma. It was a strange feeling for a man who had never counted on anyone but himself, a man who was accustomed to having others turn to him for safety. Not that he was able to provide it, but he had always sure as hell tried to.

Aching, trying to swallow feelings that seemed to be determined to be felt tonight, he tried to think of sex and not of needs. He tried to put the night down to rampaging hormones, not loneliness, not tenderness, not caring.

Yet Emma had given herself to him with tenderness and caring, whether he wanted to face it or not. She had held out a hand to him when he had been caught in a tempest of unchained needs and hurts, had told him it would be all right at a time when she should have been afraid and seeking his reassurances.

He wanted to accept all that she was offering him, but he didn't deserve it. He would never deserve the promises he had seen in her eyes after the last time they had made love. So tomorrow he was going to have to find some way to put distance between them, some way to let her know that nothing more could happen between them.

Somehow he had to stop things before he hurt her any worse than he already had.

"Gage?"

Aw, hell, he thought, he should have put on a shirt. He was standing in the kitchen in his unbuttoned jeans, watching the snow drift deeper in the dark driveway. Dawn was approaching, but it was impossible to tell. The blizzard still raged, blowing snow against the windowpanes with an icy rattle, burying Emma's small car, coming close to burying his Suburban.

She was standing in the kitchen doorway, hesitating because he hadn't responded when she called his name. He could feel her back there, could feel her eyes on his scarred back, could feel her wondering why he was standing in the kitchen in the dark like this.

"The coffee's hot," he said finally, not knowing what else to say. He kept his back to her, hoping she would take the hint.

"Is your back hurting?"

The concern in her voice was like a claw in his conscience. Damn it! He didn't deserve her caring. And she sure as hell didn't deserve the cost of that caring.

"No more than usual."

Emma edged into the kitchen, uncertain how to handle this. She had hoped this morning would bring an easiness between them, a warmth. Maybe that they would make love again. She had suspected it wouldn't be like that, and had known for certain when she found him gone from the bed.

The question was whether she should let him deal with this in his own way, or whether she should let him off the hook by telling him that she was aware there was no future for them. At least, she thought that was what might be troubling him.

Looking back at last night, she could clearly see what it had taken to break down his resistance to making love to her. She had, after all, seen him stand beside the bed, shaking from head to foot and battling his own needs. She had heard him offer her a chance to get away. She had witnessed the strength of the forces that had buffeted him.

He hadn't *wanted* to make love to her. He had *needed* to. And later, when he had been so sweet, he had been giving her something he believed he owed her.

The night beyond the windows was surprisingly bright, the light of streetlamps diffused by the glittering snow into a pale glow. That cold glow poured eerily into the kitchen. Emma felt around in the cabinet for a mug and poured herself some coffee, wondering if she should just act as if nothing had happened between them.

It was Gage who broke the strained silence. ''There's no future in this, Emma.''

''I know.'' She *did* know. She knew with agonizing clarity that no man would want her for long. She had known it for a decade now. But he didn't seem to hear her.

''I can't—'' He broke off, unable to find words.

Emma pulled out a chair at the table and sat, watching his back, aching for both of them with a depth and fatalism that astonished her even as she felt it. They were doomed, she thought. Both of them doomed by circumstances beyond their control. Was it so wrong to seek what comfort they could from one another?

Several minutes ticked by in a silence punctuated by the rattle of snow against the glass and the low moan of the wind as it whipped around the house. Finally Gage tried again.

"I don't have a future to offer you, Emma," he said roughly.

She knew better than ever to have hoped for any such thing. "I didn't ask—"

He interrupted. "I used up my brownie points with heaven a long time ago, if I ever had any."

Confused, she tried to see him more clearly. "What do you mean?"

"Just that. I've been condemned to hell."

"Gage, what—"

"Do you know what hell is, Emma?" His voice was quiet, controlled, belying the anguish his words conveyed. "It's an endless, bottomless, icy void. An infinite emptiness of the heart and soul. A gaping chasm that was once filled by everything and everyone you loved."

Emma drew a long, shuddery breath as she began to understand. "Tell me," she said unsteadily.

He tilted his head back and closed his eyes, clenching his hands into fists at his sides. He had to do this, he thought desperately. For both of them. He had to say it, and she had to hear it, before it was too late. Because he was too damn tempted to take what she offered.

"It was just before Christmas," he said, his voice low, and rougher than she'd ever heard it. "My wife and I had just finished decorating the Christmas tree."

Wife? Emma's heart began to beat painfully.

"We got the kids into their snowsuits...."

Kids? Oh, my God! She wanted to run, hide, knowing she didn't want to hear any of this. Not any of this.

"The youngest was just two months old," Gage said almost dispassionately. "We had two little girls already. Sandy was four, and Karen was two. And then we had Tommy. My wife was so thrilled with him. She'd wanted a boy from the start. I kind of liked having little girls, myself. Jan, my wife, said they had me wrapped around their little fingers. I guess maybe they did.''

"Gage..." What could she say? What could she do to stop the coming agony? Not a thing. Like a doe caught in headlights, she simply waited for the impact.

"We were..." He cleared his throat. "We were going to leave the kids with a friend of ours while we went shopping. We got everyone into the car, and then I remembered I'd left the diaper bag by the front door. I went back to get it...." He swallowed painfully. "I was halfway up the walk when the car bomb went off."

Emma closed her eyes, wishing she could somehow make this all go away for both of them.

"A piece of debris hit me in the back," he continued, his voice completely expressionless. "I fell facedown in the snow and couldn't move. I heard the roar of the fire behind me, I knew...but I was paralyzed. I couldn't help. Something hot fell on my jacket and set it on fire, and there wasn't anything I could do for them.... It was too late, anyway, they told me later. They all died instantly...." His voice broke, and he fell silent.

Presently Emma drew a shaky breath. "And the screams?" she asked, remembering what he had told her.

"My own," he said. "A neighbor managed to kick snow on me and put out the flames. I understand I didn't stop screaming for three days. I don't remember most of it." He drew a long, rough breath. "I *do* remember looking at the car when they carried me away. I remember—" His voice broke. "I remember knowing my life was gone."

Emma flew across the kitchen and slipped her arms around him from behind, knowing only that enough was enough. No one should have to bear such things alone. No one should have to be so utterly without comfort.

"Emma, I told you...."

"It's all right, Gage. You told me. I heard you. That doesn't mean I don't care. That I won't care." She pressed her cheek to his back, feeling the line of keloid tissue that defined one of his many burn scars. She drew a shaky breath, trying to ease the tightness in her throat, and blinked back helpless tears. "Did they catch the person who...bombed the car?"

"Yeah."

"Who was it?"

"You know, Em, that's the really great thing about it. It was one of the brothers of a drug kingpin I helped put away."

"Why is that so great?" His sarcastic use of the word puzzled her.

"Because I was directly responsible for the deaths of my wife and three children."

Emma gasped, stunned. The bitterness of his voice left her no doubt that he meant it, and she began to see very clearly the depth of the problem here. "How...how do you figure that, Gage?"

"It's simple. They died because of my job. No two ways about it. If I'd been a mechanic or a carpenter, they wouldn't have—they would have—" He couldn't go on. One more word and he would start crying. He'd cried enough.

"Oh, Gage, no!" The words were a horrified whisper. He couldn't believe that. He couldn't!

"Believe me, I've had a lot of time to think about it. I knew the dangers. I was just a damn fool to believe they would be directed only at me. And there are still a few people out there who would like to get at me. So that's it, Emma. I killed my family. And I'll be damned if I'm going to put anybody else in that position. Or put myself through that again."

She longed to argue with him, to insist that bad things just happened, that no one was to blame except the perpetrator. Her own life was proof of that. But she sensed that Gage wouldn't believe it. Couldn't believe it. He felt guilty for the deaths of his wife and children, and no simplistic argument was going to alter his feelings.

She told herself to turn away now, that this briefly born relationship was doomed for too many reasons, beginning with his guilt and ending with her infertility. But it was already too late.

Sometime in the last two days she had passed the point of no return. She had given him what she had given no one else, but that giving had been merely symbolic of a commitment she had already made. For her, it was already too late. Since the pain was going to be unavoidable, she made the decision to take what she could from the moment.

She stepped back from Gage and took his hand. "Come on," she said, tugging gently. "Come back to bed."

"Emma—"

"I know," she said softly. "I know. It's just a one-night stand. Maybe a two- or three-night stand. Nothing more. I know. It's okay, Gage. I promise."

Even as he was letting her drag him back toward the bedroom, he knew he was making a mistake. For her sake, for his, he ought to go upstairs right now. But she kept whispering that she understood, that he wasn't to worry, that no harm could come from a few stolen moments together. Like a siren, she drew him.

And, like a man, he followed.

Chapter 11

"I've been hearing things, old son," said the gravelly voice of Sheriff Nathan Tate over the telephone. "Maybe you'd like to tell me what the hell is going on?"

Gage leaned back in the leather chair behind the desk in Emma's study and looked out the tall window at the gray sky and blowing snow. The blizzard still raged, and the morning was waning with no sign of the storm's passing yet apparent. "I meant to call you last night, but something came up. Are you at the office, Nate?"

"I wish. No, son, I'm at home, hiding in my shop, hoping Marge and the girls don't run out of videotapes to watch. I got a phone call from Laramie. Some Lieutenant Doherty of the LPD, wanting to know if you were really one of my people. Something about a file on an old case you asked to have expressed out here. I admitted ownership of an investigator named Gage Dalton and seconded your request to have the file come by mail, not fax."

"Thanks, Nate."

"Don't mention it. So, what's going on?"

Gage hesitated, reluctant to expose Emma, but not knowing how he could avoid it now. "I don't know if you heard what happened to Miss Emma years ago when she was a student in Laramie."

"Actually, yes, I did. The judge told me about it, but I don't think he told another soul in the county. How did you find out?"

"Emma told me."

"I was under the impression she didn't remember anything about it."

"She's begun to remember quite a bit, Nate, and she's scared."

"I don't blame her." The sheriff sighed heavily. "So why did you want the file?"

Gage hesitated only briefly. "You know all these incidents—the balloon, the rabbit, the pentagram—I don't think they're pranks. I stopped thinking that when I saw the pentagram yesterday—"

"Well, so did I," Nate interrupted. "Give me something I don't already know."

"Last night Emma told me that the bastard who assaulted her in Laramie carved a pentagram on her stomach."

Nate swore. "It might be unrelated."

"I don't think so. There's something else that happened that you don't know about. Last week Emma received a photograph in the mail. It shook her up badly, which made me curious, so I sent it to a friend of mine back East. He says it's a poor copy of a dagger used by Turkish *hashshashin* in the Middle Ages."

"But—"

"By itself that doesn't mean a whole lot, Nate, I know. But why would somebody go to a lot of trouble to duplicate something like that? Why would they send it to Emma?"

Nate drew a long breath. "To scare her," he said heavily. "Just like they did with the rabbit and the pentagram."

"That's what I'm afraid of. Hell, that's what I'm convinced of. I asked an old buddy of mine to do a search on the national crime computer system for other crimes that are similar in any way to Emma's assault, and I'm waiting for information on anyone in the county who has a related criminal record. In the meantime, I don't think Miss Emma should be alone.''

The silence grew protracted as Nate pondered what Gage had told him. "I'm with you," Nate said finally. "Keep a close watch on her. Is there any other information I can get for you?"

"There's probably no connection between what's been happening to Jeff's cattle and whoever is stalking Miss Emma, but I have to admit, ever since that decapitated rabbit turned up, I've been wondering about it. Anyhow, related or not, I'm still waiting to hear from the FAA about helicopters and helicopter pilots in the area. I guess I won't hear until Monday now, unless you know some cages to rattle.''

"I know the district chief. Let me see if I can roust him out for you. What exactly do you want to know?"

"Whether we've got any helo pilots around here who have criminal records, and what kind of records they've got. Crooks are almost never completely clean, Nate. There's always something that's a tip-off to an investigator, if he just knows where to look.''

"How's Emma taking this?" Nate asked.

"Other than a few nightmares, she's handling it remarkably well," Gage said.

"Well, you tell her I said to let me know if she needs anything at all.''

"I will, Nate.''

After he hung up, Gage continued to contemplate the snowy day beyond the window. At the base of his skull there was a niggling feeling of pressure. He always got that feeling when things were about to start popping on a case. It warned him to watch his step, to take extra care, because things were going to blow wide open.

Now he felt that way and didn't know if his instincts were telling him that the stalker was about to move on Miss Emma, or if he was just feeling that way because of last night.

Too much had happened. He'd been a fool to give in to his needs, a fool to believe that he could ever simply step back and tell Miss Emma that there could never be a future for them. Of course, he hadn't counted on Emma. If he lived to be a hundred, he would never forget the way she had taken his hand this morning and urged him back to bed, as if it were the most natural thing in the world to give herself to a man who wanted to give her nothing at all. As if she understood, as if she wanted nothing in the world more than to give him whatever he needed.

How was a man supposed to resist that?

His conscience niggled at him, but at a level he had long since learned to ignore. Working undercover had numbed him to a lot of things, but in this instance he really wasn't being deceptive or taking advantage. Not now. Not after he had told Emma he had nothing to offer her.

He could, however, be a little angry at Emma for the way she was selling herself short. She deserved a whole hell of a lot more, and he felt like shaking some sense into her, except that there was no way on earth you could really shake sense into anyone. All you could do was satisfy your own need to get things off your chest.

She was an adult, he reminded himself. A mature woman of thirty or so. She was entitled to do this, if that was what she chose. And he didn't have a damn thing to say about it, except as it affected him. End of discussion.

Figuring he couldn't do any more investigating until some information started coming in to give him a direction, he went out to the kitchen, where Emma was making Christmas cookies.

She greeted him with a smile that said she was glad to see him, a smile he didn't feel he deserved. "Have a cookie," she said pleasantly, pointing to the cooling racks on the table. "They're pretty good even without the icing."

He poured himself a cup of coffee and stopped to watch her

roll out another batch of dough. "What are you going to do with all these?"

"Serve them at the open house next Sunday. I'll probably need to bake all week just for that."

"Is it worth all the trouble?"

"Oh, I think so. It's really a lot of fun, Gage. Just about everyone comes, and the caroling is so beautiful. It's..." She hesitated, seeking words as she began to cut out tree-shaped cookies. "It's Christmasy. All the warmth and friendship and goodwill most of us associate with the season is there at the open house. To me, it's the essence of the season."

She looked up suddenly, remembering that the season was a painful time for him. She bit her lip and glanced apologetically his way.

"It's okay," he reassured her. Damn, he didn't want the shadows of his life to blight hers. But how could he prevent it, when she insisted on caring?

Emma wished he didn't look so removed this morning. It was as if the past week had never happened, as if Gage had retreated into the frozen place he'd been inhabiting the night he walked her home. Hell's own archangel was back.

And why shouldn't he be? she asked herself as she worked the rolling pin with trembling hands. His losses were almost beyond imagining, and there was no reason on earth why he should ever again risk the cost of caring. But if ever he did take the risk again, he certainly wouldn't do it for a woman who wasn't a woman. A woman who couldn't give him a real family.

Feeling her lower lip tremble, she caught it between her teeth to still it. Lord, she hated to cry. Besides, she'd done all her crying years ago—unlike Gage, who evidently hadn't done his crying at all yet. Instead of giving in to the pain, he'd fast-frozen it in the depths of his soul.

Maybe hell *was* a cold, empty place, as he'd said this morning, but maybe it was also a place a person made for himself. Grief wasn't a cold emotion, but ice wasn't any emotion at all.

He would never heal until he raged, and rage was hot, a searing emotion that would surely melt all the ice he hid his feelings in. And then what?

Maybe, she admitted, he was better this way. He might never heal, but perhaps the price of healing was too high.

A long sigh escaped her, relaxing the tension that had brought her close to the edge of tears. She reached for a cookie cutter and began to make rows of bells.

Well, she'd already thrown her heart over the moon sometime in the past week, when she hadn't been paying attention and guarding her own emotions. It was too late to avoid the pain now. So, whether he liked it or not, she would just go right on giving him whatever caring she could. Everybody, no matter how frozen, needed to know that someone in this world cared.

"I guess I should try to move some of that snow in the driveway," Gage remarked. He stood at the kitchen windows looking out at the whirling snow and nearly buried vehicles. The storm seemed to have let up a little. Maybe. And maybe it was just wishful thinking.

"Don't you dare," Emma said mildly. "The boys next door and I have a contract. They'll be heartbroken to lose the money."

"Oh." Probably just as well, with his back. Even after all this time, it was hard for him to accept that there were some things he was wiser not to do. Nor did it help with the caged-lion feeling that was bugging him right now. He needed some good, hard physical activity. Ordinarily he would have gone for one of his endless walks, but he refused to leave Emma alone, and she was in the middle of enough dough to feed a hungry football team. She wouldn't want to stop now.

Jan had used to do this, too, at Christmas. Coming from the streets, just as Gage had, she had carried in her heart an image of what Christmas should really be, a picture-postcard image that she had tried her best to create each year for him and the children.

He drew a long, shaky breath and continued to stare out the window as he allowed himself to remember. The house had always smelled just like this—baking cookies, pine needles, coffee. Secrets wrapped in gaily colored paper and foil had been hidden on the highest shelves in every closet. There had been whispers and giggles, and that last year his eldest daughter had started to grow so excited at the prospect of Christmas that getting her to sleep at night had become a chore. Jan herself grew as excited as any child, and the excitement had been contagious. He, too, had come to love Christmas, to love the excitement and sense of magic.

And as he stood there staring blankly out at the stormy, snowy day, a surprising thought twisted through his sad preoccupation and turned his thoughts in an utterly different direction.

Emma, too, prepared for the holidays. She, too, created a Currier and Ives Christmas with her decorating and baking, and she spoke of the good feeling and fellowship of the season. But she would never have children to create that magic for. She would never know the excitement of buying a toy that she knew, just knew, was going to bring excited shrieks on Christmas morning. She would never know the anticipation of hiding secrets in closets, or the joy of teaching carols to her own daughter or son.

He had experienced all that. He had lost it, but he would never regret the precious episodes, the memories, the remembered joy, even if the price had been excruciatingly high. Emma would never know that. Until he had wormed past her defenses, she had always avoided men, and now he thought he knew why.

Shaken out of his self-preoccupation, he turned from the window. She might never have a family of her own, he thought, but she sure as hell didn't have to spend this Christmas alone with a man who was acting like a total jerk.

He reached for a cookie and took a bite. "Fantastic cookies, Emma," he said.

"They're just sugar cookies."

"Well, they're great. How are you going to manage to decorate them all by yourself?"

She glanced over her shoulder. "Are you volunteering?" She expected him to deny it, given his problems with Christmas.

"Sure. Except that I've never done it before and I can't guarantee I won't mess up your cookies."

Emma slid another baking pan into the oven and laughed. "We're not painting the Sistine Chapel here. If I were making just a couple dozen for a special party, I might sweat it. Making hundreds for a crowd, a smear of icing and a dash of sprinkles will do."

"Smears and dashes are right up my alley."

Smiling, Emma faced him and wondered what had changed his mood so dramatically. Hell's own archangel was gone, replaced by a friendly-looking guy with a crooked smile. Even his gray-green eyes, only moments ago as cold as snow clouds, now looked softer, like a summer rain squall.

"I'll mix up the icing, then, and you can frost while I bake."

A couple of hundred cookies later, Gage realized that something was troubling Emma. She didn't seem to be able to hold still, and if she wiped down that counter one more time, he would be tempted to growl at her. Of course, she had plenty to worry about, and he knew the need for activity when things were worrisome.

"Why don't we take a walk?" he said abruptly. "We can finish icing these things later."

"The sidewalks will be a mess," she said, glancing out the window to see that snow was still falling steadily, though the wind had let up considerably. "I don't remember it ever snowing so much or so heavily."

Gage shoved his chair back from the table and stood, stretching cautiously to ease the stiffness in his lower back. A muscle twinged, and he winced.

"Is your back hurting badly?"

He looked at Emma and shook his head. "Nope. Just a twinge. Well, if you don't want to go walking, I guess we'll have to find another way to distract you."

"Distract me?" She looked puzzled.

"Sure." He took a step toward her and gave her a lopsided smile. "You think I don't recognize the signs? What are you worrying about? Sleeping with me last night? Or about…other things?"

Emma felt her breath catch as a strange hot-cold feeling drizzled through her. In an instant he had made her aware of him again, intensely aware of his size, his shape, his masculinity. In a way she hadn't experienced since the first few days, she noticed the breadth of his shoulders and the narrowness of his hips, the long, lean power of his denim-covered thighs. And suddenly her palms remembered exactly how he felt when she clutched him to her in the delicious throes of passion.

He had taught her so much last night, she thought now as her mouth turned dry and her heart sped up, yet there was so much she still didn't know, that she still hadn't tried. She was inexperienced, not ignorant, and looking at him right now, she also discovered she was creative. There were so many ways she still wanted to touch him, so many ways she still wanted to discover him.

Was it only two days ago that she had wondered how people could look each other in the eye once they had become intimate? That didn't seem to be a problem at all. No, her problem was keeping her hands off him. She ached, actually *ached*, to feel his arms around her, to feel the smooth heat of his skin against hers, to feel the coarse hair on his thighs against hers as he fit himself between her legs.

Gage saw the longing in her darkening eyes and felt it like a punch in the gut. Being Mr. Nice Guy to her over the holidays was a far cry from being her lover for an extended period. She'd already gotten under his skin. If he gave her half a chance, she would probably curl right up in his soul and then, when he moved on, become another one of those empty places he could never fill.

"Get your boots on, Emma," he ordered harshly. "We're going out. Now."

Emma wasn't used to taking orders of any kind, and for an instant her temper flared in white heat. But she wasn't blind, and she could see the tension in his posture and the lines around his mouth. "What's your shoe size?" she asked him.

The question was so unexpected and so far out of context that his head jerked backward in astonishment. "What?"

"What's your shoe size? I think your height and weight are close to my father's...well, you're probably thinner. He got a little thick around the middle—"

"Emma, what—"

"The skis will probably be just a tad too long, but not by much. What's your shoe size?"

"Thirteen."

Emma smiled. "Good. Let's go cross-country skiing."

"When I was a kid," Emma said as they drove slowly out of town in Gage's black Suburban, "we had to wax our skis. We always carried a little backpack with all the waxes for different temperatures and types of snow, and as the day wore on and conditions changed, we'd have to stop and scrape and rewax. Waxless skis finally got to be good enough that a few years ago Dad and I bought some. What a pleasure it is to just be able to ski!" And what a pleasure it was to be sitting in the car with him without feeling the violent urge to escape that had always plagued her before. The sense of freedom was exhilarating.

The county snowplows had evidently been working long and hard, Gage thought as he steered them between pristine white drifts. Fresh powder covered the recent plowing, but the road was drivable. "I've never skied cross-country," he warned Emma.

"It's pretty much like walking. I don't go for speed, just

pleasure, and where we're going, the ground is pretty level, so you won't have to worry about control. Do you ski downhill?''

''I have, a little.''

''You'll probably notice a difference in control, then. These skis are a lot narrower.''

At several places along the road turnouts had been plowed so that vehicles could pull over or turn around. Emma finally directed Gage into one.

When the Suburban's engine was turned off, the immense silence of winter Wyoming settled over them. Nothing could be heard but the whispery whine of the wind as it blew snow-flakes around in dancing patterns. The sky remained gray, and blowing snow obscured the distance, but the scene held an incredible tranquillity. Gage could almost feel it seep into him, easing his inner tensions.

Emma, too, seemed to be caught up in the quiet. For long moments she simply sat beside him, looking out over the vast, open spaces.

''I needed this,'' she said presently, her voice low. ''That monster stole everything else from me. I don't even feel safe alone in my own home anymore, but he can't take this away from me. Short of murdering me, he can't steal this.''

''Emma...'' But what could he say? He could barely guess how much she had lost because of that assault and the terror tactics of the past week. Instinctively he started to reach out to offer comfort, but he caught himself before he touched her. If he touched her, he feared, he might never be able to let go.

She turned and gave him a wan smile. ''Will you catch him?''

''I sure as hell intend to.''

Her smile faded, and she studied him intently for several seconds. ''Thank you,'' she said. ''Thank you for staying in that house with me, and for caring what happens.'' She looked away and drew a deep, shaky breath. ''This was a great idea,'' she said with forced brightness. ''Let's go skiing.''

It was a lot easier than he had expected. The stride and

poling went naturally together, and since Emma was in no hurry, he was soon whooshing along beside her through the deep fresh snow.

"You can go a lot faster on a prepared track," she told him, sounding only a tiny bit breathless from the exertion, "but I think this is more fun."

"Going where no man has gone before, huh?"

She shot him a laughing glance. "Exactly. Is your back okay?"

"Sure. Actually, stretching out feels good." And the rise of endorphins in his blood, resulting from vigorous exercise, always eased the pain.

There were few obstacles out here—an occasional cottonwood, some brush, once in a while a boulder. For the most part they were simply able to fall into a steady rhythm and just keep going.

The exercise and fresh air were cleansing, Emma thought, as her arms and legs strained and grew pleasantly tired. The silence and the vast openness were healing, and she could almost feel the shadows withdrawing from the edges of her mind for the first time in over a week. For just this little while it was possible to believe that everything was normal and that nothing threatened her.

Eventually they reached Conard Creek, and Emma suggested it was a good time to turn back. Gage hesitated, looking beyond the creek to the rougher terrain behind it, the beginning of the foothills. Huge boulders, looking as if they had been dropped in a heap by a giant fist, rose up from the snow, a hill of nooks and crannies.

"That looks like a great place to explore," he remarked.

"It is. I used to love to come out here when I was a kid. We all did. I don't know how many hours we spent in the summers playing cowboys and Indians, or space invaders. I think our parents were absolutely sick of us asking for rides to come out here, but one of them always gave in and brought us anyway."

"The property owner didn't mind?"

"No, that section is fenced off. There was never enough grazing to make it worth risking his cattle in the crevices between the rocks. This is all Fenster land," she added, motioning with her arm. "I don't think they keep many cattle since the old man died four years ago, but the grandson keeps it running somehow."

"Don Fenster, right?"

Emma glanced at Gage. "You know him?"

Gage shook his head. "Lance Severn's boy mentioned him when I went to get your tree. He said Fenster has a bunch of real creeps staying with him. Have you heard anything about it?"

She shook her head. "Not a peep. It wouldn't surprise me, though."

He looked at her. "Why not?"

"Don was always a creep himself. Even when I was little I hated to be in the same classroom with him. He was always out here, though, and since it was his grandfather's land, we always let him play with us."

One corner of Gage's mouth lifted. "Where I grew up, that wouldn't have made a bit of difference."

"Well, it made a difference out here. Our parents were pretty strict about being good neighbors. We got up to as much pettiness and quarreling as any other kids, I suppose, but nobody ever got entirely ostracized. And certainly not when we wanted to play on his land." She shivered a little as she began to cool down from her exertion and was grateful when Gage suddenly wrapped an arm around her and shifted so that he was sheltering her from the wind with his body.

"What made the Fenster kid so creepy?" Gage asked. "Was it just the way he looked, or was he one of those who wanted to boss everybody?"

"Oh, he wanted to boss, and he was always spying on everybody. You could always count on Don to squeal to the teacher. But I didn't think he was creepy until we were about twelve. I found him tormenting a dog. Torturing, actually.'' She shivered again, this time with distaste. "He wouldn't quit it, so I beat him to a pulp. Literally. Twelve-year-old girls are generally larger than boys of the same age, and I was never a shrimp.'' She shrugged. "He never spoke to me again."

He squeezed her suddenly, hugging her tightly. "I'll bet you were something else, Red. An avenging angel." And he felt as if something icy had just trickled down his back. Don Fenster? He tucked the name away for further investigation.

Since they were both still on their skis, the hug swiftly became uncomfortable, and Gage released her. "Let's cross over,'' he suggested.

"Uh-uh,'' Emma said, gripping his hand. "It hasn't been cold enough for long enough this winter. Even if the ice is solid a little ways out, it'll be rotten by the bank. Believe me, you don't want to get your feet wet this far from home.''

He smiled lopsidedly down at her. "I told you I was a city kid.''

She smiled back, feeling her heart quicken. Surely he was the sexiest man on earth. Every time she looked at him, her body responded in a flash. "Someday maybe you can warn me about city dangers.''

"Maybe.'' He cast one longing glance over the rough terrain, aware that it was definitely the kid in him who wanted to go over there and explore. How long had it been since he'd felt that way?

Turning, they began to ski back toward the road at a leisurely pace.

"So you did all your work for the DEA in the cities?'' Emma asked.

"The vast majority of it. The trail of drugs from Southeast Asia or South America has a lot of links in it, and we go after all of them. It's not enough to knock out a single producer or a single transporter or a single deal. We work from all ends of the problem.''

"And you always infiltrated some big drug organization?''

''Not always. I did that twice. Most of the time it didn't get anywhere near so involved.''

''Why not? I mean, I would think these dealers try to keep things secret so they don't get caught.''

''They do, but it's a Catch-22, Emma. They need buyers, and as long as they need buyers, they'll keep slipping up. It's not too tough to find an informant and get him to introduce you as a big buyer. They'll be a little cautious, naturally, but it doesn't last long, because they trust the informant. And once they see the flash roll, it's usually all over.''

''What's a flash roll?''

''A big wad of money. Generally, when you want to make a big buy, the dealer insists on seeing the color of your money before he'll even agree to sell the stuff. So you arrange a meeting, flash your roll—sometimes as much as fifty grand—and then he tells you when he'll be able to produce the drugs. That's a big danger point right there. More than one agent has been killed for his flash roll.''

''But making the buy must be dangerous, too.''

''Not really, unless the dealer insists you use the drugs before you leave.''

Emma stopped skiing, and Gage followed suit immediately, stepping carefully backward until they were once again abreast. ''What's wrong?''

She looked up at him with huge green eyes. ''How do you handle that? If you refuse, they're bound to get suspicious, aren't they?''

''Oh, we've got excuses all ready to use. I'm a great actor when it comes to smoking a marijuana cigarette. When it's something injectable, I just refuse to use the dealer's shooting gallery.''

''His *what?*''

''Shooting gallery. His needles and things. It's easy to claim you've gotten sick from using somebody else's dirty needle. Depending on the situation, there're probably a dozen different excuses. And if your excuse doesn't work, you just drag your heels, because you know your backup is right outside, and if you don't come out by a certain time, they're going to come in after you.''

Emma shook her head, studying him with frank amazement. ''I don't know where you find the nerve. And you miss it, don't you?''

Gage looked away, focusing his attention on some point made invisible by the steadily falling snow. ''Maybe a little,'' he said after a moment. ''Working undercover is a drug addiction, an addiction to adrenaline. I refuse to be addicted to anything.''

Turning again, he looked at her just in time to see her shiver. ''Come on, Em. You're getting chilled. Let's keep moving.''

Back at the truck, Emma wasn't able to get her skis off. Somehow, despite the exertion that had kept her feeling warm, she had managed to become slightly hypothermic, and her coordination had suffered.

''Let me, honey,'' Gage said, squatting before her to release the bindings. Then, just as soon as she stepped out of them, he rose and steadied her with an arm around her waist. ''You need to warm up. Just get in the truck. I'll take care of this stuff.''

Honey. The word drizzled through her like honey itself, warm and sweet, touching places that had long felt cold. If only he meant it, really meant it. But it had probably slipped past his guard out of some old habit. And besides, she knew she would never really be anyone's honey.

He opened the door and helped her up onto the passenger seat. ''I'll come around and start the engine. We'll get you warmed up.''

It wasn't until a few minutes later that she began to shiver in earnest, the sudden, uncontrollable bursts that came from deep inside despite her efforts to relax. Gage loaded the skis and poles into the back, whistling as he did so. Shivering or not, Emma smiled with pleasure. Never in her wildest imaginings had she pictured Gage whistling. She liked the sound, liked the way it made her feel inside to know that for now, at least, he was feeling cheerful.

When he joined her up front, he brought a wool blanket and insisted on wrapping it around her. His movements were surprisingly gentle, making her feel suddenly on the edge of tears again. It wasn't until a person went without it that she knew just how much she missed having someone care. Bravely, she blinked back the moisture.

"This is crazy," she told Gage, to cover her roller-coasting emotions. "I never get hypothermic from a little exercise in the snow."

"You're worn out after this week, babe," he said with gruff gentleness as he caught her chin in his hand. With infinite care, he brushed a kiss on her chilled lips. "You've been having nightmares, you've been worried and scared, and then last night I only let you get a couple hours of sleep…maybe. You're exhausted, Em. Maybe you ought to think about taking a nap."

He drove slowly back to town. Gage was evidently in no bigger hurry to get back to that house than she was, Emma thought. Nor was there any need to hurry. The Suburban's heater was soon blasting enough hot air that her shivering stopped and the blanket became stifling. When she cast it aside, Gage flashed her a crooked smile and turned down the heat.

"Better?" he asked.

"Much. Thanks."

When they arrived back at the house the Haroldsen twins were just finishing up with their small snowblower and a shovel.

"We'll have to come back tomorrow and do it again, Miss Emma," Todd Haroldsen told her, "but we figured you'd want your car uncovered so there's some hope of getting to church in the morning."

"Thanks, guys. I really appreciate it. Can I interest you in some cookies?"

It was never difficult to interest two fifteen-year-old boys in food, especially junk food. Emma was almost laughing out loud a few minutes later when the twins disappeared with their booty.

"That was a major part of the Conard County high school football team, right?" Gage asked drily.

Emma chuckled. "And a good share of the basketball team, as well."

While Emma went to change, Gage slipped into the study and closed the door. His first call was to Nate Tate at home.

"Did you get anywhere with the FAA?"

"Sorry, old son, but the man's in Kansas City to see his first grandchild. Not much cage rattling I could do."

"I guess not." He swiveled the deep leather chair and looked out the window at the failing day. Unless he was mistaken, a thin golden beam of sunlight was slanting across the yard, looking every bit as beautiful and welcome as a rainbow after a storm. "It looks like the storm is breaking up."

"Yep," Nate answered. "I'm looking out my shop window right now. It's clearing over the mountains. It'll be a clear, cold night. And that reminds me. Micah called from Denver. He and Faith won't make it back today because their flight was delayed. Said he'll be back in the county sometime tomorrow."

"Good," Gage said, and meant it. He could use a little of Micah's preternatural instincts right now. "Jeff Cumberland's about fit to be tied, and I promised to bring Micah out to look at those helicopter tracks—"

"Which are now buried beneath the snow," Nate growled.

"Unfortunately. But it'll probably calm Jeff a little to know Micah's back on the case."

"I don't think anything short of a hanging is going to calm Jeff," Nate rumbled.

"Maybe not. What can you tell me about Don Fenster?"

The sudden change of subject took Nate by surprise, and it was a moment before he responded. "Don Fenster? What the hell has he gone and done now?"

"You mean he's in the habit of doing things?"

"We sent him up the river a few years back for armed robbery. Before that there were a couple of other things, but he always got probation. Anyhow, the armed robbery was the worst thing he ever got up to. He came back to live with his granny almost two years ago, and as far as I know he's been quiet. Why?''

Gage didn't answer. "What other things did he get up to?''

"Oh, hell, let me think. It was a long time ago, Gage. Joy-riding. He 'borrowed' Jill Cranston's pickup when he was still a senior in high school. Judge Conard gave him a week in the county hoosegow and six months' probation, I think. He got picked up a time or two for shoplifting in his younger days. I don't know. He was a thorn in my side back then, but until the armed robbery he was just like any of a dozen other trou-blemakers his age. I don't recall that I worried unduly about him, just that I tried to keep him from annoying everybody else in the county. About the only thing that really strikes me in retrospect is that nobody liked him. In fact, most people felt an out-and-out aversion toward him. Why?''

"I don't know, really.'' Gage hesitated and then sighed. "Hell, yes, I do. Emma told me a little story this afternoon about how she beat Fenster to a pulp when they were both twelve because he wouldn't stop torturing a dog.''

"Damn, I never knew that.'' Nate sounded disturbed.

"I don't suppose anybody but Emma and Fenster ever did. He wouldn't want anyone to know, and Emma's not the type to tell anyone much of anything. She *did* say that Fenster hasn't talked to her once since then. And that strikes me as being…a little odd. It's been at least eighteen years.''

"Yeah.''

For a long time neither man said anything. Between them, the line echoed with silence.

"Let me think about this,'' Nate said presently. "Let me think, and maybe ask a few questions. I'll call you back, but probably not before tomorrow.''

After he hung up Gage rocked back in the chair, trying to ease the growing ache in his back. He was relieved, he realized, to have shared his uneasiness about Fenster. It wasn't much to go on, a fight between two kids nearly twenty years ago, but it was the first motive he had seen anywhere for why anyone on earth would want to torment Emma. Of course, crazies didn't need motives. The worst of them had absolutely no rhyme or reason to what they did. Someone like that might be involved, but his gut didn't believe it.

It was a crazy, all right. One with a motive. One with a grudge that hadn't died in at least the ten years since he'd attacked Emma in Laramie.

There was a quiet knock at the door, and Gage looked toward it. "Come on in, Emma."

The door opened slowly, and Emma peeked around its edge. "I'm sorry to disturb you...."

"Hey, I'm sorry I closed the door. It's your house, Em. I just needed a moment to make a phone call."

"That's all right." She stepped into the room, and the way her hands were clasped before her gave Gage an uneasy feeling.

"Is something wrong?" he asked.

"I'm not sure," she admitted. "Gage...I think someone was in the house while we were gone."

Chapter 12

"I told you, I only *think* somebody was in the house," Emma snapped a short while later. "If I could absolutely pinpoint the reason, I would!"

"*Something* had to give you the feeling," Gage argued.

"I know." Emma threw up a hand and nearly glared at him. "Quit badgering me. It's nothing I can exactly put my finger on. I just *know*. As if…as if I caught a whiff of an odor and can't quite place it."

Gage frowned. "Maybe that's it. Maybe you *did* catch a whiff of someone else's odor. It'd be subtle enough to elude you, but definite enough to give you this feeling.…"

Relieved that he was evidently going to give up pressuring her to show him something that was out of place, Emma leaned back against the foot of her bed and unfolded her arms.

"You didn't get the feeling anywhere but here?" he asked.

"Here and in my bathroom. I haven't been upstairs, and now I doubt if I could tell anything for sure. My imagination is going hog-wild right now."

"Let's go up anyway," Gage said grimly. "Together. I don't want you out of my sight, Emma."

Emma was agreeable. She didn't want to be out of his sight, either. There was little, she thought, quite as horrible as the feeling that someone had invaded your home without your permission. The sense of violation was inescapable.

"I don't think anyone's in the house now," he said as he took her hand and began to climb the stairs, "but stay behind me anyway."

"Why don't you think anyone's here?"

"Because, as long as we've been back, either he'd have taken some action or we'd have heard something." That wasn't necessarily true, but for now he was counting on it.

Emma realized he was trying to reassure her, but she didn't overlook the way he kept close to the wall as they climbed and encouraged her to do the same.

There was little light at the top of the stairs. All the doors were closed, shutting out the last of the evening sun. When Gage flipped the wall switch, yellow light cascaded from the overhead fixtures.

The hall was L-shaped, and Gage led her swiftly past the closed door of his bedroom on one side and the closed door of the bathroom on the other. Rounding the corner, he headed for the bedroom at the very back of the house. There he opened the door slowly and peered in. Nothing in sight. The bed concealed nothing; stripped of any concealing fabrics, even the shadows beneath it were in plain view. A hazy golden evening light filled the room, brightening it. Gage drew Emma in with him and kept her to one side while he investigated the walk-in closet.

"Nothing," he said.

"This was my parents' room when I was little," Emma remarked. It seemed so barren and empty now, she thought a little sadly. She hated to come up here, because every time she did, she remembered when it had been decorated in the bright, primary colors her mother had so loved. "No one has been in here,'' she said with conviction. ''Whatever it is that caused me to feel uneasy in my bedroom isn't here.''

''Maybe he didn't come upstairs at all, then. Maybe he found out what he wanted to know in your room.''

Emma raised troubled eyes to his. ''Maybe,'' she agreed.

''Let's check the other rooms to be safe.''

The next two rooms were the same, empty, barren of anything except Emma's memories of her childhood and her brother. The front bedroom, the one Gage had taken as his, had always been the guest room.

It was there they found the evidence that someone had indeed been in the house.

The bottom drawer of the dresser was open, one side tugged out a little farther than the other. On the floor beside it lay the heap of jockstraps Gage had intended to deter Emma from snooping. And there, in plain sight, lay the item he had been hiding. A word escaped him on an anguished breath, a word that might have been a curse or a prayer.

Emma's breath stuck in her throat as she saw the framed color photograph. Gage—a younger, dark-haired, unscarred Gage—looked up proudly from a position behind two grinning little girls and a woman who held an infant. Beyond any shadow of a doubt, this was Gage's lost family.

For an endless moment Emma thought she would never breathe again. Pain seemed to swallow her, reminding her that he had lost what she would never have. His heart had gone to the grave with this woman and his children, and even if it hadn't…

Somehow she took a breath, and then another. Her heart began to beat again, a painful, throbbing rhythm of loss and compassion. Turning, she looked at Gage and saw the stark agony of his expression as he looked down at the photo.

And then something in his face stiffened, and his shoulders straightened. He looked at Emma. ''I'm calling in the crime-scene team.''

"For an open drawer?" For a violation of his privacy, his sanctuary, his grief? "What will they do?"

"Ransack this place looking for fingerprints or anything else."

"Oh. But I didn't notice anything else—"

Gage interrupted. "Emma, that man didn't come in here just to drag out a photograph of my family. He wanted something. We need to find out what."

Three hours later the last of the sheriff's crime-scene team trailed out the door. They'd found what the intruder had come for, and now Emma stood in her living room, staring blindly at the Christmas tree and trying not to think about the crude doll they had found hanging in its branches. A voodoo doll, badly mutilated, with unmistakably red hair. And no fingerprints. Not a one but hers and Gage's.

Shuddering, she flipped the switch and turned off all the lights. She hadn't seen Gage in the last hour, and suddenly she needed desperately to see him. He made her feel incredibly safe even when he was trying to keep her at a distance.

Thinking he must still be upstairs, she climbed wearily and turned into his open bedroom. He was there, standing by his dresser, looking down at the open drawer that held the photo of his family, a photo now dusted with black fingerprint powder. Her whole damn house was covered with the stuff, but this disturbed her as the rest didn't. It upset her, somehow, to see Gage's memories of his family tangled up in her mess.

Coming to stand beside him, she looked down at the photo. And then some instinct seized her, driving her to bend and lift the photograph into the light where it belonged. Gently, she dusted the black powder away with her sleeve and set it on the dresser.

For a minute, perhaps longer, there was no sound in the room save Gage's ragged breathing as he tried to absorb his own pain.

"They're beautiful," Emma said finally, the words painful on her lips. "Your wife was lovely. So pretty."

He said nothing, but she heard him stop breathing.

"And your daughters," she continued gently, "look so much like you. How old is your son in this picture?"

She thought he might not answer, that he might be so locked in his grief that he didn't even hear her.

But then, every syllable rusty, he answered in a low voice. "Two weeks. Just two weeks."

"You must have been so happy. So proud."

"We were." But suddenly he turned toward Emma, recognizing that his loss was not the only sorrow in this room. She was looking at the portrait, staring fixedly as if she could grow used to what it implied. And then her gaze lowered to the drawer, to the stacks of photo albums he kept but was never able to look at.

"You must hurt so badly," she whispered unsteadily. "So badly."

"I was lucky," he said, in that instant realizing the truth of it. The understanding was suddenly there as if it had always been there, feeling as if he had known it all along. "I was luckier than most people ever get to be."

Jerkily, Emma lifted her head and looked up at him. "Lucky?"

"It didn't last long," he said roughly. "Just seven years. But for seven years I had it all, Emma. I had it *all*. Some people don't ever get even half that much."

Like her, Emma thought, turning her attention back to the picture.

Like her, Gage thought, her loss piercing him as violently as his own had. All of a sudden he was very much in the present and the past was very much in the past. Emma was here, in need of things he didn't know if he could give her. But there was one thing he could definitely give her, one thing that would drive reality away for a little while. One thing that would make her forget her own sorrows. Reaching out, he took the photo and put it back in the bottom drawer. Then he shut the drawer and straightened, facing Emma.

"Come here," he said. Before she could object, he pulled her into his arms and bent his head until his mouth was pressed to her ear. "I want to make love to you," he whispered hoarsely and felt a ripple of response pass through her as she caught her breath. "I want to kiss you all over, taste you all over. I want to feel you come alive beneath my hands, and I want to come alive beneath yours."

Each word set a spark loose in Emma, and together they ignited a conflagration. Her emotions soared from sorrow to passion in an instant, and a shiver of hunger ripped through her, driving everything beyond the moment into a dark dungeon where it belonged.

"Stay here," he said raggedly. "Right here. I just want to make sure everything is locked up. Wait for me, Emma. Promise."

She opened heavy-lidded eyes and met his intense, stormy gaze. "I promise," she said huskily. "I promise."

He checked to make sure all the doors and windows were locked before he rejoined her in his bedroom. Native caution, learned from hard years on the streets and in the DEA, wouldn't let him forget such details.

Assured that the house was as secure as it could be, he stepped into his bedroom and caught his breath.

The yellowing shades held the night at bay, and she had turned on the bedside lamp. Her jeans made a dark puddle on the floor, a puddle topped by her sweater. Emma lay waiting for him in navy blue lace and satin, in a camisole and bikini panties that were an incitement, an enticement, he hadn't expected from her.

"God, Emma!" He drank her in with eyes that felt starved. "Did I tell you how lovely you are?"

Those were his hormones talking, she told herself, but her skin flushed under the warmth of his gaze, and she felt herself beginning to smile and relax, even as a deeper tension began to grow at her center.

His black sweater, jeans and briefs quickly joined the heap on the floor. He came down on his side next to her, propping himself on his elbow so that he could fill himself with the sight of her. She had freed her hair for him, and he wasn't shy about scooping up handfuls of it and sifting it through his fingers.

"Like fire," he whispered huskily. "Sweet, sweet fire...ah, Emma..."

At last, at long last, his mouth settled on hers. She was thirsty for him, thirsty for his taste and touch and smell and feel. It hadn't been that many hours since they had risen from her bed, but Emma felt as if she had spent months in a desert.

Her arms closed snugly around him, holding him as he needed to be held, as she needed to hold him. Her palms settled on the scars on his back, feeling the shiny smoothness of the grafts, the ridges of the keloids. A map of his pain and loss, she thought, and felt a wild, almost agonizing need to comfort him somehow, some way.

"Tighter, Emma...oh, God, tighter..."

So she tightened her arms until they began to ache, holding him as if she could squeeze the pain away. His tongue plunged deeply into her mouth, taking possession of her with a hunger that revealed a need far beyond simple wanting.

And she needed him every bit as desperately. The aching, yearning need went deeper than anything physical could have. She loved him, and loving him, she needed him more than she needed to breathe.

"Gage...oh, Gage..." She was incapable of silence, yet unable to say anything but his name. When his mouth closed over her breast, through the satin, she arched upward, begging for more. When he gripped her wrist and drew her hand down to his aching manhood, she curled her fingers around him greedily and relished his smooth, hard heat.

A husky laugh, almost a groan, escaped Gage suddenly, and he moved away from the breathtaking, maddening inexperience of her touch. Suddenly her arms were caught above her head, held easily in one of his large hands. Startled, she opened her eyes and looked up at him.

"You make me crazy," he told her. There was an astonishing warmth in his gray-green eyes, in the faint smile that tugged the corners of his mouth upward.

"Good," she said breathlessly.

"It's good, all right. But things happen too fast that way. I want to go slow. Easy. I want to take my time with you."

She thought she would never breathe again. Every inch of her responded to the lazy promise in his voice, his words, his eyes. Last night had been cast in a web of complex emotions, she realized, colored by so many things from outside. This time it was going to be simple. There were no shadows in Gage's eyes right now, no glimpse of the chilly wastes of hell. All she could see was heat. He was totally absorbed in the moment, totally awake to the sexuality that was steaming between them. For this little while, Gage Dalton wasn't going to be anything at all except Emmaline Conard's lover.

The understanding kicked her heart into overdrive and caused white heat to pour through her veins.

"This blue is a great color for you, Em," Gage said quietly. He continued to hold her arms above her head, but now his free hand came to rest on her satin-covered midriff, halfway between her breasts and her thighs. The touch seemed to shoot sparks through her. "It makes your skin look so creamy I want to lick it. But not yet."

Not yet. Instead he trailed a fingertip up the valley between her breasts and smiled as she undulated helplessly in response. "I want to touch you, Em," he said huskily.

"Touch me," she begged breathlessly.

"Where?" He looked up at her, a wicked sparkle in his gray-green gaze. Hell's own archangel was out on a weekend pass, and he was in a mood to play devilish games.

She caught her breath, and then a soft, whispery laugh escaped her. "Oh, Gage…you know I can't say those things.…"

"No? Why not?" His finger trailed slowly up the side of one breast, causing her nipple to harden visibly beneath the dark blue satin. He came close, but he didn't touch the pouting peak. "You want me to do it, don't you? Why is it so hard to say it out loud?"

He was teasing, she thought, catching the gleam in his eyes even as her own internal drumbeat was slowly drowning out the sounds of reason. Helpless to prevent it, she felt her hips arch upward in a search for release. He'd hardly even touched her, yet she was already losing her sanity.

"How am I supposed to know how to please you if you don't tell me?" he asked softly. Slowly, ever so achingly slowly, he ran his fingertip around her swollen nipple, never quite giving her the touch she was needing more desperately by the instant. Emma shivered, and a small moan escaped her, causing Gage to smile. It was a gentle smile, an expression so tender that it pierced her desire and made her throat ache.

"Touch me," she whispered hoarsely. "Touch my breast."

"Yes, Emma," he said just as hoarsely. "Anything you want." He slipped his hand up beneath the satin and cupped her warm flesh with his. Carefully he caught her nipple between his fingers and tugged. Emma arched like a drawn bow. "Whatever pleases you," he murmured hoarsely just before his mouth covered hers and his tongue stroked roughly against hers.

Emma felt as if she were drowning, drowning in his heat, his scent, his touch, his sheer masculinity. All her life she had read of such feelings, but until now she had never experienced them. She had never dreamed how wonderful a man's differences could be, how much pleasure it could give her to feel hair-roughened skin against her, how exciting it could be to feel his hardness against her softness. And then he released her hands.

Led by instinct, compelled by need, she began to explore him with her hands. Everywhere her fingers wandered they found hard, lean muscle sheathed in warm, resilient flesh. Her

throat began to ache again, this time with appreciation of
Gage's vitality. With wonder that he was sharing it with her.
With awe for life and its miracles.

He dragged his mouth from hers and then leaned down to
give her swollen lips a gentle lick with his tongue. "I need
you, Emma," he said on a ragged breath as he tugged her
camisole over her head.

Her breasts tightened even more as cool air brushed across
them. Bowing his head, Gage lapped at a taut nipple. Emma
groaned deeply and arched upward, forgetting about awe as
need swamped her.

"Oh, that's good, Emma." His praise was rough, ragged,
hardly more than a groan of approval. "Your breasts are so
pretty...so sweet...." He gave himself over completely to
Emma's pleasure, and in so doing he answered a need he had
only just now recognized. It was a need to drive the shadows
from this woman's eyes, a need to bring her something good
and beautiful. A need to give himself to her.

"Oh, Emma, sweetheart..." He licked and sucked and nib-
bled as if he, too, felt the pleasure he was giving her. Low in
her belly, the knot of need tightened and grew heavier, a pressure that desperately needed an answering pressure.

"Touch me," she whispered. "Please...touch me...."

"Where, baby? Where?"

Desperate, she grabbed his hand and drew it downward,
pressing it snugly against her satin-covered mound. "Gage..."
His name ended on a rising note, a plea.

"Yes...oh, baby...yes..."

Her panties vanished, tugged impatiently away, and then his
hand was on her, slipping across the aching nub and plunging
sweetly into her heated depths. With a cry Emma bucked upward, and Gage groaned.

"Tell me," he urged as his tongue swirled around her ear
and sent another shiver running through her. "Tell me...."

But she was past telling, and he was rapidly getting past the
point of listening. Again and again she rolled upward against

his hand, telling him with her body that it was good, so good, but not enough. Not nearly enough.

The world spun dizzily, and Emma suddenly realized she was above Gage, straddling him. Before the shift could shatter her mood and bring her back to sharp-edged reality, he lifted her and drove himself deeply into her. Oh, so deeply. She caught her breath as pleasure clenched her in its vise.

"Ride me, Red," he commanded hoarsely. "Ride me."

He had warned her that he was coarse, but neither of them had imagined she would like it. And she did like it. The blunt, unvarnished command sent thrills racing through her and moved her far beyond the cloak of inhibition or the reluctance of embarrassment.

Bracing herself with her hands on his powerful shoulders, she began to move, wringing every bit of pleasure she could from them both.

She rode him, hard. All the way to the stars.

"I may never move again."

Gage's muffled words brought a smile to Emma's lips. She tried to wiggle off his chest, but his arms tightened, refusing to release her. As soon as he felt her relax onto him, he ran his hands downward over her silky back and cupped her soft, round rump. For a moment he pressed her closer. It was a hug, a reminder and a promise, all in one.

"I should make dinner," Emma said, partly because her conscience was pricking her, and partly because she wanted him to object.

He objected. "Forget it. If we get hungry we'll eat cookies. Are you hungry?"

Only for you. She swallowed the words before they could spill over her lips and tell him what he had come to mean to her. Time, she thought, was irrelevant. In one short week she had come to know Gage better than many of the people she saw daily. It wasn't, after all, how many facts you knew about someone that told you the kind of person they were. "No, I'm not hungry,'' she answered lazily. ''We'll be starved later, though.''

''We'll worry about it then. I want you to stay right where you are.'' He squeezed her rump again, gently, and then tugged a blanket upward, covering them both.

''I'm heavy.''

''Not that heavy, Red. It feels good to have you all over me like this.''

It felt good to sprawl all over him like this, she admitted. Questions hovered in the wings, unspoken fears and the shadow of inevitable loss lurked right outside this cocoon, but she refused to acknowledge any of them. These stolen moments were *hers,* and they would have to last her the rest of her life. She absolutely wouldn't let anything take them from her.

But just as she had that defiant thought, the phone rang downstairs.

''No,'' she mumbled when she felt Gage stiffen.

''I have to, Em. It might be Nate.'' He brushed a kiss on her forehead. ''I'll come right back.''

Sighing, she slid off him and watched as he grabbed his briefs and yanked them on. Wearing nothing else, he trotted from the room.

Lying on her back, Emma stared at the ceiling and tried to pay attention to nothing but how good she felt right now. How beautiful and cherished Gage had made her feel. How every muscle in her body felt as if it was warm and relaxed. Unfortunately, it didn't work.

She told herself that she was prepared to pay the inevitable price of loving Gage, that she was living in a fool's paradise with complete awareness that it was just that. He would move on and she would be alone again, and she would deal with it when it happened. She could handle it, she told herself, and not for anything would she have missed the magic he had given her. Hell's own archangel had spun a fantasy of sparkling sensations and jeweled emotions for her, and the price for that would be her heart. She could handle it. She *would* handle it. And she would never regret it.

But as she lay there alone, waiting for him, the shadows moved closer, reminding her that there was a price. The chill crept into her glow, and sorrow tinged her joy.

The door opened, and Gage approached the bed. Emma found his black briefs incredibly sexy. In fact, every line of him was incredibly sexy, from his broad shoulders to his narrow flanks to his muscular legs. Until this very moment she had never guessed a man could have great legs.

Gage sat beside her and smiled crookedly when her hand rose to dive into the dark swirls of his soft chest hair.

"Was it Nate?" she asked throatily.

"Nope." His smile faded. "It was a breather."

"Breather?" Her hand stilled, and her eyes rose to his face.

"You know, one of those people who calls and then just listens."

"Oh! Oh, I've had a couple of those calls."

"You have?" He frowned. "Emma, you should have told me."

"Why? Could you do anything? Of course not." She gave him a smile that didn't quite reach her eyes. "It's probably some kid I yelled at in the library."

His frown deepened. "It could also be the person who's been pulling all these other stunts. The one who was in here tonight."

She didn't want to think about that. She didn't want to think about that horrible doll or the hate its creation implied. "Gage, he can't hurt me over the telephone."

He shook his head, as if despairing, and then sighed heavily. "No, I guess not. But, Emma, he's escalating. Surely you've noticed."

"Yes." She closed her eyes, and the hand that rested on his chest knotted into a fist. "I've noticed. But what the hell can I do about it, Gage? You tell me. I don't know who he is. I can't hide, I can't run, I can't get even. I just have to wait and count on you being here if he comes after me. There's not one other thing I can do about it! Oh, Lord..."

Gage scooped her up from the pillows and pulled her against his chest. She burrowed into his shoulder and drew a shuddering breath.

"I'll be here, Emma," he said. It was a vow.

The good spell ended during the night. After several days of relatively moderate pain, Gage awoke in the fiery grip of agony. A groan escaped him before he could swallow it, and then he forced himself to lie there facedown and accept his suffering. It was his due, after all, a purgatory of the body to match the damnation of his soul.

"Hell!" The exclamation escaped him on a breath as a fresh spear thrust through his back and into his leg. He should get up. Walk. But he couldn't leave Emma alone. Didn't dare leave her alone. Couldn't risk her getting hurt.

Couldn't risk losing her.

The realization was like a blinding shaft of nuclear heat in the barren wastes of his soul. *Couldn't risk losing her?* Oh, God, he didn't *deserve* her. She wouldn't want him for long. He was so scarred, so damaged, so...ruined. So afflicted with his losses that he didn't seem capable of living for tomorrow. What woman would want that?

No, he didn't deserve her. Didn't deserve her sweetness, her light, her warmth, her caring. Because he had failed his family.

But he wouldn't fail Emma. No, he would be there when she needed him to protect her. That determination kept him glued to the bed when he might have found some relief by rising and walking. Kept him firmly pinned to the mattress when the cold oblivion of the winter night beckoned him with the promise of solitude and miles of empty streets.

It was crazy, he thought, to feel that his body's suffering somehow atoned for what had happened to his wife and children. Even his former boss had taken him to task for his belief that he was somehow responsible for what had happened to Jan and the children.

"If you have to blame someone," Cal had argued vehemently, "blame that damn fool cop who let your real name slip to Joe Valenza. Blame the guy who built the bomb. Blame the guy who wired it to your car. But don't blame yourself for trying to do what was right!"

Cal was right. Intellectually, Gage recognized it. But his aching heart and frozen soul weren't as amenable to logic. It sounded stupid to admit he felt responsible for what had happened. It sounded incredibly egotistical, when he thought about it. He had done nothing that several thousand other agents didn't do daily. It had simply been his misfortune to send Val Valenza up the river. If Gage Dalton hadn't done it, some other agent sure as hell would have. And some other agent would have found a bomb wired to *his* car. The chances of the game. Period.

But if he hadn't been an agent...

That was the thought that haunted him. If he had been an electrician or a carpenter or a pharmacist, Jan and the kids would still be alive.

Maybe. If some other chance of the game hadn't gotten them. A car accident. A tornado. A loony like the one who seemed to be after Miss Emma.

Smothering another groan, he turned his head to one side and tried to make her out in the dark. She was there. He could hear her soft breathing, could feel her warmth like a radiance that warmed his frozen places. She deserved better than Gage Dalton. Much better.

But he wasn't able to resist her, he admitted. The sexual tension that crackled between them would have overwhelmed a stronger man than he. And the other things—her gentleness, her caring, her kindness—those things overwhelmed him even more. She had pierced his solitude and poured warm balm over some of his rawest places. She had made him start to feel that maybe it was okay that he was alive. That maybe life would be worth living again. That maybe he was worth something.

He needed her. He needed Emma in ways that had absolutely nothing to do with the incendiary sexual attraction he felt for her. Another chasm was opening in his spirit, another place that would ever afterward be empty.

Because surely Emma could not want to fill it.

A searing razor of pain slashed through his back and startled a soft moan from him. Beside him, Emma stirred.

"Gage?" she asked drowsily.

"It's okay, Emma," he whispered roughly. "Go back to sleep."

She turned slowly onto her side and reached out a hand, finding his naked shoulder with her fingertips. "Do you hurt?"

"Yeah. Nothing unusual. Go back to sleep."

For several moments she remained still, her fingertips warm and motionless on his shoulder. Just as he began to believe she had gone back to sleep, she stirred again.

"Your back?" Her voice was soft, thick with sleep.

"Just the usual, Em. Honey, just go back to sleep."

"I like that," she murmured.

"What do you like?"

"When you call me honey."

"Aw, hell," he sighed, beginning to realize that he was well and truly lost. She liked him to call her honey. Not one week ago she'd hollered because he'd called her Emma. Too familiar, she had thought. And he had answered that calling her "honey" would be familiar.

He sighed again, this time less from reluctance to face what was happening between them than from yearning. "How about sweetheart? Do you mind if I call you that?" Because he sure as hell would like to. *Sweetheart.* He'd never wanted to call anyone that, not even Jan. But that was how he felt about Emma. The admission cost him some savage twinges of conscience, but after a moment they eased, leaving him to face the future unimpeded.

''Yes,'' she whispered. ''I'd like that. If you meant it.''

He caught his breath, trying to absorb the emotional impact of what she had just told him. He didn't dare answer, he realized. If he answered, he would tell her the truth, and then she would feel obligated to stay with him. He didn't want soft words and promises made in the warm, sleepy intimacy of a bed in the middle of the night. If ever, if *ever,* he was to take Emma into his life, he had to be sure she was going into it in the bright light of day. That she saw his flaws and his scars, and still thought him worthy.

Emma didn't wait for him to answer. She didn't really expect him to. She wasn't a woman any man would ever call sweetheart, and she knew it.

But Gage hurt, and she cared deeply that he did. Throwing back the quilt, she rose and straddled him as he lay on his stomach.

''Emma?''

''Shh. You need a little rubdown.''

Her small hands settled into the small of his back and began to knead strongly, finding the knots and kinks instinctively. Another groan escaped Gage, but this time it was one of absolute relief.

''Ah, God, that's good....'' he moaned. ''Oh, Em...''

''Shh...just relax. Just let me...''

It was so marvelous, she thought, to feel free to do this. Even one day ago, she wouldn't have dared touch him without invitation. Now here she sat, buck naked herself, on his naked thighs while her fingers dug into him.

She could feel the knots in his muscles, almost rocklike in their hardness. ''Is it cramping that causes the pain?'' she asked presently.

''Some of it.'' Oh, man, she had magic fingers, he thought as knot after knot gradually dissolved. ''Some of it is from damaged nerves.''

''Is this helping?''

"Sweetheart," he said, giving up the battle against himself, "it's heaven."

The endearment settled on her like fairy dust, bringing enchantment to the night, into these precious moments of intimacy. Leaning forward, she pressed a kiss on Gage's back between his shoulder blades, then straightened and resumed the massage.

"Your hands must be getting tired," he murmured.

"Just a little." She was enjoying this too much to quit, despite the cramping of her fingers. It was rare, she thought, so rare, that one person could give another this kind of caring. Her life had been barren of such things for so long now. Too long. She needed someone to love, to worry over, to look after, to care for. Without that, life became a meaningless progression of days.

In the past week her entire life had changed—for the better, she thought. She looked forward to coming home from work in the evenings, knowing Gage would be there. Just being able to share a meal, or relate the day's doings, was a joy.

And now, now she had experienced an intimacy with him that she knew she would always crave, would always miss when it was gone. If only he wouldn't go. If only he would stay and make her part of his life. But what could she possibly offer him that he would want?

Suddenly Gage reached behind him and caught one of her hands. "Come here, Emma," he said softly. "Come here."

When she was stretched out beside him, he caught her hands in his and began to rub them gently. "You'll be sore tomorrow," he muttered. "Your hands aren't used to doing that."

Then, in turn, he lifted each hand to his lips and pressed a kiss in each palm.

Emma caught her breath. "Gage..."

"Hush," he said quietly. Wrapping her in his strong arms, he drew her into the welcoming curve of his body and settled her head on his shoulder. "My back feels a whole lot better now, sweetheart. A whole lot better." He kissed her gently on the temple and smoothed her hair with his hand. "Sleep now, Emma. Sleep."

Sleep carried her away slowly. As she spiraled down into its depths, feeling warm and cared for, she wondered why no one had ever realized that a white knight didn't have to be white. He could be dark. A dark angel. Archangel.

Turning her head drowsily, her last conscious effort was to drop a soft kiss on his smooth, warm shoulder.

Gage felt the kiss. He felt it to the very core of his being. Long after Emma dropped off, he stared into the teeth of the night and wondered why the hell he should have to give her up.

Or if he really did have to.

Chapter 13

Monday morning brought sunshine to Conard County. The fresh layers of snow lay like pristine blankets over everything, but the sun was warm, the air was calm and Christmas was only a week away.

Gage pondered that as he drove Emma to the library and personally escorted her to her desk. He needed to find something to give her, he thought. Something special. Something memorable. Because suddenly he couldn't stand the thought of Emma having a Christmas without one precious memory to store up.

"Promise me you won't go anywhere alone," he said as he helped her out of her parka.

"I promise." For the umpteenth time in the last half hour. His edginess was beginning to make her edgy, too. "Gage, I'm just going to be sitting here at this desk the way I do five days of every week. I *can't* go anywhere, because I get paid to be *here*."

"Okay." He was being ridiculously overprotective. He knew it, but he couldn't help it. You couldn't suffer the losses he had suffered and ever again be entirely comfortable with the safety of someone you cared about. No way. "I'll pick you up for lunch at one."

"I'll be ready." She would be, too. Even though she was pretending impatience, she loved every bit of his concern for her. Where once there was only a cold bleakness in his gaze, she now saw warmth. How could anyone dislike that?

"Okay." Bending, he gave her a quick, hard kiss on her mouth. "Look out, Miss Emma. I'm already hungry for you again. By tonight I'll be crazy with it."

Emma blushed profusely, but she laughed. "Me, too," she managed to admit softly. This kind of frankness was new to her, but she thought she liked it.

Gage astonished her with a broad, warm smile, a smile unlike any he had ever given her. It was a young smile, the smile of a happy man. Emma caught her breath and watched as her silver-haired archangel pivoted and strode from the library.

The report of Emma's assault was waiting on Gage's desk when he reached his office. The Express Mail envelope was still sealed, preserving her privacy.

From everyone but him.

He was reluctant to invade her privacy, even though it wasn't really an invasion. He was a police investigator working on a case, and that meant he had to look beyond every closed door and curtained window in search of information that could be useful. Still, he hesitated. His personal relationship with Emma complicated the ethics of things, but it was more than that, he realized after a moment. Much more.

He didn't want to know what had happened to her. He didn't want to read the callous, jargon-laden descriptions of every detail. He didn't want to read the cold, feelingless report of an event that had wounded Emma so terribly.

It had happened ten years ago, but for Gage, learning this all for the first time, it was going to be fresh. It was going to be today. Deep inside himself, he knew he was going to feel a rage unequaled by any except the rage he had felt over the loss of his family. He knew he was going to suffer a fresh agonizing wound.

But he had to know. He had to know in case there was an overlooked clue. He had to know because Emma was remembering, and somebody in this godforsaken world had to understand the things she wouldn't be able to say.

He opened the envelope.

The photocopies of the police file made a thick stack. At the top was the initial report detailing the discovery of Emma in a trash bin in an alley behind a bar. One of the cooks at the bar had evidently noticed something suspicious in the alley and called to report a prowler. When the police arrived, they found no prowler, but a sound from the bin had drawn their attention. Investigating, they had found Emma. The cook was unable to tell them a thing about the man he had seen except that he was large, heavily bundled in dark winter clothing, and his hair had been concealed by a stocking cap. Not one useful thing.

Following were several pages devoted to the fruitless questioning of others who had been in the area at about the right time. Then came page upon page of medical reports detailing Emma's injuries. Nineteen stab wounds. Countless small burn marks, presumably from a cigarette. A star fracture of the skull resulting from a blow by a blunt instrument. Surgery to remove a clot on the brain. Other operations to repair the damage caused by the stab wounds. Two separate operations to repair shattered bone in one arm. Eventually a hysterectomy resulting directly from sepsis of one of the stab wounds. No evidence of sexual assault.

That was truly odd, Gage thought. This type of violent crime against a woman usually involved sexual assault, as well. Ignoring the way his hands were shaking, he turned to the report by the forensic psychiatrist who had been asked to profile the crime and perpetrator. There was little there that Gage hadn't read before, but one thing stuck out: the psychiatrist believed the perpetrator had been startled before he had fulfilled his intentions, had stabbed her in an attempt to kill her immediately, and then had dumped her. Emma was most likely alive only because her attacker had panicked.

The file closed on the note that the victim, upon recovering consciousness, was unable to recall the events of that night.

Rage shook Gage, every bit as strong as he had expected and then some. He couldn't stand the thought of anyone treating Emma that way, the thought of anyone hurting her that way. He would have loved to smash something, anything, to give vent to some of his anger, but in the end it wouldn't help at all.

But he couldn't meet Emma for lunch. Not with what he had just read so fresh in his mind. Not when he was so furious he needed to destroy something. He reached for the phone and called her.

"Conard County Public Library. Emmaline Conard speaking."

Even the sound of her voice over the telephone affected him, he realized almost ruefully. Sexy. Sweet. Warm. "Sweetheart, it's Gage."

"Oh, hi!" A smile was suddenly apparent in her voice. "Did you forget to give me some warning or other? Or did you overlook a promise you want me to give?"

Her teasing warmed him, and he felt a silly, cockeyed smile grow on his face, driving his anger back into a darker place. "There're all kinds of promises I want," he growled laughingly. "We'll get to those later. About lunch…something came up…."

"Oh."

Damn, she sounded disappointed. But he couldn't face her, not yet. Not for an hour of pretending to be cheerful over lunch. He needed time to cope with his anger and his knowledge of what had happened to her. "Listen, I'll have Sara bring something over for you and keep you company. She'll be thrilled to get away from the front desk."

"Sure, that would be great. I haven't really had a chance to talk to her in weeks. One o'clock?"

"I'll have her call if that's not a good time."

But Sara thought it was a great time. She eyed Gage a little curiously when he suggested she stand in for him, but she didn't comment. But then, Sara seldom offered an opinion about the stupid things other people did, at least, not apart from her job as a deputy.

"Sure," she said, accepting Gage's suggestion amiably. "Emma and I can compare notes about you. That's always fun."

Gage paused in the midst of turning back to his office. "Compare notes?" He caught a gleam in Sara's brown eyes.

"Yeah," she said with a shrug. "Girl talk, you know? Whether you or Ed has the best buns in the department... Well, maybe we ought to consider Micah, too...."

Gage took a threatening step toward her, which sent her off into a peal of laughter. Smothering his own reluctant smile, he headed back to his office.

Micah showed up moments after Sara left. Marriage agreed with the big Indian, Gage thought as he watched Micah, ordinarily taciturn, joke lazily with Velma and Nate. Gage had only known him for a few months, but even he could see the new relaxation and quiet happiness in that harsh face.

"What's happening with the mutilations?" Micah asked Gage finally.

"Things are getting complicated. Come on back and I'll tell you about it."

Micah and Nate both followed him back, bearing mugs of coffee with them. In Gage's office they settled on chairs while he closed the door and rounded his desk. As briefly as possible, Gage and Nate brought Micah up to date on the events of the past week, including the several things that had happened to Miss Emma. And now, because it was relevant to the case, Gage gave Micah a bare-bones account of the Laramie attack on Miss Emma. Gage didn't know whether to be relieved or disappointed when Micah leaped to the same conclusion linking Emma and the cattle mutilations at the Cumberland ranch. He might have felt easier about Emma's safety if Micah hadn't also felt that the mutilator might be after her, but then, he might also have simply become more worried.

"It would take the same kind of mind, I guess," Micah said. He accepted the psychological profile of Emma's attacker from Gage and scanned it quickly. "Well, hell," he muttered. "What kind of blood was it in that pentagram on her driveway?"

"I was just about to call the lab to see if they've reached any conclusion."

"I'll do that," Nate said. "You fill Micah in on the story about Don Fenster torturing a dog. And that reminds me, I was going to pull Fenster's rap sheet for you."

As Gage told the deputy how Emma had creamed Don Fenster for abusing a dog all those years ago, Micah's brow lowered in a scowl.

"Yeah," he said. "Yeah. There could be a connection. It's sure as hell the only possibility we've got. Maybe we ought to make a little visit to the Fenster place."

"Without a warrant?"

Micah smiled faintly. "I've never needed a warrant to go anyplace I've wanted to go. Never."

Gage returned the smile with a small one of his own. "Not exactly admissible evidence."

"We can get a warrant," Nate said, startling them both as he rejoined them. "Your friend at the lab says the blood on Emma's driveway appears to match that last mutilated steer we found. They're running confirmatory tests right now."

Gage swore. Adrenaline pumped through him in a sudden surge, bringing him to his feet, creating a need to act. "That settles the little-green-men question."

"Easy, Gage," Nate said. "Fenster might seem obvious, but it could be someone else—although, I have to admit, I can't think of anyone nearly as likely off the top of my head. Anyhow, we need to explore possibilities here. Knowing there's a link helps, but—"

Gage interrupted. "Walt Severn told me Fenster has a bunch of his friends staying out there with him. 'Creeps' was the word he used."

Nate appeared struck. "Friends. Creeps. A cult?"

"That's what I'm wondering. Walt said they've been living off the old lady for months."

"I can sure as hell look into it," Micah said. "Quietly. See if there's anything to it."

Nate was beginning to nod; he knew Micah's capacity to pass over the landscape like a wraith, invisible to anyone who didn't know where to look.

Just then Gage's extension buzzed. He picked up the receiver. "What is it, Velma?" he said to the dispatcher.

"Sara just radioed, Gage. Miss Emma's gone from the library, and no one knows where she got to."

Her car was still in the lot behind the building. Mr. Craig had been there all morning, but he confessed he had fallen asleep behind the stacks and hadn't heard or noticed a thing. Emma's assistant, Linda, wasn't scheduled to show up until two o'clock, so that meant Emma's disappearance had left the library unattended. And no one believed Miss Emma would have done that by choice.

Standing on the steps of the library, Gage looked up the street through the gray lace of leafless trees, across the blindingly white snow, out toward the edge of town. Toward the vast barrenness of the wintry landscape.

Such a bright, beautiful day. Once before, on a day like this, he had lost everything. Today, faced with Emma's disappearance, realization struck him like a spear in the chest. Somehow, some way, she had become his life. She had become everything that mattered. And he was losing everything all over again.

"Son." Nate's gravelly growl hauled Gage back. "You and Micah head on out to the Fenster place. I'll have a warrant in my hands before you get there. Check in before you set foot on his property, though. I'll let you know what we're doing to support you.''

Gage didn't doubt for a minute that Nate would get the warrant. Everybody in Conard County owed Nathan Tate a few favors. He gave a short, sharp nod and headed down the steps. Micah caught up with him.

''We'll take my unit,'' Micah said. ''I've got an arsenal stashed in the back.''

As they sped away from town, Micah at the wheel, Gage squeezed his eyes shut against the painful beauty of the day and prayed for the first time since his world had blown up in his face. He prayed they weren't headed in the wrong direction—what did they have to go on except some farfetched conclusions?—prayed they wouldn't be too late, prayed Emma wasn't as terrified as she must be, that she hadn't been hurt.

There had been little in his life to persuade him that heaven ever listened, but Miss Emmaline Conard, with her gentle nature and caring heart, had taught him that heaven existed. Even an archangel from hell recognized it when he was faced with it.

Micah offered no false assurances, didn't even seek to distract him with aimless conversation. Micah understood what he was going through, down to the smallest twinge of conscience and the largest stab of fear. He just kept driving, a little too fast, but with steady hands on the wheel.

Oh, God, Gage thought desperately. Dear God, don't let us be too late.

When Tam Tennyson came running into the library a little before one o'clock to tell Miss Emma that somebody had backed into her car, Emma had no cause to doubt him. Tam was one of her favorite children, a six-year-old with carroty hair and freckles. Emma never looked at him without envying the Tennysons.

"The man said he'll wait, Miss Emma. You gotta get the 'surance stuff.''

Emma supposed she did. She never imagined it was a subterfuge, not even when she recognized Don Fenster and a strange man standing beside the pickup that had backed into the side of her car. Tam ran off, back to whatever he'd been doing earlier, leaving her alone with the two men in the lot behind the building. It was then that she experienced a prickle of unease, but she promptly dismissed it. She was always feeling uneasy about something lately, and it was broad daylight, for goodness' sake!

"I dented your door, Miss Emma," Don Fenster said, speaking the first words he had spoken to her in nearly twenty years. Stepping aside, he gave her room to look.

Emma bent, surveying the damage, wondering only if she would be able to open and close the door now. Recognizing that Don could have driven off without letting her know he had hit her, she wanted to be fair. "Let's just see if it opens and closes all right, Don. If it does, we'll just forget—"

Before the last words left her mouth, a blanket was thrown over her head, muffling her outraged cry in thick, hot wool. Her hands were seized, and a cord was wrapped around them so tightly that it cut.

"Now you just shut up, woman," a strange voice growled. "You shut up, 'cause I'll hit you every time you squeak." He gave her a sharp cuff for good measure.

She was roughly shoved into a cold, confined place, probably the toolbox in the pickup bed, she thought as shock began to give way to terror.

Don Fenster. Oh, my God, it was Don Fenster. Memory crashed through her, casting her into a prison of horror so deep that everything else receded, like a pinprick of light that grew smaller and ever smaller.

Until the only thing that was left was the dark.

Micah keyed the microphone on his radio and told Velma to let Nate know he and Gage were in place, a half mile up the county road from Fenster's gate.

Velma acknowledged, and Micah clipped the mike to the collar of his jacket. "You got a radio?" he asked Gage.

"Yeah. In my Suburban."

Micah twisted and reached behind his seat. "Here. Take my spare."

"Thanks."

The sun had sunk low, casting golden and pink light across the rippled snow. It looked like a vast sea, Gage thought, all those open spaces with occasional islands of leafless cottonwoods or rocky upthrusts. And somewhere out there was Emma. God, if he ever got his arms around her again…

He drew a deep breath, forcing himself to be calm, battering down all the urgent impulses to act. For Emma's sake, he reminded himself, he had to keep a clear head and think his actions through. Last time he had been able to do nothing for those he loved, but this time he was in a position to help. In a position to redeem himself.

What a stupid idea, he thought. What did one have to do with the other?

Suddenly Nate's voice crackled over the radio, bursting abruptly out of the silence. "We got the warrant. Three units are already on their way to help you. The Tennyson kid evidently saw who took Miss Emma. It was definitely Don Fenster."

Gage released a breath he hadn't even been aware of holding. They had come to the right place.

"If you go in there by yourselves, you be damn careful," Nate cautioned. "Walt Severn says Fenster has five other guys staying with him. And if they're running some kind of weird cult, there's no telling how many other people might be involved."

Gage shifted impatiently but kept silent. He'd been dealing with superior officers for too many years to back-talk one now.

And, as usual, he would just go ahead and do whatever he felt was necessary.

Micah was evidently of similar mind. "We're going in, Nate. Miss Emma can't wait." With a click, he turned off the radio, then released the Blazer's brake.

"We're on our own," Micah remarked as they rolled forward toward Fenster's gate.

As they had been the night they rescued Faith Parish from her former husband, Gage thought. Hard to believe that had been only a month ago. Then, however, they had been up against only one man. This time they would face Fenster and an unknown number of his cronies.

"I recommend we drive in slowly and openly," he said to Micah. "As if it's just a routine call."

Micah nodded agreement. This was the hardest part of any lawman's job, going into a situation with almost no idea of what was waiting.

They turned onto Fenster's private road and passed beneath a weathered overhead sign that was totally illegible.

"Looks like this guy doesn't put out any more effort than he has to," Gage remarked.

"Nope."

Inside, tension was drawing Gage tight, and unanswerable questions kept trying to crowd everything else out of his mind. He couldn't afford to become distracted, and he certainly couldn't give in to his worry about Emma. His hands tightened into fists on his splayed thighs, and he kept his attention firmly fixed on his surroundings.

The Fenster house was invisible from the road, hidden by dips in the land, but as they came around a bend in the rutted track it came into view. Dilapidated, in need of a good scraping and a coat of paint, it looked forlorn, abandoned.

Fresh tire tracks passed by the house, heading for the barn several hundred yards behind it.

"That must be where she is," Gage said.

"Maybe. But maybe they put her in the house. Let's check it out."

Gage couldn't argue with that, but this was one time when patience seemed to be escaping him too rapidly for his own good. He wanted to tear the door down and race through the house at full tilt.

"Stay here, man," Micah said as he halted the Blazer right in front of the house. "Watch my back while I go to the door."

Gage opened his mouth to insist that he should go to the door, then realized that was a foolish demand. Micah was the uniformed deputy, and it would look a hell of a lot less suspicious for him to walk up to the door.

Gage climbed out of the Blazer and stood waiting while Micah crossed the few yards of snow to the front porch. When he reached the door, Micah lifted his fist and hammered on it in the time-honored way of cops everywhere. Nobody inside would be in the least doubt of who was at the door, and it was not a sound that could be ignored.

Micah had to hammer a second time, and by then Gage was uptight enough to gnaw his own bones. His back had begun hurting again, a fiery ache that pulsed like a steady hammer blow, but he hardly noticed it in his anxiety for Emma. Just let him get his hands on her again. Just let her be unharmed. He would never let her out of his sight again. He would protect her from harm for the rest of his days.

Finally, what seemed like aeons later, the door swung slowly open. In the shadowy depths of the house beyond Micah, Gage saw a small, very elderly woman, leaning unsteadily on a walker. She wore a flowered housecoat, and her hair was ratty and dirty looking. She simply looked up at Micah as if she didn't know what to make of him.

"Good afternoon, Miz Fenster," Micah said politely. "I'm Deputy Parish. I'm looking for a young woman who turned up missing this afternoon. You wouldn't happen to have seen anything unusual, would you?"

An endless time passed before the old woman's eyes blinked.

"Emma Conard," she said, in a voice as dry as ancient parchment. "Don hates her."

Gage tensed and stepped forward. Micah made an almost imperceptible movement, warning him back. "What do you know about Emma Conard, Miz Fenster?" he asked with surprising gentleness. "Can you help us find her?"

"It's those boys he hangs around with," Mrs. Fenster said, her eyes strangely bewildered, almost as if she wasn't sure who Micah was, or of what she was trying to say. "They're evil, all of them, and I've told Donny so many times to tell them to go, but he just tells me to shut up and go back to my room. But they're wicked. Wicked!"

"Emma Conard, Miz Fenster," Micah prompted gently. "What about Miss Emma?"

"I heard them," she said. "I heard them talking about how they were going to...do those terrible things to her. Like they did to the cows—"

"Do you know where she is?"

"In the barn. They took her to the barn." She looked up at Micah with a kind of sad bafflement. "Why didn't you come out here before? He took the phone out so I couldn't call you.... They're wicked...wicked...."

"How many are there?"

"Donny and four of his friends."

The few hundred yards seemed endless as Micah and Gage ran toward the barn. The growl of the Blazer's engine would have given them away, so after radioing Nate, they grabbed weapons and took off at a dead run. Micah cradled a shotgun in addition to the .45 strapped to his hip. Gage carried a second shotgun and a 9 mm Browning. The fresh vehicle tracks made a packed path that was easier to traverse than the deep snow to either side, but it was also more slippery, which impeded them a little. Gage suspected that not even dry ground could have given him the speed he wanted now.

Emma. Oh, God, please...

A litany of prayers and pleas ran through the background of

Gage's thoughts as he forced himself to focus on what they needed to do now. "Donny and four of his friends" meant that if Walt Severn had been correct, there was another one to worry about. One who might not be in the barn. One who might come upon Micah and Gage at an awkward time.

The shadows of the snow dunes had grown longer and bluer. Evening was fast approaching, and Gage welcomed its advent. Less light would be an advantage for him and Micah as they cased the situation.

The side of the barn they approached had no windows and only one small door in its side. Reluctant to chance being noticed if they opened that door even a crack, they split up, heading in opposite directions in search of some means to see inside. Gage came upon a window at one point, but it opened into a tack room that was empty, giving him no clue as to what the men in the barn were up to. It would be a good way to get inside, though, once they had an idea of where their quarry was located.

On the far side of the barn he found the helicopter that must have been used in the cattle rustlings. It was hidden beneath a ramshackle lean-to against the side of the barn.

He slipped around it and encountered Micah. The bigger man was pressed to the side of the building near another door, and the way he was frozen led Gage to hope he could see inside. Hurrying as quickly as he could while still remaining silent, Gage crept up to him.

Micah glanced at him and then stepped back, motioning him to look.

There was a narrow slit between the door and frame, a place left open by a missing strip of insulation. Gage peered inside, and what he saw froze him to his soul. He could see the vague shapes of men moving about, indistinguishable in dim kerosene light, rendered completely shapeless by long robes. When he shifted a little to one side he saw what appeared to be an altar, draped in black, with a ram's head painted in gold on the front of it.

A whispered oath escaped him. No doubt, he thought. There was no doubt that some kind of ritual was about to be performed. Taking into account the pentagram and the ram's head, he would bet it was some kind of satanism. And Emma was in there. Fear squeezed his heart.

Shifting again, he tried to see in the other direction, and that was when his heart stopped utterly. Emma was there, clad only in her thin work clothes, her hands bound above her head by a rope that hung from a high rafter. Her head lolled to one side, as if she was unconscious, and he couldn't for the life of him see whether her feet touched the floor.

Gage pulled away and leaned back against the barn wall, trying desperately to find some of the detachment that was necessary for what was going to have to be done. Without detachment, he couldn't trust his judgment.

"Did you see her?" he whispered to Micah.

Micah gave a brief, wordless nod.

"She could suffocate that way." It might take time, but when you hung by your arms it became nearly impossible to breathe. Gage had had the experience once, when a dealer had gotten suspicious of him. He looked at Micah. "We can't wait."

Micah nodded his agreement. "There's still one unaccounted for."

"He might already be in there. And Emma might already be dead, or close to it. I found the tack room back there. It has a window we ought to be able to climb through."

"Let's go."

Moving in swift, careful silence, they crept around the corner to the end of the barn where the tack room was located. The sun was now a red sphere above the distant mountains, and a fiery twilight colored the world.

The window proved to be unlocked and gave only a little resistance to being raised. The cold weather had dried all the moisture from the wood and loosened the window in its frame. Gage could hardly believe their good fortune.

Micah insisted on going through first. Gage understood—Micah had had a lot more training for this kind of thing—but he didn't like it. Moments later, though, he climbed through and joined Micah by the door of the tack room. Cautiously he tried the knob and found the door unlocked. The hinges made only the quietest of creaks as he eased the door open.

Between them and the men were six box stalls, three on either side of a wide passageway. The shadows here were deep, concealing, hardly penetrated by the couple of kerosene lanterns Fenster and his friends were using at the other end of the barn.

They were confident, Gage thought, as he and Micah crept down opposite sides of the passageway, keeping close to the stalls. They were laughing and talking in normal voices as they prepared to commit their obscenities. One of them even joked about whether it would be as easy to skin a human as it was to skin a cow.

Gage closed his eyes briefly, praying Emma was unconscious and unable to hear this filth. And then, with a monumental effort of will, he returned to the ledge on the abyss where feelings couldn't reach him, the place where the cold wind kept his soul safely frozen. He couldn't afford to let his feelings interfere now.

Undetected, he and Micah reached the end of the line of stalls. As they'd agreed, Gage squatted in the shadows and waited for Micah to step out into the light and reveal himself. The intention was for Micah to ease his way around, away from Emma, drawing the attention of the five men that way, so that Gage could slip around to protect her.

And unfortunately, until somebody threatened him or Micah, they had to do this by the book. Right now Gage would have liked to burn the whole damn rule book.

That was when he heard the distant *whop-whop* of a helicopter. He cast a look at Micah and received an "okay" signal in return. It must be the sheriff's medevac chopper, Gage realized. Micah would certainly recognize the sound of the Huey.

And that meant that Nate and his units couldn't be far away. Just a few more minutes.

Emma must be freezing, Gage thought as he looked her way again. It was cold in the barn, though not quite as cold as the outdoors, and her sweater and slacks were little protection. Her feet were touching the floor, he could see now, but he couldn't tell if she was standing or simply hanging by her arms. He half wished she would move, so he could tell if she was alive, and then was glad when she didn't, because he didn't want her to remember any of this. Not any of it.

The attention of the five men suddenly shifted from their various tasks toward a clatter near the makeshift altar, where one of them dumped the contents of a black bag onto a small table. Gage caught a glint of silver, and then one of them—Don Fenster, he thought—lifted a golden dagger.

It was the one from the photograph that had been sent to Emma. Gage recognized it instantly, even though the photograph had been black-and-white. On the pommel was the ruby—probably just glass—from Emma's dreams.

''I used this on her once before,'' Fenster said, showing it around as if it were a trophy. ''I thought for sure I killed her.''

''Drop it!'' Micah's voice suddenly cracked through the barn and he stepped around the corner of the stall with his shotgun leveled at the cluster of dark-robed men. Easing around the stall, he edged slowly to the right, drawing their collective gazes from Emma's direction. ''You're under arrest for kidnapping. Put your hands where I can see them.''

Now! Gage thought, and slipped around the corner of his stall, staying low and trying to keep quiet as he crept toward Emma. The Huey's *whop-whop* was louder now, loud enough to fill the five villains with tension.

''Hold it!'' Micah barked.

Gage glanced back to see one of the men suddenly freeze in the process of lowering his arm. He kept moving toward Emma.

"The sheriff will be here in just a minute," Micah said. "It won't pay you to try something foolish."

The door just to one side of Gage suddenly burst open, admitting a blast of cold night air and the missing sixth man.

"Don, Lew, there's a whole crowd of police moving in...." His voice trailed off, and he froze as he saw Micah. Gage rolled onto his back and leveled his shotgun at the sixth man.

"Don't try anything," he said.

The man gaped down at him, then stiffened when he looked into the barrel of the shotgun.

But apparently it was the distraction the other five had needed. They all dived in different directions. Micah fired, and Don Fenster hit the floor bleeding. Micah cocked and fired again, catching another man and putting him down.

"Hold it!" screamed a frenzied voice. "Hold it or the woman dies!"

Gage's attention strayed past the man he was holding at gunpoint to Emma. One of the robed men was holding her shield-like before him, a knife at her ribs.

Gage lashed out with his foot, bringing the sixth man to the floor, where he was less of a threat. The man holding Emma jumped nervously.

"Both of you cops get out of here or she dies," the man said desperately. "Now."

"Forget it," Gage said flatly. "It's a stalemate. I'm not going anywhere, and neither is the deputy. We're both armed and ready to shoot, and all you've got is that woman. If you hurt her, there's nothing to keep me from shooting you in the groin, is there?"

The man's pale, frightened face grew even paler, but the knife never moved away from Emma. "You won't touch me while I got her."

"Like I said," Gage drawled, "stalemate. But not for long."

Micah had drawn his .45, and now he pointed it upward and pulled the trigger. The startled man with the knife spun around, exposing his back to Gage. It was all the opening Gage needed.

Heedless of his screaming back, he rolled forward onto his feet and threw himself at the man who threatened Emma.

Gage caught him around the knees and knocked him to the floor. The knife went spinning out of the man's hands when he fell. He tried to scramble away, but Gage yanked the Browning from his belt and shoved the cold barrel right in the man's belly. "Don't move."

"That goes for all of you," Micah said, his deep voice as hard as steel. "Not a muscle."

The *whop* of the Huey's blades was a loud roar now, and Micah keyed his microphone, telling Nate what the situation was. Thirty seconds later the barn was full of armed deputies and a couple of paramedics.

Gage's only thought was for Emma. He grabbed the knife that only moments before had been shoved against her ribs and hacked at the rope that held her arms suspended.

"Emma? Emma, do you hear me?" She was breathing, thank God, but she was pale, so pale, and as cold as ice. As soon as he got her down, he propped her on his lap and began to rub her icy hands. "Emma, honey, do you hear me? Oh, God, baby, answer me. Please. Just one little sound...."

A small whimper escaped her, and then she drew a deep, shuddering breath. Slowly, very slowly, her eyes fluttered open. Gage looked down into them, seeking the warmth, the caring, the gentleness—the *love*—that was Emma. It was gone. All of it.

He looked down into her hazy green eyes and realized with a terrible sense of dread that Emma had gone far away, had withdrawn to some place deep inside. Some place beyond hurt, beyond fear.

He knew that place intimately, had dwelt in it for years now. With a groan, he held her as close as he could get her and made up his mind to give her a reason to come back.

Because he sure as hell couldn't live without her.

Chapter 14

The Christmas open house had come and was nearly over. Gage watched Emma as she bade good-night to the last of the visitors, then paused in the open door to listen to one last carol from the choir that had wandered the neighborhood all evening. They stood before her steps in a semicircle and sang "The First Noel" with voices growing cracked from overuse and cold, but beautiful all the same.

Emma, too, was beautiful, Gage thought. She wore a full-skirted green velvet dress that emphasized her femininity and brought her fantastic hair to blazing life.

But ever since the night at the Fenster ranch, she had been withdrawn, hardly speaking to him or anyone else. Something had happened, something that had pulled her out of the present and cast her into some painful abyss of the soul. Gage Dalton recognized someone who was wrestling with demons when he saw her. Someone who had been there, too, couldn't mistake the signs.

After her rescue, Doc Randall had put her in the hospital for a couple of days of rest and recuperation. She had suffered from exposure and hypothermia, but Gage knew the real damage was deeper and less treatable.

He was sure she had remembered the details of the attack ten years ago. Nothing else could explain this withdrawal. She needed the time, he told himself, to deal with all those memories. She needed him to be supportive and silent.

But it had been nearly a week, a week during which he'd battled a few of his own demons, and he didn't know if he could face another day without at least a small smile from Emma. He didn't know if he could face another Christmas alone. And he had vowed he would give her a reason to come back. He'd given her time, he'd given her space, and now, no matter how it scared him, he would give her love.

"Emma?"

She turned from closing the door and looked at him. Just as it had all week, her expression looked blank, as if she was only peripherally aware of him.

Something inside him cracked wide open. He couldn't endure another day with this wraithlike woman moving silently, pointlessly, through the house. He wanted to shake her, wake her, make her look at him once again as if he mattered. He took one step toward her, then caught himself up short.

"Damn it, Emma," he said, his voice hoarse with anguish. "I hate Christmas. You know I hate it, and you know why. You know all about it. Are you going to give me another reason to feel that way?"

She blinked. For the first time in days, he believed she really saw him.

"Emma, what happened is in the past. I realize that finally. I need you to realize it, too. I need…I need you to make this Christmas joyous for me. I need you to give me—give me— aw, hell, Emma, I need you to give me all the Christmases to come."

He saw his words strike home. A long, slow shiver seemed to pass through her, and she took a step toward him. All of a sudden she didn't look remote. All of a sudden she was very much there. Very much with him.

"I remembered," she said, her voice hardly more than a whisper. A flash of searing agony showed in her eyes. "I remembered being in the car with him... I remembered what he did."

"I figured you did. God, baby, I would have spared you that if I could have."

"I know." She gave him a small, forlorn smile. "I'm sorry, Gage. It's just so much, so awful.... I can't have children because of that man!" The anguish seemed to rip her chest wide open, and tears began to spill down her cheeks. "It's his fault, and now I know it was *him,* and I think of all the times I was in the same room and never knew.... Oh, Gage—"

At last, at long last, she flew into his arms and let him give her the comfort he had ached all week to offer.

"I know, sweetheart. I know. But he's dead now, Emma. You don't ever have to see him or worry about him again." Micah's shotgun had taken care of that.

"But I feel so angry," she said into his shoulder. "So angry."

"I know. I've been angry for a long, long time, and I guess you will be, too. But, Em, are you going to sacrifice tomorrow to your anger the way I did for so long? Or are you going to put it in its place and try to make some good Christmas memories for us?"

Another long, shuddering sigh escaped her. After a few moments she raised her wet face so she could look up at him. Her hand rose instinctively to his scarred cheek, cradling it, remembering just what it was he had lost, and comparing it to her own losses. He was looking at her now with a new expression in his gray eyes. Warmth blazed out at her, warmth and something very like hope.

"But I can't have children," she said, a litany so old it came automatically.

"That's fine. I don't want any. I had mine, and I lost them, and if you want the God's honest truth, Em, I don't think I could sleep another night if I ever again had a child to worry about. In fact, it scares me sh—scares me to death to think of worrying about *you* for the rest of my days. I'll probably drive you crazy, hovering over you all the time, sending out search parties if you're fifteen minutes late...."

A small, reluctant laugh escaped her, just a puff of sound, but it reached him in his very heart. He looked intently down at her and felt nearly swamped by relief when he saw the old Emma peering up at him from sparkling green eyes. For the moment, maybe for all time, the shadows had been driven back.

"Are you trying to tell me something, Mr. Dalton?" she asked primly, Miss Emma the spinster librarian from the top of her head to the tips of her toes. Deep in her green eyes, behind the sheen of tears, was a teasing sparkle that warmed his chilly soul.

"I most certainly am, Miss Emma," he said gruffly. Then hell's own archangel bent to whisper the most seductive words of all into the pink shell of Miss Emma's ear.

"I love you, Red," he said roughly. "I'll love you all my days, and probably far beyond. I need you with every breath I draw. Say you'll marry me. Whatever comes, we can face it together."

"Oh, Gage, I do love you!" Her tremulous sigh filled his ear, filled his heart, filled his soul. With those simple words, she set him free and handed him heaven.

Hell's own archangel had found peace at last.

* * * * *

IRONHEART

To Paige Wheeler,
who is endlessly patient with my disorganization.
And to all my **P*** friends,
who are the best bunch of pals a writer could ask for.

Chapter 1

"We don't want any redskins in here," said a loud voice from the back of the room.

A whisper in the bar's sudden hush would have seemed deafening. The men at the tables forgot their drinks; the waitresses hesitated in midstep. The bartender froze in the act of wiping a glass. Every eye fixed on the doorway. Trouble had started brewing the instant the regulars spied the invader.

A tall, powerfully built man stood there, surveying the room with eyes that were the exact dark gray color of steel. His solidly muscled body was clad in a plain white Western shirt and faded jeans that clung snugly with the familiarity of long wearing. Beyond that, there wasn't an ordinary thing about him.

His boots were scuffed but expensive, hand-tooled leather with a pointed toe and the high, angled heel designed for a stirrup. The black cowboy hat on his head was decorated by a band made of silver conchos, each one unique. His leather belt, also hand-tooled, boasted an ornate silver-and-turquoise buckle.

Hair as black as the limitless night sky flowed past his shoulders.

His face was harsh-featured, hawkish, an unforgiving landscape of angles and planes that warned people away and invited no one to come nearer. He was sun-bronzed and weather-hardened, and standing there he looked as enduring and immovable as the Rocky Mountains.

Slowly, almost lazily, he scanned the room. Not a muscle in his face so much as flickered while his hard, dark eyes touched on everyone and everything.

After a moment, apparently undisturbed by the silence his arrival had caused or by the hostile stares he was receiving, he walked across to the bar, his boot heels loud on the bare wood floor. When he reached it, he placed a foot on the rail and looked at the bartender.

Just then the voice from the back of the room broke the silence, this time more insistently. "I said, we don't want any 'skins in here."

Slowly, the stranger turned, his dark eyes seeking the man who had spoken. When one of the cowboys shoved away from his table and stood, the stranger looked him over from head to foot. "Too damn bad," he said, and turned his back on the cowboy.

"Not in here," the bartender said to the cowboy. "Damn it, Alvin, keep it outside."

Several more chairs scraped back from tables, but the stranger never flinched. He looked at the bartender. "Coffee, please. And a menu."

The bartender shook his head. "Just get out of here, man. No point getting your head bashed for a principle."

The stranger smiled suddenly, a humorless, dangerous expression. "You think not? Tell that to the marines."

Then he removed his black hat, revealing a thin leather thong around his forehead that held his dark hair out of his face, and handed the hat to the bartender. "Take care of that for me."

The bartender measured him for a moment, then nodded.

"Sure." Accepting the hat, he placed it safely behind the bar. "I wish you'd hash this out in the parking lot."

The stranger shrugged. "It's up to Alvin. Something tells me he doesn't listen too good."

The bartender almost grinned. It was there, a faint twitch at the corner of his mouth, a small glimmer in his eyes. "You're right," he said.

Right then the stranger saw the bartender's eyes narrow and suddenly shift to one side. Instinctively he turned, just in time to block a punch from the cowpoke who'd first spoken. Alvin, probably.

"I'm gonna call the sheriff!" the bartender roared. "I told you jackasses—"

"Take it outside," someone said, and a crowd converged, forcing the two slugging, swinging men outside.

The Wyoming night air was chilly, the only light coming from the flashing red of the neon sign in front of the bar. A dark, silent circle of men formed, an ominous boundary to prevent escape. The stranger knew the ritual. He'd played it out countless times, always on the receiving end, because his skin was the color of copper and his heritage was native to this land. Men like these had stripped his people of everything, and had tried to strip him of dignity and pride with their fists and their words. Despite it all, his head remained unbowed.

There was a swift flurry of punches, and then one solid slug from the stranger threw Alvin onto his back. He lay there unmoving.

Crouched, hands spread, the Indian turned slowly, facing each man in the circle one at a time. "Who's next?" he asked. Red light flashed, and now a blue flash joined it. The growl of a truck came from behind, but the men ignored it. More important things were at hand.

"Me," said a brawny cowboy with a paunch that hung over his belt. Handing his hat to the man next to him, he stepped into the circle. He swung first.

The stranger blocked the blow and landed one solidly in the guy's paunch. Then he caught a hard slug himself, in the shoulder. It was a hopeless situation, and he knew it. He might manage to beat another one or two of these guys, but he was tiring, and eventually they'd have the edge. He'd get hammered to a pulp, probably. It wouldn't be the first time. But never, ever, was he going to leave a place because he was Cherokee. Never. They would have to carry him out, feetfirst.

He took another punch in the arm, then threw one that connected solidly with the other guy's jaw. The man staggered backward, and the stranger waited, fists ready, giving his opponent a chance to quit.

The sharp report of a pistol cracked the silence of the night wide open, reverberating on the chilly air.

"This is Deputy Sheriff Yates," said an amplified woman's voice. "This party is officially over. Now."

"Aw, hell, Sara!" yelled one of the cowboys. "We're just having fun!"

"I don't call it fun when ten jackasses gang up on one fool with more guts than brains. I'm giving you thirty seconds to clear the area."

The unmistakable sound of a shotgun being pumped reinforced the order. "And take Alvin with you," she added, this time without the aid of the megaphone. "Otherwise I'll book him for disturbing the peace."

The circle of men scattered, sifting into the shadows of the parking lot. One after another, pickup engines roared to life and tires spun on gravel as they pulled away.

In thirty seconds the lot was empty of every living soul save the Indian and the Conard County deputy. The Indian stayed where he was, bent over, resting his hands on his knees as he drew deep, cleansing breaths.

"Are you okay?"

Her voice was a little husky, a black-satin-sheet voice, a whisper of dark nights and forbidden things. Slowly he lifted his head and looked at a woman who was none of those things. Clad in a khaki sheriff's uniform, her hair hidden beneath a tan Stetson, her waist concealed behind the bulk of her gun belt, with a shotgun cradled casually in one arm, she wouldn't make anyone think of satin sheets or forbidden pleasures.

And in the moment before he responded, he struggled with a sense of embarrassment at being rescued by a woman, even if she *was* a gun-toting, pistol-packing peace officer.

Somewhere along the winding trail he had traveled in his life, he had developed the conviction that it was a man's place to protect those weaker than he was, and women just naturally fell into that category. Such chivalry was outdated, he knew, but that didn't keep him from feeling he had just lost another little chunk of his masculinity because he had been rescued by a female.

Stupid, he told himself. Stupid. Would it have been *masculine* to be beaten to a bloody pulp and left for dead hamburger on the gravel? A wry smile twisted his bruised mouth. Yeah, that would have been the manly thing.

"I'm fine," he said, straightening all the way. "Thanks for helping out."

"Why didn't you just clear out? Did you really think you were going to be able to handle them all on your own?"

"I figured I was going to get my butt whipped," he said frankly, "but a few of them were going with me."

Sara Yates shook her head a little and studied him. The flashing red of the neon light didn't provide much illumination. All it seemed to do was heighten the harshness of his face and create a sense of mystery. "You're a damn fool," she said flatly.

"Maybe."

"Did you really think you'd change any of their minds about Indians by beating them up and letting them beat you up in return?"

"It wasn't *their* minds I was interested in."

Silence fell again in the parking lot. For long moments neither of them said a thing, each studying the other a little warily. Then Sara spoke. "You'd better move on before someone else comes out of that bar and decides to take exception to your ancestry."

He settled his hands on his hips. "Wish I could oblige, Deputy."

Sara stepped closer, wondering if she was dealing with a madman. In her experience, most people didn't argue with the law unless they were drunk, drugged or crazy—or just plain trouble. "You're not going back in there."

"My hat's in there. It was a gift from my uncle. Custom-made."

Sara turned from him and strode back to her Blazer. "I'll get it for you," she said over her shoulder. Opening the door of the vehicle, she climbed up and turned the key in the ignition, not to start the engine, but to unlock the dashboard clamp where she stowed her shotgun. As soon as the gun was upright and in place, she removed the keys from the ignition. Nobody could get that gun now.

Climbing out again, she headed toward the door of Happy's. "What does the hat look like?"

"Black, with silver conchos on the band. The bartender's holding it for me. And thanks."

Sara paused to look at him. "As far as I'm concerned, you're never setting foot in this place again."

"Does that seem right to you?"

Sara heard the challenge despite his mild tone. "Look, mister, I don't know who you are or where you're from, but if you think you can walk into this county and change redneck attitudes in a place like Happy's just by being a stubborn cuss, it's your funeral. Just don't do it when I'm around. I get paid to keep the peace."

"Is that an invitation to leave town?"

She faced him, unconsciously adopting an aggressive posture, her hands on her hips and her legs splayed. "Conard County, Wyoming, is a friendly place, and most of the folks are good people. You're welcome to stay as long as you like— as long as you don't cause trouble. I'm just recommending that you avoid getting your head bashed in. You can take that as friendly advice, or you can take it as a warning. Either way, maybe you ought to listen."

She waited, but he seemed to have nothing more to say. Shaking her head slightly, Sara turned and headed into the bar. *Just what I need,* she thought. *An Indian with an attitude.*

Inside Happy's, the remaining regulars watched her arrival with pretended indifference. All of them knew Sara Yates. She'd lived every one of her twenty-eight years in Conard County, and her father had once been one of the regulars here. These days, she stopped in often enough herself, not to have a beer, but to hunt for her younger brother, Joey. The boy was trouble waiting to happen.

"Howdy, Sara," the bartender said, his greeting friendly. "Did anybody get hurt out there?"

"A few bruises is all, Ned." Reaching the bar, she leaned an elbow on it and looked around the room. Most everyone had gone back to their own conversations. "I came looking for a black cowboy hat with silver conchos."

"Yeah? I figured sure that Injun would come back for it himself."

"He would have. I…volunteered."

Ned gave a wheezy laugh. "I'm surprised he was smart enough to accept. He ain't the type to back off from a fight."

"Not by what I saw."

Ned reached behind the bar and brought out the black Stetson. "I haven't seen Joey, if you're looking," he told her as he passed her the hat.

"I'm always looking. He violates his probation at least twice a week. One of these days I'm going to run him in."

"Might do him some good, Sara," Ned said seriously. "That kid's got a chip as big as Wyoming on his shoulder, and some pretty dumb ideas about what makes a man. I'd sure hate to see your daddy's only boy turn out like Alvin Teague."

So would she, Sara thought, as she turned and left Happy's with the stranger's hat in her hand. Her dad had spent a little too much time in Happy's, but he'd been a good man, a hard-working man, until his wife died. The life had gone out of Ted Yates that day, but it had taken him two years to kill himself with booze. And Joey…well, Joey had been too damn young to understand. Sara had been nineteen at the time, and she wasn't sure she'd understood, either, but Joey had been barely seven.

And it's all just excuses, she told herself as she stepped out into the crisp spring night. Joey had had a better life than a lot of kids, a lot more stability, a home, plenty to eat.... It was all just excuses. There was nobody to blame for what Joey was doing except Joey.

The Indian was gone.

Sara froze, instinctively suspecting foul play. Then she saw him, squatting before the front of a long-bed pickup truck with a camper shell. Something made her hesitate, made her stay where she was. It was as if every instinct in her body screamed danger, but puzzlement held her still when fear never would have. And then she realized it wasn't her physical safety she was concerned about.

But she stayed where she was, anyway. "Trouble?" she called out.

"Yeah." The stranger straightened and turned toward her. Forty feet of gravel lay between them. "Somebody drained the oil and coolant from my truck. The bottom radiator hose is slashed, too."

Sara was a patient woman. Slow to anger, she habitually stayed calm past the point where most people were shouting and swearing. Tonight, though, she wasn't feeling any too patient. Her day had started at six with an auto accident out on the state highway and had been topped off by a domestic disturbance that had ended with a woman in the hospital and her husband in jail. She'd just been signing off duty at six-thirty when her grandfather called to say Joey hadn't come home.

Now here it was, after nine, she hadn't found Joey, and she'd gotten tangled up in this mess. For a moment she hesitated, thinking she ought to call someone else to come take care of this. She was off duty, after all. Let some other deputy write the report.

But she wasn't the type to ask others to do what she could

do herself. Stifling a sigh, she looked at the stranger. "You want to file a report?"

He closed the distance between them and took his hat from her. Not caring that she stared, Sara watched him put it on, hiding the thong that held back his long, inky hair. He looked, she thought, like a warrior of old, a character right out of the American past.

"No point in it," he said after a moment. "It would just be a waste of paper."

"What are you implying?"

"What do you think I'm implying?"

There was no mistaking the challenge this time. Sara felt her back stiffen, and her slow anger began to simmer. "If that chip gets any bigger, mister, you're going to fall flat on your face."

He stared down at her, a tall, exotic man who looked as unyielding as granite. Sara was a tall woman herself and not accustomed to looking up at many men. Some corner of her mind noted that she ought to be nervous, facing him down like this, but she stood her ground. Sara Jane Yates always stood her ground.

And then he astonished her by giving a short, soft laugh. "You're probably right."

As easily as that, he defused the moment. Turning, he studied his disabled truck. "I don't suppose there's a tow service around here."

"Not at this time of night." And there was no way out of this one, she figured. If he left his truck here overnight, one of those yahoos who'd picked on him earlier might see it and decide to even the score a little. Then there *would* be hell to pay. Sheriff Nate Tate didn't stand for shenanigans like that in his county. "I've got a tow chain," she told the man.

He looked at her again, and this time he smiled. It was a faint, lopsided expression, almost reluctant. "Thanks. I didn't mean anything about the report, by the way. I just meant there's no way to prove who did it, so why waste the paper?"

"Oh." Sara felt a little foolish and wondered if maybe she

was developing an attitude of her own. "I'll tow you into Con-ard City, but I have to make a couple stops along the way."

"No problem, Deputy." Suddenly he stuck out his hand. "The name's Gideon Ironheart."

Sara watched her smaller, paler hand vanish into his strong, warm grip. "Sara Yates."

She backed her departmental Blazer into place in front of his truck, then opened the tailgate to get at the tow chain. Gideon Ironheart was beside her instantly, his large hands stuffed into a pair of heavy leather work gloves, ready to take over. Standing back, Sara was content to let him do the work. Ranch-bred, she could do these things as confidently as anyone, but there was no point in arguing about it.

He knew what he was about. He moved with the ease and confidence of a man who was accustomed to hard physical labor. Nothing about the heavy chain or crawling beneath his truck to attach it to the frame caused him any hesitation. Glanc-ing at his Georgia license plate, she wondered what he did for a living. A man didn't get a build like that from a desk job, and he didn't develop endurance from pumping iron a couple of times a week. And this man certainly had stamina. Not ten minutes ago he'd been well on the way to having the stuffing beaten out of him, but you couldn't tell it by looking at him now.

"All set," he said as he rose from the gravel.

She noticed he didn't brush off his jeans. Dirt didn't bother him, either. A construction worker, maybe. Or a farmer…he had the sunburned look of an outdoorsman.

"I need to stop at two places on the way into town," Sara said. "Then we can drop your truck at Bayard's Garage, and I'll take you on to the Lazy Rest Motel."

"Sounds good. Except that I haven't eaten since breakfast. I went in there to get a sandwich." He indicated Happy's with a jerk of his head.

"We'll be stopping at a couple of other watering holes. You can get a sandwich to go at one of them."

He gave a nod and turned to get into his truck.

Sara stayed as she was a moment, watching him climb into the cab of his pickup, noting again the catlike grace of his movements. Something about him was familiar. Or at least she felt as if something about him *ought* to be familiar.

Shaking her head a little, she climbed into her Blazer and switched on the ignition.

Gideon Ironheart. That sure was some name.

Towing the truck slowed her down considerably, and it was more than twenty minutes before she saw the next roadhouse she wanted to check out. Signaling early to give Gideon Ironheart plenty of warning, she turned slowly and easily into the rutted parking lot.

Neon flashed in four front windows, and a lighted arrow on a signpost pointed the way to the front door. There were more than a dozen of these places scattered around the county, all doing a booming business on Friday and Saturday nights when cowpokes came in from the range with their week's pay in their pockets.

Gideon climbed out of his truck and walked up to her as she locked the Blazer.

"Are the sandwiches here any good?" he asked.

"Good enough, I guess. Let me walk in first, and you stay behind me."

He shifted his weight to one foot, canting his hips to the side in a timeless posture of male arrogance. Barely able to swallow being rescued by her, he was in no mood to accept her protection, regardless of her badge and her gun. Besides, he didn't like the idea of her going into this place alone. "Lady, I've never yet hidden behind someone's skirts."

Sara drew herself up to her full five foot eight, a good eight inches shorter than he was, and glared up at him. "Look, *Mister* Ironheart, we do it my way or you wait out here while I get your damn dinner. I'm in no mood to deal with another brawl tonight. What'll it be?"

He folded his arms across his chest and looked down at her

stonily. It was his very lack of expression that communicated his anger. "Is this Wyoming hospitality?"

That nearly did it. She'd been dealing with fools and idiots all day long, and now she wasn't even on duty. "This isn't a matter of hospitality, Ironheart. It's a matter of *reality*. You want hospitality, come out to my ranch. My grandfather will stuff you full of good home-cooking and I'll pour the damn coffee. These roadhouses are a different matter. They're loaded with redneck cowboys who've already had too damn much whiskey for their own good. If I go in first, nobody will pay any attention to you, and that's the way *I* want it, because I want to get home to my bed sometime tonight. Got it?"

His arms remained folded, and he continued to stare expressionlessly down at her. His stare was unnerving, Sara thought uneasily. Shadowed by the brim of his hat, his eyes were like two dark, glistening pools, drawing her deeper and deeper. They held her, mesmerized her, gave her the uneasy feeling that they were absorbing her and learning all her secrets. And gave her the even wilder feeling that if she just fell into those pools, a dark warmth would swallow her and shelter her.

"Who," he asked slowly, "made you ashamed of being a woman?"

It was a question to which Gideon Ironheart genuinely wanted an answer, but he knew he wasn't going to get it. Not yet. Without a word, Sara Yates pivoted on her heel and stalked toward the door of the bar. Gideon followed two steps behind, realizing what she apparently didn't: that her uniform might be scant protection in a place like this. When some men got drunk enough, they respected nothing at all. He would walk behind her if she insisted, but he'd be damned before he'd let her walk into this place alone. Happy's had been different, because the troublemakers were already gone when she went inside. Here, they were still inside and drinking.

The music from the jukebox was loud, the laughter louder. A haze of cigarette and cigar smoke filled the large room, and the bartender didn't look half as friendly as the one at the other place. Keeping close to Sara, Gideon escorted her to the bar.

The bartender nodded to her, glanced at Gideon, then dismissed him as a redskin. "Whaddya want, Sara?"

"My friend here wants some sandwiches to go. Have you seen Joey tonight?"

Kurt shook his head. "You told me the kid's on probation. He's underage besides. He comes in here, I throw him out. I don't want no grief with Tate." With visible reluctance, he looked at Gideon. "Yeah?"

Gideon ordered a couple of turkey sandwiches while Sara turned and scanned the crowded room. People were glancing surreptitiously their way, but apparently nobody was in a mood for trouble with the law tonight—except for two beefy guys in the corner who looked as if they couldn't quite make up their minds.

The bartender dumped a couple of plastic-wrapped sandwiches on the counter and threw Gideon's change down beside it.

"Walk out in front of me," Sara told Gideon as he turned toward the door.

"Damn it," he growled, keeping his voice low, "I—"

"My back is less of a provocation than yours," she said flatly. "All right?"

Over the top of her Stetson, he saw the two men who evidently had her worried. They were beginning to shove their chairs back from the table. There was no time for argument. Turning, he headed toward the door, dragging Sara right after him.

"I'm getting a really great impression of Conard County, Wyoming," he growled as he pulled her through the door after him and started tugging her across the parking lot. "I saw less trouble in dives in Chicago, Atlanta and Boston, I can tell you. What is it with these guys?"

Sara tried to yank her arm free of his grip. "Damn it, Ironheart—"

"Oh, just be quiet, woman. Those two cretins in there have got plans for both of us. I suggest you get behind the wheel and drive."

"How come you didn't have the sense to clear out of Happy's before the trouble started?" Sara demanded as she unlocked the door of her Blazer. "You're sure in enough of a hurry now."

His face was completely shadowed beneath the brim of his black hat. Not even the neon light penetrated the darkness there. "Because," he said succinctly, "at Happy's I didn't have a woman to look after."

Sara gasped, but before she could voice her outrage, Gideon pulled the Blazer's door open and lifted her onto the seat. "Drive, Deputy," he said. "I'll be right behind you."

And, damn it, he actually smiled. She caught the gleam of his teeth even in the shadows.

He got behind the wheel of his truck just as the two men emerged from the bar. Sara didn't hesitate any longer but turned over her engine and pulled out of the lot. She would deal with Gideon Ironheart later.

Fifteen minutes later, they reached the last of the roadhouses Sara wanted to check out. After this, Joey was on his own. There were limits to what even a loving sister could or would do.

Before she climbed out, Gideon was there, opening her door and looking straight in at her. "Who were those two guys back there?" he asked without preamble. "Local troublemakers?"

Sara shrugged. "I never saw them before. We *do* occasionally get strangers through here," she said dryly, wondering why she was no longer furious with him. She ought to read him the riot act for treating her like a helpless, defenseless female when she was neither. "I don't like the way you dragged me out of there, Ironheart."

"Sorry, ma'am." He didn't look sorry, though, and his eyes never wavered from her face. "Who's Joey?"

Sara sighed and averted her face, staring out through the dusty windshield at the Watering Hole. "My brother."

"He's disappeared?"

"Not exactly. He's around somewhere, probably doing something he shouldn't."

"That bartender said something about probation."

"Yeah. Grand theft auto. He's supposed to come straight home from his job, and when he doesn't, he's violating his probation." Why was she telling him all this, anyway? It was none of his damn business, and he was a complete stranger besides. Catching herself, she turned and began to slide out of the truck. Gideon stepped back to give her room.

"You wait out here," she told him flatly. "I'll only be a minute."

He didn't bother to argue. He just walked right behind her every step of the way. Sara felt him there, like a severe irritation. She could have handcuffed him to something, she supposed, but that wouldn't be legal. She couldn't, after all, prevent anyone from going anywhere they damn well pleased, as long as no law was being violated.

Damn, she hoped he was on his way out of the county by tomorrow evening. In her entire life, she couldn't remember one person ever having irritated her so severely. Or so easily. Or so continually.

Suddenly she spun about and faced him, her jaw thrust out and her hands on her hips. "What is it with you, Ironheart? This is *my* business, and I'll handle it. By myself."

He didn't answer immediately. He stood looking down at her, hips again canted in that incredibly virile, incredibly cocky way, a tall, powerful, mysterious-looking man. After a moment, he tilted his head a little to one side, almost thoughtfully. "My grandfather was a medicine man. I didn't listen to him much as a kid, not nearly as much as I should have, I reckon. But a couple of things stuck with me. He told me a man answers only to himself, but he always answers. I don't want to have to answer to myself if you go in there alone and something happens."

There really wasn't a thing she could say to that. Whatever else he might be, Ironheart was evidently an honorable man, and an honorable man couldn't be deterred. Nor should he be. Sara felt the last of her irritation drizzle away. Without a word, she turned and let him follow.

The Watering Hole was usually a quieter place than the last one they had checked, and Sara didn't really expect any trouble. The bartender was a man she had gone to high school with, and he greeted her with a ready grin.

"No Joey," he said as soon as he saw her. "You know I'd send him home, Sara."

"I know, Bill, but you're not always here. Thanks, though."

The night was growing chillier, and Sara shivered a little when she stepped back outside.

"What now?" Gideon asked.

"I'll take you on into town."

"I meant, what do you do now about Joey?"

"Not much I can do except run him in when I find him." The thought made her sick to her stomach. "He agreed to the terms of probation, and I agreed to make sure he kept them. There's no alternative. Not anymore."

"Turning him in might get his attention."

"That's what my grandfather says."

Gideon held the door of the Blazer while Sara climbed in. "That's what my grandfather said about me, too."

As she reached for the seat belt, Sara paused and looked at him. "What happened?"

"He got my attention."

Two hours later, Sara sat at the kitchen table at home, her booted feet up on the chair beside her while she sipped a mug of chocolate milk and ate the dinner her grandfather had kept warming in the oven for her. She'd traded her uniform for soft old jeans and a faded sweatshirt, and had unpinned her long black hair, giving her scalp some relief.

The Yates ranch, known as the Double Y, occupied two thousand acres in westernmost Conard County, butting right up against the mountains. Sara could get on a horse on a summer afternoon and ride up into pine forests and watch mountain brooks tumble down rocky hillsides. It was some of the prettiest land in the county, and some of the toughest to ranch. Since her father's death, the Double Y had grown little but sagebrush and grass, and Sara had taken her job with the sheriff's department in order to hang on to it. Sometimes she wondered why she bothered.

But then she would think of the pine woods and the sound of rushing water, the way the fresh, clean air smelled, and she knew she could never let it go. Whatever it took, she would keep the Double Y.

The screen door behind her slapped shut, and she looked over her shoulder to see her grandfather come into the kitchen. "No Joey?" he said.

Sara shook her head. "How's Columbine?"

"She'll foal before dawn." Moving slowly, the old man rounded the table and sat across from her. In his seventies, Zeke Jackson still stood straight and proud, but his arthritis slowed him up a little.

His face was lined and weathered from the elements and years, but his hair was still as dark as a raven's wing.

Sara had inherited his hair and a touch of his high Shoshone cheekbones, but apart from that she looked like her father's daughter: brown-eyed and ordinary. "Can I make you some coffee, Grandfather?"

The old man shook his head. "You worked hard today. You rest. I can look after myself. You'll have to turn the boy in, Sarey. A few weeks in the county jail might wake him up."

"But what if it makes him worse?" That was the fear that plagued her. The Conard County jail didn't house hardened criminals, as a rule, but just the fact of incarceration might be enough to harden his attitude rather than cure it.

Zeke shook his head slowly. "You've done all you can. We both have. Sooner or later, even a boy has to answer for what he does."

The words were so close to what Gideon Ironheart had said earlier that Sara found herself telling her grandfather about him. Zeke laughed when she told him that Gideon had said that his grandfather got his attention, but then he grew serious.

"There's nothing more you can do, Sara-child. Not a thing. You've given that boy all the loving and caring of a mother, and you've set a fine example in all you've done. You can plant a seed in the best soil, and it can still grow crooked."

Later, Sara stood at the open window of her upstairs bedroom and listened to the quiet whinnies from the barn where Columbine was in foal. Zeke and his old friend, a Sioux named Chester Elk Horn, would handle Columbine. She could sleep. She *should* sleep. But Joey was gone, out there somewhere getting into trouble, probably, and she couldn't help worrying.

And then she thought of Gideon Ironheart and wondered if he was just passing through. And hoped that he might stay a little while. He had been a splash of brilliant color in days that, for Sara, had grown increasingly colorless. Life had passed her by in some respects, but that didn't mean she was content.

Yes, it would be nice—in an interesting way—if he stayed for a while. There would be light and color and life wherever he went. He was that kind of man.

The motel room smelled like a motel room. Sickly sweet air freshener battled the odors of sweat, urine, tobacco and other things Gideon didn't want to think about. The rug looked clean enough, though, and the sheets smelled like laundry soap, so he ignored the rest of it as best he could.

The motel was located beside the state highway that ran just outside Conard City, and the otherwise quiet night was occasionally disturbed by the whine of a trailer truck as it passed at high speed. The last drunken cowboy had staggered into his room shortly after two, and since then only one truck had passed.

He was alone with the night and himself, and both were empty. Too empty.

With his hands clasped behind his head, he lay on the bed and stared up at the patterns of light on the ceiling—white from the porch light just outside the door, and green from the sign out front, softly diffused by the white curtains. The guy next door suddenly coughed, a smoker's hack, wheezy and sustained.

He'd stayed in a lot of cheap motels over the years and lived in a lot of furnished rooms, but he didn't want to think about that now. He didn't want to think about the past, and he didn't want to think about what he was intending to do tomorrow, so he focused instead on Sara Yates and the events of this evening. She was an easy out, a ready excuse not to think about important things. Not to think about all the things that had suddenly come to matter too much.

Something about her appealed to him. Maybe it was that tough exterior, that determined hardness of speech and manner that didn't fit her at all. She had all the words right and the postures down perfectly, but he didn't buy it. Someone or something had driven Sara Yates into hiding, and it was easier to wonder about her problems than it was to think about his own.

And suddenly, in the dark with no one and nothing to distract him, he thought about that brief couple of seconds when he had seized her by the waist and lifted her into her Blazer. Well, not exactly by her waist. Her gun belt had caused him to wrap his hands around her midriff. Just beneath her breasts. His thumbs remembered that all too brief sensation of warmth, weight and softness, and his palms remembered the fragile delicacy of her ribs. She might try to look like a guy, but her feel was all woman.

And all of a sudden, in the dark with nothing to distract him, his body responded to remembered sensations. A hungry ache zinged straight to his groin, reminding him he was a man—a man who'd been avoiding women for too damn long. Hell. Anyway, he knew better. He'd sworn off Anglo women half a lifetime ago, and Sara Yates looked about as Anglo as they came. Irish showed in her slightly long upper lip and rose-tinted milky skin. The kind of skin that made a man think of cool misty mornings and gentle rain. Of long, lazy, sleepy dawns full of loving. The kind of loving he'd never found.

Hell, couldn't he find a likelier woman to get the hots for?

But in the dark, with nothing to distract him except memories he wasn't ready to face, it didn't matter a damn.

Chapter 2

The sun was barely skimming the eastern horizon when Gideon left the motel and walked into town. Sleep had eluded him most of the night, and this morning he felt wired. It was the same feeling he got when he was working seventy stories up and something went wrong, the same rush of adrenaline, the same heightened senses, the same edginess of a close call. Until six months ago, he had been addicted to the feeling. These days he never wanted to feel it again.

But he was feeling it now, and it kept him walking at a brisk pace toward his goal, the Conard County Sheriff's Office. Downtown across from the courthouse, Sara had said last night. In a storefront.

He walked on the shoulder of the business detour from the state highway and into the outskirts of town. There he saw the usual businesses—gas stations, hardware stores, body shops, a veterinarian, and cattle pens and a railroad siding where market-bound steers were probably loaded.

Closer in, residential areas spread away from the business loop, older homes, mostly, with lawns and carefully nurtured trees. A nice little town, he thought. A town to grow old in, but not the best place to be young. Joey Yates probably needed a lot more excitement than Conard County provided.

Bayard's Garage still wasn't open, so he continued his way to the center of town. The courthouse was visible now, towering over the surrounding buildings, a Victorian gothic structure built of rough-hewn granite.

Maude's Diner was visible down a side street, busy even at this early hour, he noted. The coffee must be good. He'd stop there later. Right now he was too damn tense.

The courthouse lawn was large, a small park full of flower beds and benches to sit on. He found a bench right across the street from the sheriff's office and settled down to wait.

The sun rose higher and began to steal the night's chill from the air. A couple of old men, one of them leaning on a cane, took seats a little closer to the courthouse and began to read their newspapers. Pigeons strutted jerkily along the sidewalks, pecking at invisible morsels. A dog wandered by, pausing to sniff at Gideon's boots. Reaching out a hand, he stroked the dog's head absently, but he never took his eyes off the sheriff's office.

And then the day began. The first to arrive was a scrawny, leathery-looking older woman who unlocked the office and disappeared within. Only seconds behind her a sheriff's vehicle arrived, a sand-colored Blazer just like the one Sara had driven the night before. The man who climbed out was somewhere in his forties, sunburned to a permanent red and thickening around the middle.

Several much younger men arrived, all of them clearly deputies. Sara showed up but evidently didn't notice him sitting across the street. This morning she was wearing the mirrored aviator-style sunglasses that seemed to go with cop uniforms. Gideon almost smiled. Sara Yates wanted to be tough. He wondered if he would ever find out why.

The sun rose higher, and finally one more Blazer pulled up into a reserved slot. And this time Gideon tensed and sat up straighter, squinting in an effort to miss nothing.

A tall, powerfully built man climbed out. He, too, wore a deputy's khaki uniform, tan Stetson and mirrored glasses, but unlike the others, his dark hair flowed loose to his shoulders. He glanced toward the square, the quick, scanning glance common to men who never overlooked a detail of their surroundings, and then he turned to enter the office.

Gideon felt the shock of recognition like a hot punch in his stomach. He'd expected to be able to identify the man the way he would have identified any stranger who had been described to him. He hadn't been prepared for this gut recognition. It wasn't as if he'd ever met the guy.

The big man paused, scanning the square and streets again, as if he had sensed something. His eyes were hidden behind those mirrored glasses, but Gideon nonetheless felt the man's gaze scrape over him, felt it pass and then return briefly for another look.

Damn, was the man psychic? But then the big deputy turned and entered the sheriff's office. Whatever he had seen had been dismissed as unimportant. Gideon released a long breath, realizing for the first time that he had been holding it.

That was him, all right. No doubt of it. And now that he'd found Micah Parish, he had to figure out what he was going to do about it.

The sun rose a little higher and the street grew busier. The surrounding businesses opened; the courthouse parking lot filled with cars. Gideon couldn't have said why he continued to sit there. He had seen Parish, and that was what he had come here for, to identify the man. He could go down the street to the diner now and have some coffee and eggs. He could mosey on up to Bayard's Garage and arrange to get his truck fixed.

But he sat on, strangely paralyzed, and let the warm sun and cool, dry Wyoming breeze caress him. It was nice here, he thought, and he was finally old enough to appreciate it. Even six months ago he would have been impatient with the quiet, relaxed, aimless atmosphere, with the positively bucolic scene.

A battered old green pickup pulled into the last parking slot in front of the sheriff's department. Gideon watched absently as an old man with long, braided, raven-colored hair climbed out. Few full-blooded Native Americans turned gray with age, and the color of the old man's hair proclaimed the purity of his bloodline. Shoshone? Gideon wondered. Lakota? Such differences had once been critical, and to some they still were. In an Anglo world, though, they were kin.

A tall, dark-haired youth climbed out the other side, and suddenly Gideon sat a little straighter. If that boy wasn't Sara's brother, he'd eat his hat, conchos and all. Curiosity almost brought him to his feet, and then he remembered himself. If that was indeed Joey Yates, it was none of his business, and not even natural curiosity could justify his going over to the office to gawk.

Fifteen minutes later the old man came out alone and stood on the sidewalk, surveying the street as if he hadn't quite decided what he was going to do now. Then he saw Gideon.

Much to Gideon's amazement, the old man crossed the street purposefully, as if Gideon were someone he had been looking for. He came right up to the younger man and halted, staring down at him as if taking his measure.

Gideon returned the stare impassively. He knew that look. His grandfather had looked at him that way the day twelve-year-old Gideon had been brought to him from the orphanage. It had been a look that went past the surface and seemed to pry into the soul. It had made him uneasy then, but today he was a forty-one-year-old man who knew even the darkest corners of his soul. Having no secrets from himself, he didn't fear what others might see in him.

"You're Ironheart," the old man said finally.

Gideon nodded.

"Sara mentioned you. That's not any Indian name I ever heard."

"I chose it, old man."

Zeke smiled. "I'm Zeke Jackson."

"Funny name for an Indian."

"A missionary chose it."

Gideon felt a smile crease his face. "Yeah," he said.

Zeke stared down at him for another ten or fifteen seconds, then sat beside him on the bench. "Nice morning."

"Very. That boy who came in with you…Joey Yates?"

"Sara mentioned him, did she?"

"She was looking for him when we met."

"He's going to spend the next couple of days, maybe more, in jail. It'll get his attention, maybe."

Gideon looked at Zeke, and his smile broadened a little more. "Yeah. It can work that way."

Zeke nodded, the road map of lines all over his face deepening a little. "Leaves me shorthanded, though. You looking to stay in Conard County awhile?"

"Awhile. I'm not sure how long."

"What do you do?"

"I'm an ironworker."

Zeke turned and looked at him, his black eyes bright with interest. "One of those guys who builds the steel frames for skyscrapers?"

"That's right. I'm a connector."

"What does that mean, exactly?"

Gideon settled back and stared off into space, aware that his heart was picking up speed just a little. He didn't want to think about what he did. About what he *had* done. "A connector is the first guy up. He shinnies up the column from the floor below and hangs there like a monkey at the top until the derrick swings a ten-or twenty-ton beam his way. When it gets close enough, he grabs on to it, guides it into place and drives a couple of bolts home to hold it there."

"Then you're one of those crazy guys I've seen walking on those narrow I-beams up there."

"Yeah." Crazy was probably a good word for it.

"Then you're not afraid of heights."

Gideon turned his head and looked straight at him. "Old man, only a fool isn't afraid of heights."

Zeke nodded. "How high have you worked?"

"Ninety stories. My last job topped out at seventy."

"How high is that?"

"Around seven hundred feet."

Zeke gave a low whistle. "Beats me why any man wants to walk on a six-inch-wide piece of steel at that kind of altitude."

Gideon smiled. "It's almost as good as being a bird." Or had been.

Zeke studied him a little longer. "Know anything about horses?"

"A little. My uncle raises them, and when I was a kid I helped break them."

"Well, Ironheart, if you're looking for work around here, I'm shorthanded for a few days, and I've got a herd of mustangs I need some help with."

"Mustangs?"

"I can't let them all go to the glue factory, can I?" He rose and gave a nod of farewell. "Anyone can tell you how to find the Double Y, if you're interested."

Gideon hadn't learned as much from his grandfather as he should have, but he had taken a few things with him that had given him strength over the years. One of those things was the morning silence. His grandfather had called it prayer, and most other people would have called it meditation. Since Gideon didn't consider himself conventionally religious, he refused to think of it as prayer, and "meditation" sounded too New Age for his taste.

So he called it the morning silence, or going into the silence, when he called it anything at all. It was a place inside himself, an inner pool of stillness and peace, that he visited each morning before he began his day. It was like reaching inside and tapping some bottomless well full of serenity and strength. He always emerged from the silence refreshed, feeling centered in himself and ready for the day's trials. It didn't solve his problems or dull the edge of his pain, but it helped him endure.

Two mornings later, sitting in the center of the motel room on the floor, cross-legged and straight-backed, he emerged from the silence with an almost aching sense of loss. His grandfather had been a medicine man, a great shaman of the old ways, and he wished now that he had listened more closely.

"You have the power in you," the old man had told him once. "You have the gift, boy, and a responsibility. Learn to use it, and use it wisely."

But what had a fourteen-year-old boy cared for such things? A forty-one year old man cared, but now it was too late. He could only sit there in a dingy motel room and wish to God he had something more than a feeling that he had somehow lost his way, could merely think that if only he had listened to the wisdom of an old man, he might have had somewhere to look for answers and direction.

But he had only himself and the feeling that he hadn't done what he had been meant to do with the days of his life. Probably just midlife crisis, he told himself as he rose from the floor. It would sort itself out.

In the last two days, though, he hadn't learned a damn thing about Micah Parish, and learning about Micah Parish had been the main reason he'd come to Conard County. The locals, who probably gossiped avidly among themselves, were proving to be remarkably tight-lipped with the outsider. He would mention Micah casually in conversation, and all he ever got was, "Yeah. Damn fine deputy."

Two solid days, and he didn't know any more than the private detective had been able to tell him. Micah Parish had been with the Conard County Sheriff's Department for approximately five years, after retiring from the army, and just before Christmas he had married an old friend. It didn't tell Gideon a damn thing about the man. It did, however, explain why that expensive P.I. had been able to tell him so little. Judging by the way his neighbors closed their wagons in a circle around him, Micah must have made a good impression on them.

And if Gideon hung around this town much longer without some obvious reason to remain, he would probably become the subject of local speculation himself. In fact, it wouldn't surprise him if a Conard County deputy showed up at his door and started asking questions about his business. He'd already realized that people around here looked out for one another, and a stranger might be someone the community needed protecting from. Neighborliness was a far sight more than a casual wave in these parts—it was serious business.

That meant that if he wanted to stay around here without arousing all kinds of uncomfortable suspicion, he'd better take that job that Zeke Jackson had offered him out at the Double Y.

Dirk Bayard, at the garage, gave him directions, and soon he was on the road, heading out toward the western end of Conard County, driving straight toward the mountains that still bore a winter mantle of snow on their highest shoulders. Except for the six years he had spent on his uncle's ranch on the Oklahoma prairie, and a year spent building missile silos in eastern Montana, Gideon had been a city dweller because his job had demanded it. He had lived in caverns of steel and glass, and had been aware of a faint dislocation when he left them behind to travel to another city and another job across the continent, or even just when he took a week to go fishing or hunting with his buddies.

There was no way, he thought now as he drove down a long, empty county road, that you could overlook the isolation out here. Since leaving Conard City, he had passed two other vehicles, one a sheriff's unit, the other the mailman, who out here drove a white truck with the Postal Service emblem on the door. Different. It was different.

It appealed to him. Especially that line of mountains to the west, blue in the bright morning light. Everything looked so damn clean and fresh, and the quiet called to him, promising peace.

Being an ironworker had carried satisfactions that few people ever found. When Gideon had built something, he could look at it and see the actual fruits of his efforts. More, he could look at it and know it would still be there fifty years after he was gone.

People out here probably found the same satisfaction, he

thought now. The seasons might come and go, but the land remained, and they passed it on to their sons and grandsons.

He could imagine making a life here, he realized. He could easily imagine it.

The turnoff for the Double Y was marked, as Dirk Bayard had promised. Almost as soon as he turned off the county road, the terrain changed, growing more rugged. The dirt lane he traveled now rose steadily toward the mountains, and the air grew gradually chillier. One of the prettiest spots in the county, Dirk had told him, and one of the hardest to ranch. Too bad there was no market for mountain goats, he'd added.

The road ended two miles later in a hard-packed yard between a house and a weathered barn. Behind the buildings lay a large meadow that rose gently toward the trees. Part of it had been fenced for pasture, and three horses grazed there now. An idyllic setting, he thought.

In a corral behind the barn, Gideon saw the old man holding a restless stallion by his halter. The roan had the compact, sturdy build of a mustang and the temperament of a wild male. His eyes were rolling a little as Zeke Jackson tugged on the halter rope and moved closer.

Damn old man, Gideon thought, climbing out of his truck. He wasn't big enough to hold that horse down, or strong enough. If that stallion reared...

Suddenly, the stallion did just that, then pivoted in an abrupt, unexpected movement that knocked the old Shoshone to one side in the dirt. Pawing at the air with his front hooves, the horse screamed and then came down hard.

Joey wouldn't even speak to her. That glum thought had been the first one in Sara's mind that morning when she awoke, and it was still haunting her as she performed her weekly household chores. Today was her day off, so she needn't go into Conard City for that reason, and thinking of Joey's sullen silence, she told herself she wouldn't go in to see him, either. He could just sit there and sulk.

Tough words, but they didn't do anything to ease the ache

in her heart. Eleven years ago, when their mother had died,
Sara had stood beside the raw dirt of the grave and hugged her
weeping five-year-old brother. Two years later she had done it
again when they buried their father. In all the ways that
counted, she *was* Joey's mother, and like a mother, she suffered
for him and with him. At least a dozen times a day she wanted
to race into town and tell Nate Tate to let him out. Nate might
even do it, but in the long run, it was Joey who would pay for
the leniency. Somehow they had to get his attention.

No, Nate probably wouldn't let him out. The sheriff had
been preaching tough love for Joey for the last six months, and
he wasn't likely to go all soft because Sara asked him to. When
Zeke had brought Joey in the other morning, Nate had looked
at the boy and said, "Well, it's about time." And maybe it
was. Better a few days or weeks in the county jail than years
in the penitentiary.

Hearing the approach of a truck engine, she set her dust mop
aside and went onto the kitchen porch to see who it might be.
Emma and Gage Dalton, maybe. Emma had been her good
friend for many years, and since their marriage, Gage often
joined her when she came out to visit Sara.

She recognized Gideon Ironheart's truck immediately. What
had brought him out here? she wondered, and then looked
down in dismay at her worn jeans and the old khaki shirt she
had put on for cleaning. She hadn't even done anything with
her hair, had simply pulled it out of the way with a rubber band
at the nape of her neck.

And it didn't matter, she told herself sternly as she watched
him pull to a stop in the yard. It didn't matter a damn what
she was wearing or what she looked like. It hadn't mattered in
nearly ten years, and it wasn't going to start mattering today.

Just then the mustang shrieked, and Gideon leapt out of his
truck as if propelled. Sara couldn't see the corral beyond the
barn from the porch, but the sight of Gideon racing full steam
in that direction told her that her grandfather was in trouble.
Dropping the mop, she took off at a dead run.

By the time she rounded the barn, Gideon was in the corral,

holding the mustang tightly by its halter. The horse jerked his head back sharply and twisted, trying to get away, but muscles honed to steel by years of hard labor jerked right back, telling the animal who was boss.

Sara climbed the rails and dropped to the dirt beside her grandfather.

"Grandfather? Grandfather!"

The old man's eyes opened, and he drew a deep, shuddering breath. "I'm okay, child. Just got the wind knocked out of me."

"Oh, Grandfather..." Relief left her weak. When he sat up, she hugged him wordlessly as her throat tightened in reaction.

He patted her shoulder. "It's all right, Sarey. It's all right."

She helped the old man to his feet, wincing sympathetically when the pain of his arthritis flickered across his face. He was too old for this, she thought angrily. Joey should have been here helping. At that moment, she could have cheerfully boxed her brother's ears.

"I'll get someone out here to help with the horses," she told him. "I don't want you doing all this work, Grandfather. I told you—"

"I think we already have someone to help with the horses," Zeke interrupted. He indicated Gideon with a jerk of his chin.

The mustang was still sidling nervously, but he had calmed considerably. Sara watched in amazement as Gideon Ironheart murmured to the horse, standing close enough that, had the stallion taken a mind to, he could have bitten off half the man's face. But the horse didn't bite. Shivering, shifting from hoof to hoof, he listened to each and every liquid syllable that Gideon murmured.

Without missing a beat or changing his intonation, Gideon spoke to her. "Sara? Get Zeke out of here."

"I'm fine, I'm fine," Zeke muttered stubbornly, refusing to accept even a hand from her. He'd always been cussedly stubborn, Sara thought. Always.

When they were safely outside the gate, they both turned to look back at Gideon and the mustang. Horse and man seemed to have reached some kind of agreement, for now the stallion stood still, head down, and docilely accepted Gideon stroking his neck.

"Look at that," Zeke said softly. "Just look at that. There's a man who knows horses, Sarey. I'm damn glad I offered him a job."

"A job?" Sara stared in surprise at her grandfather and then looked at Gideon. "Here? Can we afford him?"

"Reckon so. He didn't ask what I was paying."

"Then maybe you'd better discuss that with him."

Zeke gave her a smiling glance. "Don't worry, gal. I'll take care of everything."

Not certain that reassurance made her feel any better, Sara looked over at Gideon. He was still talking to that damn mustang, a soft, seductive murmuring that slipped over the ears like satin over skin, enticing, mesmerizing. Promising.

And he had once again fallen into that pose of sheer male arrogance, legs splayed, one knee bent, hips cocked rakishly and thrusting slightly forward as if to draw attention to his virility. Since he was intent upon the horse, she gave him the benefit of the doubt and decided that the pose must be unconscious. He wasn't George, after all.

Thinking of George, as she had been trying not to for ten years, turned her mood instantly sour and waspish. As if he sensed it somehow, her grandfather looked at her.

"I'll take care of it, Sara."

She nodded and turned back to the house. Twenty-eight years old, and she was still taking orders as if she was a child. But that was a problem, living in a multigenerational household. To her grandfather, she would always be a child who would do as she was told.

Gideon looked away from the horse and stared at her departing back. She had a figure, that woman, he noted approvingly. Without her gun belt to conceal it, she had a waist, a tiny waist accentuated by the way she had knotted her shirttails. The ragged denim of her jeans clung lovingly to long, slender legs and a full, round rump. And her hips...well, they weren't a model's skinny ones at all. Nope, they were a woman's hips, meant to cradle a man and bear children with ease. Her hair was long, he saw, too, and he felt a stirring in places that shouldn't be stirring in broad daylight.

He glanced toward Zeke. "You didn't say she was your granddaughter."

"I don't recollect you asking."

Gideon felt himself grin in response. Damned if he didn't like this old coot. The mustang had calmed down now, and the stench of the animal's fear, while still strong, was beginning to fade in the open air. "What were you trying to do when I drove up?"

"Right foreleg looks a tad swollen just below the knee, and he's been limping. It's probably nothing, but it took me three days to coax him into the corral, and I'd like to be sure there's no real hurt."

Gideon nodded, speaking soothingly to the horse. The mustang's ears were pricked, attentive to every sound the man made, and his nostrils were still flared, but the whites of his eyes were no longer wildly showing. Not afraid any longer, Gideon judged. Just naturally wary.

Murmuring nonsense syllables in a cadence he had learned from his uncle, he stroked his hand lower and lower by small degrees, until the horse was tolerating touches to his shoulder and chest. Slowly, very slowly, Gideon squatted and began to run his fingers over first one foreleg and then the other, comparing the two as the best measure of injury.

"It's swollen, all right," he said a few moments later. "Not a lot, though, and it's not feverish. The skin's not broken anywhere."

"Probably just a strain," Zeke said. "Guess I'll keep him corralled for a day or two."

Gideon straightened slowly, murmuring soothingly again as the horse shied a little. Then he released the halter and stepped back. For several heartbeats the mustang didn't move; then he darted to the far side of the corral. Gideon laughed softly. "Reminds me of some of the street toughs I've known over the years.''

He climbed the fence and joined Zeke on the other side. For a while neither man spoke. They stood and watched the horse posture threateningly and whinny at the mares who hung back near a pine-covered ridge. The breeze stirred, carrying the scents of pine and grass and horse to them.

''How many mustangs?'' Gideon asked.

''Just these. I'd take more—certainly have enough room for 'em—but we couldn't afford to keep 'em in hay all winter. Sarey works hard enough as it is.''

The younger man nodded.

Zeke indicated the mustang with a jerk of his chin. ''What did you say to him?''

Gideon shrugged. ''Nothing but the truth.''

''And what's that?''

Steel-gray eyes met obsidian ones. ''That I didn't want to steal his fire or his freedom.''

Zeke continued to stare intently at him for a few seconds; then he looked toward the mustang again. ''So you want some work?''

''A little. A few days, maybe. A few hours here and there.''

''What kind of wage?''

Gideon had already figured that one out. ''Whatever will keep you from feeling you're taking a favor.''

Zeke laughed. ''I think you were wasted working with all that steel, Ironheart.''

Maybe he had been, Gideon thought as he watched the stallion paw the dirt. Certainly now, whenever he looked back, all he saw was a vast wasteland where his past should have been.

Sara saw them coming toward the house and immediately recognized the indefinable aura that existed between men who had reached a friendly understanding. Gideon Ironheart would be working for them, which meant she was going to be seeing a lot of him.

The thought made her at once uneasy and excited. He affected her as no man had since George, and even George hadn't given her the electric feeling Gideon did, as if the very air around him tingled and snapped with energy. Her hand flew to her dark hair, freshly brushed and loose around her shoulders. At least she'd caught herself before she had changed. That would have been too obvious.

At the very last possible moment, though, she turned and fled from the kitchen. Gideon Ironheart made her feel vulnerable, and she had to shore up her defenses before she faced him.

In her bedroom, she listened to the men come in, heard the deep rumble of their voices as they settled at the kitchen table, heard the clink of crockery as her grandfather poured coffee.

Anger flickered briefly as she recalled the way Gideon had manhandled her last night. She hadn't been a deputy sheriff for the last nine years without learning how to handle herself in tough situations, or without learning how to judge them. He hadn't needed to drag her out of that bar and thrust her into her vehicle. He certainly hadn't needed to make that remark about women needing protection. He might be eight inches taller and outweigh her by seventy or eighty pounds, but that didn't necessarily mean he could protect her any better than she could protect herself.

The memory made her steam, even as a traitorous warmth touched cold places. Apart from her grandfather, it had been a long time since anyone had wanted to protect Sara Yates from anything.

But everything else aside, she wanted nothing to do with any man who made her feel vulnerable. She was never going to be vulnerable again. Nearly a decade had passed, but she hadn't forgotten the humiliation of waiting in a church packed with people for a groom who was finally discovered to have fled to another state in order to escape marrying her. Sara Yates had awakened that long-ago morning a blushing, fresh eighteen years old. It had been both her birthday and her wedding day. By the time it was over, her heart had felt as if it were eighty. And it had been months before conversations no longer halted whenever she entered a room. No, she wasn't going to make a fool of herself again.

When Sara returned to the kitchen, Gideon and Zeke were on a second cup of coffee and making inroads on the coffee cake she had taken from the oven only an hour ago. Since she had baked it only to satisfy her grandfather's sweet tooth, she didn't mind.

She *did* mind the way Gideon's gaze followed her as she moved around the kitchen, fixing her own coffee. Her stomach was suddenly full of butterflies, and her knees felt rubbery, almost exactly the sensation she had felt during her one foray into acting in a high school play. Stage fright, all because a man was staring at her? Get real, Sara!

She reminded him, Gideon thought unexpectedly, of a sweet, small brown mouse. Evidently she dropped the tough act around her grandfather, and she even moved differently— gracefully. More like a woman and less like a boy.

She joined them at the table with her coffee, giving him a polite, casual smile. "Grandfather says he offered you a job. Did you come out to accept it?"

"Yes, I did."

Zeke spoke. "I told him he's welcome to stay in the bunk-house and eat with us."

"That was the big inducement," Gideon said, watching Sara for any sign of objection. "That fleabag motel is charging me thirty bucks a night."

Since Zeke did all the cooking, Sara couldn't much object to that, but she wasn't too thrilled at the prospect of cleaning out the bunkhouse, which hadn't been opened in almost five years. "What if the roof leaks?" she said, feeling strangely helpless.

"We'll fix it," Zeke said. "I don't reckon it does though, Sarey. I've been going in there a couple of times a year to make sure it was still okay in case we needed it. Now we need it." He looked at Gideon. "You'll bring your stuff up here today?"

"Yeah, in a couple of hours. I need to check out of the motel and give my uncle a call to tell him where to find me if he needs me."

Sara suddenly remembered him mentioning that his black hat had been a gift from his uncle. "You're close to him, aren't you?"

Gideon didn't evade. "You bet. By the time he took me in, he'd already raised six sons of his own. You'd have thought he'd have been too tired to bother, but he was never too tired for me. Now he's old and none too well, and all his boys are scattered to the four winds."

"You can call him from here," Sara said impulsively. "You can always call him from here. Anytime."

Gideon smiled, a warm expression that touched Sara almost physically. "Thanks, Sara."

"And now maybe you'll satisfy my curiosity," Zeke said.

Gideon suddenly looked a little wary, Sara thought, and was uneasy with the realization that this man might not be what he seemed. "Sure," he said, sounding almost offhand about it.

"Last night you told Sara your grandfather got your attention. What were you up to?"

"Grandfather!" Sara was appalled. That simply wasn't a question you asked anyone.

"It's okay, Sara," Gideon said unexpectedly. "He's got a right to know what kind of man he's hiring."

Which meant that Gideon Ironheart didn't have anything really serious to hide, Sara thought hopefully. Either that or he was a bigger con artist than she wanted to know. And that was unfair, she scolded herself. Why should she be suspicious before she had cause?

Gideon and her grandfather were looking at one another with a kind of seriousness that seemed odd considering that Zeke had already hired the younger man and, until a moment or two ago, had seemed quite favorably impressed. Now, suddenly, it was as if somehow another factor had been thrown into the equation. What had happened?

"I was a real troublemaker for a while," Gideon said slowly, never taking his eyes from Zeke. "Drugs. Booze. Fast cars. A little shoplifting for the thrill of it. I was lucky. I didn't get caught with weed on me, but I got caught with an expensive belt buckle I hadn't paid for. I got grand theft and sixth months on probation. Three weeks into my time, my grandfather found me out behind the barn rolling a joint. One thing led to another, and he eventually took me into town and turned me in. I did the rest of my six months in jail, fell behind a year in school, and came out a wiser man. I haven't been in trouble since."

Zeke nodded, satisfied. "Not everyone learns that quick."

"What I learned, old man, was that I can't stand to be caged. I can't stand being kept locked up away from the sun and the wind, and I can't stand having other people control me. I barely survived it once. I wouldn't survive it a second time. So I learned to get my thrills in legal ways."

Again Zeke nodded, as if he found this perfectly comprehensible. "A young man who is wild often grows into an old man with wisdom."

One corner of Gideon's mouth quirked. "I'm a long way from wisdom, Zeke. Believe me."

"A long way from old, too," Zeke said on a chuckle.

"And your grandfather?" Sara asked. "Is he still around?"

Gideon shook his head. "He passed on twelve years ago. Before I got old enough to really listen to him."

Something about the way he said that told Sara how much he regretted the loss, and she warmed a little more toward him.

"Well," said Gideon, pushing back from the table, "I'd better go check out before they charge me for another night. I'll be back in plenty of time to help with the chores, Zeke. Don't get started without me."

Sara watched him go, only half-aware that her grandfather was watching her. All man, she thought with a delicious, frightening inward thrill. Gideon Ironheart was *all* man. And he probably had a string of broken hearts behind him to prove it, she reminded herself. Still, it couldn't hurt to admire his rear view as he strolled to his truck.

"Seems like a good man," Zeke remarked.

"Maybe." She was determined to reserve judgment, and faced her grandfather with her chin stubbornly set. "Time will tell. Now I need to get out there and clean the bunkhouse. That place must be layered under inches of dust and dirt after all this time."

"I'll do it, Sarey. I offered it to the man."

"Forget it," she said, softening. "Your arthritis will give you fits, and it won't take me long at all to do a little dusting."

Zeke rose from the table and came over to wrap an arm around her shoulders. "We all depend on you too much, child."

They were nearly of a height, and Sara had to tip her head only a little bit to meet his eyes. "I wouldn't have been able to do any of it without you, Grandfather, and you know it perfectly well. I couldn't have taken a job if you hadn't come to live here and look after Joey. I would have lost the ranch for sure, and maybe I would have had to give Joey up."

And suddenly she gave a soft laugh. "Right now, that doesn't sound so awful, does it?"

Zeke joined her laughter and squeezed her in a warm hug. "No, Sarey, right now it doesn't sound bad at all."

The bunkhouse was dusty, all right, and there were plenty of cobwebs, but otherwise it was a sound and sturdy structure. It had four rooms, three with beds, and a front room with a wood stove, a couch and a couple of overstuffed chairs. A mouse had gotten into one of the chairs, pulling out a little stuffing, but the damage wasn't too bad. The plank floors needed a good dust mopping, and then a swipe with the wet mop.

A couple of hours later, she reached the last bedroom and noticed the stack of boxes and a trunk in the corner. Zeke's things, she thought. He'd stored them in here when he had come to live with her and Joey. Maybe he would want to bring them up to the house now.

Absently, not really paying attention to what she was doing, she flipped open one of the boxes. Her attention was immediately snared by a gold-framed portrait, and she lifted it with slow hands and a wondering heart.

This was her grandparents' wedding portrait, she realized, and sank onto the edge of the bed so she could study it. That would have been 1941, she thought. Just at the beginning of the war. Zeke would have been about nineteen, and his bride, Alma Dietz, would have been barely seventeen.

The photo was sepia-toned, but there was no mistaking that Alma was fair and Zeke was dark. Zeke wore an army uniform proudly, and his raven hair was trimmed close, revealing the proud shape of his skull and cheeks. Alma, with wispy blond hair and eyes so light they barely registered in the photo, looked as fragile as Zeke looked strong. Her dress was white, and her veil was trimmed with rosebuds.

Why, Sara wondered, had Alma's missionary father blessed this union? Prejudices had been even worse then than they were now, and they were bad enough now. Had Alma been so persuasive? Or had the war made other matters seem unimportant? Or had her great grandfather simply been a man of principle without prejudice?

She was tempted to ask Zeke about it, then hesitated. This photo was out here, after all, hidden away with things he evidently had no need of. Maybe it was better left hidden. Perhaps the memories were still too painful for him in some way.

Sara devoted another couple of minutes to looking at the face of the grandmother she had never known, then slipped the framed portrait back into the box. Maybe she would just mention the boxes casually and see what Zeke said. Maybe he wouldn't want them out here where Gideon could rummage through them.

And maybe he would tell her why they weren't in the house with him.

The bathroom took a little longer to clean, partly because it had been years since anyone had scoured the scum from the tub, and partly because Sara kept coming face-to-face with memories of her father. Ted Yates had worked nearly a solid month one summer to bring water and modern facilities to the bunkhouse. Sara, ten at the time, had worked right alongside him, getting her first lessons in plumbing, soldering, welding and good, old-fashioned ditch digging. The ditch, to lay pipe from the well, had taken most of the time, needing to be pick-axed out of rocky ground and made deep enough so the pipes wouldn't freeze in the winter. Looking at her hands now, Sara remembered her blisters and her wonderful sense of accomplishment.

And remembered her dad hugging her to his side, saying, "You're a great gal, Sarey. Some man's going to love you to death."

But George had panicked at the mere thought of loving her and marrying her, and Sara, at twenty-eight, had given up hope of any man loving her at all, never mind loving her to death.

Then, slowly and softly, as easily as the words he had whispered to that damn mustang hours ago had slipped into her ears, the memory of Gideon Ironheart slipped into her mind. A woman would give a lot to be loved by a man like that, Sara thought. A whole lot.

But not her. Damn it, she was never again going to be any man's fool. Never!

Chapter 3

"Steady, boy. Steady." Gideon spoke soothingly to the wary mustang, patting the horse's shoulder reassuringly. In the four days he had been working for Zeke Jackson, he had spent some time coaxing the roan stallion to accept him. It was important, he thought, to get the horse to tolerate at least one person, because if the animal ever got truly sick or badly injured, he was going to need human help. So far, Gideon thought, he seemed to be gaining ground. The horse no longer shuddered so violently at his proximity and now didn't even attempt to evade his touch.

The horse had fire in his eye, Gideon thought. He'd survived the wilderness, capture and the BLM corrals, and yet he hadn't sacrificed any of himself.

"You sure haven't, boy," Gideon murmured, stroking the sleek neck and shoulder, and almost fancied the horse snorted an affirmative. "Still just as free and independent as day one, aren't you? Still you, through and through."

The stallion bobbed his head and whinnied, then butted Gideon's shoulder. Gideon chuckled.

The horse, he thought, with a deep, private pang, had achieved something that he himself had failed to. It was hard to put into words, this sense that the horse had fulfilled itself while he, Gideon, had not. Hard to explain even to himself the feeling that his life had somehow been bent out of shape, that he had sacrificed himself to goals that hadn't mattered. Hard to find words to tell himself that this horse had become the best horse he could be, but that Gideon Ironheart was a long way from being the best man he could be.

He clucked soothingly to the animal and let liquid syllables tumble over his tongue, the sounds and cadences learned so long ago and somehow never forgotten. And thinking of his uncle brought his reverie around to his grandfather, and the old man's warning.

"Boy, a life is a portrait. It's a picture you paint every day, every minute, every second, with the palette you were given at birth. It's an expression of yourself, whether you want it to be or not. Make sure it's a picture you're proud of."

Well, Gideon thought now, he sure as hell wasn't proud of his portrait. Not that he was ashamed of it. No, he hadn't done very much that he was ashamed of, because he'd realized a long time ago that he had to live with himself first of all. But he hadn't done a whole hell of a lot to be proud of, either. What did a few skyscrapers amount to, after all? They sure didn't measure up to a Sistine Chapel, or a *Mona Lisa*. They didn't even measure up to a guy who could raise a good crowd for his funeral.

Suddenly his lips quirked and he almost laughed out loud. God, talk about sinking into self-pity! What had gotten into him? He was almost never like this.

"You've got that damn mustang mesmerized."

Gideon glanced toward the fence and saw a man he didn't recognize. Tall, lean, well-built, the guy was dressed like everyone in these parts—jeans, Western shirt and straw cowboy hat. Gideon himself had traded his black felt hat for a straw one, in concession to the warmth of the day.

"Howdy," Gideon said quietly. "Something I can do for you?"

The man shook his head. "I'm here to see Sara, but I caught sight of you and couldn't resist watching. Where'd you learn to whisper a horse?"

"My uncle taught me when I was a kid." Realizing that his time with the horse was over for now, Gideon gave the stallion a friendly pat and then headed for the fence himself. "Does Sara know you're here?"

"Not yet. I'll go up to the house in just a minute. I don't recall seeing you around here before. You're new in these parts."

Gideon nodded. "Lately from Georgia." This guy was good-looking, he thought, just the kind of man women seemed to go for. What was he to Sara? "The name's Ironheart."

"I'm Jeff Cumberland." He stuck his hand out and shook Gideon's briskly. "I own the Bar C, up north from here."

Gideon had heard of the Bar C. It was the biggest, most successful ranching operation in the county, and Zeke must have mentioned it at least twice, as had other people around town when they thought he might be looking for work.

Jeff continued speaking. "I don't have a man who can talk a horse that way. In fact, I don't think I've seen anyone do it in a dozen years or more. If you get tired of the Double Y, come see me."

"Trying to steal my hired hand, Jeff?" Sara asked. She had come up almost silently, and both men started a little at the sound of her voice. The first thing Gideon noticed was that she was annoyed. Not at him, but at Cumberland.

Jeff smiled and shook his head. "Nope. Forget I said anything."

Sara put her hands on her hips in a posture Gideon recognized. Sara, who hadn't shown him the tough side of herself since he started working here, was showing it to Cumberland now. What had this man done to her to make her feel she had to be tough around him?

"What brings you up here?" she asked Jeff.

"I wanted to make our usual arrangement about summer pasturage. Are you agreeable?"

Sara nodded. She needed the money, even if she hated dealing with a Cumberland. Of course, it wasn't Jeff's fault that George had turned tail like a yellow-bellied skunk. In fact, Jeff had been as sympathetic as a big brother, had even offered to date her for a while to save her face. No, she told herself, she shouldn't be mad at Jeff. But every time she saw him, she remembered George and her humiliation at his hands.

"I brought the papers with me," Jeff said. "It's the same as always, except the fee has been upped five percent, if that's agreeable?"

"That's fine. Come on inside and I'll give you some coffee while I look it over."

Gideon watched them walk to the house, wondering what the story was between those two. And he was surprised to feel a rather hot irritation at the idea that Sara had a past with that man—the biggest rancher in the county.

He looked down at himself, at his dusty jeans and scuffed boots, and tried not to remember that he wasn't even a connector anymore. Tried not to feel as if he were falling, tried not to see the flashing, splintering images of spinning blue sky and wildly careening beams.

Dizzily, he reached out and grabbed the fence rail for stability. It would pass. The vertigo always passed, because it wasn't real. It was imagined. It was just a psychological reaction, that was all.

Breathing deeply, he kept his eyes open to counter the vivid, spinning mental images and the sensation of tumbling end over end. Nausea welled in the pit of his stomach, and he swallowed it.

It would pass. Everything passed eventually.

In the kitchen, Sara poured two mugs of coffee and carried them to the table where Jeff Cumberland sat. "I wish you'd refrain from stealing Gideon Ironheart, at least until Joey is back out here to help my grandfather. Zeke can't handle it all alone.''

"I got the feeling Ironheart isn't in a mood to go anywhere." Jeff smiled and gave a little shrug. "Maybe I can borrow him for a few hours here and there?"

"That's up to him." She took a seat across from him and reached for the contract.

"What about Joey?" Jeff asked. "How long will he be locked up?"

Sara shook her head. "I guess it's up to Nate, from what Judge Williams said when she revoked Joey's probation. With the way Nate feels about it, I guess Joey's going to spend some time there."

"I'm really sorry, Sara," Jeff said. "I know how hard you've worked and how hard you tried to bring him up right. I guess not everybody turns out okay. Like George."

Sara drew a sharp breath and looked at him. She and Jeff had studiously avoided mentioning his brother for nearly ten years now. "George?"

Jeff grimaced. "He left his wife. Can you believe it? He left her and their kid because it wasn't what he wanted. I could kill him."

"What—what will she do?"

"I've asked her and the kid to come stay with me. Just because my brother is a reprehensible, good-for-nothing jackass doesn't mean his wife and kid should suffer."

"Is she coming?"

"I don't know. I think she's in pretty much of a state of shock." He shook his head. "She loved him, Sara. Just like you did. What the hell is the matter with him?"

"I can't imagine, Jeff. I really can't." And for the first time it occurred to her that she might have gotten off lightly when George left her at the altar.

"Well, I didn't come up here to saddle you with my troubles," he said after a moment. "I guess I just wanted you to know that you were never the problem."

Just as Sara turned her attention back to the contract, Gideon opened the screen door and stepped in. "Just wanted a mug of that coffee, Sara."

"Help yourself." As soon as he had moved into the bunk-house, she had told him he was welcome to come into the kitchen anytime for coffee or a soft drink. So far, apart from mealtimes, he hadn't availed himself of the invitation, but here he was. Helplessly, Sara watched him saunter across the kitchen to the coffeepot. There ought to be a law, she thought, against men who looked like that walking like that. It was an almost animal prowl.

Glancing away, she found Jeff regarding her curiously. Before a blush could betray her, she fastened her attention on the contract.

Gideon poured a cup a coffee and leaned back against the counter as he sipped it. He was acting like a fool, he thought, coming in here this way, but he couldn't seem to make himself walk out. Well, he admitted, Sara was a damn attractive woman, at least according to his lights. He'd been trying to ignore the attraction because he was only passing through, but right now that didn't seem half as important as making sure Cumberland didn't put the make on Sara, especially consider-ing how she had bristled. Since she had something against the man, it seemed wise to be protective.

"What brought you up here from Georgia?" Jeff asked him while Sara read.

"Vacation," Gideon replied promptly. He'd answered the question so many times that he had a stock answer. "I finished off my last job and decided it was as good a time as any to do some of the sight-seeing I've always wanted to do."

"Last job?" said Cumberland. "Where was that?"

Sara answered without looking up from the contract. "Gid-eon's an ironworker. I think he's only here because he likes Zeke and Zeke asked for his help." She scanned the last page, then looked at Jeff. "Looks good to me. My only qualification is that I don't want your cowboys crossing the fence line at the falls. That meadow up there is one of my favorite places.

If their horses chew up the ground, the place will get full of sage and maybe choke out the wildflowers.''

"I'll make a point of telling them, Sara. If you have any trouble about it, let me know.''

Declining an offer of more coffee after they had signed both copies of the contract, Jeff said his good-byes and left. Gideon was still standing against the counter with his coffee, and Sara glanced at him.

"Something wrong?" she asked.

Only with him. He shrugged. "Just wanted some coffee. What's this about him leasing your pasture?"

"I don't have a lot of grazing land, but I've got a lot of water. Come June, Jeff moves part of his herd into my pasture so he doesn't overtax his own water supplies and grazing.''

"If you've got the water, why can't you raise your own herd?''

"Because I don't have enough good grazing to raise enough cattle to make it economically worthwhile. I could raise a few head, maybe, but not enough to make this a going concern.''

"You've sure got some beautiful land here. I can see why you don't want to part with it.''

Sara almost smiled at him. Most people thought she needed her head examined for working so hard to keep a nonproductive piece of land. "This place is part of me," she admitted. "Leaving it would be like cutting off my arm. But it sure would be nice if I could figure out some way to make it self-sufficient without sacrificing the beauty or the privacy.''

"You could board horses," Gideon said, the words popping out before he considered them.

"But everyone around here…''

"Not everyone around here," he corrected her. "People in town, for one. They have no place to stable them. People who might want their horses broken before they take them to more convenient stables nearer their homes. Maybe some people who'd like to save a mustang but have no place to put one.''

She instinctively opened her mouth to disagree, but then she stopped, reconsidering. "Maybe," she said after a moment. "It's an idea. I'll give it some thought."

"Good." He put his mug in the sink and headed toward the door. "Zeke wants me to go to town and pick up some stuff for him. I'll be back before dinner."

They couldn't possibly, Sara thought as she watched him go, be paying him enough to work as hard as he worked. Gideon Ironheart evidently preferred not to be idle, and jobs that had needed doing for years around here were beginning to finally get done.

The woman was getting under his skin, Gideon thought as he drove into town with Zeke's list in his pocket. For a minute there, when she had opened her mouth to object and then had changed her mind, he'd had an almost overwhelming urge to bend over and plunge his tongue into the warm, silky depths of her mouth.

He didn't like this at all. He was forty-one, not sixteen. It had been almost that long since the last time his hormones had ruled him, and he didn't like the idea that some woman could make a mockery of his restraint and self-control. He didn't like the feeling that some complete innocent, with no such intention at all, could cause his loins to stir and his heart to race.

If she'd meant to attract him, he wouldn't have minded half so much that he had responded. But Sara Yates honestly wasn't interested in attracting a man. She didn't send significant looks or make tempting little gestures, didn't put on makeup or do any of those other things a woman did to advertise her availability. He couldn't quite make up his mind whether she was unaware of such things or just wasn't aware of him as a man.

No, he thought after a moment, that wasn't quite it, either. A couple of times he had caught her gaze following him. She knew he was a man, all right, and flickers of interest showed from time to time. Sara just didn't want to be interested. Fine. He was willing to let it rest.

For now.

He had hoped that his frequent appearances in town would

start putting him into the category of a familiar face, but while shopkeepers nodded and chatted with him, they still didn't respond in any detail to his gambits about Micah Parish. He'd better let that drop for a while, he decided, or somebody might notice his interest and get suspicious.

And maybe he was going to have to break down and meet the man. That was something he'd wanted to avoid, because, once done, it was irrevocable. Once Micah became aware of him, matters would no longer be under Gideon's sole control, and he wasn't at all sure he wanted that to happen. And then there was the matter of meeting him. He couldn't just walk up, introduce himself and tell the truth. No, he would need some kind of cover.

And there was always Sara, he found himself thinking. She worked with Parish and would be the likeliest person to introduce him if he decided to go that route. So maybe, if he worked at it, he could just get her to talk about the man.

Columbine, a sorrel mare, and her new foal were frisking together in the pasture near the barn, while the roan mustang stood in the corral and watched them, hooves planted widely, ears pricked forward and nostrils flaring as he sought their scent. When Gideon pulled his truck into the yard, Zeke and his lifelong friend, Chester Elk Horn, were standing at the fence and watching.

Gideon joined the two men at the fence and gave Chester, whom he'd met the other day, a nod. "What's up, Zeke?"

Zeke chuckled. "Boy meets girl. Same old story. That mustang has been putting on quite a show trying to get Columbine's attention."

"And she ain't giving it." Chester grinned.

Columbine wouldn't be interested for some time yet, but that didn't seem to faze the mustang, who now reared a little and then pranced along the fence, tail held high.

Shaking his head a little and smiling to himself, Gideon went to unload his truck. Zeke and Chester made a pair, he thought. Something about those two would never be old.

After he unloaded the truck, he went to wash up at the faucet out behind the bunkhouse. A cup of coffee was sounding real good right about now. Maybe he would venture into Sara's territory and get one.

It was as he stood shaking water off his hands and arms that a flash from the trees farther uphill caught his attention. Sort of like sun catching on glass.

There. Again.

That wasn't right. A piece of glass lying on the ground would have made a steady reflection. Whatever was reflecting the sunlight was moving.

Somebody was up there.

Without giving it another thought, he started trotting in that direction. A hiker probably, gone astray. As the weather warmed, every bit of wilderness in America became overrun by hikers and campers from all over the world. He would just check things out, make sure everything was okay. Sara and Zeke wouldn't mind a hiker or two crossing their spread.

What they didn't like was dirt bikers. "They tear up the ground, kill the vegetation, pollute the atmosphere with fumes, and ruin the peace and quiet with their racket," Zeke had said. "They scare the horses, drive the deer and elk away…damn vandals, that's all they are." The Double Y was posted against trespassers primarily because of off-the-road vehicles.

They also didn't like poachers, and from time to time they had trouble with out-of-season hunters who wanted to bag an elk or a moose.

So he would just go up and check things out.

Before he got halfway across the meadow, however, his quarry figured out he'd been spotted. With a roar of his motorcycle engine, he took off into the trees, giving Gideon a view only of a flash of sun off metal.

Dirt biker, Gideon thought, listening to the engine roar fade with distance. He stood there for a minute, clenching and unclenching his fists, angry at the intruder. For a long time he'd lived in cities, and he'd never owned property, so his territory had been limited to his personal space. Suddenly the Double

Y seemed to have become his territory, and it irritated the hell out of him that some idiot had flouted the signs and ridden his bike all over Sara and Zeke's property. What was it with people like that? he wondered. Why couldn't they respect other people's rights?

He turned at the sound of boots moving through the grass and saw Zeke approaching. "Dirt biker," he said.

Zeke nodded. "I heard him. Don't go after them yourself, Ironheart. You never know when one might be armed. It just isn't worth it."

"Makes me almost want to string wire here and there as a lesson."

Zeke shook his head. "Think of the horses. They'd be the ones to suffer. Come on. It's just one biker. Let's go get some coffee."

"Where's Chester?" Gideon asked as they walked toward the house.

"He headed back to town."

"Why doesn't he just stay up here in the bunkhouse? I sure wouldn't mind."

"Chester hasn't taken a dime from anybody in his life," Zeke said. "He'd feel like he was taking charity, and he wouldn't like it. Besides, he'd miss playing checkers over at Bayard's Garage."

That was another one of the local charms, Gideon thought. A bunch of old coots settled on chairs beneath the tree at the corner of Bayard's Garage and played checkers with each other by the hour, weather permitting. On the couple of occasions he'd gone by, he'd stopped to watch them play. They sat there, chewing tobacco, telling tales as tall as the Rockies, and laughing the hearty, wheezy laughter of old men. Dirk provided a spittoon and kept the price on his soft-drink machine at cost for them.

Just another one of those things that got a man to thinking that Conard County wouldn't be a bad place to grow old.

The house was quiet when they entered, no sound issuing from the other rooms or the upstairs. Sara must have decided to take a nap, Gideon thought. He'd been a little surprised to see her up and about at noon when Cumberland had arrived, because she'd worked the graveyard shift last night.

He didn't like her working graveyard. He'd stewed about it the last two nights while she did it, and it hadn't helped to tell himself that it was none of his business and that she'd been doing it for years. It didn't help to remind himself that she was a trained, experienced cop and that she carried a gun she knew how to use.

Simple fact was, Gideon Ironheart was old-fashioned in some ways. Some women might even consider him a male chauvinist, though they would be wrong. He was perfectly willing to acknowledge that a determined woman could do anything a man could. And Sara was a determined woman. He had no doubt she was a damn good cop, too. That wasn't the problem. The problem was, he had been raised to believe that a man owed a woman his protection. The nuns hadn't been plagued with any notions of female equality. They'd raised the boys to be chivalrous and protective. His uncle and grandfather had done little to disturb those ideas. Men were the warriors. Period.

All of that made it hard to stand back and be silent when a woman went ahead and did something dangerous. Something a *man* ought to be doing. That was all.

But he kept his mouth shut, because it really wasn't any of his business, because he knew that women felt differently about such things, and tried to ignore his discomfort.

Zeke made a fresh pot of coffee and then joined Gideon at the table. With little in the way of livestock, the pace at the Double Y was sometimes downright lazy.

"You getting restless yet, boy?" Zeke asked.

Gideon shook his head. "Not at all, old man. I don't get restless that easy."

"Then how come you never settled down?"

Gideon turned his head a little, looking out the screen door, across the porch and yard to the mountains behind the barn.

Wildflowers bobbed their colorful heads along the corral fence, adding color to a green-and-blue world.

"Did you know," he said slowly, "my people—the Cherokee—had a democratic government and a constitution before Jackson drove them from Georgia? One of my people created an alphabet for our language without even being able to read English. All he did was understand the *idea* of written language. We built brick homes and schools. We had our own newspaper. We married and intermarried, farmed, and trusted Andy Jackson because he was our friend."

He turned and looked at Zeke. "Then they drove us out of our homes and sent us on the long walk, the Trail of Tears. They drove us clear to Oklahoma, and we died in the thousands on that march. But some of us survived, and we built homes and farms and married and had children.... And then came the discovery of oil. They drove us out of our homes again, and we rebuilt again. We're not restless by nature, old man. We're builders, survivors. Adaptable and strong. But not restless."

"And you?" Zeke said.

Gideon shrugged. "I moved on because I never found anything that made me want to stay once the job was done. I hate to be idle."

When the coffee was ready, Gideon rose to fill their mugs. He hadn't missed the stiffness of Zeke's movements, and while the old man didn't let his arthritis keep him from doing a single thing, Gideon couldn't see any reason not to spare him some of the little stuff.

"Thanks," Zeke said.

Gideon returned to his seat, crossing his legs loosely and fixing his attention on the world beyond the open windows and screen door. He didn't know why he'd brought up all that stuff about Cherokee history except that it was about the only thing he had that gave him a sense of his place in the scheme of things. He sure as hell didn't know a damn thing about his European half. The half that was probably responsible for the way he moved on when the job finished. The half that was undoubtedly responsible for his inability to feel that he belonged anywhere.

Zeke startled him out of thought. "You need a vision quest, boy."

Gideon turned, facing Zeke directly. "You've done it?"

"Many times. I had my first vision when I was ten, and my second one before I asked Alma to marry me." Zeke gave a faint, rueful smile. "A man has to give serious thought to what he's about to do when he considers marriage to any woman, but most especially when she's of another race and culture. My mind and heart were both troubled, so Chester took me to a *wichasha wakan*—holy man—and I followed the Lakota rite."

"You've known Chester all this time?" The thought of a friendship spanning more than fifty years was rather awe-inspiring.

"We were orphans together in the mission school. I don't know if you know anything about it, but most of the Lakota religious practices were outlawed in the last century. In fact, the massacre at Wounded Knee came about as an attempt to prevent a Ghost Dance. Then, in 1923, Congress passed the Religious Crimes Act, which outlawed the practice of all Indian religions, so things got even worse. I was a small child at the time, but the primary effect of it for me was that I needed a friend to direct me in secret to a holy man, one who wasn't even of my own people. All of it was done in such secrecy."

"And you married her?"

Zeke smiled. "I married her. I guess the most surprising thing was that her father didn't raise any objections. There are times when the strands of destiny weave together seamlessly, and without the least struggle your dreams come to pass. But first you must dream."

First you must dream. Maybe three or four times in a lifetime, if a man was lucky, he heard a truth that he recognized in his soul. This was one of those times, and Gideon sat perfectly still as he let it fill him and settle in. When had he last dreamed? he wondered suddenly. When had he last dreamed anything at all?

"Just let me know," Zeke said presently. "I can arrange it all."

The sound of footsteps alerted them to the fact that Sara was up and about again. A few moments later she appeared in the kitchen, her cheeks still flushed from sleep and her long, inky hair caught back in a loose ponytail. Smothering a yawn, she bent to kiss her grandfather's cheek, then joined them at the table with a mug of coffee.

"Where's Chester?" she asked her grandfather. "I thought you were going to ask him to dinner."

"I did, but he had other plans. You're stuck with just the two of us again, Sarey."

She gave her grandfather a teasing smile. "I don't know if I can stand it."

Zeke chuckled and reached over to pat her thigh, while Gideon wrestled with a sudden surge of the desire he was trying to ignore. She looked so sweet just now, softened by sleep, and her black-satin voice was even huskier than usual, brushing over his nerve endings like the seductive touch of warm, smooth skin.

Maybe, he found himself thinking, he ought to ask her out. Just one date, on which he could kill two birds with one stone. He could tease himself a little, which always felt good, however frustrating, and maybe he could get her to talk about Micah Parish. His conscience objected a little at his mixed motives, but he reminded himself that having mixed motives was a far cry from dishonesty.

Sara looked at him. "You look like you're pondering the fate of the world."

"He's giving some thought to *Hanblecheyapi*," Zeke said, using the Lakota word for the ceremony, speaking of it as if it were a natural thing, not an embarrassing one at all.

Sara looked at Gideon with renewed interest. "Really? You're thinking about crying for a vision?"

Gideon squirmed uncomfortably. After a lifetime in the Anglo world, some things just didn't feel comfortable. He wanted to change the subject—fast. "Partly. And partly I'm thinking about asking you to have dinner with me."

Over the years, Gideon had experienced all kinds of reactions from women when he asked them out, everything from borderline ecstasy to utter indifference, but he didn't think he'd ever made a woman turn as white as bleached cotton.

Sara felt as if something inside her were about to splinter. No man had asked her out in ten years, and she had come to believe she was completely unattractive. She had also come to believe that she liked it that way. Abruptly, she knew she didn't like it that way at all, but she also couldn't suddenly believe that she *was* attractive. That any man could be interested. That Gideon Ironheart could be doing anything except making fun of her.

"I… No!" Rising swiftly, she left the room, and her footsteps could be heard mounting the stairs.

Gideon looked at Zeke. "What the hell did I do? Apart from maybe moving too fast, that is."

"That's for her to explain," Zeke said impassively, dark eyes almost watchful.

"Then how about some advice, old man?" He was troubled by Sara's reaction, by the inexplicable feeling that he had harmed her in some way. A partly guilty conscience didn't help.

Zeke chose his words carefully, betraying nothing. "Maybe you haven't given her any reason to think you find her attractive."

Gideon's mouth opened to answer, but no words emerged. He had been about to argue that a dinner invitation was ipso facto a declaration of interest but he realized that wasn't necessarily so. "Does she date at all?"

"No."

Well, that didn't shock him. He wouldn't date at all himself, except it was part of the mating game, and a man had a biological urge that had to be satisfied occasionally. He tended to avoid women like Sara, though. Women who didn't know the rules. Maybe he ought to just drop this now.

But he remembered her shocked expression and the way she had paled, and he knew he couldn't drop it. He had hurt her somehow, however unintentionally, and he just wasn't capable of leaving things that way. He looked at Zeke. "She's upstairs? In her bedroom?"

The old Shoshone nodded.

"What will you do if I go up after her?"

The faintest of smiles touched the corners of Zeke's mouth. "I'm an old man. What would you expect me to do?"

"Fight like a warrior to protect your own."

Zeke gave a small nod. "But sometimes true protection is not always doing the obvious thing."

Gideon pushed back from the table. "I'm going up."

From the kitchen he walked through a dining room that was graced by a scarred but polished cherrywood table and eight chairs with worn embroidered seat covers. Probably as old as this house, he thought as worn carpet silenced his steps. The dining room opened directly onto a living room furnished with the overstuffed pieces of another era, and everything—everything—showed signs of age, wear and care. Poor but proud, that was the history of the Yates family.

The staircase rose at the far end of the living room, along the wall right beside the front door. As soon as his booted feet hit those wooden treads, they were no longer silent. Sara could hear his approach, and he wondered if she would lock her door. Damn, why hadn't he thought this through a little more before he blurted out that invitation? What had seemed like a good idea five minutes ago suddenly looked like the ultimate in stupidity.

She didn't lock him out. She hadn't even closed her door. Maybe she didn't really believe he would have the gall to follow her. Maybe she had thought those footsteps on the stairs were her grandfather's. Whatever, he found her in the first bedroom on the left. She stood with her back to the door as she stared out the window. Sheer curtains waved lazily in the breeze, wrapping from time to time around her jean-clad legs.

Her arms were tightly wrapped around herself, a defensive posture he felt as much as he saw.

"Sara?"

She sighed, a heavy, sad sound, but didn't turn around. "I'm sorry, Gideon. I was unforgivably rude."

"Not to worry." He stepped into the room and looked around with quick curiosity. If a woman lived here, no one would ever guess. The room was sexless and sterile—except for the tiny pink stuffed cat tucked away on the corner of the dresser. "I guess I took you by surprise."

"Mmm." Still she didn't face him. "Did my grandfather tell you to come up here?"

"Not exactly."

"Well, I apologize, but I'm not going to change my mind, so you might as well go."

He stared at her stiff back, noticing its graceful, slender line, noticing just how small the bones beneath her creamy skin were. She was a woman, all right. A woman in hiding for some reason.

"Thanks for telling me," he said quietly. "For a minute there, I thought I was going to have to beg."

It took a moment, but at last a chuckle rose in her, shaking her shoulders and spilling over her lips, a gentle cascade of sound. God, he thought, that laugh was an aphrodisiac! She turned, still chuckling, to face him. Her cheeks were flushed, and her eyes sparkled with amusement.

"Nothing throws you, does it?" she remarked.

"Very little." He stepped closer. "I have to admit, it throws me a little when I ask a woman to dinner and she turns as white as a sheet."

Her smile faded. "Are you asking for an explanation?"

She was looking wary again, he noticed. A lot like that mustang outside. "Naw," he said casually, easing closer, keeping his voice soothing. "It's none of my business."

"That's right."

"But I wondered if maybe you have something against Cherokees."

She blinked, obviously astonished. "Why would I? And how was I supposed to know you're Cherokee?"

He shrugged and moved a little closer. "You're at least a quarter Shoshone, right? Well, for all I know, there's bad blood between our tribes."

She was watching him in helpless fascination, so distracted by his crazy suggestion that she was utterly oblivious to his close approach. Sleight of hand, that was what it was, and she was falling for it.

"I never heard of any bad blood," she said. "And really, I didn't know you were Cherokee until just now, when you told me."

"Actually, I'm *half* Cherokee."

"Like Micah Parish. He's half Cherokee and half European."

"Yeah?" He was only a foot away from her now, and he halted. "So you didn't turn me down because of my blood?"

She blinked. "Good Lord, no!"

"Then why?"

"Because I don't want to be a fool again." The words were out before she could stop them, and before she could take them back, he covered her mouth with the hard, callused palm of his hand.

"Shh," he said, calming her as he had calmed the mustang. "Easy, Sara. I don't want to make a fool of anybody. Not you. Not me."

"Then why...?" The words vibrated against his hand, and her wide brown eyes never left his face.

"Because you turn me on, lady," he said bluntly, watching color flood her cheeks all the way to the roots of her hair. "I figure that's worth looking into." He dropped his hand, but she didn't attempt to speak. "Maybe it'll wear off in a couple of hours and I can forget about it. Maybe it won't. There's only one way to find out. Go out with me tonight, Sara Jane Yates."

Sara stared up at him, unaware that every bit of her yearning, every bit of her uncertainty, was showing in her eyes right now. Gideon Ironheart said she turned him on, and her insides clenched when she thought of him saying that. This incredibly virile man, so much older and more experienced than she, wanted to take her out because she turned him on. Oh, God! It was at once a dream come true and a terrifying threat. Whatever it was that men really wanted, Sara Yates knew she didn't have enough of it. George's defection had made that clear.

She licked her lips. "I don't think—" She couldn't finish. She couldn't bring herself to say no.

"Please?" He coaxed her the way he would have coaxed a shy horse. He didn't mind asking. A man too proud to ask never got anything.

Finally she nodded, apparently unable to voice even so much as a yes.

"Good," he said with a broad smile. He turned and walked to the bedroom door, where he paused and looked back. "Tonight at seven," he told her. "Wear jeans and bring a warm jacket."

Chapter 4

The whole damn county was going to hear about this, Sara thought unhappily as she waited for Gideon that evening. Being a deputy had brought her into contact with nearly everyone in the county, and there wasn't a restaurant or a diner for a hundred and fifty miles in any direction where she could be sure she wouldn't be recognized. By this time tomorrow, everyone would know that Sara Yates, who hadn't dated since George Cumberland had left her standing at the altar, had been seen dining in the company of a stranger.

She could just imagine the curious looks, the speculation, the outright smirks she would get from some of the lowlife she had to deal with in her job. And come Sunday, the Bible Study Group would probably give her the third degree. Oh, Lord, why hadn't she refused to go out with him?

This close to the mountains, the sun vanished early, leaving the ground in twilight while the sky remained bright overhead. There was still plenty of light to see by when Gideon's truck pulled into the yard, returning from his second trip to town that day, but the shadows that gave depth were gone.

Taking Gideon at his word, she had dressed in fresh jeans, a chambray shirt and her denim jacket. Stubbornly she had refused to use even a dab of makeup, and she had plaited her hair into two braids that fell to her breasts. Nobody was ever going to say that she had gussied herself up for a man.

Gideon climbed out of his truck and walked toward her across the hard-packed earth with surefooted ease and grace. Watching him, Sara suddenly imagined him walking along one of those incredibly narrow beams at those incredible heights. His every movement was controlled, she realized. Fine-tuned and accurate. Ready to deal with any unexpected obstacle or change of terrain. She had never seen a man move that way before, so fluidly and precisely.

He reached the porch and stayed at the bottom of the two steps, looking up at her. "I really didn't think you'd be here," he said.

Sara caught her breath as she unexpectedly saw all this from his point of view. She had been looking at it from her own perspective as a possibility for him to humiliate her, but she had utterly failed to consider just how much he had exposed himself to embarrassment. He had laid himself open by asking her out in the first place, then had done it again by coming to get her when he thought she might have fled.

"It's just a date, Sara," he said quietly. Reaching out, he caught her cold fingers in his warm hand and tugged gently. "We'll eat and we'll talk, and maybe we'll start to become friends."

Why? The question was there in her eyes as she looked at him and hesitated.

Why? Damn it, he thought, it was too early for questions like that, all those complicating questions he'd managed to avoid for nearly twenty years. What he wanted, *all* he wanted, was a simple, uncomplicated evening in the presence of a woman who somehow turned him on. Maybe he would steal a kiss or two and get himself really hot and bothered, but that was as far as it would go. Ever. A woman her age ought to be able to handle that, surely. But, as he looked up into her uncertain gaze, he knew she was no ordinary woman, and her age had nothing to do with anything.

"Okay," he said, and let go of her hand. Turning, he headed back to his truck. "Tell Zeke I'll see him in the morning."

Sara felt again that painful splintering sensation, as if somewhere deep inside she knew she was making a mistake, even though her mind told her she was avoiding one. Watching Gideon walk away, she suddenly saw the long years stretching in front of her, years that would grow increasingly empty unless she filled them with friends.

"Gideon?"

He paused and looked back over his shoulder. "Ma'am?"

"I thought we had a date."

He turned to face her then, settling his hands on his hips and cocking his pelvis to one side. Sara felt her breath catch, and her hand suddenly tingled with the memory of his warm, dry touch.

"We do," he said, "as long as you understand that I don't put out. One good-night kiss is as far as I'll go, Sara Yates."

The laugh rose from the pit of her nervous stomach and popped from her lips like a bubble breaking the surface of a still pool. His remark had been outrageously absurd, so absurd she couldn't prevent the laughter. But she had also taken his point. She was leaping to conclusions, crossing bridges they might never reach. Taking too seriously what was only meant to be a little bit of fun.

This time when he held out his hand, she stepped down from the porch and joined him.

"It's a beautiful evening," he remarked as he handed her up into his truck. "Is that jacket going to be warm enough against the chill later?"

"It'll be fine. It's lined."

"How's Joey handling his incarceration?" he asked as he guided the truck down the rough, rutted private road.

"Not well. He hasn't spoken a word to anyone since Zeke brought him in."

Gideon glanced at her, giving her a slight smile. "That's a

good sign, Sara. He's thinking, not shooting his mouth off. Give it time."

"Is that how you acted when your grandfather got your attention?"

He shook his head. "I think I was a lot further gone than Joey probably is."

"Why?"

"Well, from what I see, your brother comes from a pretty good home. I grew up in an orphanage until I was twelve, and I had a serious attitude problem."

Sara turned on the seat to better see him. "Were you adopted finally?"

"With that attitude? Not likely. About the time I turned eleven, Sister Mary Paul came to the orphanage. She was one of these energetic types who could hardly hold still and could never leave well enough alone. She was looking through old files one day and saw my birth certificate, which showed that my mother had been born in Oklahoma. She was off and running with that, and finally, more than a year later, tracked down my uncle, William Lightfoot. He came for me before the week was out."

"Why—" Sara bit back the question before it fully emerged. It was none of her business, and he would tell her what he wanted her to know.

"Why did it take him so damn long? You know, I used to ask myself that question. It was all explained to me, but at that age I didn't listen very well. I'm a hell of a lot older now, and I understand some things a hell of a lot better. My mother was disowned by my grandfather when she insisted on marrying my father, who was Anglo. The old man told her she was dead to her family, and she believed him."

"How awful!"

"Oh, it gets better yet. The marriage didn't work. When they split, my mother didn't go home to Oklahoma but took me to Atlanta instead. No one knew where she was, and I guess my grandfather was still insisting she was dead. By the time he got over that, she and I had both vanished into smoke."

Sara had the worst urge to reach out and touch him. "What about your father?"

Gideon's hands tightened around the wheel. This was the part of the subject he didn't want to discuss. Still couldn't discuss fairly. Too many years of hurt, anger and bitterness lay there. "Who knows?" he managed to say finally. "Who knows?"

He turned them onto the county road and headed away from town.

"Where are we going?"

He glanced at her and smiled. "That's a surprise. It took a lot of ingenuity, I want you to know, to come up with someplace we could go where the whole county wouldn't be discussing the lady deputy's date."

A laugh escaped her. "You've figured this place out."

"I lived in a place like this once." Years ago, miles ago, when he'd been cocky and too angry to recognize the good things that he *did* have.

The road wound higher into the mountains, and the air grew chillier as day faded even more. Sara knew there was nothing up this way for fifty or more miles, but she was content suddenly to let the evening unfold as it would.

"You must have been so angry," she remarked.

"I spent a lot of years being angry. Too many. My grandfather lived to regret what he'd done, and he made it up to me by straightening me out when everybody else gave up. My uncle loved me like a son. Still does. But I'll admit, understanding has been a long time in coming."

He pulled off the highway on a narrow track Sara recognized well. It led to a small glade through which a mountain brook tumbled and where, at this time of year, wildflowers made a thick carpet.

"It's your land," he remarked. "I guess you can throw us off if you want to."

"Why would I want to? This is my favorite place. How did you ever find it?"

He flashed her a smile. "An old Shoshone whispered in my ear."

Gideon Ironheart was a truly exceptional man, Sara thought as he parked the truck. He just kept right on shattering all her expectations.

Since he wouldn't let her help him, she wandered in the glade, admiring the Indian paintbrush blooms that seemed to glow in the twilight like tiny fires. The brook tumbled wildly over rocks, hissing and splashing with spring vigor, still icy cold from the snowfields that had given it birth.

"Ready for supper?" He had to raise his voice a little to be heard over the noisy rush of the water.

Sara turned to him with a smile. "I'm famished." And she was. Her nerves had settled down finally, probably because he had gone to the trouble of bringing her to her favorite spot on earth.

And then she looked beyond him and gasped with pleasure. The darkening glade had become a fairy-tale setting. He had lit a campfire, and beside it dinner had been laid out on a colorful blanket. She had expected paper plates, but not champagne served in plastic goblets. She hadn't expected to see fresh strawberries heaped in a bowl, or that he would actually be planning to cook over the fire. She had anticipated sandwiches, or cold chicken from Maude's, not T-bones freshly cooked and foil-wrapped potatoes baking in the fire.

Gideon liked the expression on her face as she surveyed his efforts. She looked…enchanted. Until this very moment he would have sworn the expression could have appeared only on the face of a five-year-old on Christmas morning. And it was the first time in all his forty-one years that he had ever brought that look to someone's face.

Uncomfortable suddenly, he cleared his throat. "Grab a seat," he said roughly. Damn, what was so special about a stupid picnic? "Eat some strawberries. It'll be a while before those potatoes are done."

A little startled by his sudden gruffness, Sara glanced at him but couldn't tell what had disturbed him. Forcing herself to shrug it away, she sat cross-legged on the blanket and reached for a strawberry. "This is fabulous," she told him sincerely.

"It's nothing." He squatted and poked at the potatoes. "I travel a lot, because I have to go where the work is, and when I'm on the road, if the weather's good, I like to camp out and cook over an open fire."

"I would have thought there would be enough work to keep you in one major city."

He shook his head. "It comes and goes. And when you top off a job, there may not be another one ready to start just then. Guys with families pretty much stay put, but a lot of us travel like Gypsies. There's always another job, another thrill, another big one over the horizon." He sent her an almost amused look. "You can finish a skyscraper one day and the next start building a bridge. Or maybe you can work on a nuclear power plant. Or you can work on a radio telescope, or the launch tower at Cape Kennedy, or a missile silo…just all kinds of opportunity out there if you know how to walk the iron."

Sara popped the last of a strawberry into her mouth and then drew her knees up, wrapping her arms around them. "You must have seen all kinds of things."

"I've seen a lot of the country," he agreed easily. "And a lot of interstate highway."

"I've never even left Wyoming," Sara admitted.

"I don't see any reason to leave. Seems like you've got everything that matters right here, and I don't recommend city life. When I was a lot younger, I thought it was exciting, but these days…" He shrugged. "It just irritates the hell out of me."

He lay back on the blanket, propping himself up on one elbow to keep an eye on the fire. From time to time he glanced at Sara and smiled, but she was grateful that he didn't look steadily at her. She was far more comfortable with the feeling that he was only casually aware of her.

Because she was not casually aware of him. There was nothing at all casual about the way her gaze kept returning to his long powerful limbs, his broad chest, his long dark hair. Something about him kept pricking her with a sense of familiarity, but there was nothing familiar about the heat he stirred in her. Her blood felt as if it were turning to warm molasses, and she was developing a pulsebeat in the most unusual place.

Frightened, she tried to look away, to calm herself and her own treasonous body, but her eyes just wouldn't behave. He was a harsh, hard-looking man. His flowing black hair only added to the warriorlike power of him. It didn't matter that he might never have fought in a battle. He had been born to be a warrior, and while modern times had made him into something else, there was no doubt he had everything he needed to be one.

So why, Sara asked herself uncertainly, had this hard, harsh, *experienced* man, who was at least a decade older than she, asked her to spend this evening with him? Because she turned him on? That was what he had said, and it was probably the last thing she could really believe.

He looked so utterly relaxed lying there, sipping champagne from a plastic goblet too small for his large hand. The strawberries were huge, but he popped them whole into his mouth as he ate them. He couldn't possibly lie there eating and drinking if he felt one-tenth of the arousal he elicited in her just by being there.

And thinking about those things was making her condition worse. Desperately, she forced herself to speak.

"You told Jeff you're on vacation."

He glanced at her. "Yep. A *long* vacation. I'm...getting too old to connect anymore."

"Too old? You?" The thought was stunning. She had never seen a man more in his prime.

"Most connectors change to something easier by the time they hit thirty. It's a young man's job, and I've lasted longer than most by far."

"How old are you?"

"Forty-one."

Forty-one. Thirteen years her senior. He couldn't possibly be interested in someone her age. Lord, he must look at her and see a child. He was up to something, but she couldn't imagine what in the world it could possibly be. "What's so hard about connecting? I mean, what exactly do you do?"

He gave her a half smile. "Well, on an average morning I'll shinny up a few columns, guide a few ten-or twenty-ton beams or headers into place, line them up by levering them with a two-foot-long connecting rod or hammering with a sixteen-pound hammer, and drive a bunch of bolts home. In between I'll do my tightrope walk along the headers and beams with fifty pounds of tools strapped to my waist. It's physical, it's wearing, and you need to be absolutely sure in everything you do. Finally…" His voice trailed off, and he looked away briefly. "Finally you realize you're not as fast as you used to be. Not as sure. Not quite as strong or enduring. A smart man comes down then. Before he *falls* down."

Sara was troubled by some indefinable sadness in his expression. "I suppose," she said softly, "that people do fall."

"Oh, yeah," he said quietly. "People fall."

He sat up suddenly and reached for a long-handled fork. Prodding the potatoes baking in the fire, he tested their doneness. "Soon," he said a moment later. "More champagne?"

Sara shook her head. "Thanks, but I don't have any head for alcohol."

He smiled then, an expression that creased the corners of his hard eyes in the most attractive way. "Time to break out the soft drinks, huh?"

He had an ice chest full of them, and a selection nearly as good as the supermarket's. Sara felt an urge to laugh again. Really, he was the most surprising man!

He took other things from the ice chest: a lettuce salad in a clear plastic bowl that was chock-full of good stuff like cucumbers and tomatoes. Two different bottled dressings. Another foil-wrapped package that he set near the fire.

From his truck he brought a rack on legs and set it directly over the fire, turning it into a barbecue. Then he put the steaks on to cook, and the most delicious aromas filled the glade.

"You're prepared for just about everything," Sara remarked.

"I just do this a lot, mainly by myself."

They dined on perfectly cooked T-bones, broccoli that had been steamed in foil, baked potatoes with sour cream, and the crispy salad that he admitted he'd coaxed Maude Bleaker, of Maude's diner, into preparing for him. When they finished, he burned what trash would burn and stuffed the rest into a garbage bag for later disposal.

And then there was no longer the excuse of a meal to eat to keep them lingering by the fire. Gideon showed no sign of wanting to leave, and Sara grew quietly anxious, wondering what came next. Her entire experience of dating had been with George, when they had both been little more than children. Never had George gotten any more forward with her than a few careful kisses. Gideon Ironheart, however, was a man, and she was sure he didn't play children's games.

"You're getting tense, Sara," he said. The low rumble of his voice held a teasing note. "I told you, I don't put out, so quit thinking about pouncing."

But this time she couldn't laugh. This time she could only feel embarrassed and achy, and certain that he must see every humiliating longing she'd ever tried to hide from herself.

"C'mere, Mouse," he said suddenly, his voice a rough whisper.

Before she knew what was happening, he had her stretched out on her side facing the fire and he was pressed warmly to her back. One arm settled around her waist, and the other pillowed her head. Her heart started beating double time as nervousness battled with need. She ought to get up right now, she thought, but it felt so incredibly good to be held like this. Surely this couldn't hurt?

She had totally forgotten these sensations, she realized. Had forgotten the tentative, nervous thrill of wondering what would happen next. Had forgotten the warm, edgy satisfaction that came from being held. Had forgotten that the brush of old denim against skin could be so pleasant, or that the subtle scents of a man could be so good.

"There," he said. "It's a beautiful campfire and a beautiful night, and they deserve to be enjoyed. That's all we're here for—the fire and the night.''

He could feel the hammer of her heart with the palm of his hand, which rested just below her breast. She was frightened and excited all at once, and confused about it.

He had enough experience to tell, to read her, to know. The thought of all that experience sickened him a little, and he wished, too late, that he could capture a little of the innocence and excitement he'd once had. Wished he could remember the time when getting this close to a woman would have had his hands shaking and could forget all the game-playing women between then and now. He was kind of soured on women, he guessed, but Sara Yates didn't fit into that category. Tonight he would hold her a little and excite her a little, and maybe he'd remember, just a little, what it was like when life was still a miracle.

And she hadn't once tough-talked him in the last few days, he realized suddenly. That tough, little sheriff's deputy he'd met the other night in a dark parking lot hadn't been in evidence once since he'd started working with her grandfather. She was out of her depth with him, he realized. She knew how to handle people on the job, but she had no idea what to do with a man in a social situation. The understanding tickled him.

But he wasn't here to get tickled, he reminded himself. He was here to get a little hot and bothered by toying with something he could never have, and to get her to talk about Micah Parish.

''So I'm not the only half-breed Cherokee you know,'' he remarked a little later, when she finally seemed to have relaxed.

''No, I work with one. Micah Parish...I told you.''

He lifted his head a little and leaned closer, so that his mouth was right beside her ear. When he sighed, she shivered in response. ''I hope he hasn't given you a bad opinion of breeds.''

''I'm a breed myself.''

He gave a quiet laugh, a soft puff of air that tickled her ear and made her shiver again. ''Being a quarter Indian is interesting, like having a cattle rustler somewhere in your family tree. It's safe and doesn't seem to bother anybody much.''

"But being half-Indian does?"

"Believe it, lady. Believe it. Especially when it's stamped on your face like an old Indian-head nickel. I'll bet Micah Parish would tell you the same thing."

"Maybe he would. He's one of those silent types, though. Never says much—well, these days he talks more often, ever since he got married. You should see him with his wife."

"Why?"

"She's such a little bit of a thing, hardly much over five feet, and he's huge, taller than you, I think. And she's one of those fairy-tale blondes, with hair so light it's almost white, and these really blue eyes...."

He slipped his hand a little higher and let his lips brush lightly against the shell of her ear. "Don't tell me you want to be a fairy-tale blonde, Sara. Do you really think hair or eye color makes a difference?"

"Men seem to think so." And she was too aware of the man who held her to realize how much she had just revealed.

"*Boys* think so. Men know better." He let another warm puff of air pass from his lips into her ear and felt the minute, almost undetectable movement of her hips in response. For an instant he had to hold himself tense, so that he didn't respond as he wanted to, by rubbing his rapidly growing arousal right against that soft little rump. He'd known he was going to get hot and bothered, but he hadn't expected to ache quite this badly.

And he still had a mission to accomplish.

"So he married an Anglo," he remarked casually. His tongue swept across her earlobe. She shivered delectably.

"Mmm...it's not a dirty word, Gideon. And Faith loves Micah so much. Anybody can see it. She makes him smile a whole lot more, and he's so proud of the baby...."

"Baby?" He lifted his head a little. The investigator hadn't mentioned that when he'd said Micah had married in December. And wasn't it too soon?

"Well, it's not really Micah's baby. Everyone knows that. But it doesn't seem to make any difference to Micah."

This was a story he *had* to hear. "Do you know how weird what you just said sounds?"

She hesitated a moment, and then a soft laugh escaped her. "I guess it does. Okay, Faith's former husband was abusive, and she came up here to her father's ranch to escape him after he nearly killed her. They were divorced already.... Are you following?"

"So far."

"Anyhow, the guy followed her up here, and Micah and Gage Dalton barely managed to rescue her from him. Micah married her a couple of weeks later, and it never seemed to bother him that she was already six months along with her ex-husband's child."

"That's unusual." Damn, he couldn't imagine doing that.

"Micah's an unusual man," Sara said. "I think...I think he's known some pretty hard times, but he has this inner strength, a kind of inward serenity—oh, I don't know how to describe it. You just know, somehow, that he's made peace with himself and life."

As his grandfather finally had, Gideon thought, recognizing her description as one that would have fit the old Cherokee medicine man who had forced him to wake up and take responsibility for himself. As he would like someday to do himself, if he ever figured out how. The older he got, the more he ached to find whatever it was that had put that look in his grandfather's eye. Sometimes, in the morning silence, he almost thought he touched upon it, but then it slipped away, elusive as a wraith.

"I think I'd like to meet him," Gideon said.

"Well, sure. I'll introduce you." She was having trouble hanging on to her thoughts, and she suddenly couldn't remember why they were discussing Micah Parish, anyway. Gideon's hand had wandered higher, finding the valley between her breasts, where it lay in perfect innocence, as if he wasn't even aware of where he was touching her.

And why should he be? she asked herself. She was overre-acting, like the inexperienced woman she was. Her sexuality hadn't had the opportunity to grow or change very much since high school, but this man was long past high school. He prob-ably didn't find anything at all erotic in the way he was holding her, and if he wanted erotic he wouldn't hesitate to touch her intimately. He was no uncertain boy in the back of his dad's pickup.

Besides, she didn't want to be touched intimately, so she was a fool to let it affect her at all. Nothing good could possibly come of losing her head over a man like Gideon Ironheart. The most she could ever be for a man like him was an amusing back-country diversion before he moved on. She couldn't sur-vive that kind of humiliation a second time.

But before she could stiffen her resolve, Gideon's lips found an exquisitely sensitive spot behind her ear. A shudder of sheer sexual delight ran through her, and she caught her breath.

Oh, yeah, he thought, forgetting purposes and mixed motives and guilt. *Oh yeah!* She smelled so good, like baby shampoo and woman. Her hair was as soft as silk against his cheek, and he wished she hadn't braided it. The skin behind her ear was as smooth as a baby's, and fragrant, and the sound of her caught breath when he kissed her there was an aphrodisiac for a hungry soul.

And he was hungry. Oh, God, he was miles hungry, years hungry, lifelong hungry, for things he had never had and never admitted he wanted. All the things he'd been running from were trying to catch up, and he needed to find a warm, soft sanctuary.

Gently, knowing he shouldn't but needing to, anyway, he tugged her shoulder. There was no hesitation when she rolled onto her back, her head resting on his arm, and looked up at him. Her eyes were dark, catching a touch of flickering orange and yellow from the fire. Her bottom lip was caught between her teeth.

She wanted this, too, he realized. She wanted *him.* But she was afraid of her feelings and afraid of him, with good reason.

He leaned over her on his elbows, taking care not to let his arousal brush against her.

"I'm a traveling man, Mouse," he said softly. "I ride the wind from one place to another, like a tumbleweed. No roots, no baggage. I've got nothing to give you but a few moments out of a lifetime. But you've got something I want very badly."

Her gaze had grown almost sad as he spoke, and now, surprising him, she reached up and lightly touched his cheeks with her fingers. "What's that, Gideon?"

"A kiss, baby. Just a kiss." Just a warm, soft kiss to put in his soul to keep the dying fire there alive. Just a touch of lips and tongue given freely to tell him he was still a man, and that a woman could still want him. Just a small, soft reminder of an innocence he'd never really had. Just something *good* in a life that had known so little.

She lifted her chin a little, reaching for him in consent, and he lowered his head until their lips barely touched.

Warm, thought Sara at the first touch of his mouth. Warm and soft, surprising in a man who looked to be essentially hard and cold. Gentle, unexpectedly gentle, as he touched, retreated, then touched again. His tongue, warm and rough, found her lower lip and traced it, causing another shiver of growing awareness to shudder through her. Instinctively, she tipped her head, reaching for a stronger pressure and a deeper touch.

She hadn't expected this seduction of her mouth. Dimly, she realized that the long-ago kisses she remembered had never been kisses at all. *This* was a kiss, this cautious touch and retreat, this exciting sweep of tongue over highly sensitive lips.

"Open for me, Mouse. Let me in."

The gruffly whispered command was as thrilling as anything in her life. On a softly whispered moan, she opened for him and felt her heart stop as his tongue found hers. He moaned then, as if he liked it every bit as much as she did, and she felt, for the first time in her life, the weight of a man's chest on her aching breasts.

He was forgetting, and he tried to call himself back, but he couldn't, just couldn't, draw back yet. Her mouth was sweet and fresh and shy, and that shyness was maddening him. He'd never kissed an inexperienced woman; he had never imagined that shyness could be so damn arousing. He had taken practiced gestures for the real thing for so long that he was stunned to realize they were mere parodies.

This was the real thing, he realized. This, a woman awakening to her own needs and not quite certain of them or herself. He had never realized what a turn-on it could be to have a woman get genuinely turned on by him. He'd had women who gave because it was expected, and women who gave because they needed it, and for any of them he could have been anyone at all. Sara wasn't making him feel that way. Oh, no. Sara was discovering her passion because of him, because *he* turned her on enough to make her forget whatever it was that had her hiding behind a facade of toughness.

The realization terrified him.

He was kissing her with unabashed eroticism, thrusting his tongue into her rhythmically, and she was responding as if…damn it, as if she was going to find satisfaction from his kiss alone. He felt the minute movements of her body as she lay half-beneath him, and they told him how close she was to the pinnacle and how easy it would be to take her right this instant. She wouldn't even whimper a protest. So hot. So fast.

Oh, God!

With more strength than he would have believed he had in him, he broke the kiss and rolled onto his back, separating them. After a few moments, when the chilly night air had cooled his head a little, he reached for her and pulled her close.

"I'm sorry," he said roughly. "That damned well got out of hand."

"That—that's all right." She didn't know what she was going to do with all these wild feelings he'd awakened in her, with the hard ache between her legs that needed something he wasn't giving. She wondered if it would go away, or if she was going to feel like this forever.

"No, damn it, it's not okay," he said angrily. "I made you miserable!"

A few minutes passed in silence, but finally he seemed to relax. "I'm sorry," he said again. "I ought to be shot. First I get you all wound up, and then I shout at you. Damn!"

Suddenly Sara sat up. "Let's put out the fire and go."

Gideon sat up, too. "Wait a minute. Sara, don't..." Don't what? Don't get mad at him? Don't feel hurt and rejected? Damn it, Ironheart, you're an ass! And that made him furious.

"Damn it, woman!" He was on his feet in an instant and took her by the shoulders so she couldn't escape. "What do you want me to do? Throw you on the ground and have my way with you? Do you really want a fantastic one-night stand? I could give you one, baby, but would you be able to look yourself in the eye tomorrow morning?"

At first she had glared up at him, every bit as mad as he was, but when he asked that final, damning question, she averted her face, and a tremulous sigh escaped her.

He heard that sigh, and his anger fled. "I'm sorry, Mouse," he said quietly. "I wanted you so badly that for a minute I forgot and let things go too far."

No woman on the planet could stay mad when faced with an excuse like that, she thought as she darted an uncertain look his way. He'd wanted her so badly that he forgot? Any normal, red-blooded woman would be glad to hear a confession like that, especially from a man like Gideon Ironheart, who looked as if he didn't forget much and could have his pick of women. But she wasn't a normal woman, and she knew better than to believe any man could want her that much, least of all Ironheart.

He caught her chin with his index finger and turned her face toward him. "Forgive me?" he asked.

It was like watching a mask slip over her face. The shy, uncertain woman who had come on this picnic with him vanished. In her place was the tough deputy he had met the first night. With a sick sense of his own iniquity, Gideon realized that he had driven her back into hiding.

"Sure," she said briskly. "No problem. Look, I need to get back. I've got to be on duty at 7:00 a.m."

With the fading of her anger had come humiliation. There was no one to blame for this but herself, Sara thought. She'd broken every promise she'd ever made to herself and tangled with a man. Of course she felt like a fool. He had coaxed her into revealing things—needs, desires, yearnings—that could only be embarrassing when exposed. And then, having exposed her vulnerability, naturally he pulled away. A man had done that once before. Fool me once, shame on you. Fool me twice…

Grimly, she helped Gideon pack up the picnic. At least he didn't give her any more hassles about forgiving him.

It was small consolation with tears of humiliation burning in her eyes and throat, and her heart aching for what could never be. Sara Yates now knew, beyond any shadow of a doubt, that she was a failure as a woman.

Chapter 5

It was nearly ten o'clock when they pulled up beside the house. Afraid that Gideon might speak, Sara hurried to open the truck door. "Thanks," she managed to say. "It was fun. See you tomorrow." She wished she never had to see him again.

"Sara—"

She slid quickly out and turned to give him a brittle smile. "Good night."

"Sara, wait!"

But she turned again and headed toward the house. She couldn't stand another minute, she thought. It was too humiliating.

And then she froze, staring at the back door of the house. Her heart seemed to stop.

"Sara." Gideon reached her side. "Let me go in first."

He'd seen it, too, she realized. The way the back door was crooked on its hinges and not quite closed. "Nonsense," she said tensely. "I'm the cop."

"But I've got the only weapon."

She turned and looked at him. In his work-gloved hand was a two-foot-long steel bar with pointed ends. It looked deadly.

"I know how to use it, too. I'll go first."

This time she didn't argue, and when he handed her a long wrench with a handle that tapered to another point, she hefted its weight gratefully. These must be his connecting tools, she thought. Her weapons were locked in the Blazer, and the keys were upstairs in her bedroom. But who the hell carried a side-arm on a date in Conard County? she asked herself almost wildly.

She was scared, she realized. Terrified of what she was going to find. Her grandfather— She couldn't even stand to wonder about it. He had to be all right. He *had* to be.

Gideon touched her arm briefly. "If anyone is in there, they know we're here," he warned her.

Of course. They would have heard the truck drive up. She nodded without looking at him. "I know." She stared at the house, forcing herself to think, despite her nearly paralyzing fear for her grandfather. "We go in together. It might allow them to get away, but they won't be able to overwhelm us as easily."

He nodded and spared her a long, intense look. Tough, he thought. Despite the fact that she was scared to death. Admiration flickered in him again.

"But I go first," she said, stepping forward. "I'm trained—"

His hand closed on her upper arm, almost painful in its grip. "I'm trained, too. Marines." So what if it had been a long time ago? He'd had plenty of opportunity to keep in practice in holes like Happy's Bar the other night.

Relief touched Sara like a gentle breeze. She was glad to know he had some training. Glad for both of them. Glad for her grandfather. Glad that they could back each other up.

Angled as it was, the screen door would no longer swing open. Sara stood to one side as Gideon lifted the sagging end and moved the door out of the way. The interior door was open a couple of inches. They stood on opposite sides of it, their backs to the wall, as Gideon reached out with his connecting rod and shoved it open.

After a heart-stopping moment of apprehension, Sara leaned to the side and peered into the kitchen. Seeing nothing in the shadows, she reached slowly around the door frame and felt for the light switch. The fluorescent bulb hummed, flickered and sprang to blinding life.

Nothing.

Gideon slipped past her into the room, and after a quick look around headed immediately for the dining room beyond. Sara's heart lodged in her throat, but she was right behind him, giving him just enough lead space so that they wouldn't walk into a trap together.

The dining room was a mess, the chairs knocked aside from the table as if someone had run through here too fast to avoid obstacles. The sight caused her heart to skip a beat, and the absence of any normal sounds filled her with dread. Her grandfather...

"Sara?" Gideon's voice came from around the corner of the living room. "Sara, Zeke's hurt. Come watch over him while I check out the upstairs."

Sara nearly ran around the corner, then halted in horror at the sight of her grandfather lying in a pool of blood. "Oh my God..." she said in a whisper.

"He's breathing okay," Gideon said softly. "Sara, he's alive, just unconscious. The bleeding has stopped, so it's been a while and they're probably gone, but I need to check...."

Sara nodded and came swiftly to kneel beside her grandfather. This was no time for horror or any other feeling. Right now there were things that needed to be done. She had to draw a couple of deep breaths to steady herself, but she managed to find a core of internal calm. "Okay."

Gideon gripped her shoulder briefly, then started up the stairs. Sara's gaze followed his prowling movements until he disappeared. Then she looked down at her grandfather and started praying.

Gideon was back in under three minutes. "They were up

there,'' he said, ''but they're gone now. What's faster? Calling for help or driving Zeke to the hospital?''

Sara looked up bleakly, measuring minutes in her mind. ''Call the sheriff's office and tell them we need the medevac flight. Then we'll need to position my Blazer to illuminate a landing pad and guide the chopper in.''

The nearest patrolling sheriff's unit arrived in the yard in under ten minutes. Gideon went out to the porch to greet the deputy and found himself face-to-face with Micah Parish.

Damn, thought Gideon, the man was even bigger than he'd realized, at least two inches taller than Gideon, and built of solid muscle. And Parish's eyes were familiar, so familiar that Gideon felt his stomach knot.

''You must be Ironheart,'' Micah said. ''Where's Sara?''

Gideon stepped aside, letting the deputy see Sara kneeling beside her grandfather. ''He's hurt pretty badly, from what I can tell.''

Micah nodded and brushed past, going to Sara's side, where he squatted and gripped her shoulder. ''The chopper'll be here in just a couple of minutes, Sara,'' he said. ''Yuma said to tell you that old Huey is going to break speed records.''

Sara tilted her head and gave Micah a wan smile. ''Thanks, Micah.''

''Ironheart and I are going to position the Blazers so they can see where to set down. Where are your keys?''

''Top drawer of my dresser.''

''I'll get them,'' Gideon said.

Sara glanced up at him. ''Thanks.''

Micah and Gideon parked the Blazers facing each other with the wide expanse of hard-packed yard between them, providing a flat, lighted area for the helicopter to set down on. They turned on the flashers of both vehicles so the pilot could use them as a guide.

''Who's Yuma?'' Gideon asked Micah as the two of them listened for the *whop-whop* that would signal the Huey's approach. What he really wanted to ask was how Micah had known who *he* was. Had Sara mentioned him? Or had Micah heard that Gideon was asking about him around town?

"The best damn chopper pilot this side of the Mekong," Parish said.

Gideon had heard that kind of remark before from men and was easily able to fill in all the unspeakable blanks that arose from Vietnam.

Suddenly Parish's dark eyes riveted him. "You a vet?"

"Marines."

"Nam?"

"I was there during the evacuation."

For a moment Micah's black-as-night eyes seemed to impale him. "I missed that," he said finally. "Damn filthy duty."

So filthy it had given Gideon an unalterable distaste for military life, but all he said was, "Yeah. Filthy."

The distinctive whopping of the Huey drew their attention to the east and the approaching helicopter. With navigation and landing lights on, the Huey was highly visible against the star-strewn sky.

Yuma set the Huey down as gently as a feather. Two medics piled out of the side bay doors, carrying a back board between them as Micah pointed to the front door.

Yuma climbed out, too, and crossed the dirt toward Micah. He was a moderately tall, lean man who walked with a limp and had a face that looked as if it had been ravaged by night-mares. Deep lines scored it, and hell looked out of his eyes, Gideon thought. He'd seen that look before. Some nightmares never ended.

"I spotted two more units on the road headed this way," Yuma told Micah. "They'll be here within five minutes."

Micah nodded approval. "Good."

"How's Sara?"

Micah shook his head. "Stunned. She'll go with you."

"Of course. I've got room." He gave a nod to Gideon, then limped back to the helicopter to be ready to take off as soon as the patient was loaded.

Micah looked at Gideon. "I want you to stay here. You can help us check things out."

Reluctantly, Gideon nodded. His impulse was to go with Sara, to be there if she needed anything, but he understood the deputy's concern. Someone had to be here to show the cops around and to answer questions.

He watched them carry Zeke carefully out and load him into the helicopter. Sara didn't even glance toward Gideon. Of course not. She had room for only one thing on her mind right now.

He watched the helicopter lift off with a roar of its engines and stared after it as it shrank into the distance. And he realized, quite suddenly, just how much an old Shoshone Indian had come to mean to him.

"Let's go," said Micah in the sudden silence left behind by the chopper. "Show me what you saw and walk me through exactly what you and Sara did. Start at the beginning."

So he started at the beginning.

Sara shivered and drew her denim jacket closer around her. It wasn't really chilly in the waiting room, but the early hour made her feel cold.

In the past several hours she had experienced a whole gamut of emotions and had finally reached a plateau of relative calm resulting mainly from weariness. Now she waited only to hear whether they needed to send her grandfather to a larger hospital where he could receive more specialized care. Zeke hadn't come to yet, and a neurologist from Laramie was consulting over the phone with Dr. MacArdle, trying to determine the seriousness of Zeke's injuries.

Her hands knotted into fists deep within her pockets, and she closed her eyes against the sting of tears. She really didn't know how she would stand it if her grandfather didn't recover. She simply couldn't imagine life without Zeke's warm humor and steady support. The ache that image brought was nearly intolerable.

"Sara?"

She looked up through a blur of tears and saw Gideon standing uncertainly in the doorway. Her throat was too tight to speak, and she could only make a small, almost helpless gesture to acknowledge him.

It was enough. He closed the distance between them in two long strides, then sat beside her and gathered her into his arms. "Oh, baby," he said softly. "Oh, baby..." He pressed her cheek to his chest and rocked her gently, listening to her swallow again and again as she fought her tears.

Even through her worry and grief, Sara felt a dim sense of astonishment at how ready Gideon was to hold her comfortingly. The men she worked with would have offered an awkward pat to the shoulder and a few gruff words of concern. And that was all she would have expected.

He didn't offer any false hopes or assurances. Not once did he say it was okay or would be all right. Because both of them knew it wasn't okay and might never be all right.

She drew a few shaky breaths and managed finally to subdue the urge to cry. The weary calm returned, a muffling blanket.

"What do they say?" Gideon asked presently.

"They don't know for sure. Zeke is stable but unconscious, and Dr. MacArdle is consulting by phone with a neurologist. They may have to move him to a bigger hospital."

Gideon nodded, forgetting that she couldn't see the gesture with her cheek pressed to his chest. Stable but unconscious, and seventy-plus years old. Zeke was in great shape, and probably as tough as old shoe leather, but he was also getting on in years. How much could he stand?

It would have been impossible, Gideon thought, for minutes to move any more slowly without time coming to a complete halt. It had been like this the night his own grandfather had died, he remembered. His uncle had called him to tell him the old man wouldn't make it through the night. Seven hours and three connecting flights later, Gideon had sat in a room something like this and waited as the minutes dragged by.

His grandfather, he thought now, should never have been in

the hospital. It hadn't been the place for a man who had devoted the better part of his adult life to healing through the old ways. Yet Adam Lightfoot had never mocked the white men's medicine, he remembered.

"You can't heal the body unless you heal the spirit, too," the old man had told him. "Anglo medicine heals the body, and heals it well, but the people keep getting sick because the spirit is forgotten."

Another one of those things that Gideon hadn't really heard until it was too late. *The spirit is forgotten.* He felt as if his own had not only been forgotten, but lost somewhere, as well.

Sara sat in her corner of the couch, folding into herself with her shoulders hunched and her hands tucked up under her jacket. She looked so small and lost right now, nothing like the deputy who'd saved his butt from that gang of rednecks.

"How about some coffee?" he suggested, and glanced at his watch. A little after three. No place would be open right now, so it would have to be the vending machine. "I'll get it," he said, when she didn't answer. "Be right back."

The machine was only a short way down the hall. He leaned against it, resting his forehead against his fist as he watched the stream of coffee pour into the disposable cup. When it was done, he moved it to one side and shoved his hand into his jeans pocket, looking for a couple more quarters.

"Here," said a deep, gravelly voice behind him, and quarters were slipped into the slot. "You must be Ironheart."

Gideon straightened slowly and turned to face a ruddy, stocky man of maybe forty-five. He wore ordinary jeans, a zipped-up nylon jacket and a battered straw cowboy hat. "That's my name," he agreed, thinking he had seen this man somewhere from a distance.

"I'm Nate Tate," the man said. "Sheriff Nate Tate."

Ah! thought Gideon. At last the inquisition. "Pleased to meet you."

"I've been hearing about you here and there," Tate said noncommittally. "You planning on staying awhile?"

"Awhile. At least until Zeke is better. Sara doesn't seem to have a whole lot of help."

Tate's unwinking gaze raked him from head to foot. "Sara's never had a lot of help, not since her ma died. And she doesn't need any more trouble than she's got."

"I'm not planning on making any."

After a moment Tate nodded. "She's here, I imagine."

"In the waiting room."

"Well, get the coffee, son, and let's go."

Feeling that he had passed the first hurdle with the sheriff, Gideon followed him into the waiting room.

"Nate!" As soon as she saw him, Sara rose to her feet. And then she hesitated, clearly uncertain whether he was here as her boss or her friend.

Nate settled it. "I'm sorry, Sara. I just heard." Closing the distance between them, he wrapped his arm around her shoulders. "How's he doing?"

"We don't really know yet. He's stable, but he won't…wake up." Her voice trembled a little and then recovered.

Nate gave her a little squeeze and let her go. Gideon offered her one of the cups of coffee, and she accepted it with a wan smile of thanks before returning her attention to Nate. "What have you found?"

"Not a whole hell of a lot, I'm afraid. Micah says it looks as if nothing was stolen, but very definitely as if they were looking for something. Something big, because they didn't bother opening any drawers, but they checked out all the rooms in your house, the bunkhouse and the barn. Maybe the most suspicious thing is that they left the valuables alone."

"I don't have any valuables."

"Ironheart here does," Nate said. When Sara plopped back down onto the couch, Nate sat in a chair across from her. "According to Micah, they passed on a Zuni belt buckle that's worth a small fortune and a few other things of that kind."

Gideon shifted uneasily, not sure he liked the way that

sounded. "A lot of people don't have any notion of the value of Zuni jewelry. Or of Indian jewelry as a whole."

Nate nodded. "I realize that. It's still funny. Micah said something about a dirt biker you saw earlier?"

"I didn't exactly see him. I saw sun glint off metal or glass, and when I headed up toward the trees to investigate, he took off. It sounded like a dirt bike, or a small motorcycle."

"There might not be any connection," Nate said after a moment. He looked at Sara. "Anyhow, I need you to go through the house in the morning with one of the other deputies and tell me if anything is missing. You're the only one who can do that, Sara."

She drew a long breath and nodded. "Okay. Unless something happens with my grandfather."

"And you," Nate said, turning to Gideon. "I want you to show us exactly where that biker was. There has to be a reason Zeke Jackson is lying in a hospital bed right now, and no stone is going to be left unturned."

That might almost be a threat, Gideon found himself thinking. If a man wanted to take it that way. "No problem," he said. "I can show you right where it's at. And what's more, unless one of your deputies poked around up there, it hasn't been disturbed, because Zeke and I didn't even bother to check it out once the biker was gone."

Nate nodded approval. "Good."

"Sara?" Dr. MacArdle entered the room looking rumpled, tired and concerned. Giving Nate and Gideon only the barest of nods, he went to sit beside Sara. "Your grandfather's condition hasn't changed at all. No, wait," he said when she opened her mouth. "Actually, that's a good sign at this point. If he'd suffered any kind of serious neurological injury, say a blood clot in the brain, we'd expect a deterioration of his neurological signs. That's not happening. Dr. Brandeis and I have decided to keep him here in intensive care for a while longer, unless something changes. In the meantime, why don't you get some sleep? We'll call you if anything changes."

"You can stay with Marge and me," Nate said as MacArdle

left the room. "We've got an extra bunk in Janet's room, now that Cindy's in college."

Sara shook her head, thinking that the last thing she could tolerate right now was the well-meaning concern of friends. She would much rather just stay here and wait. "Thanks, Nate, but really, I'd rather not."

"Holler if you change your mind." The sheriff rose, patted her shoulder and left.

"I could get a room for you at the motel," Gideon said. "And I packed some of your clothes, in case. They're out in my truck. You can go get some sleep, and I'll sit right here and wait, and I'll call you the minute anything happens." He leaned over and touched her arm. "Mouse, that old man is going to wake up, probably in just a few hours, and it's not going to make him very happy to see you looking like this."

Her eyes were blurring again, with tears and fatigue, and she didn't even argue when he drew her against his side and tucked her face to his shoulder.

"Okay," he said. "Okay. You sleep right here, then. Sleep, baby. You won't miss a damn thing, I swear."

All her life, Sara had had to comfort others. Her father when her mother died, her brother when their father died. Friends who had lost loved ones. Survivors of accidents. The injured and battered innocents of the world. Looking back, she couldn't remember one time in her adult life when anyone at all had simply held her as Gideon Ironheart did through the endless predawn hours.

She didn't see why he should do it. He had only entered her life a few short days ago, yet he seemed somehow to have taken root. Zeke really liked him, that was obvious. Something had clicked between the two men, almost as if they had been friends from another time.

She could imagine them in another time, too, the old warrior and the younger one, dressed in buckskin, surveying the plains and mountains, riding free....

She sighed and snuggled closer to Gideon. He was so warm,

so hard, so big, so comforting. He made her feel safe, and Sara honestly couldn't remember the last time she had felt safe. It was an illusion, of course. He was a tumbleweed, he'd said, moving on when the whim took him. But for right now he made her feel safe, and Sara was reluctant to fight a feeling she'd known so rarely.

This afternoon, sitting in the kitchen when Zeke had mentioned the vision quest, she'd had the strangest feeling that her grandfather had a greater purpose than simply helping Gideon find a vision to guide him. Almost as if…as if he had wanted to pass something on to the younger man.

What a crazy idea, she thought drowsily. What could possibly be passed on? An idea? A dream? A vision of…what? The future? She was aware that her grandfather had a mystical side to his nature, but it was something he kept closely private, because it was so intensely personal. Why had he mentioned such things to Gideon, whom he hardly knew?

But then, Gideon was different. It didn't take a genius to feel his…difference, for lack of a better word. It wasn't exactly charisma, it wasn't exactly…anything. Just this sense of power, of invisible whirlwinds around him, of silent lightning and thunder. Things beyond normal ken.

When she'd first met him, she had labeled him an "Indian with an attitude." But that wasn't it. Whatever it was that made a man face down ten other men rather than leave a place, whatever it was that made him take a stand rather than yield to overwhelming odds, was not an attitude. It might be foolish, it might even be suicidal, but it was also admirable.

Her grandfather must have sensed these things, she thought, unconsciously snuggling closer, enjoying the way Gideon shifted to accommodate her, the way his arm tightened around her shoulders. His heartbeat beneath her ear was steady, comforting, and his breathing was slow and regular. Soothing.

The gentle rise and fall of his chest was as relaxing as being rocked, and little by little she slipped into sleep.

"Sara? Sara, Zeke is awake."

She was never sure afterward whether Gideon or Dr.

MacArdle had roused her, but it really didn't matter. What *did* matter was that fifteen seconds later she was standing beside her grandfather's bed in intensive care, and he was smiling at her.

That was when, for the first time, she realized just how old and frail Zeke really was. He was always so active, always so firm, that she hadn't really noticed, but now she did. He had aged considerably in the nine years since he had come to help her and Joey, and he was an old man now. She should be caring for him, not the other way around.

"I'm fine, child, just fine," he said in answer to her question. "Just a little headache is all. You go on home and get some rest. Is Gideon with you?"

"Yes, he's been here most of the night. I was so worried...."

"Sh-sh-sh," he said, and brushed away her tears with his fingertip. "My time has not yet come, child."

Sara looked away, biting her upper lip and blinking rapidly. Little by little the tightness around her throat loosened, and breathing became easier. Finally she found her voice.

"Do you remember what happened, Grandfather?"

"No. Dr. MacArdle already questioned me about that. He told me what happened."

"But you don't remember?"

Zeke shook his head slightly. "The last thing I remember is stepping outside to watch the sunset."

"He doesn't remember a thing," Sara was telling Nate only a short time later. The sheriff's office was gearing up for the day, a steadily rising level of activity apparent as they talked. Gideon stood over by the front window, waiting patiently. "Dr. MacArdle says that's normal, but that he might never remember what happened."

"That's probably best for Zeke," Nate rumbled, "but it sure as hell handicaps the investigation. At this moment, hon, we don't have a damn thing to go on."

Sara nodded, glancing toward the windows and the sun-drenched square beyond. Marigolds in the courthouse flower beds bobbed gaily in the gentle morning breeze, and old Bill Haldersen and Al Loomis were already out there reading the morning paper. Those benches ought to have their names on them, she thought vaguely.

"Maybe," she said after a moment, "I'll notice something when I get back up there. I'm the best person to know what's out of place."

"That's what I'm hoping," Nate agreed. "Micah will meet you up there a little later this morning. He especially wants to check out the area where the biker was spotted."

"But he worked swing shifts last night," Sara argued automatically, which meant he shouldn't work today at all.

"Yeah, but he figures this is his case. Hours don't mean a thing to Micah when he gets on something."

Sara nodded, remembering other times. "I'll need a few days off."

Nate half smiled. "You never needed to ask. You're off the schedule already. You can make up for it when Ed's wife has the baby."

Sara almost chuckled at that. Ed Dewhurst had been the first deputy in Conard County history to request paternity leave. Nate had granted it without a moment's hesitation, but the subject had been hotly debated in the Bible Study Group, over coffee at Maude's Diner, and probably in most of the bars. Opinion was pretty evenly divided, and not along lines of gender.

"I'd better go up and tell Joey about Grandfather," she said after a moment.

"He's still not talking," Nate warned her. "Sullenest so-and-so I've ever seen."

"Well, that's just too damn bad," Sara said, her ordinarily quiescent temper snapping. "He doesn't have to talk, but, by God, he's going to listen!"

Nate and Gideon watched her stalk up the stairs toward the jail, which was in an armored room on the second floor.

"That girl," Nate remarked, "was always a damn sight too

patient with that boy. She should have kicked his butt out of the house at least two years ago.''

He looked at Gideon. "Just so you know, I did a priors check on you."

Gideon nodded, undisturbed. Given the circumstances, Nate Tate would have been a lousy sheriff if he hadn't checked up on the stranger who was involved.

"One felony when you were sixteen and a couple of misdemeanors for barroom brawling don't make me nervous, Ironheart," Tate continued. "I've got people in this county who did a whole lot worse in their youth and lived to become upstanding citizens."

Gideon gave a brief nod, waiting, sensing more.

"But you make me nervous, anyway, son," the sheriff continued. "Something about you is ringing my bells like mad, and I get the definite feeling you're not just vacationing here. So I'm going to keep an eye on you."

Well, he'd been anticipating that all along, ever since he arrived and started asking questions about Micah. Conard County was so thinly populated that a stranger was bound to draw attention. "Fine with me, Sheriff," he said easily.

Nate studied him a moment longer, then turned away to greet Velma Jansen, the department's dispatcher, as she walked in the door.

Gideon turned to face the window, staring out over the courthouse lawn and flower beds, his mind wandering over the events of last night. There didn't seem to be any rhyme or reason to it, he thought. Unless somebody out there just got their kicks terrifying people or beating up old men.

And Micah Parish. The man was calm, assured and silent. Enigmatic. Not an easy man to know. But a man Gideon nevertheless wanted to know.

Last fall, on the seventieth story of the job he had mentioned to Zeke, there had been an accident. He and his partner, Barney Witt, had shinnied up opposing columns and waited for the derrick, resting on plank flooring thirty feet below, to swing a beam toward them. Connectors needed to have an almost telepathic understanding of their partners, needed to know them well enough to anticipate every move, needed to feel absolutely comfortable with them. Barney and Gideon were such a pair, and they *always* worked together.

As close as brothers, Gideon thought now. Facing the sunlit square, he forced himself to remember.

The beam had swung into place slowly, cautiously, guided by a tag line held by a man below. It was his job to keep the beam from swinging wildly or spinning out of control. To guide it into the right place. Below them, he braced his feet and leaned backward so far his shoulders were only a foot above the plank flooring as he kept that beam steady.

Gideon and Barney, clinging to their opposite columns, watched it come closer. Barney's end arrived a little sooner, and he reached out, grabbing a corner to help guide it toward his column. Gideon got ready to grab his end.

The tag line snapped suddenly. Without warning. The beam, released abruptly from the guiding pressure of the tag line, swung the other way and caught Barney Witt right in the chest and flung him from his precarious perch. Then it swung back, but Gideon had had just enough time, barely enough time, to slide downward on his column and get out of its way. He was safe even before Barney hit the ground.

Gideon broke into a cold sweat every time he thought of it. Every time he remembered clinging to his column with one hand and watching that beam spin and swing until he got dizzy. Every time he remembered hanging there while his heart stopped beating and his soul quieted. While everything inside him froze with the knowledge that Barney was falling. Barney was dying.

And then the instant Barney died. He hadn't seen it. Hadn't heard it. But he had felt it. A black, roiling wave had crashed through him suddenly, and he had known Barney was dead. Only then did his heart start beating again. Only then did his body move, his brain think. Only then.

But he would never, ever, walk the iron again.

He had lost a brother that day. The only brother he had ever really had. He had gone home to his uncle's ranch, and his uncle, as always, had given him a sanctuary. Gideon worked with the horses, mucked out their stalls, performed all the mindless labor he could manage, trying to silence his grief and loss and nightmares with bone-deep fatigue.

And then he had learned of the existence of Micah Parish. His *real* brother.

Joey wouldn't even look at her. Sara stood outside the cell, fighting for patience and strength, and got madder and madder at her brother. He was sixteen, handsome as sin, with just enough of his grandfather's looks to make him exotically attractive. Up until two years ago she had always imagined a bright future for him. Girls flocked like bees to honey around him. Teachers had always praised his intelligence and creativity. He'd seemed only normally rebellious, normally difficult, for his age.

All that had changed. Not all at once, but rapidly enough. What had at first been called a phase by teachers, other parents and the minister, had finally become a serious problem. Detention and expulsion from school had only seemed to make it worse. He'd run up against the law any number of times, and time and again some deputy let him go with a warning. Sara heard about it all, of course. Her fellow deputies felt she needed to know what was going on. She hadn't been able to prevent it, though.

Now this. Grand theft auto and jail. A felony record. And no sign that he was going to turn around.

He still wouldn't look at her. She glanced at her watch and realized that she'd been standing there for five minutes, waiting for that sullen brat to look at her so she could tell him what had happened. She had stood there for five minutes, trying to rein in her rising temper. Why the hell should she?

"Okay," she said, not caring that her voice vibrated with anger. "Okay, don't look at me. I'm going to tell you this, and I'm only going to say it once. Somebody broke into the house last night and beat Grandfather badly. He's in the hospital with a fractured skull and some broken ribs. Right now he's in intensive care, but they think he's going to be all right.''

No response. Nothing. Except that she thought, just maybe, he had stiffened a little. She couldn't be sure.

"Joey." With difficulty, she kept her voice level. "You wouldn't have any idea why anyone would break into the house, would you?"

Again there was no answer. Sara stood there for another moment, feeling as close to despair as she had ever come. And as close to violence. Her hands knotted, and she turned away, mentally washing her hands. That was it, she thought. No more. He could just sit there and rot.

Her hand was on the heavy steel door when he called her. "Sara."

His voice sounded rusty from disuse, and something in her ached for the boy he had been and the man he might never be now. For her baby brother. She hesitated only a moment, then turned to look back.

"Sara, tell him…tell Grandfather I love him."

"I will." Torn, she stood there, wondering what to do now. Go back to him? Try to talk some more? And then she decided not to push it. "I'll tell him," she repeated. "We love you, too, Joey." Then, before he could reject her again, she hurried away.

Sara, Gideon thought as he watched her cross the room toward him, had just about reached her limit for now. Her eyes were red-rimmed with fatigue and unshed tears. The corners of her mouth were drooping, and she was trembling. At her limit or not, though, she walked with her head up and her gaze steady.

She didn't say anything as they stepped outside and he opened the door of his truck to help her in. She didn't say a word as he backed out and headed out of town. She didn't say anything until Conard City was well behind them and the truck's engine strained a little harder as they began to climb gently toward the mountains. The early morning air was crisp; the sun was warm and bright.

"Gideon?"

"Ma'am?"

"Will you…can you…" Her voice trailed away, and she sighed.

"I sure can," he answered. "I plan on sticking around at least until Zeke can manage. Somebody's got to look after those dang mustangs of his, and I kind of promised I would."

"But you're on vacation."

"I don't like to be idle. Besides, I'm in no hurry to get anywhere."

"But…" Again her voice trailed away.

This was not like Sara, he thought. He might only have known her for a few days, but she wasn't one to tiptoe around things. And then he realized what might be troubling her.

"Last night?" he said. "Is that worrying you? Forget it, Mouse. I'm not going to jump your bones without an invitation, and I honestly don't expect to get one. Relax."

She averted her face, aware that worry and lack of sleep were making her stupid, fogging her brain and scrambling her words. If she were feeling anything like normal, she never would have brought the subject up, but she wasn't feeling normal. Her whole world had managed to get turned upside down in just a few hours, and strange things were going on inside her. Things that compelled her to pursue a subject she should have dropped like a hot potato as soon as it crossed her mind.

"No," she said, leaning her cheek against the chilly glass of the window. "I mean the way I acted. I'm sorry I blew everything out of proportion. I acted like…like…"

"A frustrated woman?" Gideon suggested, and a warm, teasing chuckle escaped him. "Hell, Mouse, I'm feeling like a bear with a sore paw myself. Self-control is miserable, isn't it?"

Slowly Sara turned her head and looked at him. He was so incredibly frank, she thought. No hidden agendas with him. A woman would always know where she stood with him, and to

Sara that was an incredibly attractive attribute. "Don't you have any shame, Ironheart?" she heard herself say, surprised to hear the uncharacteristic teasing note in her voice.

He glanced at her and smiled. "Shame about what? I don't see why I should be ashamed of being a normal, healthy male, or why I should try to pretend that you didn't get me all hot and bothered last night. You're dynamite, Sara Yates, and I'm not at all ashamed that I reacted to you." He paused as he downshifted and turned into her driveway. "I don't see why people are so afraid to admit that."

Sara might be groggy, but her brain hadn't completely failed. "They're afraid of being manipulated."

They had reached the yard before he responded to that. "I guess," he said, as he braked and switched off the engine. "Fear is a terrible thing, isn't it? Messes up things that ought to be perfectly natural and perfectly easy." Like telling a man you're his brother. What the hell would Parish do, anyway? The worst he could do was tell him to get lost. He turned and looked at Sara and realized he had let things get serious. He flashed her a smile. "You're welcome to manipulate me anytime, Mouse."

His meaning was clear, and wild color blossomed in Sara's cheeks. He didn't wait for her answer but climbed out, chuckling, and came around to open the door for her. His laughter had faded by the time he handed her down, though.

"You go in and catch a nap," he said. "I'll take care of the animals and keep an eye out for Parish."

"But you haven't had any sleep yourself!"

He shrugged. "I feel okay. Second wind. Go on. I'll wake you if anything comes up."

He watched that nicely rounded bottom of hers sway as she walked toward the house, and he wondered if he was losing his mind. He had come to Conard County to learn something about the brother he had never known, not to get tangled up in the personal problems of the Yates family.

But here he was, anyway, promising to stick it out until Zeke

could manage again, worrying about Sara and how she was
going to handle Zeke's temporary disability and Joey's attitude.

And wondering who the hell would want to beat up a harm-
less old man.

Chapter 6

Mucking out stalls was filthy, backbreaking work, and Gideon threw himself into it with a will. In addition to the mustangs, which were wild, Sara kept three horses for riding. Zeke had brought them in last night, and this morning they were eager to escape their stalls. He put them all, plus Columbine's foal, into the fenced east pasture and stood for a few minutes watching them gambol.

They were sure feeling frisky this morning. He smiled and leaned against the rail, giving himself a few minutes to soak up the warm sun, the dry air, the pristine beauty of the mountains, trees and grasses. There was something about this place that had a quieting effect on his soul. Despite everything that had happened, everything that was worrying him, despite even his concern for Zeke and Sara, something deep inside him was opening, expanding, trying to flower in response to the sunlight and beauty of the mountains.

He was forty-one years old. In those years he'd experienced an awful lot, some of it things that other people would never experience. He'd had good times, he'd had bad times, and he'd seen hell more than once. He'd laughed with friends and had plenty of fun when he had a few extra bucks in his pocket.

But he'd never once been happy.

Right now something inside him said he *could* be happy. That all he had to do was let it happen.

"Ah, hell," he muttered, and turned from the pasture toward the barn. Stalls needed cleaning, a mustang needed some attention, and happiness was a mental Shangri-la, a delusion, a place people kept trying to reach and never did.

He was just spreading straw in the last stall when Micah Parish found him. Gideon straightened, tensing inwardly as he faced the man. His brother.

Damn. Micah's eyes were the eyes of their grandfather, not just in shape and color, but in their quiet intensity. Shaman's eyes. Eyes that could see past facades, into the soul.

Tell him. But the words wouldn't come. He wasn't ready. He had to deal with his own tangled feelings about this before he would be ready to deal with Micah's reaction, whatever it might be. Leaning on the pitchfork, Gideon studied his brother and said nothing. Today, he realized suddenly, Micah wasn't in uniform. It was the first time Gideon had seen him in anything but khaki, but jeans and a red shirt didn't make Micah any less intimidating.

Micah tipped back the brim of his straw hat and then leaned against the stall gate. "Morning, Ironheart."

"Parish." Feeling wary, Gideon waited.

"Is Sara around?"

"She was going to take a nap."

"Good." Micah's eyes flicked over him, missing nothing, coming to rest finally on the hand that held the pitchfork handle in a white-knuckled grip. "Zeke's doing pretty good this morning, I hear. I called the hospital before I came up here."

"That's good."

Micah's gaze returned to his face, and eyes like obsidian impaled him. "What are you doing mucking out stalls in Conard County, Wyoming, when you could be building a skyscraper in Dallas or Atlanta?"

Gideon's breath caught deep inside for just a split second. This man didn't pull his punches. And suddenly Gideon didn't give a damn who knew the truth. A punch for a punch, he thought. "My partner fell from the seventieth story last fall. I don't walk iron anymore."

Micah was very still and very silent for a moment. When he spoke again, there was a slightly different note in his voice. "Things like that can play hell with a man. You got a minute to show me where you saw that biker?"

"Sure." A feeling close to relief settled over him. He set the pitchfork aside and led the way. "Out behind the bunkhouse, up in the trees."

"What were you doing when you saw him?"

This time, Gideon realized, the accusing tone was missing. Somehow his answer about Barney's accident had settled doubts in Micah's mind. "I was washing up at the spigot in the back."

"And Zeke?"

"He and Chester Elk Horn were at the corral there." He pointed. "I guess Chester was just getting ready to leave. I went around to wash up, and just as I was finishing—shaking the water off my arms—I looked up and saw the glint from the trees."

They reached the back of the bunkhouse, and Gideon pointed. "I knew right away it wasn't a piece of glass lying on the ground, because it flickered and winked. Had to be moving to do that. So I started up that way to investigate. Zeke and Sara don't mind hikers, but they hate ATVs and dirt bikers."

Micah nodded. "I feel the same myself. Some of those folks seem to think that just because they *can* go off the road, they have a right to go anywhere, including private property."

Halfway across the grassy pasture to the trees, Gideon paused. "Right here is where I was when the guy took off. It sounded as if he went up and to the left."

"Toward the county road, probably three miles as the crow flies."

Gideon nodded. "About that far. Zeke caught up with me here right then. Said to ignore it, that it was only one biker and not much we could do." With his thumb, he shoved his hat farther back on his head and looked up into the trees. "I was kind of mad," he admitted. "Anyhow, we went back to the house and had coffee."

"So nobody's been up there?"

"Not as far as I know."

Micah nodded and began to stride upward toward the trees. The pasture was on a gentle slope, not particularly taxing, but Gideon hadn't fully adjusted yet to the altitude here, though he was better adapted than a week ago. He got a little winded by the time they reached the line of trees, but Micah wasn't even breathing deeply.

Micah gestured for him to stay back a little, and Gideon complied, understanding that the deputy didn't want any tracks or other signs disturbed. Micah moved in slowly, crouching often to study what appeared to be only a blade of grass or a twig.

Watching him, Gideon realized that his brother had training in tracking that far exceeded the ordinary. "LRRP?" he asked suddenly, pronouncing it "lurp."

Micah never even glanced up. "Special Operations Branch. Twenty-one years."

Special Operations Branch said more than Special Forces. Special Operations covered a lot of things the public never heard about, and included the most elite units. Gideon looked at Micah with new eyes. "That's a long time."

"Seemed like it upon occasion." Micah eased forward again, checking out some more blades of grass.

Ten, maybe fifteen minutes passed while Micah studied the area. Gideon, left with nothing to do but hook his thumbs in his belt loops, tipped his head back and watched a couple of fluffy clouds grow slowly in the deep blue sky. Maybe they would get some rain later. They sure could use it. The pasture was beginning to look a little dry, and the dust was getting thick in the yard.

"He was here for a while," Micah said abruptly. Straightening, he came back to Gideon.

"He?"

Micah nodded. "Size-eleven shoe, maybe 180 or 190 pounds, probably between five foot ten and six feet. Lots of prints, tramped back and forth for some time. Long enough to smoke half a pack of butts." He held out his hand, showing Gideon the filter tip of a popular brand of cigarettes. "He kicked dirt over it, but not carefully enough."

"Not just a dirt biker, then."

Micah shook his head. "Somebody was watching this place. Looking for someone or something, or looking for someone to leave."

Together they walked back to the house. Micah spoke again.

"I'll have to go check along the road and see if I can tell where he came out of the woods."

"That'll take forever."

Micah glanced at him. "Probably not. I doubt he was being as careful out there as he was up in those trees. If Sara's not awake yet, I'll go out and look into that first. No point getting her up unless I have to."

But Sara was already up. She had heard Micah's vehicle pull into the yard and now was waiting for them in the kitchen with a fresh pot of coffee.

She looked a lot fresher, Gideon thought. A few hours of sleep had done wonders, bringing the color back to her cheeks and the sparkle back to her warm brown eyes. She wore a denim skirt and white blouse. Gideon, who had never seen her in a skirt, couldn't help taking an eyeful of slender calves, delicate ankles and pink-tipped toes peeking from her sandals.

God, he thought, looking away, she was some woman. An armful. No twiggy model with legs so thin they were practically sticks. No, Sara was curvy. Curvy calves that led right up to thighs that would be soft and… He sighed and forced himself to pay attention to business.

"How are Faith and the baby?" Sara asked as she filled three mugs with coffee and joined the men at the table.

"Doing great," Micah replied. "Sally's just about the happiest baby ever born. Takes after her mother, I reckon."

Gideon thought about that for a minute, taking in Micah's obvious pride and pleasure in both his wife and child, and decided that even if the baby wasn't Micah's, it didn't matter to Micah. Unexpectedly, he thought of his uncle, William Lightfoot, and how delighted he would be to learn there was a baby girl in the family. He wouldn't have a problem with the baby's paternity, either. He would welcome the child as readily and warmly as he had long ago welcomed Gideon.

"I've got some chores to finish up," he said abruptly, rising from the table. "You let me know when you want to go through the bunkhouse, Parish."

He climbed the fence into the corral with the mustang and then stood still, giving a coaxing little cluck. The stallion's ears pricked and he took a tentative step toward the man.

Ironheart. He'd taken the name shortly after his eighteenth birthday. The judge who granted the request had been bored with the proceeding and had hardly glanced at the boy. Gideon had taken it with purpose, refusing any longer to bear the name of the father who had abandoned him. At the time the name Ironheart had been a statement of the man he intended to be. Now look at him, getting all bent out of shape over Sara and her grandfather, over the brother he had just met, and the child his brother hadn't sired but was fathering. He swore under his breath.

It wasn't that he wanted to be hard so much as it was that he didn't trust all those soft feelings. They were fleeting, fanciful, and all they did was weaken a man, make him vulnerable to some shaft or other. They were aberrations, not to be relied on. People said they loved someone, and the next thing you knew they were moving on without a backward glance. How many times had he seen it?

So it was just best not to let yourself be deluded by the momentary soft feelings.

He clucked again, and the mustang pranced a little closer. A game, he realized suddenly. That damn stallion was teasing him.

Gideon grinned then, suddenly feeling pretty good, forgetting all his musings about the unreliability of gentler feelings. "You better look out, boy," he told the horse. "I'll ride you yet."

Sara went to town to visit her grandfather right after Micah finished up and left. She invited Gideon to join her, but he told her he didn't want to leave the place unattended.

"There's no reason why they should come back," she argued. "They know we haven't got whatever they wanted."

He shrugged. "Say hi to Zeke. Tell him I'm thinking about the vision quest, but I'm going to need some convincing."

She took two steps toward her Blazer, then turned again to face him. "I don't feel easy about you being here alone. If they come back—"

She bit the word off as if she wished she could take it back, but Gideon had heard her, anyway, and the fact that she was concerned about him touched some long-locked place in him. He ignored the warm, syrupy feeling that tried to bring itself to his attention.

"If they come back, I'll hold 'em for questioning," he told her teasingly. "Go on, Sara. I'll be okay."

She looked at him standing there in the bright afternoon sunlight, his hands on his rakishly cocked hips, and realized that she had come to care for him. Foolishly, stupidly, she cared. She wanted, she realized with a sad, desperate ache, to always see him standing in the sun like this with his hips cocked and his hard, harsh face shadowed by the brim of his hat. She wanted to know that he was going to be there tomorrow and tomorrow.

And he had already told her that he wouldn't be.

"Sara?" His hands fell from his hips, and he stepped toward her. "Sara? What's wrong?"

She caught her lips between her teeth and shook her head. "Nothing. Really. I'll see you later."

Too late, she thought as she tooled the Blazer down the rutted driveway. Too late. She had been sabotaged by all the years that she had refused to have anything personal to do with men. The one man who had refused to be put off by her barriers had managed to slip beneath her guard because she hadn't been prepared. She'd had no defenses against a man who wouldn't take no for an answer. A man who could tease her out of her fear of him simply by being outrageous.

Well, she promised herself shakily, she wouldn't let him know she cared. And if she didn't let him know, didn't let anyone know, he could hardly make a fool of her, could he?

Gideon's image seemed to dance before her all the way to town, and all she could think was that all that raw masculinity ought to come with some kind of warning. *She* sure as hell didn't know how to handle it.

The clouds that had started out as a few white puffs in late morning had, by late afternoon, turned into the dark gray steel of thunderheads. Gauging them, Gideon decided to stable the saddle horses. The mustangs would manage on their own. Even the stallion would do better, so he let the horse out of the corral. The mustang hesitated only a moment before trumpeting his approach to the mares and then taking off across the pasture toward the woods.

That horse would have gone crazy if he were trapped during a bad storm, Gideon thought as he watched the roan disappear into the trees. He was a wild creature, more terrified of confinement than the elements. The saddle horses, used to stabling, would feel safer indoors.

Thunder rumbled hollowly, bouncing back and forth on the mountains and out of ravines higher up. The wind picked up a little, blowing a cold gust or two right off the snowfields above the ranch. He had to reach up to hang on to his hat and then decided to ditch it in the bunkhouse and get his slicker out. It would be a far sight more useful if those clouds dumped.

He had no sooner finished securing the barn and the bunkhouse when it hit. Hail fell, stones the size of marbles pelting the yard and denting his truck as he watched from the porch of the house. The roar of falling stones and rolling thunder was almost deafening, and he hoped to God it didn't panic the mustangs too much to take shelter beneath trees.

As suddenly as it had started, the hailstorm stopped. The hush was almost unreal after the racket, and only the rumble of thunder kept Gideon from thinking he'd gone deaf. The sky was leaden from horizon to horizon, and clouds seemed to scud along the very treetops. The temperature must have dropped fifteen degrees, he thought, feeling chilled and damp.

Well, he would go in and close up Sara's house completely before it started to rain, and then he'd settle in for the night. Little else could be done today.

The phone rang just as he was walking through the kitchen. Reaching out, he snagged the receiver and leaned against the wall. "Double Y Ranch," he said.

"Gideon, it's Sara. I'm at the hospital with Grandfather."

"How is he?"

"He's doing really well. They're going to move him into a regular room tomorrow morning. But that isn't why I called. One of the nurses just told me the weather service has issued a stockmen's advisory and a storm warning."

"Hardly surprising. We just had five minutes of marble-sized hail. I don't think my truck is ever going to look the same again."

"Oh, Gideon…"

He laughed. "Hey, Mouse, if that's the worst that ever happens…! The saddle horses are safe in the barn, and I assume the mustangs are safe under the trees. I was just going upstairs to check the bedroom windows before the rain hits. The temperature must have dropped fifteen degrees. You're going to wish you'd worn a jacket."

She gave a small laugh. "The Blazer has a good heater. I'm going to be down here a couple more hours, I guess. I forgot to tell you that there's a pot of stew in the refrigerator for dinner, and some homemade bread in the bread box. And ice cream. Just help yourself to whatever looks good."

She'd thought of him, he realized a few moments later as he hung up the phone. She'd thought of him and worried about what he would do for dinner. That warm, syrupy feeling returned, and this time he didn't find it quite so easy to dismiss. With all she had on her mind right now, the woman had still worried about *him*. That was pretty damn special, and for once he didn't argue with himself about it.

Upstairs, he walked from room to room, closing windows and securing the latches. In Sara's room, he found a loose latch. It wasn't much to worry about on the second story, but he pulled a screwdriver out of his back pocket and went to work on it, anyway. He didn't like leaving things undone, and it gave him a sense of satisfaction to fix what was broken and mend what needed mending. He always had a screwdriver in one hip pocket and a tape measure in the other, and as often as not a small wrench tucked somewhere.

Beyond the window, heavy dark clouds moved slowly, looking almost low enough to touch. Above the pasture, the pines had turned almost black in the gray light, and beneath them shadows loomed mysteriously.

It was beautiful, he thought, pausing. Beautiful. Wild. Thunder boomed hollowly, lightning forked dazzlingly in the distance, and thunder cracked again. A fat raindrop hit the window with a splat, and moments later another joined it.

Something—a sense of unease—made him look toward the spot under the trees where the biker had hidden. There was no one there now, he was sure, but he reached for the shade anyway and lowered it. He didn't want Sara walking in here after dark and flipping on the light, becoming visible to anyone who might care to watch. He knew she would just cross the room and draw the shade—from the porch of the bunkhouse he'd watched her do it every night—but he didn't want anyone else to watch her. See her. Know that this was her room.

The feeling was rooted in some deep, dark instinct, and he didn't analyze it. Once the shade was closed, he was done, and he left her room without another glance, without in any way trespassing on her privacy.

He checked all the downstairs windows, too, and found a couple of other loose latches. He fixed them, then drew the blinds everywhere except the kitchen. She would be here alone, he thought, and he damn well didn't want anyone else to know that.

And maybe, he found himself thinking, he shouldn't stay in the bunkhouse tonight. Maybe he should sleep on the couch or get his sleeping bag and curl up on the porch.

Damn it, he didn't like this at all. If something valuable had been taken, he could at least feel easy about the motive for the break-in and be at least reasonably certain that the creep wouldn't return.

On the kitchen porch, he took the screen door down so he could work on the bent hinges. Thunder rolled down the hillside, bringing another gust of frosty air from the snowfields. Occasional big drops of rain continued to fall, one or two at a time, making little craters in the mud of the yard between the slowly melting hailstones.

The hinges were only a little bent, he saw, but the screws had been stripped out of the wood door. He would need some glue and sawdust, and both were in the barn. Grabbing the hinges, he shoved them into his pocket and snatched up his slicker. While he was there he could check on the horses and straighten the hinges, too.

The barn was still warm, redolent of horses, hay and manure. In the workshop beside the tack room, in the golden light from the overhead fixtures, he forgot the storm, forgot his worries for Sara and Zeke, and lost track of time. Once the hinges were fixed, he didn't stop. There was a broken kitchen chair, solid oak, that needed mending, an old dresser that needed new drawer bottoms, and a dozen or more other things, big and small, that needed fixing.

He lost himself in the smell of the sawdust, the solid feel of the wood, the pleasure of holding and using tools. Thunder rolled, rain hammered loudly on the roof, and the horses whickered softly. They were good sounds, a soothing background to his satisfaction in working with his hands again.

* * *

Sara found him there. It was after nine, dark, windy, cold and wet outside, and she had arrived home to find no sign that Gideon had even eaten his supper. She waited for a while, sure that he must have heard her Blazer pull into the yard and would come over to ask about Zeke, but he didn't show. Finally, concerned that he might have gotten hurt somehow, she went looking. The bunkhouse was empty, his bed untouched. That left the barn, she thought.

Lightning zigzagged through the dark, illuminating the puddled ground briefly as she hurried that way, guided as much by instinct as the little bit of light from the house. The lights were off in the barn, so she saw the yellow glow from the workshop immediately. Flipping the switch just inside the side door, she checked the horses quickly, noting they'd all settled for the night. Columbine snorted a little when the light came on, but other than that, all four animals ignored her.

On the threshold of the shop, she stopped in amazement. Gideon had his back to her, and he was singing quietly, in a deep, resonant voice, some country ballad of lost love. He wore her father's old safety goggles, he was covered head to foot in sawdust, and he had repaired two chairs, a table and her grandmother's old cupboard, by the looks of it. And now he appeared to be building drawers for the old dresser.

He'd taken the leather thong from around his forehead and used it to tie his hair back loosely at the nape of his neck. Something about that made Sara quiver deep inside with an almost urgent desire to pull that piece of leather free and sink her hands into that long, black-as-night hair. God, what fool had ever thought men were less masculine with long hair? There was nothing at all unmanly about that warrior's mane, or the man who wore it. As he moved, muscles flexed beneath his plain white shirt, muscles developed by moving mountains of steel and building the cities that were the hubs of this country.

He'd rolled back his sleeves, and as he reached for the planer and used it to smooth the edge of a piece of wood, she watched his powerful hands and forearms flex and bulge. She could have watched him for hours, she realized. Could have simply stood there and soaked up the sheer magnificence of Gideon Ironheart with her eyes until some empty spot in her was filled with it.

But she was concerned that he hadn't had his supper, and before she started heating food for herself, she needed to know if he was going to join her. She rapped on the doorframe, a quiet knock.

He broke off singing and glanced her way. A smile creased his dark, dusty face. "Hi. How's Zeke?"

That smile curled her toes in her sandals. "He's doing really well. He asked if you might come in tomorrow and see him, once they get him moved out of ICU."

"Sure. I'd like that." He tugged the goggles off and tossed them onto the workbench. "I'm sorry. I meant to be out front when you got home. I didn't like the idea of you coming home to an empty house."

"It looks like you've been busy."

He smiled, an almost sheepish expression that touched her deep inside. "I forget myself when I get tools in my hands."

"At the rate you're going, things that haven't been fixed in years are going to be fixed in no time at all." Lord, how she wanted to reach out and touch him. Was it only last night that she had lain in his arms before the campfire and felt long-dead urges awaken? How had he become such a craving? "I was going to make some supper. You haven't eaten, have you?"

"Nope."

"Then join me. It'll be ready in fifteen or twenty minutes." She turned before she could betray herself somehow, remembering her promise that nobody would ever know that she had come to care about this man. As a friend, she reminded herself. She cared for him as a friend and nothing more. He was, after all, going to move on.

"I need to shower," he called after her.

"Fine," she called back. "I'll make it thirty minutes."

That sounded casual enough, she thought with satisfaction,

although at the thought of him standing naked beneath a shower, her heart had climbed into her throat and begun to beat like a pagan drum. Gideon Ironheart naked was bound to be even more magnificent and a hell of a lot sexier than Gideon Ironheart dressed. Too bad she couldn't peek.

Gideon left his muddy boots by the back door and stepped into a kitchen filled with rich aromas of stew and coffee. Sara had already set the table and was placing the stew pot on it when he entered.

"Grab a seat," she said, pointing. "Just let me get the bread out of the oven and we'll be ready."

She was still wearing that denim skirt. It wasn't a sexy skirt, but a perfectly plain little A-line that had obviously seen a few washings. It didn't have a flounce or a ruffle or anything else to enhance it, and it was just about the sexiest thing he'd ever seen.

Because *she* was wearing it, he realized. Because it was curving over her sweet little rump and her rounded hips and brushing against her soft knees and exposing her gently rounded calves. She had pretty knees, he noticed now. Very pretty knees. Not bony, not pointy, but nicely shaped with a little dimple on either side. He had a wild urge to kiss those dimples.

With effort, he dragged his attention away from her legs and focused on the plate in front of him. She joined him and passed him a basket of hot, buttered bread.

"Boy, does this smell good," he told her.

"Do you often forget to eat?"

He looked at her and saw a teasing gleam in her warm brown eyes. She had, he realized with relief, forgiven him for last night. All day long, though he had tried not to think about it, he had been worried about that. "No," he said in answer to her question, "I almost never forget to eat. Do I look under-nourished?"

Actually, Sara thought, he looked *perfectly* nourished. But tired though she was, she had sense enough not to say so out loud.

"I don't think I should sleep in the bunkhouse tonight," he said, startling her out of her preoccupation with her attraction to him.

"What?" Confused, she stared at him. "Why not? Is something wrong?"

He shook his head. "I just don't like the idea of you sleeping here alone. I know you have a gun, and I know you know how to use it. I know you're a deputy and all that, but—" He shook his head. "But you're still only one person. Two of us even the odds better if something happens, but I wouldn't be much help all the way out in the bunkhouse. Short of utter mayhem, I'd never know anything was happening over here. So I'll sleep on the couch. Or the porch, if you don't want me inside."

An honest-to-goodness Galahad, Sara thought, not quite certain what to say. She had been raised among chivalrous men and had worked daily with some of the best for the last nine years. She was accustomed to seeing their courtliness to their wives and girlfriends, but not since Jeff Cumberland had offered to date her after George fled had anyone been so gallant on her behalf.

No, she thought suddenly. Not true. Gideon Ironheart had, in his own way, been gallant toward her from the start. He might not have been courtly in his manner, but it was pure chivalry that had refused to let her walk alone into those bars, gun or no gun, badge or no badge.

"On the porch?" she repeated. "You've got to be kidding. You'll freeze." Spring nights were chilly in the Wyoming mountains, but the cold front that had brought the storm had made it chillier than usual. There would probably even be some fresh snow higher up come morning.

"I've got a good sleeping bag." Satisfied, he rose and carried his dishes to the sink where he began to wash them as naturally as if this was his kitchen and he did it every day. "I won't freeze. Look, Sara, I don't want to press you and I don't want to make you uneasy by forcing myself on you, but I'd feel a whole lot better if those guys had stolen something. The fact that they hurt Zeke and then didn't take anything leaves a really bad taste in my mouth. I don't want you facing them alone.''

Sara was never sure why she said what she said then. Later, thinking it over, she decided it had more to do with her feelings about Gideon Ironheart than any fears for her safety. It sure didn't have anything to do with some female desire to put a man on an ego trip, though. *That* was definitely the last thing on her mind. ''I'll be glad to have you here. You look like you could handle just about anything.''

Gideon, with his back to her, stiffened visibly and for an endless moment didn't respond. Sara stared at his back, growing acutely embarrassed as she realized how that might have sounded. What it might have revealed. But before she could turn completely crimson, or embarrass herself further by trying to explain her remark, he turned from the sink, tossed aside the towel he'd been using to dry his hands and faced her.

Leaning back against the counter, he folded his arms across his broad chest and smiled. Grinned, actually. There was no mistaking the sudden teasing gleam in his steel-gray eyes. ''Thank God you noticed. I'm getting tired of sucking in my gut to impress you.''

Inevitably, instantly, her eyes were drawn to his incredibly flat stomach. ''What gut?'' she asked, realizing he'd done it again. He'd said something so outrageous that all the embarrassment was gone as if it had never been. He was good at saying things no one else on earth would have the nerve to say, saying things that lightened the atmosphere.

That troubled her a little, she realized suddenly. He was good at evading uncomfortable feelings, good at diverting attention. How had he learned to do that? And why?

And then she realized she was doing it again, drawing his attention to the fact that she was noticing such things. And now, worst of all, she was simply staring at a belly that probably looked like a washboard, and was inevitably noticing the male bulge lower down, a bulge thrust into prominence by the way he was leaning back against the counter.

Oh, Lord, she thought almost weakly, he was such a fine-looking man. Just looking at him made her intensely aware that she was a woman, made her intensely aware of her body in ways she hadn't felt in a decade.

God, thought Gideon, she was stirring him up into a roaring blaze just by looking at him. It was the *way* she was looking that got to him. He was used to being noticed by women, used to speculative looks, used to outright sexual invitation. Sara's look was different. In it there was no speculation, no blatant, knowing curiosity. In her face was simple yearning, and it ripped his soul, unleashing a torrent of needs and wants he had never acknowledged before and didn't even know how to name.

"C'mere," he said, his voice a rough whisper, a breath of sound barely forced past a dry throat. He was burning. Burning. "C'mere, Mouse." She had to come to him, he thought. Had to. He didn't want to ever wonder whether she really wanted to be in his arms. He didn't want to wonder later if he'd somehow...

The thought was never completed. Licking her dry lips in an unconsciously sensual way, Sara rose on shaky legs. She stood there, looking at him with huge brown eyes, yearning so plainly written there that his heart throbbed in response.

"C'mere," he whispered again. "Closer...."

She moved toward him. It wasn't even a full step but more of a tentative edging his way.

"Oh, God, Sara," he said hoarsely. "Closer, baby...." He unfolded his arms, widened his stance, aching for her... aching.... "Sara..."

Just the way he whispered to that damn mustang, she thought dazedly, edging closer...closer.... Except that there was something so sexy, so sensual, about the grittiness of his voice just now that everything inside her clenched in response.

And then, with a little sob, she was there in his arms,

wrapped in him, surrounded by him, and it felt good, so good, to be held....

"Oh, God, baby..." The words escaped him on a ragged sigh of relief as he bowed his head and buried his face in her hair. He couldn't remember the last time he had wanted so badly to hold a woman, to feel her softness pressed to him. Just to have her there, to hold her, to feel her close, eased yearnings so deep he didn't have words for them. Maybe he was losing his mind at long last, but for now, right now, he didn't give a damn.

Sara's arms stole around his narrow waist and hugged him back. He widened his stance a little more, drawing her deeper into his embrace, and for a moment she didn't breathe as she realized how intimately she was pressed to him. Her breasts were crushed to a chest as hard as iron, and nestled against her lower belly was that bulge that had earlier fascinated her. She could feel every hard, masculine line of him, and all she wanted was to burrow deeper and deeper.

Easy, he told himself. Easy. This woman was the same one who hid behind a deputy's uniform and mirrored sunglasses, who talked tough and pretended to be one of the guys. Here at the ranch she softened up, as if here she felt safe, and she had softened up considerably with him. He didn't want to ruin that by hurrying her or pushing her. For whatever reason, she was as shy as that mustang.

His hands ran slowly down her back, a soothing, gentling touch, halting at her waist and then returning slowly upward. Her hair was caught in a ponytail again, and without a word he snapped the rubber band and freed it.

"You have beautiful hair," he murmured against her temple. "Soft and silky." Gently, he combed his fingers through it. "So soft."

"You have nice hair, too," she said, feeling terribly, painfully shy, wanting whatever he might give her so badly that she could hardly stand it, and sure that he couldn't really want to give her very much. She was such a plain Jane after all, so dull and ordinary and unappealing. The kind of woman men fled from.

Reaching up with one hand, Gideon released the leather thong that tied his hair back and dropped it on the counter. Somehow that was, she thought as her insides twisted pleasurably, one of the most shatteringly intimate things a man had ever done in her presence.

It was also a silent invitation, as was the way he tugged one of her small hands up until her fingers were in his hair. "Touch me," he whispered, the slightest tremor in his breath. "Don't be shy, Mouse."

But she was, miserably so, and it was there in her soft brown eyes as she tilted her head back and looked up at him. But there also was the yearning, the longing, the need. Seeing it, he bent his head and touched her petal-soft lips with his.

"Sweet," he murmured. "So sweet." She *was* absolutely the sweetest thing he'd held in so very many years. Gently, so, so gently, he brushed his mouth back and forth across hers, coaxing and teasing. And little by little her hands slipped into his hair, stroking and finally gently pulling him closer.

Another ragged sigh escaped him, each of her tentative touches detonating along his nerve endings like dynamite. He opened his mouth over hers and ran his tongue along her lips, along the exquisitely sensitive seam between them. He needed to be inside her, needed the taste of her and the heat of her.

She gave it to him. With a soft little moan she opened to him and eagerly accepted the thrust of his hot, rough tongue. She knew now the kind of pleasure his kiss could give her, the way the stroking of his tongue seemed to reach every nerve in her body and cause a twisting, clenching thrill to run through her, making her ache for more and more.

She clutched handfuls of his hair, of his soft, silky, sexy-as-sin hair, and pulled him nearer still. The tug didn't hurt him, but it electrified him, causing his arms to tighten almost painfully around her as he heard all that she was unconsciously telling him.

She wanted him. Oh, God, she wanted him. He felt it in her

clutching, tugging hands, in the way she molded herself against him, and the way her head sagged back beneath the onslaught of his mouth.

She wanted him as he'd never been wanted before, with a passion flaming every bit as hotly as his own, with a passion for *him*. He knew it in his very bones. Sara Yates was reaching for Gideon Ironheart and no one else. If he'd been anybody else, she wouldn't have wanted him. And that was the most seductive thing he'd ever known.

For a moment his passion flared even hotter. With a tug he yanked her blouse free of her skirt and sent his hand foraging beneath, across soft, satiny skin until he found the beckoning hill of her breast. Soft, simple cotton encased it, without even a trim of lace. As plain and everyday as Sara Yates herself. Finding the bra clasp between her breasts, he twisted it and freed her. She gasped and tore her mouth from his, but her head fell back in surrender as he covered her soft, small, aching breast with his large, warm hand.

"Gideon..." His name escaped her on a tremulous sigh, at once a plea and a sound of pleasure. Her breasts were small, just another one of the things that made her feel inadequate, but Gideon's touch almost made her forget such concerns.

"You feel so damn good, Sara," he muttered roughly. "I'll bet your breast is every bit as pretty as it feels. Do you like that?" He tugged gently on a small, hard nipple.

A rippling shiver passed through her and escaped her as a soft moan. The sound of her desire sent a shudder of pleasure racing through him, making him even harder and heavier than he already was.

He wanted her...wanted her...wanted her. The need was a drumbeat in his blood. And she wanted him. Just him.

And that was why he didn't give in to himself or her. The conviction that she wouldn't be responding this way to anyone else, the belief that she wanted *only* him, was the very reason he couldn't take her. She didn't offer herself cheaply, so he couldn't take her that way. It was just that simple.

For a long moment he held her, his hand on her breast,

feeling his brain try to kick into gear through the muzzy red haze of his hunger. With just a single, ruthless effort he could have silenced reason, but he didn't. Sara had touched some place deep inside him, and concern for her overrode his hammering hunger. He couldn't hurt her. Wouldn't hurt her.

Gently, carefully, he withdrew his hand and pulled her snugly against his chest. Wrapping his arms around her, he hugged her tightly and rocked her tenderly, giving her time to return to reality and wake from the daze of passion.

Oh man, he thought, now she was really going to hate him. He was showing himself for a real fool. Getting carried away was an excuse that sounded pretty damn lame the second time.

But Sara didn't get mad. Leaning against him, soaking up the comfort of being held, she acknowledged that his withdrawal had been the result of his concern for her. Even now she could feel his tension and his arousal, and she'd listened to enough men talk over the years to know that an aroused man didn't call a halt because he didn't feel like proceeding.

"I'm sorry, Sara," Gideon said finally, still holding her and rocking her. "I did it again, didn't I? Damn it, woman, you turn me on like a switch. It's as embarrassing as hell at my age, but around you I seem to have about as much control as a sixteen-year-old."

She still ached, and she still yearned, but common sense told her that she was going to be very glad later that Gideon had as much self-control as he did. More, apparently, than she could claim for herself. It wasn't as if she hadn't been an eager and willing participant. "That's okay," she managed to say.

"Is it? Is it really?" He caught her chin and urged it up so he could read her face. "You're not furious?"

"I think I'm flattered," she said, and blushed. "I mean…well, I never thought of myself as being…" How had she gotten into this? There was nothing she could say that wouldn't embarrass her.

"Irresistible?" he supplied. A smile began to dawn on his dark face, and a twinkle came into his dark gray eyes. "A femme fatale? A sex object?"

"Gideon...!" Squirming, blushing wildly, she tried to break free.

"A siren," he said relentlessly. "Yeah, that's what you are. Something about you is an irresistible lure. It might be those legs of yours. You've got great legs, Mouse. Or maybe it's those warm brown eyes. A man gets an urge to drown in them. Beautiful."

"Gideon, please!"

Laughing softly, he pressed her hot cheek to his shoulder and let it alone.

Later, much later, he lay on the living room floor, his sleeping bag wrapped around him. The storms outside had moved on, leaving the night utterly silent. He could almost feel the emptiness around him, feel the vast spaces outside this house where not another human soul breathed for miles. Closing his eyes, he tried to reach within for the silence in himself, the place that gave him strength and what little peace he'd ever known.

But he couldn't find it. Every time he looked inside himself, he found memories of Sara. Remembered how she had felt in his arms. The woman was easy to hold. Too easy.

A man might forget himself and start building castles in the air with a woman like that in his arms. He might forget that it was all just illusory, and that love was a meaningless word.

He might find himself standing in quicksand with no way out—if he were a deluded fool.

But Gideon Ironheart was nobody's fool.

Chapter 7

The wind blew down off the high snowfields and rippled the grasses of the pasture with its chilly breath. Storm clouds were brewing over the peaks again, promising late afternoon rain.

"Need a jacket?" Gideon asked Zeke. More than a week had passed, and Zeke was getting around pretty well now, except that his ribs pained him if he moved the wrong way. Gideon was still doing all the chores, steadfastly refusing Zeke's help and insisting that the older man take it easy.

"I'm fine, boy," Zeke answered. "It'll take a little more than a breeze to chill me." He still didn't remember what had happened the night he was beaten, but other than that, he insisted he was just fine.

Gideon smothered a smile. "You're just a damn tough old bird, Zeke. And about as hardheaded as they come." He glanced toward the tree line, waiting. They waited every afternoon at this time for the mustangs to make their appearance. He would feel their approach first, through the earth beneath his feet. They always came into the meadow at a dead run, their hooves making thunder on the ground. And it always caused his heart to race and his spirits to soar in some primitive way.

"Have you thought any more about a vision quest?" Zeke said suddenly.

Gideon hesitated, reluctant to admit that he *had* been thinking about it. Simple fact was, the longer he stayed here, the less he wanted to move on. Even his primary purpose in being here, getting to know Micah Parish, had somehow become less pressing. "Why is it so important to you, old man?"

Zeke raised a hand, resting it on the top rail of the corral. He stared past Gideon, beyond even the trees and mountains to someplace only he could see. "You were meant to be *wichasha wakan,* a holy man."

Gideon felt his scalp prickle, as if a chilly wind had touched him. His grandfather had told him the very same thing.

"A holy man is not necessarily a good man," Zeke said presently. "He doesn't have any rules to follow or a certain way he must live. He is an ordinary man living an ordinary life."

"Then why—"

Zeke shook his head. "Listen. A holy man is special only because he has power in him. You have power. I can feel it in the air around you. I'm sure others have told you the same."

Gideon couldn't deny it, but this conversation was making him distinctly uneasy. What *power?* He had never understood what was meant by that.

"You see the grass, how it grows? You see the trees that stand so tall? Each thing must be itself. Must fulfill itself. You have not fulfilled yourself, Ironheart. And you don't need me to tell you that."

No, he didn't need to hear it from Zeke, Gideon thought uncomfortably. But a vision quest?

Before he needed to say anything, he felt the hammering of approaching hooves through his feet. "They're coming," he told Zeke.

The eight horses emerged from the trees at a full, thundering gallop. Reaching the center of the unfenced portion of the meadow, they turned abruptly, circling before coming to a halt.

God, Gideon thought, they were beautiful. Sleek coats, losing some of the winter's protective thickness, glistened in the sun as the seven mares tossed their heads and waited for their stallion to take off again.

Gideon clucked softly, and the roan's ears pricked forward. The game again. Man and horse appeared to enjoy it equally. This time, though, Gideon changed the rules a little. Instead of waiting for the mustang to edge closer, he left the corral fence and walked out into the grassy meadow.

The stallion snorted and reared a little, warning. Gideon halted, then clucked again, softly. "Come on, boy. You know I'm not going to hurt you. Come on...."

Whispering, murmuring, he called the horse to him. Behind him, he heard the sound of Sara's Blazer coming into the yard. She was off duty early, he thought, but both he and the horse ignored the intrusion. They were too absorbed in one another to be distracted.

"Come on, boy. Come on." The meaningless liquid syllables, learned so long ago, tripped over his tongue as he willed the mustang to approach. And little by little the roan pranced nearer, pausing often to snort and visibly hesitate.

But the man, it seemed, was an irresistible lure to the horse. Finally, minutes later, the stallion stood with lowered head right before Gideon and accepted the affectionate touch of the man's hands along his neck and shoulder.

Something swelled in Gideon, a golden bubble of feeling so warm that it was like internal sunlight. The horse trusted him. For an instant he closed his eyes against the emotion and told himself the feeling would pass, that it was just fanciful, that the tightness in his throat was just...

Ah, hell, he thought, and drew a deep, shaky breath. He was having a lot of these feelings lately, feelings he'd never had before, and it was getting harder to tell himself it was a reaction to Barney's death. Parts of himself that had been walled off since childhood were breaking loose, and he was beginning to feel as if he were standing in the middle of shifting sands.

The horse nudged him gently, then laid his head over Gideon's shoulder, just as he often did with his mares. Just as if he felt the man's need.

A sudden, sharp, piercing whistle shattered the quiet. The stallion snorted, jerked away and ran into the trees with his mares hot on his heels.

Gideon swung around angrily, unable to believe that either Sara or Zeke would have done that, and looked into a pair of dark eyes that might have been his own twenty-five years ago.

"Joey!" Sara's horrified exclamation was ignored by her brother. The boy stood there, a black-leather-clad maternal nightmare, and looked at Gideon with all the resentment and anger only a sixteen-year-old boy could feel.

Gideon knew that look. He knew it in his heart and soul, knew his grandfather and uncle had faced it from him nearly every day for years. And he knew what lay behind it. Without a word he began walking toward the youth.

Only the slightest movement betrayed the boy's uneasiness as the tall, powerfully built man bore down on him. Gideon halted just two feet from the boy.

"Why'd you do that?" he asked, his voice deceptively soft.

Joey shrugged. "Hell, it looked like you were going to f—"

The word never escaped the boy's mouth. Before he finished his obscenity, Gideon had lifted him off his feet by the front of his leather jacket.

"Let's get something straight here, boy," Gideon said softly. "You're nothing but a little punk until you prove you're a man, and nobody around here is going to take any crap from a punk. You make your sister or your grandfather upset, and you and I will be talking out behind the barn. And while we're on the subject, clean up your language."

For an interminable moment he stared into the blazing hatred in the boy's eyes and saw the fright behind it. Then he set Joey on his feet.

"With that out of the way," Gideon said quietly, "I'm sure

we'll get along just fine. I'm Gideon Ironheart.'' He held out his hand and waited.

For an endless time it seemed that Joey would ignore the gesture. Sara watched, torn between a feeling that Gideon had had no right to handle Joey that way and the realization that her brother had deserved it. More, that he had *needed* it. And now she could hardly breathe for fear that her brother would refuse to shake hands with Gideon. What then? If Joey made things too uncomfortable around here, Gideon might leave, and Sara honestly didn't think she could stand that.

But Joey reached out at last and shook Gideon's hand.

"My pleasure, son," Gideon said as if nothing at all had happened before the handshake. Then he touched the brim of his hat to Sara, nodded to Zeke and headed for his truck.

"I'll be out late," he tossed over his shoulder. "Don't wait dinner." He had to get out of here, he thought. Absolutely, positively had to get out of here. It was getting too easy to hang around, getting too comfortable to be here. Why should he give a damn about what was going on inside Joey Yates? Why should he feel any urge at all to straighten the boy out? The kid wasn't his problem.

And Sara. Sara *was* his problem. The woman was living, breathing temptation. Well, that was one ache he could ease in town.

If he could make himself sink that low.

Somewhere around two in the morning, Sara gave up all pretense of trying to sleep. She pulled on her jeans and a sweater, and tiptoed downstairs with her boots in hand. Thank goodness she didn't have to work in the morning.

Outside, clouds had buried the stars, leaving the night inky. Wind shifted restlessly, a lonesome sound in the dark. The air smelled of pines and grass, and was soft with a promise of rain.

She pulled on her boots and wished there was moonlight so she could take a walk. Instead, she had to settle for standing in the yard and soaking up the scents and sounds of the night.

Gideon hadn't returned yet, and she guessed she wasn't going to sleep until he did. He'd walked off, leaving the evening chores for her and Joey to take care of, and that wasn't like him. The Gideon she had come to know these past couple of weeks was an extremely responsible man, not the kind to forget evening chores or assume someone else would do them. For all he claimed to be a tumbleweed, he never left a thing undone. Not a thing. He was a finisher, not a quitter.

Something had been troubling him, and she didn't think it was Joey, obnoxious as he had been. Gideon had been mad, not shocked by the boy. And whatever was bothering him, she suspected, had been coming on for some time. Any number of times in the past week she'd caught him staring pensively at nothing in particular, and once or twice she'd seen him grab on to something and just stand there for several minutes, as if he was in some kind of pain. And then he would straighten and carry on as if nothing had happened.

She wished—oh, how she wished!—there was something she could do for him. And wished he would touch her again, kiss her again, hold her again. She wanted to be in his arms so badly that she ached nearly every moment of every day. Ached so badly that sometimes she was even able to convince herself that it didn't matter that he'd eventually leave if only she could have him right now.

Which made her a fool again, she thought with a sigh, whether anybody else knew it or not. And why should he want her, anyway? George had been so chilled by the prospect of bedding her that he'd fled all the way to Denver. So scared of being stuck for life with her that he'd tried to hide. Maybe Gideon hadn't backed off out of some sense of nobility, after all. Maybe he, too, had found her in some way repulsive.

Hardly thinking about it, she walked to the bunkhouse and sat on the porch step, knowing that she wouldn't sleep until Gideon returned, so she might as well make sure he got back in one piece.

He'd probably be full of beer or whiskey and smelling of cheap perfume, she told herself. Nine years as a deputy had taught her the uglier side of male pastimes. She knew every dive, every hooker and every easy woman in town. Sooner or later she'd had to deal with every single one of them. Even in a county this underpopulated, there was plenty of work for prostitutes. Cowboys in from the range made sure of that. Gideon would probably have to fight the women off. If he even wanted to.

That thought caused her a serious pang, but she shoved it aside. She knew men, and she wasn't going to let herself fall into some delusion that Gideon Ironheart was different. There was no reason why he should be. He wasn't married and didn't have kids to worry about, after all.

She heard his truck on the drive long before his lights punctured the darkness. There was plenty of time for her to escape, to run back to the house so he would never know she had waited for him, but something kept her where she was, holding her as surely as if she were nailed to the spot.

If he was drunk and reeking of some woman, she told herself, it would free her of this need she felt for him. She would be so disgusted that she would never want him to touch her again. Men in that condition always revolted her.

And if he wasn't...if he wasn't, she might be in serious trouble.

The truck pulled into the yard, and its headlights pinned her in their glare. Slowly Gideon pulled up and stopped. For a minute he let the engine run and stared at her sitting there on the bunkhouse porch. Waiting for him. Looking a little lost, a little sad and a whole lot frightened.

If he had a single ounce of common sense, he told himself, he would drive out of the yard right now and head back to town. But he evidently didn't have any common sense, because he switched off his lights and his engine and climbed out.

She didn't move. For a moment neither of them moved, waiting for their eyes to adapt to the darkness.

"Is something wrong?" he asked her finally.

She shook her head. "I just couldn't sleep." He didn't sound drunk, she thought with relief.

"Yeah." He hesitated a little longer, then came to sit beside her on the porch step. "I'm sorry I stomped off the way I did. I know I left you with all those damn chores."

"Joey helped. That's why he's back here, you know. He managed to convince Nate that he wanted to come home and help out because Grandfather was injured."

"And I was here. No wonder the kid was so mad. Maybe I should just move on." He'd been thinking about that all evening but couldn't quite convince himself to do it.

"No," said Sara, battling a wave of panic. "No. Not unless you want to. Nothing around here is going to get bent out of shape for Joey ever again. It's time he started learning to accommodate himself to other people."

Gideon nodded, granting her that. It was a lesson everyone had to learn sooner or later. "Well, I'm still sorry I tore out of here and left you to cope. I don't usually do that."

"I know you don't."

The quiet conviction in her voice caused him to turn his head and peer at her in the dark. Her confidence in him was like a warm touch. "Thank you," he said, meaning it.

"I've had nearly two weeks to learn a few things about you," she told him, brushing it aside. "You're honest, you're honorable, and you don't leave things undone."

"A regular Boy Scout, huh?"

She surprised him with a soft, rippling laugh. "Not quite."

"That's a relief. A man likes to think he's at least a little bit of a rogue." He wanted to reach out and catch a handful of her hair, reach out and pull her close until her mouth was under his and her small breasts were crushed against his chest. Three times tonight he'd sent an interested woman away because he just couldn't stir up any interest in anyone but Sara. He'd been thinking about that, too, when he thought about moving on. "Why are you sitting out here, Sara Yates?" He meant here on the bunkhouse steps instead of her own porch. She could ignore that distinction if she chose to.

She didn't choose to, maybe because it was the middle of the night and her mind wasn't as clear as it should have been.

Maybe because deep inside she wanted him to know, wanted somehow to close the distance between them. "I was worried about you."

He wanted to dismiss her concern with some easy, flip remark, but the words wouldn't come. "Thanks," he said gruffly. "Thanks." God, nobody had worried about him in more years than he wanted to think about. Nobody had waited up for him; nobody had even wondered where he was. "Sometimes... sometimes I just have to be by myself."

Sara bit her lip, afraid to press him, yet concerned enough to be unable to let it alone. Finally concern won out. "Sometimes...sometimes I get the feeling that you...hurt very badly."

Gideon's heart stopped. He didn't even draw a breath as an extraordinary stillness filled him. All his life, whenever he hurt, he had been expected to go off by himself and lick his own wounds in private. Nobody wanted to hear, nobody wanted to know. Even his uncle, forever understanding about such things, was silent about them. He gave Gideon the place and the privacy, but left it to him to manage his own pain. It was the way a man was supposed to do it.

Nobody ever, not once in his entire life, had wanted to hear about it. To share it. And he didn't know if he could even talk about it. Not really. Not in any meaningful way. "I, um..."

Sara reached out and touched his forearm. "I know it's none of my business, Gideon. I just...worry."

And suddenly the world was spinning again. Even though it was pitch-dark, he saw spiraling blue sky, saw the beam swinging and spinning, felt his grip on the steel slipping, felt as if he was falling....

"I felt him die."

The words seemed to be torn from Gideon's throat, and he bent over until his head was between his knees. Sara hesitated only a moment and then reached out instinctively to wrap her arm around his back. She felt the horrible tension in him, felt the subtle tremors of violent emotion suppressed.

"I keep feeling it," he said, his voice little more than a raw whisper as the pain erupted from the deep well in which he tried to hide it from everyone else. "Over and over and over."

For the longest time he stayed as he was, doubled over and silent, buffeted by waves of anguish. And then, almost as swiftly as he had been overcome, he overcame it. He straightened, looking out into the dark as if he could see something there. When he spoke, his voice was once again normal—or close to it.

"Sorry. I get these flashbacks and feel like I'm falling."

"You fell?" Sara asked tentatively, trying to understand what was happening, why he was so torn up.

For the space of several heartbeats he didn't answer, and Sara began to think he wasn't going to. And that was his right, she told herself. Absolutely his right.

"Connectors work in pairs," he said suddenly. "It's absolutely essential to be able to read your partner, to know what he's going to do, how he operates. You have to be able to trust him with your life. So when you find a good partner, you tend to stick together. Barney and I worked together on every job for the last thirteen years. We were…close. Really close." He drew a long breath. "Last October, Barney fell. Seventy stories."

"Oh, my God!" She reached out again, covering his hand with hers and holding on tight. "Oh, Gideon!"

"I felt him die, Sara. Maybe nobody will ever believe that," he said rawly, "but I felt him die. And there wasn't a damn thing I could do except hang on to the column and wait for it to be over. But I felt it, Sara. *I felt it.*"

"I believe you. Oh, Gideon, I believe you."

He turned suddenly and gathered her to him, crushing her to his chest, hanging on as if she were a lifeline in a world gone mad. There just weren't words to tell anybody how it had felt to have Barney *gone*. There was a hole in him where Barney had been, and in the moment of his friend's death he had felt something ripped out of his soul by its roots, leaving nothing but a bleeding wound.

For thirteen years he and Barney had worked together, drunk

together, fished together, hunted together. Brothers. Even Barney's marriage hadn't come between them. They'd simply packed Jolene up with the tent or the boat and taken her with them. Jolene had loved it. She had even loved moving from town to town, wherever the jobs took them.

"What happened to Jolene?" Sara asked softly.

Her question jarred him out of his memories, and back to the chilly Wyoming night and the restless sighing of the wind in the trees. Only when she spoke did he realize he'd been talking. Rambling. Spilling his guts about Barney. He started to pull away, but her arms tightened, clinging, and honest to God, he needed her touch. He stayed.

"She...uh...she told me she didn't want to see me again for a long time. Said I made her...think of Barney every time she set eyes on me."

Oh God, Sara thought, pain ripping her heart. Even then, the person who could have most shared his grief had left him on the outside. He'd been on the outside his entire life, never belonging, never fitting. Always looking in but never asked to come inside. Except for his grandfather and uncle, she amended. They'd asked him in, but she suspected he was so used to being on the outside that he didn't know any other way to be.

Squeezing her eyes shut against the ache in her heart, she had a sudden memory of Gideon Ironheart as she had first seen him, standing at the center of a group of men who wanted to beat him to a pulp. Refusing to give an inch. Fighting for the right to stand at a damn bar and order a sandwich. Refusing to be cast out because of his skin.

But he was already an emotional outcast, and he didn't even know it. Didn't even realize that he had accepted that he should always be on the outside looking in.

That was the moment when Sara realized that she had already invited him in. He was there, in her heart, as not even George had been. But how could she tell him that? she wondered miserably, aching for both of them. He would rear up like that damn mustang and dash for the trees, believing himself to be a wild creature. He would shy away and tell her that he was a tumbleweed, that he didn't believe in love.

And he didn't. That was the really odd thing about him. He didn't believe in it, but he practiced it with nearly every breath he took. Look at the way he took care of Zeke. The way he had fretted about her safety, the way he looked after the ranch when Zeke couldn't. The way he whispered to that damn mustang. The way he called his uncle every few days to check on the old man.

She couldn't tell him, she realized, tightening her hold on him. But she could certainly show him.

When at length he eased away, she let him go. You couldn't hold a wild thing, she reminded herself. It had to want to be held.

The wind whispered of things lost, and the night yielded no secrets. It was lonely out here, and empty. The vastness of the Wyoming night was awesome.

"I'm sorry, Sara," he said after a bit. "I didn't mean to dump all over you."

"That's what friends are for."

"You've got enough problems of your own. Joey's a real handful, isn't he?"

She let him change the subject. "He can be."

"What exactly do you think is eating him?"

She sighed then and lifted her feet to a higher step so she could hug her knees. "I'm not sure. He was little when we lost our parents, but he was never a problem until just about two years ago. I keep thinking something must have happened, but I sure don't know what. I've tried talking to him. I've suggested counseling. I've begged his teachers for clues and patience and help, and nothing changes."

She wiggled her toes in her boots and shivered a little as the breeze snaked into the neck of her sweater. "Nate didn't really want to send him home," she said after a few minutes.

"Why not?"

"He doesn't believe Joey's really turning over a new leaf.

He said Joey's just scared right now, but not scared enough to change.''

Gideon thought about what little he'd seen of the boy during their confrontation this afternoon. "He's scared, all right. More than a little scared.''

A small laugh escaped Sara. "Frankly, Gideon, I think anybody would be petrified to have you lift them right off their feet with one hand the way you did Joey. Lordy, I couldn't believe I was seeing it!''

He chuckled and raised his arm, making a muscle for her inspection. "These arms have moved more tons of steel than Schwarzenegger. Joey's a snap by comparison.''

She reached out and touched the bulge of his biceps through the chambray of his shirt. "Hard,'' she said approvingly. Like steel. Like iron.

He let his arm relax beneath her hand, and the firm resilience of his flesh proved far more seductive than the bulge of taut muscle. She snatched her hand back as if burned, realizing that friendly play might turn into something else. Much as she wanted him, she wasn't yet convinced she should take that step.

"It's late,'' she said, telling herself that she really ought to go back to bed. She was still restless, but the excuse of wanting to be sure Gideon returned safely was no longer even an excuse. She had absolutely no business being out here with him like this. He was bound to be wondering about it, and what if he drew the wrong conclusion? Not that she was sure there was a wrong conclusion.

The crazy spiraling of her thoughts suddenly stopped dead when Gideon claimed her hand and held it between both of his. His touch was warm but innocent. She could have sworn he was hardly aware of what he was doing. But *she* was aware—acutely, exquisitely aware of the dry, callused heat of his palm against hers.

"Just a few more minutes,'' he said.

"All right.''

"You never told me why you're hiding, Sara Yates.''

She stiffened and tried to yank her hand away, but he held

on tightly. The reminder of George was as good as a fall into an icy river. In an instant she was very much alert and very much wary.

"Come on, Mouse. I bared my soul. Now it's your turn."

She turned her head and looked straight at him, wishing she could see him better, could read his expression. It was so dark, though, that she could barely make out the deep-set hollows of his eyes. "Who said this was a trade?"

"Me. I've been wondering since I clapped eyes on you." Keeping his grip on her with one hand, he raised the other to touch her cheek. It was a touch so exquisitely tender that her throat tightened. "Someone hurt you," he said. "Someone wounded you, and now you talk tough and wear a badge and hide behind a shotgun and mirrored glasses."

"Gideon—"

"Hush, little mouse," he said softly. "Hush. I've been living here for twelve days, and the Sara Yates who lives at the Double Y is not the Sara Yates the rest of the world sees. You put on a shell when you leave here. Why?"

She licked her dry lips and tried not to lean into his fingers, which were now tracing the curve of her cheek. He was leaving, she reminded herself for the umpteenth time. At any moment he would get bored with ranch life and go back to building skyscrapers. "Why do you call me 'Mouse'?"

He chuckled softly. "Changing the subject, Mouse? I call you Mouse because you remind me of something very small, very soft and very warm." He hesitated, and then thought what the hell. Sara would understand. "When I was in the orphanage, there was this little brown mouse who used to come into our dormitory at night. It took a long time and an awful lot of bread crumbs, but he finally would climb onto my knee when I sat on the floor. And sometimes he would let me touch him. That little brown mouse is the only really good memory I have of those years."

Her hand was suddenly gripping his hand as tightly as he gripped hers. She *did* understand.

"So," he said quietly, "who hurt you, Mouse?"

He wasn't going to let it go, she realized. And maybe, she thought, it was only fair. It was just that it was so humiliating to remember, so humiliating to speak of. She kept telling herself she shouldn't feel that way, that she hadn't done anything wrong, and that it was George who should be embarrassed, but the fact was, rejection was humiliating. No two ways about it. And no woman wanted to admit that she'd sent her fiancé into panicked flight.

A sigh escaped her, and at the sound Gideon slipped his arm around her shoulder. "What happened?"

"Oh, it sounds so stupid," she said, her voice little more than a shaky whisper. "I dated this guy all the way through high school, you know?"

He squeezed her, letting her come at things in her own way.

"We went everywhere together, did everything together. It was just...accepted, I guess, that we'd marry. Everyone thought so. His family. My family. All our friends. The date was set before we even graduated."

"Weren't you kind of young?"

Sara shrugged. "We're behind the times out here. People don't think it's unusual to marry out of high school. I mean, if all you're going to do is ranch, why wait? And there sure isn't any fast lane around here to dabble in."

"No, I guess not."

"It's changing, I guess. Not so many people marry right away now. A lot more of them go to college than even ten years ago."

She was changing the subject again, he realized. So he pulled her back. "What happened?"

"We set the date for my birthday, August third. His mother and father were still alive then, and they wanted a big bash. I think everybody in the county was invited, and an awful lot of people from Laramie and Cheyenne. They weren't going to be able to get everyone into the church, so a lot of people only got invited to the reception, which is unusual, I guess. It was to be a big barbecue at the Bar C, the Cumberland ranch."

Gideon tried to look down at her, but the dark defeated him. "We aren't talking about Jeff Cumberland, are we?"

She shook her head. "His younger brother. George Cumberland." Even the sound of his name made her stomach roil. "Things were out of my control right from the start. I remember feeling like a doll. I got pushed this way and pulled that way by Mrs. Cumberland. I didn't even get to say two words about my wedding dress. She dragged me to Laramie and picked it out herself. Sometimes I think—" She broke off.

"Think what, Mouse?" he prompted gently. "What do you think?"

"That maybe George wouldn't have gotten so scared if his mother hadn't taken over the way she did. I mean, I hardly even got to see him from graduation day until our wedding day. When I did, there were always a dozen other people there. It was like riding a runaway train."

"Didn't you get scared, too?"

"A little. I threw up my whole breakfast the morning of the wedding." She blushed and averted her face, forgetting he could barely see her in the dark, anyway. "I'm sorry. You didn't need to know that."

He gave a soft laugh. "It kind of completes the picture, Sara. My stomach is knotting in sympathy. Okay, here we are, the morning of your…eighteenth birthday, right?"

"Eighteen," she agreed. "That morning Dad gave me my mother's necklace, a gold chain with a tiny diamond pendant. I felt so grown-up when I put it on." She sighed again and unconsciously leaned against him. "To make a long story short, I dressed, I went to the church, everybody arrived, and people squeezed in until you could almost hear the place groan. And George never showed up."

"Never?" He let go and put his other arm around her, holding her tight. "What happened?"

"He chickened out. Only we didn't know that at first. At first we just waited. Then we got scared something had happened to him. I think I must have cried a couple of gallons of tears. Nate had the deputies searching high and low. Honest to God, Gideon, we expected to find a corpse.''

''I imagine so.'' His heart squeezed for her, imagining the hell she must have gone through.

Sara drew a deep breath and plunged ahead, needing now to finish it. ''He finally called around midnight and told Jeff that he was in Denver and he was never coming back, that he wouldn't marry me if I were the last woman on earth....''

''Jeff told you that?'' Gideon wanted to sock the rancher right in the jaw.

''No, oh no. We were all sitting in Jeff's study by that time. Mr. and Mrs. Cumberland, Jeff, my father, Reverend Fromberg. Waiting to hear from the sheriff. When George called, Jeff put it on the speaker. When George started talking like that, Jeff switched off the speaker, but not before I heard—'' Not before she heard. Not before the scar had been hacked even wider and deeper by George's tongue. ''I was mortified,'' she whispered. ''I wanted to die. And everyone was so nice, so sweet. Jeff offered to date me.... I think he'd have married me on the spot if I'd wanted it. And his parents were wonderful. But... conversations came to a dead halt whenever I entered a room for months afterwards. And I felt...I felt...''

''Violated? Wounded? Emotionally raped?'' Gideon would have liked to wring George Cumberland's neck.

Somehow her head had come to rest in the hollow of his shoulder, and now both his arms cradled her gently. ''All of that and a few other things besides,'' she admitted. ''I hid out here on the ranch for a long time, but then Dad died, and I really needed to go to work if I was going to hang on to this place. Nate hired me, and the rest, as they say, is history.''

Well, that sure explained it, Gideon thought. She had been publicly humiliated, so, naturally, for the last ten years she'd put on a tough facade that told everyone she didn't care and couldn't be hurt.

Some tender little place in him, some private little corner that hadn't been blighted by all the abandonments in his own life, ached for her. He wanted so badly to soothe her pain, to wipe away her embarrassment, but he didn't know how. Her rejection by George had left a deep wound, a wound made all the deeper by the fact that he had blamed his defection on her.

"The bastard didn't know what he was throwing away," he said gruffly.

Sara almost smiled into his shoulder. "You're sweet."

"Sweet? Me? Hell, no."

He sounded so uncomfortable with the idea that Sara chuckled softly and let it go. Telling him about George, crazily enough, seemed to have lifted some kind of load from her shoulders. Somehow she no longer felt quite as humiliated.

The wind rustled in the treetops and blew a chilly breath across her cheeks. "It's late. I really ought to get to bed." She started to pull away from him, wishing like mad she could stay, knowing such a wish was in vain. He'd made it clear enough over the last week that he wanted to avoid involvement with her. Since the night in the kitchen, he'd tried very hard not to even brush against her by accident.

"No," he said, surprising her by tightening his arms around her and preventing her escape. He'd been holding this woman for the last half hour, and now his throbbing, aching, hungry body was doing the talking. "No. Stay with me, Sara. Please."

Chapter 8

At the instant he spoke, the wind ceased and the world grew hushed. In the silence, he heard her sharply indrawn breath.

Oh, God, he thought, wishing he could take back the words. How could he have said it so baldly? How could he have asked such a thing of her without even a kiss to sweeten the words? Why had he said it at all? She deserved a lot more than he could offer, and he had no right to ask this of her.

But he *had* asked, and the words lay between them in a world that seemed to be holding its breath. Sara didn't move, didn't try to pull away, but she, too, seemed to be holding her breath, waiting for something more.

He had little experience of women like Sara. She was a cut above him in so many ways, aeons removed from the easy women he'd met in bars when the need got too great to ignore. They had been lonely, too, and hungry, and looking for a night of forgetfulness. Sara wasn't like them.

So what now, Ironheart? he asked himself as the whole night seemed to wait with bated breath. If she stays, will I be able to please her? If she stays, will she hate me tomorrow?

It would be better, he told himself, if he just laughed and told her he'd been teasing. Except that he'd waited too long to laugh now. The significance of his words grew with each passing moment.

Stay with me, Sara. Please. The words echoed in her mind, resounded in the hollow emptiness of her heart. A moment ago she had been wishing she didn't have to leave, and now he had asked her to stay. Wisdom dictated that she flee. Years of avoiding the pain and humiliation urged her to run as if all the hounds of hell were in pursuit. Her heart, empty for so long, begged her to stay. And her body…her body was on fire from little more than the roughly murmured plea to stay.

If she stayed, she would eventually hurt, because Gideon would eventually leave. She was honest enough, even as longing drizzled through her to the most private of places, to admit that she didn't know if she would be able to endure being a spurned lover. The pain of losing Gideon, she suspected, was going to be far worse than the pain of losing George, even if they never made love.

Yet if she turned away now, she would probably spend the rest of her life regretting it. Lately it had been occurring to her off and on that the last ten years had been a wasteland. Someday she was going to run out of future, and it would be awful to look back and see nothing but missed opportunities.

But even that didn't sway her as much as her need. Every cell in her body yearned toward Gideon. Her heart reached out to him; her soul recognized him. If heaven granted her only one night, it was a night for which she would be forever grateful.

And then, for one agonizing moment, it occurred to her that he might have been teasing her.

"Do you—" Her whisper fractured, then steadied. "Do you mean it?"

Now. Tell her it was a joke. Tell her that he'd momentarily lost his senses but was sane again. Tell her.

"With every cell in my body," he said roughly. "With

every single aching inch of me. Damn it, Mouse, I'm on fire for you. Now get out of here before I do something about it.''

She should have run. He was surprised when she didn't. He was stunned when she put her hand on his thigh. "Is this—is this where your little brown mouse perched?''

Sara's heart was in her throat, hammering so hard she could hear it. Resting her hand on his thigh was the most daring thing she'd ever done, more daring by far than breaking up a brawl or chasing a speeder. Dying, she thought, would be easier than exposing herself this way. George had fled, and perhaps Gideon just hadn't yet noticed whatever it was that made her so repulsive.

But the feel of denim and taut muscle beneath her palm was as exciting as anything she had ever felt, and she couldn't bring herself to be wise. Scared to death, hoping against hope, she waited.

Maybe she didn't understand what he meant. He had to give her one last chance, one last warning. "I won't stop.''

"God, I hope not,'' she said shakily.

She understood, and he had run out of nobility, restraint and self-control. Rising, he pulled her to her feet and drew her toward the bunkhouse door. Toward his cave. Toward the dark warmth of a private place where he could claim her as men have claimed women since time immemorial.

He wanted a light. He wanted to be able to see her, but he ignored the wall switch as he tugged her into the bedroom, then ignored the lamp on the nightstand. He wanted nothing, absolutely nothing, to jar her and cause her to rethink her decision. He didn't want any harsh light of reality to pierce the darkly sensual mood that stretched between them.

What he most wanted right now was the feeling. The feeling of closeness and caring, of need and hunger. Later he could fill his eyes with her, but right now he wanted to fill his hands with her, his lungs, his mouth, and to fill her body with himself.

A shaky little sigh escaped her as he tugged the sweater over her head and discovered she wasn't wearing a bra. He growled softly with pleasure as he found her small breasts and covered them with his callused hands. Her hardening nipples pressed his palms, and recognition of her growing arousal zinged straight to his groin, making him throb.

''I'm...so small,'' she whispered apologetically.

That almost inaudible confession punched him in the gut. For an instant he froze, absorbing a truth about Sara Yates that he'd somehow managed to miss. Somehow he hadn't seen the fears and inadequacy she felt, hadn't realized that George Cumberland had done more than humiliate her. He had gutted her womanhood, leaving her frightened, uncertain and full of self-doubt.

''You're so exactly perfect,'' he corrected her gruffly. ''You have no idea just how good you feel to me. Just take my word for it. You're exactly right for me. And I can't tell you...'' Still cupping her breasts, he bent and pressed a kiss to her shoulder. ''Oh, babe, I can't tell you what it means when you let me touch you like this. Especially when you're shy about it.'' And that was true. The fact that this was not a casual, easy thing for her to do aroused him as little had, piercing the armor plating around his heart.

She drew another shaky breath, and then a soft little moan spilled from her as he brushed his thumbs over her beading nipples. The sigh and the moan passed directly into his ear as he kissed her smooth shoulder, and his loins clenched with deepening need.

Pretty little breasts. He didn't need to see them to know that, and it didn't matter whether they were crowned in pink or brown. What mattered was that her nipples rose eagerly to his touch, and her body moved restlessly in response. What mattered was that she let him bend and draw her swollen nipple deep into his mouth, and then clutched wildly at him as the pleasure ripped through her.

''Oh, baby,'' he whispered raggedly when he tried to catch his breath. No woman had ever responded to him this way, so quickly, so hotly, so artlessly. Her hands tugged at his shoulders, and she whispered something. ''Hmm? I didn't hear you, Mouse.''

"Your hair," she whispered breathlessly.

"My hair?" He had once again tied it at the nape of his neck with the thong.

"Untie it," she demanded on a gasp. She wanted all of him, and that included his unbound hair. She couldn't have begun to express why that aroused her so much, except that it seemed like such an intimacy. Except that his hair was never completely free but was always tied back, or restrained by the thong around his forehead. Except when he was loving her.

Lifting a hand, Gideon yanked the leather from his hair and threw it across the room. Then he grabbed the snaps of his shirt and ripped them open. Sara's hands were there immediately, reaching out to help him pull the cloth from his shoulders. A violent shudder ripped through him as her breasts brushed the smooth skin of his chest.

"Sara..." Her name emerged on a deep groan as he gathered her closer.

She raised her arms and plowed her fingers into his long, dark hair, finding his scalp and then grabbing handfuls of his mane to tug his mouth down to hers. He liked it. Oh, God, he liked the way she demanded from him, liked the way she grabbed and pulled him closer. And now she was stretched against him, her breasts crushed to the hard wall of his chest. Roughly, almost urgently, his palms swept the long, silky length of her back and closed on her soft, full rump. With another groan he tightened his grip and lifted her against him.

Sara tore her mouth from his and threw back her head, arching against him, still clutching handfuls of his hair. A moan escaped her as for the first time in her life a man's body fitted intimately to hers. Two layers of denim were suddenly all that lay between her and fulfillment. Wanting more, so much more, she wrapped her legs around his narrow hips, settling the hard ridge of his arousal even more snugly against herself. And even that was not nearly enough.

If it were possible, his powerful arms tightened even more around her, pressing her so close now that she could barely breathe. The world spun wildly, and then she found herself lying on her back on the quilt of his bed. Her knees were still locked around his hips, and he knelt over her, bearing his weight on his elbows.

"Lord, Sara," he muttered, and began dropping hot little kisses over her cheek and neck. "You turn a man inside out."

Fear struck her, freezing passion in an instant. "Is that—is that bad?"

Her words stilled him. For what felt like an eternity, Gideon didn't move, didn't breathe. Finally he spoke harshly. "I'll kill him. If I ever lay eyes on that son of a bitch, I'll kill him."

"Who?" Sara asked, confused, afraid that she had somehow revolted him.

"George Cumberland, that's who. The man— Man? Hell, I won't even dignify him with that. The *creep* who made you feel something is wrong with you. There's not a damn thing wrong with you, Mouse. Not a one. As for being turned inside out, it's never happened to me before, but I'm loving every minute of it."

Except that now he was mad. Growling with frustration, he rose from the bed and stripped off the rest of his clothes—the boots, the socks, the jeans, the briefs. Sara couldn't see a thing but dark shadows flying this way and that, but she heard the thumps and muttered curses.

And then he was with her again. Reaching out, he pulled her against his naked body and settled one hand on her denim-clad bottom.

"Let's talk about this, Mouse," he said roughly.

"Talk about what?" Her voice was little more than a tentative whisper. He was mad, and she knew it was her fault, and something inside her squeezed painfully as she waited for Gideon to tell her what she had done wrong. To enumerate her failures. God, she was no good at being a woman. Hadn't George said that? How could she have forgotten?

"This. Cumberland. How you feel. How you make me feel. And whether you really want to do this."

"But—" He silenced her with a finger over her mouth before she could protest that she did, indeed, really want to do this. That she thought she would die if she didn't.

"Relax," he said softly. "I'm here, and I'm not going anywhere. Believe me, Mouse, you'll have to *throw* me out. But there are obviously a couple of things that need clearing up."

She wished she could see his face. Wished she could see him as he was now, completely nude. And was glad the darkness hid her from him. "Such as?"

"Such as how you make me feel. I've been wanting to make love with you since the night you rescued me from those rednecks. I kid you not. I was standing there, hating having to be rescued by a woman, and getting so turned on by your voice I was worried you'd notice."

"My voice?"

"Your voice is husky and sexy and enough to drive a man out of his mind. From the first word you spoke, I was having visions of being with you like this. Before I even noticed what a beautiful rear end you have. Before I realized that you've got the sexiest little sway when you walk. Before you wore that denim skirt and I got an eyeful of your legs. I've been wanting to kiss your knees for a solid week now. And as for your breasts…"

Sara gasped and arched as his mouth suddenly closed over the aching mound of her breast and his tongue teased her nipple into hardness.

"As for your breasts," he said huskily a short while later, "any more than a mouthful is wasted. I don't know what was the matter with George, Mouse, but there sure as hell isn't a problem with your sex appeal."

Shivering with longing and heat, Sara lay against him and hung on for dear life, waiting for the world to settle down again. He didn't give it much chance.

"Now, about turning me inside out," he continued, his voice deep and throaty as he reached for the snap of her jeans. "Babe, I love it. I love it when you grab me and pull me closer. I love it when you kiss me, when you touch me, and I hope to heaven you'll be making a lot more demands on me before this night is out. Get bossy. Tell me what you want and make me give you enough of it, because, sweet little mouse, there's no bigger turn-on in the world for me than knowing you want me, too.''

His words were as arousing as any touch he had given her, and spirals of shimmering need swirled through her, reaching her core and leaving her damp. ''Gideon,'' she whispered achingly. ''Oh, Gideon…''

He tugged the snap on her jeans and released it. At the sound, her entire center seemed to clamp with an almost painful throb of need.

''Tell me now, Mouse,'' he said. ''Tell me now. Another thirty seconds and nothing will stop me.''

''Don't stop,'' she said hoarsely. ''Don't ever stop.''

The husky demand nearly pushed him right over the edge, but he caught himself before he acted on it. Liquid fire lapped at his loins, and his lungs strained for more air, and he hadn't yet even removed her jeans. God, had he ever gotten so hot so fast? So easily?

Her boots resisted his tugs, but only briefly. He peeled her jeans and panties down her legs without regard to modesty. It was dark, after all, so there was no reason why she should be embarrassed or shy.

And then they were pressed together, naked skin to naked skin. Sara drew a shuddering breath and dug her nails into his shoulders. ''Oh, you feel so good….''

And it was so unbelievably intimate to be pressed to him this way. She could feel every line of him, including his hard arousal and the thicket of hair from which it sprang. And almost as if it had a mind of its own, her hand slipped downward and closed around him. She had never touched a man so boldly, but the need to touch Gideon that way overwhelmed every inhibition. He was big. He was hard. He was built like a warrior, she thought dizzily.

Gideon sucked air through his teeth as her curious touch unleashed rivers of fire in his blood. Slowly, helplessly, he rocked his hips and rubbed himself against her palm.

Grasping the idea, her natural shyness warring with an equally natural desire to drive him out of his mind, Sara mimicked the motion with her hand. And smiled into the dark when Gideon groaned. "You like that?" she whispered. Even that much was hard to say when she felt so breathless, so hot, so excited.

He was in little better state. He answered in a whisper that sounded as if air was in short supply. "Oh, yeah!" Sara's hands were not a soft woman's hands. They were hardworking hands, callused and strong, but the roughness was just a new titillation, and for a few moments he let himself enjoy the sheer magic of her touch.

Pleasuring Gideon was the most powerful aphrodisiac Sara had ever experienced. A low, steady throbbing began in her, seeming to time itself to the motions of her hands and the slight, subtle movements of Gideon's hips as she touched him. Unconsciously, she clamped her legs together tighter and tighter, trying to ease the growing ache, trying to banish the increasing sense of emptiness. Unconsciously she began to rock her own hips, seeking more.

Then suddenly, almost before she knew it was happening, Gideon pushed her onto her back and captured her hands above her head. One of his long, powerful legs settled between hers and began to move slowly up and down, pressing, retreating. Sara caught her breath and clamped her legs together, catching Gideon between them.

He gave a soft, deep laugh. "Ah, she likes that." Before Sara could manage a response, he covered her mouth with his and stole her breath in a stunningly erotic kiss. His tongue and leg moved in matched rhythms, causing her womb to throb in response. Forgetting everything but what she was feeling, Sara arched, pressing herself to him. More. Harder. Deeper. She clutched at him with her legs, undulated against him and made little sounds deep in her throat.

And he loved it. Oh, damn, did he love it. With one hand he held her wrists above her head, using the other to prop himself above her. After a quick nip at her lower lip, he took his mouth from hers and moved lower, seeking those small, shy breasts. When his tongue found her, she arched as tightly as a drawn bow and moaned his name.

The sound was like liquid heat pouring into his ears and running to the farthest, darkest reaches of his body. Of his soul. The sounds of this woman's pleasure affected him as no other's had. The feel of her silky skin beneath his palm was warmer, smoother, than any he had ever touched. Each slender, graceful line of her seemed precious, perfect.

He wanted her...wanted her...wanted her. The desire was like a drumbeat in his hot blood, hammering at him, driving him. Not sure he could wait much longer, he slipped his hand downward, heading toward her womanhood, needing to feel her heat. Needing to measure her readiness.

She stiffened at the first touch of his fingers, stiffened and grew utterly still. He was past stopping now, though. Well past. He found slick folds and pressed further, drawing a gasp from her as he slipped a finger into her. Just a little way. Just enough to feel her wetness.

She panted. Once. Twice. Again. Then he drew his now wet finger upward until he found that tiny knot of nerves, that one place that could push her to the brink. Gently, carefully, he stroked her.

"Do it for me, Mouse," he whispered huskily. "Do it for me."

She had no idea what he meant, but she was in no condition to care. Each touch of his fingers sent ribbons of electricity through her and built the growing ache at her center. When he released her hands, she reached for him, needing him closer. Needing to be filled by him, crushed by him. Needing him... needing him...needing him...

"Gideon...oh, Gideon, please...please..."

Her broken whispers and pleas, her clutching hands, snapped his last thread of control. With fumbling fingers he grabbed the protection he had stashed in the night table a week ago when it began to seem he might lose his head over this woman.

"Gideon..."

"Just a second, Mouse. Just a—" There. Ready now, he eased her legs apart and knelt between them. She stilled, and a moment of perfect clarity settled over him. For an instant he rose above the swamping haze of passion, moved away from the throbbing of his own body. This was, he recognized, no simple act of passion gone out of control. Like a crystal note, the understanding resounded in his soul. This was special.

But his body's demands surged again, muddying thought and bringing him back to the elemental level of a man loving a woman. Leaning forward, he pressed the heel of his palm to Sara's mound and rubbed gently until her hips were arching, reaching for him, and she was whispering his name brokenly, again and again.

"That's it, Mouse," he whispered encouragingly. "That's it." Leaning forward, he found her moist opening with the tip of his shaft. Pleasure swept through him like an electric shock as he leaned into her. Pressed into her. Sought relief and release in her hot, slick depths.

And then he swore.

Sara felt the light like twin knives in her eyes. Confused, startled, she blinked and tried to see the face of the man who hovered over her, the man whose body was partially embedded in hers. Why had he sworn? Why had he switched on the light? "Gideon?"

Eyes closed, he muttered a string of imprecations that turned the air blue and made Sara's cheeks rosy. She'd heard plenty on the job, but Gideon knew all of the worst ones.

"Gideon?"

His eyes snapped open, and dark gray steel bore down into her. "Why the hell didn't you tell me you'd never done this before?"

"Why the hell did you think I had?" she demanded, frustration fueling her normally somnolent temper.

"Because...because you almost got married!"

"So? Nice girls don't—"

He caught her face between his hands and shook her. Just a

little. With incredible gentleness, considering he looked mad enough to kill. "Nice girls don't?" he repeated roughly. "Then what the hell are you doing in bed with a naked half-breed savage?"

"Good God!" Sara stared at him in complete astonishment. "Who called you that?"

He went utterly still, shocked by what he had just revealed. Briefly he closed his eyes, seeking internal stability before he continued with the issue at hand. Then he glared down at her. "Quit changing the subject."

"I didn't change the subject. You said something horrible, and I want to know who called you that."

"Just answer the question, damn it!"

"What am I doing here?" *Loving you,* she wanted to say, *loving you with my whole heart.* "Making love with you. Or I thought I was."

"But nice girls don't," he reminded her.

"So? So maybe I'm not so nice anymore," she said hotly, her temper flaring again. "Maybe I don't want to die a nice virgin. Maybe I want to find out what it's all about. Maybe you just turn me on so damn much that all I can think about is—" She broke off. "Gideon Ironheart, if you stop now, I'm going to get my .45 and...and..."

A little trickle of amusement ran down his spine. Just a tiny trickle, but it washed the anger right out of him. She was as mad as a wet kitten, he thought, studying her flushed face and sparkling eyes. Mad and frustrated, and who the hell was he to argue if she wanted to get rid of her virginity? It was her decision, not his. And he was still hot for her, still heavy and hard.

"And what, Mouse?" he asked, one corner of his mouth hitching up. "Force me at gunpoint? Damn, that's kinky. I think I could learn to like it, though. With *you.*"

She caught her breath, and all the harshness of anger slipped out of her face, leaving her looking soft. In an instant she was throbbing from head to toe again, acutely aware of the tip of him just barely inside her.

"You should have told me, Sara," he said huskily. "I don't want to hurt you. I might have, by going too fast."

"You're killing me by not going fast enough," she said raggedly. "Damn you, Gideon, don't do this to me."

"Tell me you're sure." Even as he spoke, he pressed just a little deeper into her. Impulses were zinging through his body, every one of them zeroing in on his hips, trying to drive him into making one great thrust. "Tell me."

"I'm sure. Damn it, I'm sure."

"Why, Mouse? Why?"

"I want you." She was almost sobbing. Reaching up, she grabbed his hair and tugged. "Every time I look at you I ache. I need so badly for you to touch me, fill me, take me...."

And he needed so badly to know it. He took her then, with one long, smooth thrust that transformed her, and he never once took his eyes from hers. He saw the flash of pain and felt it in his heart. He heard her caught breath and felt it in his soul. And he saw pain slowly transformed into revived passion as he moved again, just a little. In and out.

And then her hands slipped down and grabbed his hips, pulling him closer, urging his pace to quicken. Reassured, he gave her all he had and moments later listened to her keening cry as she crested the peak. An instant later, in an explosion so violent he heard it in his brain, he followed her over.

She didn't want to let go of him, so he took care of necessary matters with one hand and then pulled her over him like a warm, soft blanket. The light was still on, and he debated a moment whether to turn it off and let them both fall asleep, or to wait a little and make sure that Sara was all right. He'd never made love to a virgin before, but he suspected this was a momentous event for her that she wouldn't want to let pass without a little talk.

Nor did he, he realized. He wanted to hear her sexy, husky voice, wanted to see her smile and wanted to look into her warm brown eyes to be sure she wasn't regretting this. Man, how he hoped she didn't regret this.

"Mmm…" Sighing, she stretched a little, rubbing against him as if she thoroughly enjoyed the sensation.

"Feel good?" he asked her huskily.

"Mmm." She lifted her head and smiled down at him, a lazy contented smile. "I feel fabulous." Then the shadow of doubt flickered across her face. "You?"

He spared a moment to imagine kicking George Cumberland's butt, then reached up to sweep Sara's tousled hair back from her face. "I feel like somebody just made me king. I feel…special. Very, very special."

"You *are* special." Bending, she kissed his chest. "I wouldn't be here otherwise."

His throat tightened, and he found himself wondering why it seemed that she was reassuring him, when he should be reassuring her. When he should be telling her just how special she was.

"And I should be getting back," she said shyly, not wanting to put him in an awkward position. Now that they'd made love, he probably didn't want her hanging around. "You need your sleep, and I—"

He silenced her with a deep, almost savage kiss. "You're not going anywhere. I want you right here. I want to wrap myself around you while you sleep in my arms. I want to open my eyes at dawn and find you right beside me."

A soft, warm glow came to her face, telling him how good he had just made her feel. And he was sure in trouble now, because he'd never wanted a woman to spend the night in his bed. In fact, he always went to *their* beds so he could leave when he was ready.

But Sara was different, he admitted. Very different. Sooner or later she would want more than he could give, and that would be the end of it. But for now, right now, he wanted everything *she* could give, and he wanted to give her anything he had to offer in return.

Reaching down, he tugged her legs to one side and then sat up with her still on his chest.

Sara drew her head back and stared at him. "I don't believe you just did that."

"Just a sit-up."

"With about a hundred pounds of me on your chest."

"Stomach muscles," he said with a shrug.

She looked down and saw that he did indeed have a washboard belly. And farther down... Quickly she snapped her gaze to his face. He was grinning, damn him. "All this from connecting?"

"Yep." In one easy movement he stood with her in his arms. "You don't weigh anything compared to a beam or a header, babe." He headed down the hall toward the bathroom, liking the way she looped her arms around his neck and pressed her face to his shoulder.

"You smell good," she said, sighing.

"You too." Reaching the bathroom, he set her gently on her feet and bent to turn on the water in the tub.

"What's this?" she asked.

He smiled over his shoulder at her. "A warm, soothing shower. I get to wash you, and you get to wash me."

That was when she saw the blood on him. Her blood. Just a little. And when she looked down at herself, she closed her eyes. "Oh my!" Her voice sounded thin.

"Now, don't be embarrassed, Mouse," he said, tugging her under the spray with him. "It's just one of those things that can't be avoided the first time. Besides, you're supposed to be proud of it, not ashamed."

Her eyes snapped open. "Next you'll want to hang the sheets over the balcony."

He tipped back his head and laughed, then shook his head. "Oh, no," he said lowering his voice. "That's our special secret."

Then he put the soap in her hand and, taking her by the wrist, guided her hand all over him, making it clear that there were no more barriers between them, no more boundaries that couldn't be crossed. That she was free to explore, touch and look however she wanted.

She wanted. Oh, how she wanted. When his hand fell from her wrist finally, she never noticed. She was too absorbed in the incredible male beauty of Gideon Ironheart. His chest was broad and smooth, powerful with muscle, sleek without hair. The twin points of his dark nipples fascinated her, drew her like magnets. When at last she licked one with her tongue, he shuddered and groaned softly.

He liked that, she realized, recognizing other changes in his body as well. Standing back a little, she looked down. Oh my, but he was magnificent!

Gideon chuckled at the way she smiled. He recognized female satisfaction when he saw it. "See what you do to me?" he asked. It was important for her to know that. She needed to know it, and he didn't mind at all that she did.

He would have loved to let her continue, but he figured the hot water couldn't last forever. Taking the soap from her, he treated her to the same slick caresses and exploration she had given him.

Nor did he spare her modesty. While she had washed him, she had forgotten herself, but now she grew painfully aware of her nakedness and her every imagined flaw. Gideon hushed her broken protests and brushed aside her whispered apologies. He touched her everywhere and did it with his eyes wide open. He told her how she excited him, how pretty she was, how sleek, how slender, how perfect....

Until with a growl he shut off the water and grabbed a towel. She could barely stand on her own legs, but he didn't mind. Excitement had made her weak, but it had made him strong.

And that was exactly how it was supposed to be.

The first pink fingers of dawn found their way through a crack in the curtains of Gideon's east-facing bedroom window. They trailed across Sara, who was awake, and Gideon, who slept soundly.

Her head propped on her hand, Sara watched him slumber. Sometime during the night he had kicked the quilt away, and now he sprawled in magnificent nakedness. He was, she thought, beautiful.

She ought to leave, to spare herself and him any morning-after awkwardness. She didn't know the protocol, after all—what to say, what to do. What if he opened his eyes and she saw regret?

And if she slipped away now, no one would know she had been here. But as soon as she thought that, she knew better. Joey wouldn't know, because Joey never stirred until someone made him. Zeke would know, though, because Zeke somehow knew everything. She sometimes thought the wind whispered tales in his ear.

She stayed, facing the possible awkwardness that would come with Gideon's awakening, because she couldn't bear to leave before she absolutely had to. Because she hoped, wildly, that he would draw her to him one more time. Because she needed another kiss, another touch, another smile.

God, she had it bad. She was like a thirsty woman faced with water. Her eyes drank him in, and she felt that she would never get enough. And if he ever suspected such a thing, he would be gone before she could say "scat."

A naked half-breed savage. Someone must have called him that at one time or another. Those weren't words most people would apply to themselves. Nor were they words Gideon would have taken to heart if they had been hurled at him by some drunk in a bar. No, he probably heard crap like that all the time from idiots who'd had one too many.

Someone else had spoken those words, had made them so hurtful that they had come out of him in a moment of intimacy and anger. Just the memory of them made her want to cry for all the hurts he must have suffered. Why, she wondered for the umpteenth time, were people so cruel to one another?

Almost unconsciously, she reached out and rested her hand on his chest. She was so pale against the beautiful copper of his skin. Her father's Irish heritage had run true in her, giving her a fair, milky color with an undertone of roses, a smattering of freckles everywhere and a sensitivity to the sun that kept her in broad-brimmed cowboy hats and long-sleeved shirts most of the summer.

Why, she wondered, would anyone object to a skin as beautiful as Gideon's? To hair so black and beautiful? How could anyone call a man who was more civilized than most a savage?

Oh, yes, she really had it bad.

Suddenly a prickle of awareness penetrated her preoccupation. Looking up, she found Gideon watching her study him. She felt her cheeks heat as she realized he had caught her gawking like a star-struck kid.

"You're beautiful in the morning," he said roughly. "Beautiful."

Before she could do more than register his words, he tugged her gently toward him and kissed her deeply. Relief caught her and then gave way to sheer erotic bliss, to a warm feeling of being wanted, being needed. To the deep satisfaction of Gideon's arms around her, holding her tightly.

"Ah, babe, don't do that," he whispered when her hands began to roam. "Don't, Mouse. It's too soon for you...."

Understanding poured through her like warm, golden honey. He had kept her with him because he had wanted her there, not because he expected to make love again this morning. Slowly she lifted her head and looked him right in the eye.

"Gideon Ironheart," she said huskily, "you are one in a billion."

For an instant, just an instant, he looked embarrassed. Then his face stiffened and he said, "You don't want to start thinking that way, Mouse. I'm just another one of a billion tumbleweeds, is all."

"Right," she said. Right, she thought as she let her cheek come to rest on his smooth, powerful shoulder. Absolutely. "I hear you." She did, too.

But damned if she could make herself believe it.

Chapter 9

Zeke was in the kitchen pouring coffee when Sara entered. The early morning light filled the room with the clarity of a day just beginning and seemed to etch the moment in glass. Her grandfather looked at her, intently, she thought. She had the uneasy feeling that he could read every thought in her head. Then, giving a small, almost imperceptible nod, he turned and reached for another mug.

"It's going to be a beautiful day," he remarked.

"Yes. Yes, it is."

He handed her the freshly filled mug. "Take it up with you while you change."

Well, Sara thought, he'd said all he was going to say on the subject, and she didn't know whether to be surprised or not. Zeke had always been extremely protective of her. But he had also allowed her to grow up and take risks that many grandfathers or fathers would certainly have objected to. He had let her become a deputy, after all, without a word of argument.

"You do what you must, Sarey," he had told her. He had told her essentially the same thing just now.

Dressed in fresh clothes, still too high to feel the lack of sleep, she knocked on Joey's door and told him to hop to. "We're late getting the garden in," she called through the door. "Come on. I want it done today."

A muffled curse answered her, but she ignored it and headed downstairs. Joey had just started tilling the acre on which she raised vegetables before he'd had to go to jail. If they delayed planting much longer, they would run out of growing season for some of the things she liked most.

Downstairs, she found the kitchen empty. Beyond the windows, she saw Zeke and Gideon standing in the yard, talking, and almost in spite of herself she stopped and watched them. They talked a lot, those two, each of them seeming to have found in the other a good friend. It pleased her to see them together, to know that there was genuine liking there.

That was when she remembered that Gideon had wanted to meet Micah Parish, another Cherokee half-breed. They might have a lot in common, Sara thought, watching the way the sunlight seemed to disappear in the absolute black of Gideon's hair. Micah's work on Zeke's assault case had brought the two of them together, but not in the kind of capacity that would allow them to become friends. And that, Sara thought now, was probably what Gideon would have liked. And if he had friends around here, perhaps he wouldn't be so quick to leave.

Well, it would be easy enough to ask Micah and his wife and daughter to dinner. She'd entertained them once before, just after Micah's marriage, and had really liked Faith. And perhaps she should ask Gage and Emma Dalton, too.

A little chill touched her heart as she realized what she was doing, that she was in fact going to present this man to her friends in the hopes that they would like him. She was setting herself up to be played for a fool again.

But almost as soon as she had the thought, she dismissed it. No, she was doing this because Gideon had asked her to, no more, no less. As for asking her dear friend Emma and her new husband, well, that was just because more people would make the situation less awkward. Because Micah and Gage appeared to be good friends. Because she thought Gideon would like Gage, too.

Certainly not because she wanted her friends to like him. Certainly not.

Joey came down and ate his breakfast in a silence so sullen that Sara's palm itched with the wish to turn him over her knee.

"I'll come help with the tilling," she said.

That got his attention. "No."

Sara stared down at him, torn between wanting to shake him and begging him to tell her what she had done wrong. Finally, aching, she turned her back. "Fine. Do it by yourself. But get it done, or the vegetables I have to buy are going to come out of your paycheck."

Unable to stand another minute in the same room with the boy without losing her temper, she went outside to join Zeke and Gideon.

"You have to send a sacred pipe and tobacco," Zeke was saying to Gideon. "That's the proper way to ask a holy man to perform a ritual for you."

"But if the vision quest is done alone, why do I need the holy man?"

"You need to purify yourself first. He'll hold a sweat for you, cleanse you. Then you're ready."

"And the pipe? Where do you get a sacred pipe?"

"You carve it yourself."

Sara looked at Gideon, wishing she could touch him, but not certain how he might react. "You're going to seek a vision?"

Gideon shook his head. "I don't know. Not yet. I was just asking about it. Like most kids, I never listened to my grandfather when I had the chance. Now I'm bugging Zeke about it."

"It is different from tribe to tribe," Zeke said. "The way of your people may be different."

"Well, I don't know a whole hell of a lot about it," Gideon said. "One way is as good as another from where I stand. I never listened and never participated in anything my grandfather did. I wasted a lot."

They all turned as the kitchen door slammed and Joey came out of the house. The boy said nothing, merely scuffing his way across the yard to the barn. A few minutes later he returned, pushing the tiller ahead of him. When he reached the battered 1963 pickup, Gideon went over to him.

"Let me help with that, Joe."

Joey didn't answer immediately. He fiddled a moment with the gas cap and tightened down a screw with his thumbnail. At last, though, he nodded. "Thanks," he said.

Sara almost stopped breathing as man and boy hoisted the tiller onto the pickup bed. Then, as if they had reached some kind of agreement, Gideon simply walked around and climbed into the passenger seat. Joey hesitated only a moment and then got behind the wheel.

The field Sara always planted was only a couple of hundred yards from the house, but she had chosen to plant there because the groundwater level was higher and the land dipped a little into a hollow that reduced the wind's drying effects. It was, however, visible from the house, and she watched in amazement as boy and man climbed out and set to work together.

"I don't believe that," she said.

"That Ironheart is a unique man," Zeke said from beside her. "Joey feels it, too." He glanced at Sara, and suddenly his dark eyes were twinkling. "Of course, it helps that they settled who was boss."

Sara felt herself smiling back. "I suppose it does," she agreed, and then laughed, because this was, after all, one of the best days of her life.

Sunset in these mountains happened in stages. After dinner that night, Gideon watched the last stage, when the twilight that had blanketed the world for several hours was suddenly shot through by streamers of pink-and-orange clouds as the sun, long hidden behind the mountains, really set. It was a strange effect, he thought, sitting in the near dark while sunset blazed in the sky above his head. Beautiful. Unforgettable.

He wondered if Sara would come by tonight. He had tried

to let her know she would be welcome, but between Zeke and Joey, they hadn't had a private moment all day. And now Sara was on duty and wouldn't be home until after midnight. No, she would probably go on up to the house. Sara wasn't the kind to impose, and she'd probably figure that she would be if she came without invitation.

Hell, he thought, and sighed. That was for the best, wasn't it? He didn't want to hurt the woman, and from the way she looked at him sometimes, he figured tough Sara Yates would be remarkably easy to wound.

A sound snagged his attention, and he looked around, spying Joey standing in the yard. The boy looked lost, Gideon thought. Probably the same way he had looked at that age, pretending to be tough and uncaring to hide the hurt.

They had worked together well enough throughout the day, tilling the field and planting the vegetables. And Joey had, without being asked, helped with the other chores this evening. Not a bad kid at heart, it seemed. Just a troubled one. A worried one.

A frightened one.

Gideon wasn't sure how he knew that, or even that he was right about it, but several times today he had gotten the feeling that Joey Yates was scared to death and didn't know what to do about it. That he was in worse trouble than violating his probation. But nobody could help Joey if Joey didn't talk, and Joey had no intention of talking.

Sighing again, Gideon almost let it go. Then, feeling a twinge of conscience, he called out, "Nice evening."

A moment of silence preceded Joey's answer. "Yeah."

Well, that was hopeful, Gideon thought. At least it could pass for courteous. Anything more, though, would have to come from Joey. And then he decided to make one more stab at it, anyway. "Jail is the pits, isn't it?"

That caught the boy's interest. Joey tensed a little and looked at him, although he didn't come any closer. "You been there?"

"Six months, when I was sixteen."

"What for?"

"I stole an expensive belt buckle. They gave me probation right off, but I blew that, too, so I spent six months in a cell." He hesitated, then volunteered a little more. "I swore I'd never again do anything to get myself locked up like that. I can't stand being caged."

Joey's answer was a long time coming. Just about the time Gideon was ready to give up, he said, "It's awful."

And whether he knew it or not, Joey was edging closer. Just a shuffling step here and there, but he was closing the distance. From the corner of his eye Gideon watched and remembered a brown mouse long ago. Suddenly he smiled into the night. Two little mice in one family. Must be genetic.

There was an old refrigerator in the bunkhouse, one so old it more closely resembled an icebox, and in it were soft drinks. When Joey edged up to the end of the porch, Gideon asked him if he'd like one.

"Uh, yeah. Thanks."

That response had come more easily, Gideon thought. "Cola, orange or ginger ale?" he asked the boy.

"Cola, please."

When Gideon returned with the soft drinks, he found Joey sitting on the opposite end of the porch step from where Gideon had been sitting. Offering no comment, he simply handed the boy the aluminum can and returned to his own seat.

For a long time the only sound was the sighing of the wind in the pines and the occasional whinny of a horse. It was soothing. Peaceful. A man could easily get addicted to it, if he let himself. He could grow used to the quiet, the lack of human ruckus, the nose-tickling scent of pine on the air.

Joey spoke suddenly, startling him. "You like my sister?"

Gideon turned his head and tried to read the boy in the fading light. No such luck. "I like your sister," he agreed. "I like her a whole lot."

"She tell you what George Cumberland did to her?"

"She did." Gideon waited, wondering if he should halt this conversation right now. Sara sure as hell wouldn't like knowing they had discussed her. On the other hand, for once Joey was talking instead of glaring sullenly, and shutting him up might be a big mistake.

"She needs someone to be good to her," Joey said after a moment.

"I couldn't agree more." Nor could his conscience, which was pricking him right now. "She's also old enough to make her own decisions."

"Yeah." Joey sipped his drink and didn't say any more for a while. Then he asked, "So you're Cherokee?"

"Half of me is." He suddenly wondered why he always qualified it. *Half-breed.*

"Gramps is Shoshone. But you know that."

"Yeah."

"He says because he was raised in that orphanage he knows more about being Sioux than about being Shoshone. Shoshone aren't one of the Seven Council Fires of the Sioux."

"I didn't realize that." Interested, he leaned back against the porch pillar and turned to look at Joey.

"There are really seven bands," Joey said. "Grandfather knows the ways of the Oglala mostly because of Chester Elk Horn. I think Chester sort of adopted him." Even in the dark, Gideon saw the flash of Joey's smile, quickly appearing and just as quickly gone.

"Well, he sure knows more about being Oglala than I know about being Cherokee. I was a hardheaded kid, I'm afraid."

"Like me," Joey said.

"Worse, believe me."

"I went to a Sun Dance the summer before last with Chester's grandson," Joey said after a little while. "Over at Pine Ridge. I thought it was a little…commercial. Tourists and things. But I hear they do it more privately on the Rosebud Reservation. The real thing, for religious reasons."

"Hmm."

"Chester's grandson wants me to go with him this summer. Maybe dance this time."

Gideon sat up a little straighter. He *did* know a little something about the Sun Dance. "That's…rough."

"It kind of scares me a little," Joey admitted.

"I imagine so." He hesitated, wishing his familiarity with the subject were a whole lot greater. "Why would you want to do it? I, uh, understand that it has great religious significance."

"That's the point." He looked at Gideon. "It's meaningful. More meaningful than going to school and making money."

Gideon stared at him hard and then gave a quiet laugh. "Joe, you smartened up about twenty-five years younger than me. So you're going to do it?"

"I don't think I can. I'm on probation, and they won't let me go anywhere." He looked away.

A couple of minutes passed. Gideon listened to the sorrowful murmur of the wind and wondered how this boy had gotten so messed up. "Why'd you do it, Joe? Why'd you steal the car?"

"I was dumb!" Shouting the words, the boy stood up and hurled his can across the yard. "You look bad and everybody believes it! Even your own family believes it!"

Gideon watched him tear off into the darkness and wondered what the hell he had meant.

Clouds were scudding across the moon when Sara pulled into the yard after midnight. More rain, she thought, tasting it on the breeze. The mountainous part of the county always got more rain than the eastern sections, but even so, they were having considerably more than usual. But the whole year had been that way, she reminded herself.

All evening long she had thought about Gideon, wishing she could go to him when she got home, and knowing she couldn't. He'd gotten what he wanted last night, and men seldom wanted more than that, judging by what she had seen. They certainly didn't want to feel things were getting sticky, and it would probably feel very sticky if she showed up on his porch. No, she had to let him know that she wasn't going to pressure him or demand anything.

And then she caught sight of movement at the edge of the beam of her headlights. Looking, she saw Gideon walking across the yard toward her. He was still up, as if he had been waiting for her. And he was walking like a man with a purpose.

He opened the door of the Blazer and reached in to switch off her lights. Then he looked at her, simply looked, with a hunger that seemed to reach out and touch her.

Everything inside her went into instant meltdown. She could feel herself softening, dissolving, liquefying, and somehow she was leaning against him, wrapped in his arms and cuddled to his chest.

"Oh, babe," he whispered. "Oh, babe." He lifted her down and waited patiently while she locked the Blazer. Then, as easily as if she were a wisp of the night air, he lifted her from her feet and carried her toward the bunkhouse. He'd figured she would want a shower and something to eat, and he had it ready for her, but the way she had softened against him and wrapped herself around him told him the shower and food might well have to wait.

He needed her. As the hours of the endless evening had ticked by, the need had grown, a need for more than the warmth of her body. He'd never felt this way before and didn't like it at all, but, like a man driven, he'd waited and hungered, every cell in his body focused on the moment of her return. The Wyoming night spun away, and nothing existed for him now except Sara, warm and willing in his arms.

The sound of his huskily whispered "Oh, babe" in her ear caused shivers of longing to pour through her. He'd waited up for her. He wanted her. It was more than she had dared hope for, and all she had been able to think of for hours.

She had been so afraid that she might have allowed herself to be used like some disposable tissue. So afraid that once had been enough, that in some essential way she had failed to give him anything that he would want again. Now here he was holding her and carrying her as if she were infinitely precious.

The bedside lamp was already on, and the bed was already turned down. When Gideon set her carefully on her feet, Sara looked from the bed to him and felt her chest tighten with emotion. He had taken a risk she would never have had the courage to take herself, she realized. He had come to her risking rejection, and now he'd brought her in here and let her see that he had indeed been waiting for her. She would have done anything to avoid exposing herself that way.

Aching, yearning, needing, fighting back tears of emotion, she leaned into him and wrapped her arms around his narrow waist. He was so hard, so solid, so strong. So warm, so alive. So real. She couldn't imagine why he should want her at all, but she wanted him with a depth and breadth that was terrifying. He drove away a loneliness that she hadn't even been aware of until he had completed her. She couldn't bear, absolutely couldn't bear, to think how empty she would feel when he moved on.

"Sweet Mouse," he murmured in a voice so passion-roughened that it was as sensual as a caress. "Sweet, sweet Sara." He hugged her tightly for an instant and then set her back a little so he could undress her.

First there was the gun belt. Never in a million years would Gideon have imagined himself removing a gun belt from a woman so that he could make love to her. Unexpected humor tugged the corners of his mouth, giving him a cockeyed smile.

"What's so funny?" Sara asked.

"Me taking this gun off you," he replied, and gave her a teasing look. "Not quite *High Noon,* is it?" He set the heavy belt and gun on the battered wooden dresser.

"Does it bother you?"

He faced her, taking her gently by the shoulders. She was feeling inadequate again, he saw. Worried that she was somehow wrong. "No, it doesn't bother me," he said softly. "I was just amused, because it suddenly struck me that out of all the fantasies I've ever had about taking something off a woman, I never imagined a gun belt."

He reached for the buttons of her khaki uniform shirt. "Now, a shirt was on my list," he said, his voice dropping huskily. "And slacks and jeans and even boots, but not a .45. Just goes to show you that life can always rustle up a little surprise." He pushed the shirt from her shoulders and let it flutter to the floor, and saw her small breasts cupped in the plain cotton bra—the same bra he had discovered the first time he had touched her breast, that night in the kitchen.

"No lace," he said. "Not a smidgeon. Damn it, Mouse, it's the sexiest darn thing I've ever seen."

Startled, she looked down at herself, unable to imagine that he would find such a utilitarian garment appealing. Only this afternoon she'd considered stopping in at Freitag's Mercantile to see if they had something prettier. "Sexy?"

"Yeah." Reaching out, he ran his finger along the top edge, causing sparks deep inside her. "It's not playing any games. It's doing its job without pretenses. Like you, Mouse. Just like you." With a twist he undid the front clasp and released her small breasts. "You're the sexiest woman I've ever seen."

He meant it, too, as he slipped the bra from her shoulders and then bent to flick each pink nipple with his tongue. She gasped and grabbed his shoulders in response.

She was absolutely the sexiest woman he'd ever known, and he suspected that had a lot to do with the fact that, for her, sex was most definitely *not* a game. And he'd played games for too many years.

Lifting his head, he looked into her slumbrous eyes and nearly smiled with delight when he saw the glowing coals of passion there. "You've had a long day," he said roughly, even though he hated like hell to say it. "You must want a shower and something to eat."

Sara's eyes widened. She couldn't believe it. Her damp nipples felt chilled from the air and cheated by the absence of his mouth, her lower half was aching in a steady, clenching throb for the feel of him on her and in her, and he was talking about food and a shower?

Tonight he wore the leather strip around his forehead. Sara reached up and pulled it off, tossing it away. "The only thing I'm interested in right now is *your* gun."

He laughed. A low, throaty sound, it spilled from him as he tumbled them both to the bed. Springs creaked, slats groaned, and Sara's giggles joined his.

"God, you're a handful, Sara Yates," Gideon said, his dark eyes smiling down at her. So different, so special, so unique, he thought, lowering his head so he could find her mouth with his. Special....

Heat flared swiftly; licking flames danced along nerve endings as passion spread. So right, Sara thought as she tugged at Gideon's clothes. So right. This was how she was meant to be, who she was meant to be. He had opened the self-made coffin in which she had been hiding and breathed new life into her with his hands, his mouth, his body.

She had been made for this man. The certainty filled her as surely as the coming of dawn. She had existed and endured until now just so that she could be here at this place and this time to become part of the man who now held her.

Gideon groaned deeply as he slid down the bed, trailing kisses from her small, sweet breasts to her tummy. Hot. He was so damn hot for this woman. Years of experience had taught him to expect waning passion with familiarity, to know that he would want less the second time than the first. That wasn't true this time. Not at all.

It had been many years since he had wanted a woman more than once. Not since his one ill-starred love affair in the green days of his youth had he felt this degree of longing and need, this constant, unremitting desire for a particular woman. He'd given up hope of ever rediscovering this clawing hunger, this sharp thrill of excitement. This groaning, wrenching, aching need.

His exploring mouth ran into her belt buckle, and he gave a low groan of frustration. Propping himself on his elbows, he tugged at the buckle, at the button and zipper of her khaki slacks. Then he reared up on his knees and impatiently tugged slacks and panties down.

Sara caught her breath as she watched him. So big, so dark, so hard, so wild-looking. His shirt hung open, one tail pulled out by her hungry hands. He straddled her, worn denim cupping his aroused masculinity, molding to his powerful thighs, revealing each muscular flex as he struggled with her clothes.

His long black hair spilled forward, making him look as if he came from another time.

His impatience with the obstruction of her clothing excited her even more. Never had she felt so wanted, so prized, so special.

He muttered an oath as he dealt with her stubborn cowboy boots and then dragged her pants off her. At last she lay completely naked for him, sprawled wantonly on the bed, her soft brown eyes never leaving him. And then, damned if she didn't lift her arms and whisper, "Hurry."

He hurried. He cast off his clothes and lowered himself to the bed between her legs. He heard her gasp as he propped himself on his elbows and cupped her soft rump, lifting her to his mouth.

"Gideon…" She sounded shocked, excited, only faintly protesting.

"Let me, Mouse," he said hoarsely. "Let me give you this." This, something he had never given any woman. Something he had never wanted to give any woman until this one. How could he explain his absolutely overwhelming need to love her in every way possible, to leave the memory of him on every inch of her? Lowering his head, he claimed her.

He took her to a place where pleasure was so intense it was nearly pain. She writhed wildly, clutching the sheets, then clutching his head, afraid he would stop, afraid she would die if he didn't. She whimpered and twisted and suddenly drew taut, arching up from the bed as a sharp-edged wave of excruciating pleasure ripped through her and carried her over the edge.

Dimly, from the other side of oblivion, she felt Gideon slide up over her, felt him slowly, surely, fill her. And then he was lifting her yet again, carrying her away as if he were winged Pegasus heading for the stars.

"Now," she heard him say hoarsely. "Now!"

And in some fantastic, unbelievable way, she turned into a supernova in a burst of light, heat and joy that seared her very soul.

* * *

Cold roast beef sandwiches had never tasted so good. Having finished hers, Sara sat in Gideon's bed, wrapped in one of his flannel shirts, her hair still damp from her shower, and thought that dreams really could come true. Despite all that had happened between them, she still couldn't believe that this powerful, virile, attractive man, wearing nothing but unbuttoned jeans, was lying propped on an elbow beside her on his bed. That he had just loved her to the edge of sanity, and that now he was calmly pulling the stems from green grapes and popping the grapes one at a time into her mouth. Smiling each time he did so.

Impulsively, she reached out and touched the corner of his lips. Immediately he turned his head and drew her finger into his mouth. Feeling the rasp of his tongue on her sensitive flesh, she caught her breath. Remembering what that tongue had so recently done to other tender flesh, she stopped breathing entirely.

Gideon bit her finger gently and released it. Smiling, he popped another grape into her mouth. "Full yet?" he asked. Sara's appetite for food was as healthy as everything else about her.

"Getting there," she managed to say.

The corners of his eyes creased with a deepening smile as he gave her another grape. "Have y'all figured out anything about who attacked Zeke?"

Sara shook her head. "There isn't a whole lot to go on. No fingerprints. The yard was too hard to take a tire impression. About the only hope we have is that Zeke will remember."

"Those cigarette butts and boot prints Micah found weren't useful, then?"

Sara shook her head and declined another grape. "I'm stuffed. We'd probably never catch him even if we did have something more. Nate's pretty much convinced it was just some drifter looking for money, probably on drugs or something, and he got mean when he didn't find what he wanted."

"Since we haven't had any more trouble in a week, I guess he's right."

Sara shrugged. "What else could it be?"

"Nothing." He took the bowl of grapes from the bed between them and twisted to set it on the night table. Then he was looking at her again, head propped on his hand, a faint smile on his firm mouth. "You've enchanted me," he said unexpectedly.

For an instant everything inside Sara stilled to perfect quiet in a moment of exquisite awareness. Then she shook loose, reminding herself that this man was a tumbleweed, and that nothing he said mattered beyond the moment. "Must be those newt eyes and toadstools I threw in your lunch earlier."

"Must be." The corners of his eyes crinkled. "Or it could be I'm a sucker for little brown mice with warm eyes and a need to be stroked. I talked to Joey earlier this evening."

The swift change of subject distracted her, as he had intended. "Joey?" she repeated. "Has he done something?"

"No, nothing. We just got to talking. Some of the things he said... Sara, I just can't figure how he went bad."

"Me, either," she admitted. "I never thought...I never *saw* anything in him that made me think he was bad. But the way he's been acting..."

"He's mad. Something has really hurt him." Gideon paused, then added, "He was talking about doing the Sun Dance this summer."

"He was?" Sara was clearly astonished, but after a moment she looked thoughtful. "He went to the Pine Ridge Reservation two years ago for the annual powwow. Chester Elk Horn and his grandson took him."

"He told me."

"I remember he was irritated by all the tourists. Not so much that people were interested, I guess, but rather that they didn't understand the religious significance of the Sun Dance. He didn't feel it should be performed as a public spectacle. Grandfather reminded him that tourists attend religious ceremonies all over the world. Catholic Masses in missions around San

Antonio. Processions in Mexico.… That kind of thing. I'm not sure it calmed him any. You know how passionate kids get about things at that age.''

''About some things at *any* age,'' he said, and leaned over to kiss her wrist. He smiled when he felt her shiver faintly in response. ''He mentioned Pine Ridge to me, too. He said he wants to participate in the Sun Dance that's held privately on the Rosebud Reservation. And he appears to think he won't be allowed to go because he's on probation.''

''He's probably right. Unless Nate agreed to let me take him. He's Joey's probation officer now.''

''Would you take him?''

Sara's gaze rose from her lap to his dark eyes. ''I don't know,'' she said truthfully. ''I was raised with a foot in two worlds, but mostly in the Anglo world, and so was Joey. Zeke has always spoken of these things, the way he does with you, but he has always recognized that this is a white man's world now, and Joey and I are more Anglo than not. I have to question why Joey wants to do this.''

''Maybe he needs a sense of who he is that he hasn't discovered so far. Maybe he needs a purpose he hasn't found. Maybe he needs it to find his manhood.''

Sara's head jerked a little, and she stared hard at him. ''Gideon?'' There was more in his words than a casually considered group of possible reasons for Joey's desire to participate in the grueling Sun Dance.

''Ah, hell.'' At the back of his mind, a flashback was trying to happen, a sense of splintering blue sky that kept dancing in the corners of his mind, a sensation of falling when he was lying perfectly still. ''Ah, hell,'' he said again. He needed to talk. His whole life long, he'd never really talked to anybody. Even Barney, his best friend, had never been a confidant. ''You're tired,'' he said, making one last attempt to keep from spilling his guts.

Somehow Sara knew. The impassioned speech about Joey finding himself had said an awful lot about Gideon Ironheart. Not so much in words that her ears had heard, but more in feelings that her heart had sensed. She lay down facing him, and before he could react in any way, she threw her long, bare leg over his denim-clad hips and wrapped her arm around his neck, drawing his head into the dark, warm hollow created by her shoulder and cheek. "I'm not too tired to listen."

"Ah, hell," he said roughly. "You don't want to hear this crap."

"I do," she murmured, tunneling her fingers into his long hair. "I want to hear anything you need to tell me. It's about Barney, isn't it? About his fall and your flashbacks."

"What are you? A mind reader?"

"Grandfather always taught me to see with my heart, not my eyes," Sara answered softly, while every cell in her body tensed for his inevitable rejection. She was pushing him, she knew, pushing him hard, and he would probably step down hard on her. But somewhere in her helpless, headlong tumble into love with this man, she had discovered a new kind of courage in herself, a courage to take emotional risks. For him she would expose herself to the reopening of the scar that had kept her in hiding for a decade.

To see with her heart. Slowly, slowly, Gideon relaxed against her, giving up the battle with himself. If she saw with her heart, then perhaps she could see through the pain that scoured him raw. Perhaps she could point the way to the other side of the spiritual chasm that yawned before him.

"I'm afraid," he said, his whisper husky. "It's not unusual for a man to be scared after a near miss. It happens to us all, and for a time we work on the ground, until we feel ready to go up again. Nobody thinks anything of it. It's normal. Natural."

Sara's hand never stopped moving, just kept combing soothingly through his hair. "I should think so," she murmured when it seemed he needed some kind of response. "Only a fool wouldn't have some kind of reaction."

"Yeah. Most of the time it only takes a week or two. But...I can't go up at all anymore. Hell, I even get vertigo in the barn loft. I'm not sure I could handle a drainage ditch, to tell you the truth.''

None of this sounded so very terrible on the face of it, but, listening with her heart, Sara heard something else. Something more. She heard what had happened to his self-confidence, his self-image, his identity. In one fell swoop Gideon had lost his best friend, his career, his belief in himself, and an essential part of his manhood: his courage. Or what he believed to be his courage.

It was on the tip of her tongue to point out that going up to the top of those buildings to walk those narrow beams in the first place had displayed a kind of courage few people ever had. And that in losing that courage he had merely come down to the level of the rest of the world. But that was easy to say, and it wouldn't help Gideon at all. He had lost something of himself, something he'd once had, something that had been an integral part of him. The fact that it was something most people never had was hardly going to mitigate the loss.

Finally, she said the only thing she could. "I'm sorry. That must really hurt.''

He nuzzled her shoulder, inhaling deeply of the scent of warm woman, the scent of Sara. Then, relaxing even more, he wrapped his own arms around her waist. After a while he spoke again.

"It's not that I want to be a connector again,'' he said slowly. "I'm too old, and there's no way on earth I'd do it even if I found a partner as good as Barney. I'd be a danger to him, because I'm slowing down. Barney and I would have had to quit soon. We both knew it. We were getting older, slower. Not enough to be dangerous yet, but enough that we couldn't pretend we weren't. We'd even begun to talk about working on the ground.''

Sara made an encouraging sound and let her hand wander lower, to the smooth, warm skin of his back.

"It's just that…'' He didn't know if there were even words to encompass all that he had lost along with Barney. "It's just that everything I ever knew, everything I ever believed about

myself, turned out to be an illusion. All of a sudden, there I
was with nothing. Absolutely nothing. As if everything I'd
done with the first forty years of my life was absolutely pointless. Why am I telling you this?''

"Because you need to. Because I want to listen."

He tilted his head back and looked her right in the eye. He
was suddenly angry with himself for spilling all this ridiculous
tripe on her, but just as suddenly his anger died. Something in
her soft brown eyes killed it. Something of understanding and
caring and concern. In that instant, he knew he had words to
say what he felt, and that she would understand them.

"Mouse," he said hoarsely, "I lost myself."

Her expression grew sad; the corners of her mouth turned
down. Her hand lifted from his shoulder to touch his cheek
gently, to trace the line of his strong jaw, then to cradle the
back of his head and draw him closer.

"Let me hold you," she whispered. "Let me hold you, because I've only just found you."

Somehow that seemed to make perfect sense. He wrapped
himself around her, wrapped her around him, and neither let
go of the other until the night was over.

Chapter 10

"We're going to have guests for dinner tonight," Sara announced. Three masculine heads at the breakfast table lifted from plates full of ham and eggs and looked at her. "I'll do the cooking, Grandfather."

"Don't be silly, child. I've been cooking for this household since you started working. *I'll* cook, and you'll help."

Sara laughed at the twinkle in her grandfather's eye. "I invited Micah and Faith Parish over. I asked Emma and Gage, too, but they couldn't make it. Emma has to speak to some library meeting or other in Cheyenne, so they'll be gone for a few days."

"Well, just ask them for next week," Zeke said. "It's been a while since we had guests." He was always pleased whenever Sara invited any of her friends over, and always encouraged her to do it more often.

"I'll do that." She glanced at Joey and found her brother looking indifferent. Well, he would probably just vanish right after dinner, so it wouldn't make a whole lot of difference to him. Looking past him to Gideon, Sara said, "You're invited, too, of course." In case he didn't realize that. "You said you wanted to meet Micah."

Gideon nodded briefly and fastened his attention on his plate. "Thanks," he managed to say. Moments later he shoved his chair back from the table and carried his half-eaten breakfast over to the sink. "I need to see to some stuff in town, Zeke. I took care of the livestock already, so there's nothing that can't wait until I get back." Snatching his hat from the peg, he stomped out of the kitchen.

"Well, what got into him?" Sara wondered aloud.

Zeke shrugged. "Time will tell, Sarey. Time will tell."

Muttering every oath he knew, Gideon drove down the rutted drive to the highway and wondered if he carried a personal curse of some kind. Maybe the fates were after him because he'd never listened to his grandfather, never lived up to the responsibility of the "power" people kept telling him he had.

All he knew, all he could remember, was holding Sara in his arms the night of their picnic, gently seducing her and himself, and asking about Micah. Silently encouraging her to offer to introduce him to Micah. He swore again and spun loose gravel out from beneath his tires. He didn't need to be a genius to know what Sara was going to think if she learned Micah was his brother.

But surely, he told himself, she would remember that he hadn't mentioned Micah again since that night almost two weeks ago. She *had* to realize by now that he wasn't making love to her because he wanted her to introduce him socially to Micah Parish. Surely.

Cursing again, he pulled off onto the road that led to Sara's favorite glade. Once there, he climbed out of the truck, walked through the thick wildflowers, yellow ones now joining the paintbrushes, and sat cross-legged on a rock beside the snow-fed stream. Farther up the slope, a waterfall provided a soothing rush of sound.

He needed to go into the silence, he thought. It had been days since he had taken the time for his morning meditation, and he was sorely feeling the lack. His center seemed to be escaping his grasp along with his identity and his manhood. He was losing his hold on everything. Everything.

So he closed his eyes and dove inward, seeking the deep, quiet pool of his innermost self, that place from which all the rest of him sprang. He was in desperate need of an anchor to hang on to, a piece of solid ground on which to stand. Without that, he couldn't even hope to begin rebuilding his life.

Gideon watched from the window of the bunkhouse as Micah Parish and his family arrived. Faith Parish was every bit as small and blond as Sara had said, so tiny beside her large husband that she looked like a sprite, almost insubstantial. And it was obvious from the way the big man hovered over her that she was the center of his world and the light of his life.

Gideon smiled in spite of himself and felt a painful yearning tug in the vicinity of his breastbone. He ignored it, wondering what he was going to do about Micah. The question had settled onto the back burner lately while he'd been busy working the ranch, worrying about Zeke and getting to know Sara. Now it couldn't be ignored any longer.

He had come to Conard County with the best of intentions, wanting only to learn something of the brother he had never known, never intending to disrupt any lives. He had convinced himself that if he said nothing, no one would be hurt.

With each passing day, however, his silence looked less like wisdom and grew closer to deception. At the beginning he had told himself that he only wanted to know a little about Micah, to see him for himself, but not to establish any kind of relationship with him. After all, if Micah or their father, Amory Parish, had ever had any interest in what had happened to Gideon, surely it would have showed by now.

He felt, he thought, something like a kid who'd been adopted, needing to know something about his real roots, but aware that his interest might be very unwelcome. Coming anonymously to Conard County and saying nothing to Micah had initially seemed like a matter of respecting Micah's privacy. It had also seemed like a way to protect his own. What if Micah had turned out to be a man he wouldn't want to know?

Gideon sighed, thinking his reasons sounded awfully flimsy now. And the closer he grew to Sara and Zeke, the worse it got.

His grandfather, he felt suddenly, would probably have had his hide for a stunt like this. For all his faults, the old Cherokee medicine man had been unfailingly honest with himself and all those with whom he dealt. Without a doubt, he would have told Gideon that nothing justified deception.

"Ah, hell." And he still hadn't decided whether to tell Micah the truth. All he knew was that the longer he waited, the tougher it was going to get.

"Hell," he said again, and turned from the window. Time to go up to the house before his tardiness became remarkable.

Everyone except Joey had gathered in the living room. For a moment Gideon stood unnoticed on the threshold between the dining room and living room, and he took the opportunity to study his new sister-in-law. She was every bit the fairy-tale princess Sara had said, tiny, blond and lovely. She watched Micah with adoring eyes when he spoke, and cradled her child close to her breast.

And again Gideon felt that strange pang of longing.

"Gideon!" Sara spied him and smiled. "We've been wondering where you were. You know Micah, of course, and this is his wife, Faith, and their daughter, Sally."

Micah rose to shake his hand. For an instant, a split second so brief it might almost never have happened, their eyes locked, and Gideon felt something pass between them. Something beyond words.

Then he was treated to the full effect of Faith Parish's shining blue eyes and brilliant smile. And, irresistibly, he was drawn to squat and bend over the baby. A pair of blue eyes stared back at him from a frame of pink blanket and fragile skin. A tiny rosebud mouth opened in a yawn.

"She's beautiful," he told Faith, and reached out to touch one tiny fist. "Three months?"

"Three and a half. How could you tell that? Most men aren't very interested in babies."

He glanced at Faith's smiling face and felt himself grinning back. "I have six cousins who have a slew of kids. Every time I go home to Oklahoma, I wind up baby-sitting, and so far there's always been an infant or two in the bunch."

"Wonderful," said Faith, and she leaned forward, depositing Sally in Gideon's surprised arms. "I'm not above taking advantage of you." She laughed and smiled winningly. "If you don't mind, of course."

"I don't mind." He looked down at the small bundle he now held and felt a stupid grin grow on his face. "She's a heartbreaker, all right. I'm already in love."

Conversation resumed and flowed around him, but he only half heard. He supposed it wasn't something most men would admit—or even feel—but he got a kick out of babies and kids. That was why he always wound up baby-sitting when he went home, and it was never a chore. His cousins' wives had swiftly learned that Gideon was a sucker for babies, and there was never a family gathering where his arms weren't full of one infant or another.

He was still holding Sally when they moved into the dining room for dinner, and he assured Faith that he was quite content to continue holding her. He felt Micah's eyes on him, but the man didn't say anything. Sara seemed equally fascinated by Gideon's fascination with Sally, and when he glanced her way, he saw a soft warmth in her brown eyes that made him ache in some indefinable way.

Conversation wandered around the weather, passed over the assault on Zeke, and finally settled on the plans being made for this year's Fourth of July celebration. There was to be a picnic down by Conard Creek, where the Cattlemen's Association was planning to barbecue beef ribs for all comers. The Jaycees were organizing a parade, and a memorial service would be held afterward in the Courthouse Square.

The only fly in the ointment appeared to be Micah himself.

He was refusing to don his uniform, his green beret and all his medals, and give a speech.

"I don't give speeches," he said now.

"It's more than that," Faith said, utterly unintimidated by the dark look her husband sent her. "You'll never convince Micah he's any kind of hero, so he doesn't want to be treated like one."

Micah scowled and said, "Actually, I just don't want to cut my hair."

Gideon chuckled. "After twenty years of G.I. haircuts, I can understand it."

Micah flashed him a faint smile.

Sara spoke. "I really don't think anyone would expect you to cut your hair just for a couple of hours in uniform."

"I would," Micah answered.

Faith threw up her hands. "You see, Sara? He's impossible!"

Just as dessert was served, Sally decided she was hungry and began to holler for her mother. Faith immediately came to the rescue, taking her daughter into the living room to feed her. Gideon's arms felt empty without the baby.

"I miss her already," he said to Micah. "She's cute as a button."

Micah fixed him with a stare. "She could sure use an uncle."

Heat, then cold, washed through Gideon in waves as he stared into obsidian eyes. Shocked, he understood.

Micah already knew they were brothers.

Zeke refused all offers of help cleaning up the meal, insisting that he and Joey would take care of it. Sara and Faith he shooed into the living room with coffee. Then he looked at Micah and Gideon, seeming to know they had a secret they had not yet shared.

"You two need to take a walk. Go."

Micah and Gideon looked at one another, Micah impassive,

Gideon uneasy, uncertain whether he was angry or relieved. As one, they turned toward the kitchen and the back door.

Outside, the spring night had already settled in, and a chilly breeze blew off the mountaintops. Micah wore a flannel shirt and seemed impervious. Gideon doubted he would ever feel any colder than he had felt in that moment of shock.

"Want to walk?" he asked. "Or go talk in the bunkhouse?"

"Walk," Micah said. Then, "You know."

"Yeah, I know." And now he was feeling angry that Micah had known about him and done nothing. It was the rejection he had felt all his life long, and now it was being inflicted again.

"Did you know when you arrived here?" Micah asked.

"Yes." They headed down the driveway, each walking in a separate but parallel rut.

Micah shoved his thumbs into his front pockets, looking for all the world like a man out for a casual stroll. "Why didn't you say anything?"

For a minute Gideon didn't know how to react to that. In the depths of his hurt anger, he realized that Micah was asking him the question he wanted to ask Micah. And somehow he managed to shrug, as if none of this was as important as it suddenly felt. "None of it seems to make much sense right now. I wasn't sure you knew you had a brother. I wasn't sure that, even if you did, you would want to meet me. I wasn't sure I would want to know you. It just seemed more sensible at the time to wait and do a little reconnaissance before taking an irrevocable step."

"I can see that." For a while they walked on in silence; then Micah spoke again. "That doesn't explain why you stayed silent."

Gideon halted abruptly and faced him, old hurts suddenly fresh and sharp. Micah, too, stopped, and they stared at one another, separated by a gulf that neither was really sure he wanted to cross.

"Our mother," Gideon said tightly, "died when I was just over two. I was raised in an orphanage until the age of twelve, when one of the nuns managed to track down my uncle. From then until now, there was never any indication that our *father* gave a damn if I was alive or dead.''

Micah nodded and tipped his head back, studying the stars. ''I felt the same way about our mother.''

Gideon was struck. Somehow he had never imagined that, and now he felt stupid because of it.

Micah continued his survey of the heavens. ''I knew you existed, probably because I was older and had some kind of memory of you before our mother left with you. I asked Dad about it once when I was maybe seven or eight. He said they had agreed to each take one child rather than one of them having to lose us both.''

Gideon yielded a long breath and let go of an old, old tension. It somehow didn't sound as bad when put that way. ''But he didn't keep in touch?''

''He said he tried once but was told she was dead. I don't know if that's true or not.'' Micah lowered his gaze to Gideon. ''Our father was not... Well, hell. Fact of it is, he wasn't much of a father. Oh, from time to time he got his father duds on and gave me a lecture about something. Once he even told me not to be ashamed of my ancestry, because on our mother's side I was descended from powerful medicine men.''

''That's true.''

Micah shrugged. ''The point is, that was the extent of his fathering. He was a cold man, Ironheart. If you want the honest truth, he didn't have enough heart to make an attempt to keep after you or our mother. He would probably have been just as happy if she'd taken me, too, the way it felt at times. At best, I think he never forgave her for leaving. Anyhow, by the time I got old enough to ask any serious questions about you, he didn't remember anything useful, and then he died. And truthfully, it seemed like a lot of water over the dam at that point.''

Gideon nodded his understanding. Except for Barney's death, he never would have felt compelled to look for Micah. He started walking again, and Micah followed suit. What he had learned was hardly a blinding revelation, but it helped him understand.

"Our grandfather didn't help matters," Gideon said. "He declared our mother dead when she married our father. Maybe that explains why he only once attempted to get in touch with her."

"Could be. Did the old man ever come around?"

"By the time my uncle took me from the orphanage, he'd lived to regret banishing her."

Micah swore. "Never ceases to amaze me how people can mess things up. Things would just be so simple if folks would let them."

They walked on a little farther in silence, then Gideon asked, "How did you know who I was?"

"I heard there was a half-breed Cherokee named Gideon Ironheart in town. That got me wondering, because I knew I had a brother named Gideon. Then I saw you. Don't know if this will bother you or not, but you got our father's eyes. I'd've recognized 'em just about anywhere."

"You've known that long?"

"Yep." He glanced over at Gideon. "You weren't saying anything, though, and I wasn't sure you knew. Faith was sure, though. That's why she dumped Sally in your arms tonight. She's been fretting that Sally wouldn't have any relatives, and now she's bound and determined you're going to be the baby's uncle. And I'd better warn you—when Faith makes up her mind, there's no deterring her. I've tried."

Gideon couldn't help the chuckle that escaped him. The image of Micah being helpless before the determination of his tiny wife was inescapably amusing. "I'm being adopted?"

"Reckon so," Micah agreed.

Gideon tilted his head back, pretending to study the stars while he tried to cope with an unexpected tidal wave of feeling. His throat ached, and his chest felt almost too tight to breathe, as some ancient hurt began to let go. Then Micah astonished him by briefly clapping a hand to his shoulder.

"I told you," he said to Gideon, "life is really very simple.

It's pointless to make it complicated. We're brothers. Whether that will become anything more than a word is something only time will tell.''

Gideon managed at last to draw a long breath. He faced Micah. "Just play out the hand and see what happens?"

Micah nodded. "I spent my whole life telling myself I preferred to be alone. Faith convinced me I didn't really mean that. Reckon there's room for a couple more good folks, too.''

Sara was right, Gideon found himself thinking. Micah Parish had made peace with himself. And Gideon felt a stab of painful envy. He forced it down. "Faith is quite a steamroller, huh?"

Micah laughed, a rare sound from the silent man. "You wouldn't believe one little moonbeam could throw her weight around the way she does. Take a word of advice, Ironheart. Don't even *think* of arguing with her about anything.''

Sara's face was full of questions, but Gideon ignored them. After saying good-night, he turned and headed toward the meadow, thinking he would take a stroll and try to get his thoughts in order. He hadn't asked Sara to come to him tonight, so he was pretty sure she wouldn't. She didn't have enough self-confidence to push him. Another time that would have bothered him, but right now it was merely a relief. He had too many personal demons he needed to face tonight. He didn't have anything left over for anyone else.

On the far side of the meadow, well away from curious eyes, he settled onto a flat boulder at the base of a tall pine and leaned back, drawing one knee up to rest his elbow on it. Around him the pines whispered of things lost and found, of things to be learned and unlearned. An owl hooted eerily from somewhere above, and then the sense of something silent passing in the dark came to him.

The sense of anticlimax was inevitable, he supposed. His discussion with Micah had been fraught with little of the intensity he had expected. Instead, they had behaved like two civilized men discussing the antics of people they had never understood. And somehow, as a result, the bitterness he had carried with him for so many years suddenly felt childish, self-indulgent, foolish.

They would never know, now, what had driven their parents to behave as they did. Nor did it really matter. All of that was water over the dam, as Micah had said, and that was the realization that made Gideon feel foolish.

Sitting there in the dark with only the stars, the wind and an owl for company, he faced the fact that he had allowed his life to be ruled by a confluence of events that had occurred at a point so early in his childhood that he could not even remember the time. He had no memory of his mother, and his father had been an ogre built out of childish resentment and a terrible sense of rejection. He had for a time even hated those who had come to his rescue, who had taken him in and tried to make up for their mistakes.

For his entire life, he had worn his hatred, anger and bitterness like a shield to keep others away, to prevent anyone getting close enough to reject him again. The way he had once believed everyone had rejected him.

But his mother hadn't rejected him; she had died. And his father had not rejected him either; he had simply failed, through a variety of reasons, to be there. Nor had his grandfather or uncle rejected him. Just as soon as they had learned where he was, they had come to get him.

Ironheart. That was what he had wished for. He had buried his feelings in places so deep he could hardly find them anymore. He had skimmed the surface of every damn thing like some kind of water skate, until Barney's death had yanked him down into the depths of painful reality.

He hadn't lost himself because of Barney's death. No, he'd lost himself a long, long time ago. Barney's death had just made him aware of it.

He wasn't sure what alerted him. He was still sitting on his rock, doing some long-overdue thinking, when it was as if the atmospheric pressure changed. The wind was rustling in the treetops too loudly for any but the loudest sounds to reach him, but still he felt as if he had heard something.

Leaning forward intently, he strained every sense, convinced somehow that he was no longer alone out here. And the first thing, the very first thing, that occurred to him, was that Zeke's attacker had come back for some reason.

But why would he? Zeke and Sara had very little apart from their land. There wasn't a thing in that house worth stealing, as the perpetrator had evidently discovered his first time through. And if he had wanted anything of value, why hadn't he taken Gideon's Zuni belt buckle?

He strained his eyes, telling himself that it was late, that he had probably just dozed and dreamed without realizing it. But still he couldn't shake the conviction that someone else was out here.

All the lights below were out now, indicating that everyone was in bed. Glancing at his watch, tipping it this way and that, he finally managed to see that it was after midnight. Definitely too late for someone to be stirring.

Sara. Perhaps Sara had gone to the bunkhouse looking for him, after all. The thought brought him instantly to his feet. He was halfway across the meadow before a warning prickle caused him to stop and stare into the dark ahead of him. The starlight provided scant illumination, but enough to make the familiar shapes of the house and barn visible.

And then, against the light tan color of Sara's police Blazer, he saw a low, crouching shadow move.

There was no way on earth Sara would be skulking like that in her own yard. Moving as quietly as he could, counting on the rustling wind to cover any inadvertent sounds he made, Gideon hurried forward. Whoever was down there in the yard wouldn't be expecting anyone to come from this direction, and he was counting on that to keep him undiscovered until he got closer.

And it did. He made it to the rear of the bunkhouse without being spotted. Then, working his way carefully around, he looked into the yard. The shadow was still there, and he could swear it was checking out Sara's vehicle, looking for something.

Or tampering with something....

A flicker of light betrayed that the shadow was using a small flashlight. He was definitely looking around under the Blazer.

Gideon measured the distance between himself and the vehicle. Maybe twenty yards. If he alerted the guy to his presence right now, the man would probably get away. Gideon might be in great shape, but he was no world-class sprinter, and cowboy boots were the devil's own invention when it came to running. He spared an instant to wish he was wearing his work boots instead.

He eased out of the shadows around the bunkhouse and headed across the yard at a steady, quiet walk, figuring to get as close as he could before he was noticed. *Then* he'd charge.

Later, Gideon was to consider his own stupidity with disgust. At the time, though, he was merely amazed that he got as close as he did without the other man becoming aware of him.

But the other man *was* aware of him, and when Gideon was almost on him, he rose in a fast, blinding whirl and struck out, catching Gideon in the side of the head with something hard and heavy. Then he took off at a dead run down the driveway.

Gideon swore, battling a momentary confusion resulting from the unexpected blow. Then, damning his cowboy boots, he charged after the assailant.

For a hundred yards, two hundred, they ran down the rutted driveway, the other man managing to keep a good lead. And then Gideon began to gain on him. The other man was tiring, he thought, ignoring the fire that seared his own lungs as he struggled for added oxygen. Damned if that bastard was going to get away!

Just as he was almost close enough to make a leaping tackle, the guy swung around. Gideon had just enough time to throw up his left arm in front of his face to block the blow. Something as solid and heavy as a lead pipe connected with his forearm, and shock waves of pain shot up his entire arm. He glimpsed another swing coming his way and ducked, but as he did so, he stepped into a rut and went sprawling, getting a solid, crippling blow to his solar plexus when he hit the ground.

His assailant took off again, evidently not having murder on his mind. Gideon lay there, struggling to get his diaphragm to work, struggling to get air into his lungs, and wondered why he had ever been so stupid as to think he might be cut out to be a hero. He should have scared the guy off and gone in to call the cops. Or at least to get Sara to unlock her damn gun and go after him in a vehicle. That would have accomplished a hell of a lot more than chasing after him on foot in the dark. Idiot!

"Oh, God," he muttered as he dragged in the first few lungfuls of blessed air. "Oh, God." But now that he could breathe, his arm sent excruciating signals flashing to his brain. For a moment all he could do was roll onto his side and hold his arm like a baby while a long moan escaped him. Fighting ten guys in a parking lot had never hurt quite this badly.

Some damn hero!

At last he rolled to his knees and managed to get to his feet while cradling his arm. The damn thing was broken. Of that he had not the least doubt. Over the years he'd managed to break a bone or two, and he knew the sensation. Well, once it was set it wouldn't be much of a problem.

He was feeling a little ragged, he thought as he made his way back to the house. Not quite with-it. When he reached the yard, he considered going to bed and waiting until morning to ask someone to drive him to the hospital. But then he staggered to one side and realized he was feeling a little drunk. Maybe it wouldn't be smart to wait.

Just then the kitchen porch light flipped on and Sara stood there, .45 in hand, looking ready for anything, even in her terry-cloth bathrobe. Damn, she was one hell of a woman, Gideon thought groggily. If he'd known they grew them like her in Wyoming, he would have headed this way years ago.

"Gideon?" Sara stepped out onto the porch. "I heard something— Oh, my God! What happened to you?"

She was off the porch in a shot, and the next thing he knew, her arm was around his waist and she was guiding him up the steps, across the porch and into the kitchen.

"Sit down," she said, helping him ease onto a chair. "My God, your head...."

His head? He looked at her, wondering what she was talking about. "My arm's broken, I think."

"We'll take care of that if you don't bleed to death."

Bleed? That was when he realized his head was aching fit to burst. Turning a little, he looked at himself and saw that his entire right side was covered in blood. "Where'd that come from?" he said.

"Oh, my God," Sara said again, and this time she sounded as if she was going to cry. Taking a clean dish towel, she pressed it to the side of his scalp. "I've got to get you to the hospital. Can you hold this towel on your head while I wake up Joey?"

"Sure." Anything the lady wanted. "Don't drive your car," he said, wondering why his words seemed to be running together.

"What?" She leaned back and stared at him. "Why not?"

"Somebody...fooling with it."

"The person who hurt you?"

"Yeah." Then he set his broken arm on the table and reached up with his right hand to hold the towel. "I'll be okay, Sara," he said seriously.

"Oh, Gideon," Sara said, and leaned forward, kissing his cheek. "Of course you will," she whispered. "You have to be. I only just found you."

Then she turned swiftly and disappeared from the kitchen.

He never lost consciousness, although for a while he wasn't very far from losing it. He was aware of Sara calling the sheriff's department to report the incident while Joey went out to the bunkhouse to get Gideon's truck keys. He'd managed to get the point across that they needed to take his truck, not Sara's vehicle, which might have been tampered with. He was too far out of it to realize that his own might have been tampered with also.

Joey, however, wasn't. He took a flashlight out and went over Gideon's truck while Sara talked to a deputy on the phone and Zeke applied pressure to the wound on Gideon's head.

He was aware of a low-voice fight between Zeke and Sara.

"I don't want you staying here alone, Grandfather. Something is going on, and I don't want you hurt again."

"I'll lock the doors and get the gun, Sarey," Zeke told her. "I'll be just fine until the deputy gets here."

"But, Grandfather—"

"Look, Joey's ready. Just get Ironheart to the hospital."

By the time he'd been x-rayed, had his scalp stitched up and a cast put on his forearm, Gideon's head had pretty much cleared up. Doc Randall was agreeable to releasing him, so Gideon was able to pull on his blood-crusted shirt and skedaddle.

Joey was out in the waiting room, and he eyed Gideon doubtfully, shaking his head. "Man, you don't look so good."

"I'm better than I was a little while ago. My head still feels like somebody's beating on it, though. Where's Sara?"

"Ladies' room. She'll be right back. So your arm's broken? But not your head?"

"Not my head. I think it's almost as hard as yours."

That surprised a crack of laughter out of Joey, who grinned at him. No, thought Gideon, this boy wasn't bad at heart. So what was going on?

Sara smiled when she saw him, relief and concern apparent in her face and eyes. "How do you feel? Are you okay? What did Doc Randall say?"

"That my arm is broken, that my head is harder than steel, and that I'll live. We both agreed that guy must've been swinging a lead pipe, though."

Sara drew a sharp breath. "Do you want to tell me exactly what happened?"

Gideon looked down at her and thought of all the things he

wanted to do, and none of them involved discussing the night's events. They were more like curling up in his bed with a naked Sara Yates beside him, with her soothing, enticing, wicked little hands doing soothing, arousing, devilish little things.

"Now?" he said. "Here?"

Her chin took on a mulish set, belying the worry in her eyes. She had her moments, Gideon thought. "Or at the office."

He sighed. "This is official, huh?"

Sara nodded. "You can talk to another officer, if you prefer." And if he did, she would kill him. This had happened on *her* property, after all, and had already involved her family.

"Why would I want to talk to anybody but you, Mouse?" he asked, ignoring Joey's interested look. "Okay. But can't we go someplace where we can sit and have some coffee?" Truth was, he was still feeling a little ragged, maybe from blood loss.

"Let's go over to the office, then. I can fill out the paperwork while we talk."

"Fair enough." Anything was better than hanging around in this lobby looking like an escapee from *Halloween.*

The coffeemaker at the Sheriff's office had been cleaned out and stood ready to brew. Sara asked Joey to make the pot while she and Gideon settled down at the front desk. Sara found a yellow pad in the bottom drawer and pulled it out, and from a cup at the dispatcher's desk she retrieved a black felt-tip pen.

Gideon held up his injured arm and said with all the appeal of a small boy, "Will you sign my cast? Please?"

It was as if he had pulled a plug. All of a sudden the tension went out of Sara, and she looked at him with huge, luminous eyes. "I was so worried," she whispered. "So worried."

Gideon lowered his arm. "I'm sorry. I acted like a grade-A jackass, going after the guy, and I probably got less than I deserved. All I could think of was that somebody was tampering with your Blazer, maybe with intent to do harm, and I guess I saw red. Or something. I sure wasn't thinking clearly." He had in fact reacted instinctively to protect Sara. He wasn't sure thought had entered into it at all.

That wasn't like him. He had fast reflexes and swift responses to danger, developed by twenty years at the top, but as a rule, he didn't go leaping *into* danger without thinking things through first. No connector did, if he wanted to live long. But tonight he had. For Sara.

The awareness settled into him uneasily, but he was too damned tired to think about it now. Nor was he sure he wanted to think about it at all. He suspected the reasons behind his behavior were not going to make him happy.

"Tell me what happened," Sara said, drawing the pad closer. She was all business now. All deputy.

So he told her. From the moment he was hit in the side of the head, though, his memory of events had become fuzzy, and he could give her only the highlights of his ill-fated chase. One concern stuck forcibly in his mind, though.

"Has someone checked out your Blazer?"

"Not yet. It's too dark. They'll look it over in the morning. You don't remember anything at all about your assailant that might help us identify him?"

It had been dark—too dark, really—to get more than a blurred impression of anything. He shook his head slowly, only saying, "Just that he was big, maybe my height. Heavyset."

"Fat?" Sara queried.

Gideon hesitated, and shrugged as he looked at Joey, who was listening intently. "Not really. Broad, solid." He gave Sara a rueful smile. "Of course, my mental image of him may have been affected by the damage he did to me. The guy who beats you bloody is *always* bigger, by definition."

By the time they arrived back at the Double Y, Gideon felt as if he'd tangled with a gorilla. His arm ached fiercely, his head ached worse, and the bruise on his solar plexus was beginning to throb in time to his pulse. All he wanted to do was crawl into his bed and sleep off the worst of the pain.

In no mood to wrestle one-handed with his clothes, he simply lay down on his bed fully clothed and closed his eyes. It was nearly dawn, and he should have fallen asleep effortlessly, but his mind was in high gear and wouldn't slow down.

Fact: Little more than a week ago, Zeke had been brutally attacked, and the house and bunkhouse had been searched but nothing taken.

Fact: Tonight someone had been prowling around Sara's vehicle and possibly other vehicles in the dead of night.

Conclusion: Somebody was looking for something at the Double Y.

But what? Something that might be hidden in the undercarriage of a vehicle? Something small?

Hell, it could be just about anything, he supposed. The real question was what anybody on the Double Y might have that would arouse such interest. And why they had beaten Zeke so badly, yet tonight had come stealthily. Had they thought Zeke might tell them something? But Zeke seemed to have no earthly notion what anyone could be looking for.

"Gideon?" It was an almost soundless whisper.

Opening his eyes, he saw Sara standing hesitantly in the bedroom doorway, just visible in the first early glow of coming dawn. She was still fully dressed, and he suspected she wasn't sleeping any better than he was. Too much had happened that shouldn't have happened.

"I'm awake, Mouse. Come here."

Moments later she was curled up against his good side, her head tucked on his shoulder. Turning his head just a little, he could feel the silkiness of her beautiful hair and fill himself with her wonderful scent. Now, he thought, he could sleep.

An alarm sounded somewhere at the back of his mind, but sleep was already washing over him, muffling it, making it seem unimportant.

Sara was here, and now he could sleep. Nothing else mattered.

Chapter 11

Zeke and Chester were building a sweat lodge, and Gideon had the not quite comfortable feeling that he was going to be drafted into using it along with them. After last night's events, the two elderly men had evidently decided that some help was needed, and that started with *Inipi,* Chester explained. Purification. Then he and Zeke would ask for help in *Yuwipi,* a spirit-calling ceremony.

With his arm in a sling, there wasn't a whole lot Gideon could do except watch. Not that anyone would let him. Joey took care of the chores, and Zeke and Chester took care of the Stone-People-Lodge, as they called the sweat lodge. Together they cleared a circle of ground at the back of the meadow, and in it measured another circle, which was dug out to make a shallow bowl. Then they paced off ten steps to the east and dug another hole, this one deeper, in which they would heat the rocks for the sweat, they said. This was called the Fire of No End. By this time, both men were so busy they quit explaining, and anyway, Gideon was content to watch and offer his one good hand where he could.

"The lodge must always face east," Chester said as he and Zeke began erecting the willow saplings that would frame the building. "From there comes the light of knowledge."

Gideon helped hold one of the saplings in a bowed position while Zeke tied it to another. "Don't you need a holy man to do this?"

Zeke chuckled, and Chester regarded him with dark, twinkling eyes. "I *am* a holy man," Chester said. "I'm all we need. Offer me a pipe, Ironheart, so we can get you started on your quest."

Hell, thought Gideon, now Zeke even had Chester doing it. Disgruntled, he walked back to the house to get himself a glass of water. Just as he reached the porch, thinking about filling a water jug and taking it up the meadow to Chester and Zeke, Sara returned to the yard in her own Blazer. Early this morning it had been towed to town to be checked over, and apparently now had a clean bill of health.

"Did they find anything?" he asked Sara when she climbed out.

"Nope. Somebody looked, but he didn't mess with anything."

"No prints?"

"Nope."

He realized suddenly that he was watching her stiff back as she stalked toward the house. Something was wrong. This was not the woman who had smiled sleepily in his arms only a few hours ago and then proceeded to take his battered, aching body to heaven with nothing but the gentle touch of her hands and mouth. God, the mere memory of that zinged through him like wildfire!

But...she was disappearing stiffly into the house, and he had to find out what was wrong. She had her back to him when he entered the kitchen.

"Sara?"

She didn't turn to look at him. "Yes?"

"What's wrong?"

For an endless time it seemed she would not answer. When

finally she did, she still wouldn't look at him. "I saw Faith Parish in town this morning."

His stomach sank to his boots, and he no longer had any doubt what was coming. Nor did he have any defense.

"She thought I knew you and Micah were brothers," Sara said tightly. "Do you have any idea how embarrassing it was that I didn't?" Even now she remembered the cold sensation of shock that had made her nearly dizzy as she realized that she knew nothing about this man to whom she had given her heart. As she realized that he was keeping secrets. That he was using her.

"Sara, I—" Oh, God!

She whirled suddenly and faced him, angry and hurt beyond belief. "Shut up, Ironheart! I don't want to hear your excuses. I felt a little better when I learned that you hadn't even told Micah, but that didn't last long because I...because I—" She broke off and drew a long, shuddering breath before she could continue. "Then I remembered how you wanted me to introduce him to you. How you used me—*seduced* me—into doing what you wanted."

"Sara, please—"

"No, Gideon. I don't want to hear it. Were you ever going to tell any of us? Or were you just going to use us all?"

She hadn't given him an opportunity to answer, and he supposed at this point she wasn't really interested in anything he had to say, anyway.

He considered leaving. He even went so far as to dig his duffel bag out of the closet. It didn't seem right to stay around when Sara was so hurt and angry at him. She would feel better if he moved on and got out of her life.

But as he reached for the bag with his one good hand, he hesitated. He was always assuming people would be better off without him, that they would prefer him to vanish from their lives. And always, when he felt that way, he moved on.

But maybe Sara *wouldn't* feel better if he left. Maybe that would only confirm for her that she had meant nothing at all to him. Maybe it would harden her belief that he had simply used her. Maybe it would humiliate her every bit as much as George's defection years ago.

Maybe Sara Yates needed somebody to stick around and fight back. Maybe she needed some proof that he'd forgotten all about using her long before he had made love to her. Maybe she needed to know she meant something to him, meant enough that he would stick around through the rough times.

Slowly he sank onto the edge of his bed and thought about it. Maybe Sara needed from him all the things he had always wanted for himself.

All the things he didn't believe in.

Sara had thought that George had taught her what it meant to be hurt. Now she knew better. Nothing on earth could possibly hurt as much as Gideon's betrayal. Her throat felt as tight as if a noose were tied around it, and she was sure she would never dare speak again for fear of bursting into tears.

Sorrow tightened her chest, too, like a vise, and made even the simplest act seem difficult. From her bedroom window she could see Gideon crossing the meadow to where Zeke and Chester were building the sweat lodge and wondered if he would tell them of his deception. He had used them all.

Etched in acid on her brain was the memory of Faith Parish this morning on the sidewalk, her baby in her arms, bubbling cheerfully and obliviously about how wonderful it was that Micah and Gideon had found one another, how simply fantastic that Micah had a whole family he had never even met. How, if Gideon were any example of the Oklahoma Lightfoots, they would all be wonderful people.

And how she herself had stood there listening to Faith, frozen almost to ice in the middle of a day that had turned into a nightmare. How she had since wondered how many other secrets Gideon was keeping. A wife, perhaps? A dozen children? Maybe that was the real reason he was a "tumbleweed."

And then the horrible, horrible realization that she had been used. That Gideon had sought her out because she worked with Micah.

She drew a long, shaky breath and tried to tell herself it didn't matter. This had merely been a reinforcement of a lesson she had learned long ago, and she had only herself to blame for giving her heart to a drifter. At least he'd warned her about that much. At least he hadn't tried to make her think he would stay.

In fact, she admitted with bitter honesty, he hadn't promised her one damn thing. *She* was the one who had given him more than he had ever asked for. If she had heeded his warning, she wouldn't be hurting half so badly right now.

Like so many women before her, she had fallen into the oldest trap in the world, she thought miserably. She had been foolish enough to think her love could make a rolling stone stay. Foolish enough to think that he would become what she needed him to be.

Lies or no lies, what she was feeling right now was all her own fault.

That knowledge didn't make it one bit easier to take.

By midafternoon Zeke and Chester had nearly finished the lodge. Neither man had any buffalo skins, which would traditionally have covered the frame, so trade cloth was used.

"Tomorrow," said Chester finally, nodding approval. Then he got into his thirty-year-old pickup truck and departed.

"Now," said Zeke, looking at Gideon, "you'll make your *Chanunpa,* your own sacred pipe."

Gideon shook his head. "I've got other things on my mind, Zeke."

For a long moment the old Shoshone regarded him intently, with black eyes as piercing as arrows. Gideon knew that look and felt as exposed as an upended turtle. "Zeke, Sara is...furious with me. With good reason. And right now I just don't want to think about sacred pipes and vision quests and sweats."

"I don't want you to *think* about sacred pipes or any of the rest of it," Zeke said. "I just want you to *do* it. So I'll give you the pipe I started for you, and you can finish it."

"I've only got one arm."

"It's enough. You only need to do a little carving. I even have the knives for you to use."

"Zeke…"

Zeke silenced him with a wave of his hand. "You do it, boy. You carve something on the pipe and it'll be yours. Do it. And while you're doing it, stop thinking with your head. It's been getting in your way for as long as you've been here. I'll get the pipe."

Frustrated, Gideon stared after him and resigned himself to his fate. It appeared he was going to carve a pipe whether he wanted to or not.

Several paces away, Zeke suddenly halted and faced him once more. "Ironheart."

"Mmm?"

"Sara's thinking with her head right now. In a little while she'll start thinking with her heart. Be sure that *you're* doing the same."

Thinking with head or heart, what was the difference? Gideon wondered irritably. Either way, Sara would be furious, and any explanation he could offer sounded pretty pathetic, even to his own ears. What had made so much sense two weeks ago right now seemed to fly in the face of all common sense.

Zeke showed up ten minutes later with the damn pipe. Settling on the bunkhouse step beside Gideon, he removed the hide wrapping from the half-made object. There were two pieces, the long, straight wood stem, and the red stone elbow that was the bowl.

"I drilled out the center of the stem and carved the bowl for you already," Zeke said. "I figured you wouldn't know how to do it."

"I don't know how to do *any* of this, old man."

Zeke chuckled softly. "You'll learn, boy. You'll learn. This first pipe you don't have to make entirely by yourself. When you make your next one, I'll show you step-by-step, including finding the right ash branch for the stem and getting the red stone for the bowl. Did you know there's only one place on earth where you can find that stone?''

Zeke shook his head. "Never guessed."

"White men call the place Pipestone, Minnesota. The Lakota say the buffaloes died there and shed their blood so that we could live. But I'll tell you all that at another time. Or better, get Chester to tell you. He knows a lot more than I do.

"Right now, all you have to do is carve something on the stem. A buffalo, or an eagle. Maybe a turtle. Whatever. Choose something not too difficult. All that matters is that you make it yours."

Then he picked up a second bundle and brought forth another pipe. In spite of his sour mood, Gideon drew a long, appreciative breath. This pipe was a work of art, intricately carved, decorated with feathers, stained and painted in beautiful colors.

"I made this," Zeke said. "I spent many, many hours on it when I was lonely, after my wife died, before Sarey needed me to come here. The work helped me to see with my heart when my head would only grieve. Someday, Ironheart, you will make a pipe this beautiful. But for now, just make a pipe. Any pipe. Tonight."

Gideon picked up his pipe stem and moved it around until he figured out how best to brace it so he could work on it. Anything, he told himself, was better than doing nothing.

Sara had already started dinner when Zeke returned to the house. Industriously, she was chopping and peeling and dicing for stew. Zeke paused to wash his hands at the kitchen sink.

"I'll do that," he said.

"I'll do it. You worked hard this afternoon on the sweat lodge."

"And you work hard all the rest of the time."

Sara turned and pointed at him with her peeler. "Sit down, Grandfather. Have some tea."

The old man smiled. "Yes, Granddaughter. How very respectful of your elders you are."

"I didn't say one disrespectful thing."

"No, but you were thinking of it."

Sara's smile appeared reluctantly. "Go on. Relax."

He didn't speak again until he was seated at the table with a tall glass of ice tea. "Joey's taking longer than I thought he would, fixing that fence."

"Where'd he go?"

"Up by the falls." Every spring, snow runoff softened the ground and made the fence near the falls sag, and every spring it had to be shored up again.

"Well, he probably got hot and decided to take a little dip. Or just to play hooky." It wouldn't be the first time.

"Maybe."

"I wish he hadn't gone up there by himself."

Zeke sighed. "Sarey, we can't live like prisoners because of what has happened. Besides, whatever they were looking for is something they expected to find in the house or one of the cars. And they always come in the dark. There's no reason why they should bother Joey when he's mending the fence."

True, thought Sara, and let it go. She was only trying to distract herself, anyway, from thoughts of Gideon's betrayal, from noticing how badly she hurt and how empty she felt. "Did Gideon tell you about Micah?"

"Yes."

"You don't feel used or betrayed?" She turned to look at her grandfather.

"No. I can see why he wanted to keep his secret until he was sure of the kind of man Micah is."

"But he used me to meet Micah!"

Zeke's expression never changed. "Did he? Did he really?"

Frustrated, Sara turned back to making the stew. Zeke could be absolutely infuriating when he got into one of his inscrutable moods. Sometimes she felt as if she were living with Socrates and was caught up in some kind of philosophical dialogue. It was maddening!

A little while later her thoughts wandered over to the bunk-house, and she wondered what Gideon was doing. Packing his suitcases, maybe. And that made her think of the trunk of her grandfather's belongings.

"Grandfather? Why do you keep all your things over at the bunkhouse? Why did you pack your wedding picture?"

"Those things are keepsakes for you and Joey. They're meaningless to me."

She turned and looked at him. "How can you say that?"

"Because it's true. All that is important is in my memory, but the past is the past, Sara. One learns from it, perhaps cherishes it a little, but then must leave it behind. I loved your grandmother, child, but I cannot allow my grief over her death to color all the remaining days of my life. No one should allow the past to govern the future."

Sara swiftly turned back to her task, while a niggling little voice in the back of her mind asked: was that what she was doing? There seemed to be no answer beyond the uneasy sinking of her stomach.

Gideon looked down at the pipe stem in his hands and decided that the damn buffalo head looked as much like a buffalo as it ever would. At least the horns, however crooked, were identifiable. He set the knife down and brushed wood chips from his jeans, realizing with a sense of shock that several hours had passed. Now it was supper time.

He wasn't sure he should go up to the kitchen. Sara, he suspected, would be relieved if he didn't, and given his sense of iniquity, he wasn't sure he *ought* to. On the other hand, he was feeling more strongly than ever that he really needed to stick this one out, that for once in his life he shouldn't bail out of a relationship without making a stab at repairing the damage. That it was time to stop skating on the surface and face the currents underneath. Time, perhaps, to face the possibility that someone might need something from him...and that he might need something from them.

On the other hand, he found himself thinking, Sara hadn't

even given him a chance to explain what he'd done, which just proved the premise under which he had always functioned: people were fickle and wouldn't hesitate to drop you at the first provocation. She had drawn all her conclusions without asking him his side of the story.

And it hurt. Closing his eyes momentarily, he admitted to himself what he'd been refusing to face for two weeks now. He cared what Sara Yates thought of him, and it hurt that she had judged him without even asking his reasons. Not that his reasons justified his actions, he admitted with painful honesty, but if she cared about him, wouldn't she at least want to hear his side of it?

All of which led him right back to where he had begun years ago. Caring hurt, so he didn't want to care too deeply. And *love* was a word people used to manipulate one another. He'd fallen into that trap long, long ago. So long ago that the woman was only a dim memory of a blond, blue-eyed hussy he'd initially likened to a fairy princess, only to discover she more closely resembled a succubus.

Part of that mess, he acknowledged now, had arisen from his own youth and an overwhelming desire to be…loved. The word nearly stuck in his mental craw. Love had turned out to be a blond bimbo who was taking him for every cent he earned and ridiculing him to her friends. One who, when he had overheard her denigrating him, had turned on him with a scornful smile and proceeded to inflict verbal wounds to his soul. One who had come to know him well enough that she knew exactly what to say, exactly how to hurt him.

He had thought himself well past that episode until the other night when the words "half-breed savage" had spilled out of him. Some wounds, it seemed, never healed.

They were the legacy of love.

Sara Yates wasn't anything like that blond bimbo from twenty years ago, so he'd fallen into the trap again, he realized, the trap of wanting to be loved. And it was obvious now that she didn't love him. Not with the kind of love he'd always longed for and never believed in. If she had loved him that way, she might have been angry at his deceit, but she wouldn't have turned her back on him.

He looked down at the rough pipe he held and fit the stem into the bowl. The bowl represented Woman, Zeke had said, and the stem represented Man. The Tree of Life.

Sometimes they sundered, Gideon thought, separating the pieces and looking at them. And when they did, they were incomplete. Useless. No one could smoke a broken pipe. But he had never found the glue that could hold the pieces together.

And once again he faced the dark possibility that it just didn't exist.

Joey appeared at dinner with a dark bruise mottling his cheekbone.

"What happened?" Sara asked immediately.

Joey shrugged. "I wasn't paying attention and tripped, that's all. Forget it."

"Did you get that fence all braced?" Zeke asked.

"I need to go up again in the morning. I'll have it done before lunch." He shifted irritably and stabbed at a pea with his fork. "It'll get done. You don't need to ride me."

"No one's riding—" Sara broke off at a sharp gesture from Zeke. Silence reigned for a couple of minutes.

"Where's Gideon?" Joey asked suddenly.

"Guess he's late," Zeke remarked.

Joey looked at Sara. "What did you do? Drive him off? Every other guy who's ever—"

"Joey Yates, you be quiet right now," Sara said sharply. "It's none of your—"

"It's my business, all right!" Joey shouted, causing Sara and Zeke both to stare at him in astonishment. "Ever since George dumped you, you treat men like rattlesnakes. Even me! You never believe me! Never! You're always so damn sure a man is lying or cheating or—"

"Silence, boy," said Zeke. It was a tone that cut through Joey's tirade and brooked no argument.

"You never even *listen*," Joey shouted and jumped up from the table, heading toward the door.

"Joey." Zeke's voice stopped him. "Ask Gideon to join us. Then come back here and finish your supper. I'm giving you ten minutes."

Joey stomped out without answering.

Sara looked at Zeke, aware that her lower lip was trembling and that she wanted to cry again. This day had been hell, and she felt as if she was losing everything she loved. "You should have just let him cool off," she said to her grandfather.

"It's time he learned self-control," Zeke said. "High time."

Sara nodded, knowing he was right about that. But... "What do you suppose he meant, that we never listen? That I don't believe him?"

"I guess one of us didn't hear something we should have. And maybe we'd better ask him when he calms down."

Joey found Gideon still sitting on the bunkhouse steps with the pieces of the pipe in his hands. Gideon looked up and greeted him with a nod.

"You argue with somebody?" he asked the boy.

"Tripped."

Gideon seriously doubted it, but he let it go. Joey sat beside him.

"Grandfather talked you into making a pipe?"

"Your grandfather is an irrcsistible force."

A soft snort escaped Joey. "Yeah."

Gideon held up the pieces. "My carving leaves a lot to be desired."

"It looks like my first pipe," Joey said. "Actually, I think mine was a lot worse. The bowl wasn't as straight."

"Zeke carved everything except the buffalo."

Joey leaned over for a closer look. "Oh." Then he snickered.

Gideon chuckled in spite of himself. "Yeah, I know." He picked up the square of hide in which Zeke had originally kept it and wrapped the pieces.

"I'm supposed to bring you back for dinner," Joey said.

"I wasn't sure I ought to show up."

"I wondered. What happened? Did Sara give you hell over something? She's impossible. I think George made her hate men. Or at least never trust them."

And I made it worse, Gideon thought. "Well, I gave her cause," he said to Joey. "I wasn't exactly up-front with her."

"So?"

Gideon looked at him, a little startled. "So?"

"Well, it's not like you've known her for years or anything. It's only been a couple of weeks. It takes longer than that to tell somebody everything, especially the important things." He shrugged. "Not that she would have listened, anyway."

Gideon turned to look straight at the boy. "What didn't she hear you say?"

Joey looked down at his scuffed, dusty boots. "Oh, hell, it doesn't matter now."

"Sure it does. That's the second time you've mentioned it to me. What was it, Joey?"

Joey hunched his shoulders. "I told her I didn't steal that damn car. I didn't even know it was stolen. I thought it was Les Walker's car. He said his dad gave it to him, and he let me drive it. But nobody believed me. Everybody believed Les when he said he never saw the car before."

"Why do you think that happened?"

Joey shrugged, then finally looked at Gideon. "Probably because I'd been cutting up so much at school and Les never got into trouble. Probably because I look like a punk. Probably because I was the only one in the car. But *Sara* should have believed me. *Grandfather* should have believed me."

"And what about Les? Why did he set you up like that?"

"Because of Daisy Halloran. She said she'd go to the prom with me, and Les thought she was going to go with him. He was pretty pi—ticked off about that. We even had a fight over it in the school parking lot. I won." He shrugged. "Daisy went to the prom with him."

So much for love.

"I believe you," he told Joey.

The boy turned and looked doubtfully at him. "Why? Just because I said so? Nobody else did."

"Just because you said so."

Joey almost grinned. Gideon could see it. Then the boy suddenly looked away and scuffed nervously at the ground. "Maybe we better go up for supper. Grandfather only gave me ten minutes."

"Let's go, then," Gideon said, rising with the pipe still in his hands. He felt a little like Daniel going into the lion's den, except that Daniel had had virtue on his side. And Daniel had only had to face a lion, not an angry woman.

Chester Elk Horn spent most of the next morning by the sweat lodge, praying. Gideon looked over to that end of the meadow a number of times and had the eerie feeling that he could feel a gathering of forces in the air. The hair on the back of his neck stood up a little even as he tried to tell himself his imagination was running away with him.

And then the mustangs showed up, hours earlier than usual. The mares, as always, hung back by the trees, but the stallion came prancing right over to Gideon and butted him gently on the shoulder.

Touched by this display of unequivocal trust, Gideon reached up with his one good arm and patted the horse awkwardly.

"It's hell sometimes, boy, isn't it?" he heard himself whisper huskily to the horse.

He'd had plenty of time during the long, dark hours of the night to face the unexpected loneliness of Sara's absence. Plenty of time to consider how much misery he was suffering from an emotion he didn't believe in. Plenty of time to wonder how he was going to cope with the emptiness from here on in.

He'd been ripped up before in his life. Hell, it was the primary reason he tried not to care. Barney's death, he had thought, had completely gutted him. Now the loss of Sara showed him he hadn't been gutted, after all. There was still enough feeling in him, still enough caring, to ache for that woman. God, he thought, pressing his cheek to the stallion's sleek neck. God, it hurts so bad.

The mustang nickered softly and then pulled away, trotting off toward his mares.

Gideon watched him go, wishing he were a mustang rather than a man, and then turned toward the bunkhouse, intent upon working on his pipe. He wanted that buffalo to look like a buffalo before he offered the pipe to Chester later.

Because he *was* going to offer the pipe. He was going to do the sweat and seek a vision, because he needed answers and direction, and neither seemed to be coming from the meanderings of his own mind. Minute by minute he flopped back and forth between trying to force Sara to listen and waiting until she calmed down enough to be willing to hear reason. He could understand that she felt betrayed. If that had been the sum of it, he would have known exactly what to do. But that was only half of it. The other half of it was that Gideon was feeling betrayed, too. By her.

Instinct said to turn his back on the whole mess and walk away right now. His heart said otherwise. Sara Yates and her soft brown eyes had somehow become more important to him than protecting himself.

And it was time to figure out just what that meant.

"Gideon! Gideon!"

Sara called to him from the yard, and the insistent, almost panicked note in her voice brought him across the meadow at a full run from where he'd been listening to Chester explain the strips of colored cloth, called *Shina,* that he was hanging over the altar in the lodge.

His first thought was that the mugger had returned in broad daylight, but then he realized Sara would hardly be standing in the yard shouting for him if that were the case. His long legs ate up the ground as he ran down the hill to her, ignoring the pain in his shoulder and arm as his cast bounced in the sling.

"Joey's gone," Sara said just as soon as he got within talking distance.

"Gone? You mean he went someplace?"

"I mean *gone*." Her eyes were wide, worried. "Zeke took him up to the falls this morning to finish fixing the fence."

Gideon nodded. "I know."

"Anyway, Zeke left him working there and went out to check on another section where we have trouble sometimes and the mustangs might get out. When he came back, Joey wasn't there." She bit her lip and shook her head. "There's no place he could have *gone*. Not by himself without a vehicle. Not from there. Zeke said his hat and gloves are there by the fence, along with all the tools. Zeke called and called and called...."

Instinctively, he reached out and drew her into his arms. She came without resistance, surprising him. "Where's Zeke?"

"Inside calling the sheriff. Oh, Gideon, I'm so worried!"

After the other things that had happened, so was Gideon. Especially after his conversation with Joey last night. He really didn't think the boy intended to get up to any mischief right now. "Micah will be able to tell if he wandered off—"

She shook her head, interrupting him. "Micah's up in the mountains looking for that woman who disappeared from her campsite yesterday." It would take hours and hours to get him out of that wilderness and back to Conard County, she thought. Too many hours. They had to find Joey before nightfall, because if he was hurt and out there all alone, exposure might kill him before morning. The nighttime lows were still falling into the forties and fifties, depending on altitude.

She refused to even consider the possibility of abduction.

"Take me up there and show me the place," Gideon said after a moment, feeling an overwhelming need to do something. "My eyes are better than Zeke's. Maybe I'll be able to see something he missed."

Sara hesitated only a moment. "All right," she said. "Just let me tell Grandfather."

At that moment Zeke stepped out onto the porch. His expression was impassive. Too impassive, Gideon thought. Sara, who had just turned from Gideon, froze when she saw him. "What are they going to do?" she asked.

"Not much," Zeke said. "It's not as if the boy has never disappeared before. One of the deputies is going to come up and look things over, but without some evidence that he didn't just walk off on his own, they're not going to do a damn thing, Sarey."

Chapter 12

Gideon found the blood. It was spattered across the grass and brush not ten feet from where Joey's gloves lay. There had obviously been a struggle of some kind, judging from broken branches and trampled grass. Deputy Charlie Huskins agreed, and by midafternoon search parties were combing the vicinity for some sign of Joey or his attackers.

By nightfall, nothing helpful had been discovered. The search parties returned to the command post that had been established near the place from which Joey had disappeared, all with negative reports. Nor could the search continue after dark. Important clues might be trampled, but just as importantly, someone might get hurt stumbling around in terrain full of gullies, crevices, gorges and boulders.

Gideon and his search partners returned to the command post just as the last light faded and turned dusk into night. Sara had been manning the communications base station at Nate's insistence and despite her own overwhelming urge to participate in the search.

"It's better this way," Nate had told her. "This way you'll

know everything we find the minute we find it. You won't have to wonder.''

So she had stayed, and now she watched as Gideon's party, the last to return, emerged from the shadowed woods into the light of kerosene lanterns.

''We'll start again at dawn, Sara,'' Nate promised her before he left.

Gideon approached and stood beside her as they watched the last of the searchers pack up and drive off. A few minutes later they stood alone in the eerie silence and darkness of the deserted wood.

''He's got to be all right,'' Sara whispered, as much to herself as to him. ''He's got to be all right.''

Unable to offer any other comfort, Gideon turned her into his arms and stood hugging her as night drew more deeply around them. He didn't want to think about how it was already growing chilly up here and would grow even colder before dawn. He didn't want to think of Joey lying unconscious somewhere out there and dying of exposure. He didn't want to think of Joey already dead and buried in a shallow grave.

And Sara was surely thinking of those things herself, right now, as she shuddered in his arms. He would have given anything to spare her this anxiety.

''Come on,'' he said presently. ''Let's go back. Zeke's probably going out of his mind wondering if we found anything.''

''He would know.''

Gideon tipped his head back and looked down at Sara. ''He'd know? How?''

She shook her head distractedly. ''Zeke always knows. Sometimes I think the wind whispers to him. Oh, God!'' she exclaimed in a burst of utter frustration. ''Oh, God, I'm so scared! What if he's out there somewhere? What if he's hurt and…'' She couldn't even make herself complete the thought.

''Come on,'' Gideon said after a moment. He squeezed her and urged her toward the truck. ''I haven't eaten since breakfast and I bet you haven't either. I don't know about you, but my head works better when I'm not starved.''

Stupid, he thought, to discuss food at a time like this, but necessities had to be dealt with, even when they felt out of place.

As he helped her into the passenger seat of his truck—a formality that she accepted awkwardly, as if it embarrassed her—a huge fist suddenly gripped his heart.

"Sara?"

She turned her head to peer at him in the dark. The moonlight cast mysterious shadows over her delicate features, darkening her eyes to bottomless wells. Catching her chin gently in the palm of his hand, he turned her face up just a hair.

"I'm sorry," he said.

"Sorry?"

"For not telling you—"

She covered his mouth swiftly with her fingertips. "No," she said.

"No?"

"I don't want your apology."

Until that instant he hadn't realized just how much he had been hoping she would forgive him. Hadn't realized just how much he had been counting on it. With those words she ripped hope from him and left him standing in an icy void of the heart unlike any he had ever imagined.

Slowly, suddenly feeling very old, he dropped his hand from her chin and closed the truck door. *I don't want your apology.* That said it all, didn't it? The words, the denial in them, cast him back into his solitude with a pain so old it seemed part of his skin. With a pain so new and so huge that its magnitude was beyond comprehension.

His feet felt like lead as he walked around the truck and climbed in behind the wheel. He would stay until Joey was found, he told himself. And then he would move on.

When they returned to the house, they learned that Chester had hurried up his timetable and was just about to begin *Yuwipi*, the ceremony to ask for help.

"He's going to ask where Joey is," Zeke told Sara and Gideon. "Come if you want, but once he starts, you mustn't disturb him."

Chester had taken over one of the rooms in the bunkhouse. Everything had been moved out, and the floor had been covered with sage. In the center, a square had been marked out by small twists of cloth all tied together on a rope. Inside the square stood a can full of dirt with a red-and-black stick poking up out of it. Tied to the top of the stick was an eagle feather. Beside that were a buffalo skull and some gourds, and some other items that were difficult to see in the poor light.

By the illumination of a single lantern, the arrangement looked eerie. Not even moonlight penetrated the room, for the windows had been covered by blankets.

"Sit against the wall," Zeke said, motioning Sara and Gideon to one side. "Keep your thoughts pure and don't be afraid."

Chester was bundled mummylike in a blanket, and tied inside it by Zeke, who then rolled him over so he lay facedown on the floor.

"Okay," said Zeke. "Now it begins." He doused the lantern.

Gideon wondered how Chester could even breathe. Beside him, he felt Sara shift restlessly, and then, causing his breath to catch in his throat, she leaned against him. Closing his eyes tightly against an unwelcome uprush of emotion, he wrapped an arm around her shoulders and waited tensely for her to stiffen or pull away. But she didn't. Instead, she snuggled a little closer, and his heart nearly stopped.

For a long, long time, the room was silent. Then the drum began to beat, steady and low, and Zeke began to sing.

It was hypnotic, Gideon thought. Slowly, gradually, tension seeped away, and in its place came a sense of restful expectancy. And little by little he felt himself going into the silence.

The climb was long, arduous. The air grew thinner with every step, and overhead gray-green thunderheads boomed and rumbled as they swallowed the sun. The sound of his own breathing was loud in his ears, and from time to time he slipped on loose rocks.

There were no shadows, he realized as the sun vanished in the leaden clouds. It was the Black Light, the light that cast no shadows. Around him, trees swayed and groaned in the wind, and then he left them behind. Ahead, above, there was nothing but rock. And a red buffalo that stood far ahead, looking back at him as if it was waiting. Waiting.

Calling.

Fluttering wings brushed his face, invisible wings, the wind, yet more than the wind. From behind, someone pushed him forward, a silent command to climb. Glancing back, he saw nothing but darkness. Even the trees and the slope below had vanished into the pit of night.

Ahead, the buffalo looked back at him, glowing now, a red as brilliant as fire, as beckoning as flame on a cold, empty night.

"Come," whispered the voice of the breeze. "Come see."

Pressing forward, he toiled upward, struggling against gravity, against the slippery rock, against the force of weariness that dragged him down. The air seemed to grow thick, fighting him, too.

And always, always, the buffalo stayed exactly the same distance ahead.

But finally, aeons later, he reached the pinnacle, a small point of land high above the sea of night below, and there the buffalo awaited him. The beast looked at him with sad, knowing eyes, with a sorrow beyond words, and said, "Ironheart, below you lies the sea of your making, and in the midst of the void you stand alone. You have been given all the colors of the universe, yet you have chosen to paint your world in only one tone. Take out your palette now, and paint the colors of the rainbow into your void."

As the buffalo spoke, the black sea below began to shimmer, at first like the dim rainbow colors of an oil slick. But as he watched, the colors blossomed into brilliant, blinding hues of gold and red and green and blue, colors so bright they drowned the stormy sky and made his eyes sting.

"These are your colors," the buffalo said. "Take them with you."

He watched the buffalo turn away, and the great beast began to walk off into the rainbow colors as if they were a road made for his feet.

"Wait!" Gideon cried. "The boy. Joey!"

The buffalo glanced back. "The deer will show the way."

Just then a huge wind blew, toppling him from the narrow peak and throwing him down the rocky slope. He bounced against rocks and felt the bite of their sharp corners, felt the tearing of his flesh and the breaking of his bones. Only when he lay again in the dark void did the pain cease. But this time, inside him, he felt the rainbow.

Turning, struggling to bring the colors inside him back out into the world, he saw the deer.

The pounding of the drum was loud, seeming to reverberate from the walls. Zeke's singing had long since stopped, and now the drum fell silent, too. And into that silence came the rattle of the gourds, a hissing sound like a rattlesnake. First it came from here, then there, seeming to fly around the room. Light flashed near the ceiling, a small blue burst. Another flash burst near the floor, revealing Zeke and the drum for one blinding instant.

Sara curled closer to Gideon, frightened at the strangeness of all that was happening. Lightning seemed to have come into the room with them, lightning and thunder and the rattle of hail. These were powers her grandfather and Chester had spoken of all the years she could remember, but not until now had she truly tasted them.

And then, as abruptly as it had begun, it ceased. Silence reigned for several minutes; then came the flare of the match as Zeke lit the lantern. Chester now lay unwrapped within his square of tobacco ties. Sara wondered how he had gotten untied. A glance at her watch told her the night had passed, and that dawn was less than an hour away.

Chester sat up, and he and Zeke sang softly. Sara looked at Gideon.

"I know where Joey is," Gideon said quietly. "I saw him."

Sara caught her breath as her heart climbed into her throat. "Saw him?" She hardly dared believe.

"I saw him," Gideon said again. "He's hurt, cold and hungry, but he's alive. Up the mountain. Near a tree that was blasted by lightning and then grew into two, like a *Y*."

"I know that place," Sara said excitedly. And there was no way on earth Gideon could have known about that tree. It was on one of the most remote parts of the ranch. She started to rise, in her eagerness, but her grandfather motioned sharply. His meaning was clear. She was to stay until he finished the song of thanks and farewell to the spirits who had aided them.

And for the first time in her life Sara Yates honestly felt she had something to thank the spirits for. Slowly she turned to look at Gideon. This man had had a vision during the night, and even as he spoke of it and prepared to act upon it, he didn't look very happy about it.

"Grandfather said you have power," she murmured.

"We'll see how much damn good it does anyone," he muttered back. "It hasn't ever done *me* any good that I can see."

Impulsively, she lifted her head and stretched until she could brush a kiss on his cheek.

The kiss struck Gideon like a bolt of lightning. Why was she kissing him? Because she thought he was going to find her brother? Was this the same woman who had told him just last night that she didn't want his apology?

"Ironheart." Chester had come over to them, and now he knelt facing Gideon. "The blasted tree is a power place. The boy is alive because of it. Don't break your neck trying to get there. He'll be alive."

A half hour later, with dawn just a faint gray line of promise at the horizon, Sara and Gideon started up into the mountains on horseback, to a place they could get to no other way.

"Except on dirt bikes," Sara said.

Gideon glanced at her. "What? Did I miss something?"

"I was just thinking that the only way to get to this tree is on horseback. Or on dirt bikes."

"Yeah. Well, I kind of suspected our dirt-biking friend might be involved. The question is, what is he after?" Feeling almost helpless against himself, he watched Sara, who was riding to one side and just a little ahead of him, as hopelessly as any sixteen-year-old in the throes of a major crush. The crystalline light of dawning day began to wash across the world, bringing sharp-edged clarity and color to their surroundings.

Watching her, he drank in every graceful line of her face, her neck, her thigh. Thought how lovely she was. How achingly, sweetly lovely. How badly he wanted to hold her again and tell her just how much she meant to him. To admit that she had become the only rainbow in his colorless world.

"Sara?"

She glanced back at him and smiled, just a small smile, but one that warmed his soul. Considering that she had been up all night, she looked awfully fresh, he thought.

"Sara, I really want to apologize for not telling you about Micah."

"That's not necessary. I told you that last night."

"But I…" Not necessary? How was he supposed to interpret that? "Of course it's necessary."

She shook her head. "In the first place, it's none of my business how you choose to handle your personal affairs. In the second place, it was presumptuous of me to think I had a right to know anything so personal about you."

"Presumptuous?" Now that was a word he hadn't heard anybody actually use in his entire life. He looked at Sara, taking in her crisp khaki uniform, the sage nylon jacket, the tan Stetson and the .45 riding on her hip, and thought what a unique delight she was. A black-satin voice in a black-satin woman who hid behind a tough-as-nails veneer.

"Now wait one minute," he said, heeling his mount forward until he was right beside her. "Spending a few nights in my bed gives you certain rights." Damn, he thought, feeling a little shocked at himself. Was he actually saying that? "You can't be presumptuous."

"No?" She glanced at him, and from somewhere in the depths of her anxiety over Joey came a glimmer of humor, just a faint sparkle in her brown eyes. "Well, it doesn't matter, anyway. I accept that you had your reasons. I shouldn't have gotten mad."

He frowned at her, feeling off-center and unsure of what was happening. "You had every right to get mad."

Sara shook her head. "Not really. The truth is, I wasn't really mad at you. I was feeling…uncertain, I guess. Scared. Afraid that I was making a fool of myself again. Sort of a knee-jerk reaction because of George. After he left, I always wondered how many secrets he'd had that he never told me about. I guess that was part of the worst of it, besides the humiliation. Thinking I had known this guy, and having it turn out that I didn't know him at all."

Everything inside Gideon winced as he realized the magnitude of the wound he had dealt this woman. "Mouse—"

"Let me finish. Please?"

Meeting the uncertainty of her gaze, seeing her determination to say difficult things, he nodded and fell silent.

"My reaction to you was filtered through my experience with George," Sara said after a moment. "When I calmed down enough, I realized that your being Micah's brother wasn't just your secret. It was Micah's secret, too, and you had no business sharing it with anyone before you shared it with him. And I got to thinking about how I would have felt in your shoes.… Honestly, Gideon, I'm not at all sure I would have done anything different from what you did. When I really thought about it, I saw how complicated and scary and difficult it would be, and why maybe you wouldn't want anyone at all to know, ever.

"And that business about using me? Well, when I thought

it over, I realized that you asked me some questions about Micah, but mostly I did the talking, and *I* was the one who came up with the idea of introducing you. So you weren't even being bad in a big way.''

Feeling terribly shy, terribly afraid, Sara dared a glance at Gideon. She had realized, somewhere in the hell of the last thirty-six hours, that she had jumped off the cliff all on her own. Gideon hadn't pushed her, hadn't abandoned her, hadn't done a damn thing except keep an intensely personal secret. And she, who had promised herself that she was going to love him regardless, had succeeded only in showing him once again that you couldn't trust the people closest to you, because they could turn on you at the slightest provocation.

Gideon thought his heart was going to burst. Emotions locked his throat tight, made words impossible, as he looked at Sara's shy, uncertain face and realized she didn't think there was anything to forgive. That kind of acceptance had been so rare in his life that he could count on one hand the number of people who had given it to him. He swallowed hard and managed some gruff words. ''After we find Joey, we'll talk.''

She nodded, then pulled her sunglasses from her pocket and slipped them on. The morning sun was strong now, dappling the open spaces between trees with a brilliant golden light. Gideon found himself remembering his dream, his vision, or whatever it had been. The red buffalo had spoken his grandfather's words, he realized now—that business about colors.

But his life hadn't been colorless, he thought. At least, not until Barney's death. Maybe he hadn't painted it in *all* the colors of the rainbow, but he sure hadn't painted a black void. There had been Barney, of course, and good times, and plenty of excitement and thrills. Some of the colors had been missing, though, he admitted now. And since Barney's death, there hadn't been any color at all.

Until now. It almost seemed the world was glowing from within this morning, as if trees and grass and even rocks were brighter than ever before. As if edges were clear and sharp and perfectly etched. As if he had suddenly donned a pair of new glasses that brought everything into focus. As if such beauty had always been there but he had simply failed to perceive it.

"How much farther?" he asked Sara.

"Another hour or so. We can't make a straight line because of the terrain, so it takes a long time to get to the tree."

"I imagine you know every inch of the Double Y."

"Just about. Exploring was one of my favorite pastimes as a kid. I never much wanted to hang around the house, and once I got my own horse, that was all she wrote. As long as I got my share of chores done, Dad didn't seem to mind, and Mom gave up all hope of turning me into a cook and housekeeper."

"I can't imagine you as a cook or housekeeper," Gideon said after a moment. "I didn't quite know what to make of you when I first saw you, though. Not because you were a cop—there're women cops everywhere nowadays—but because something…didn't quite fit. It was as if you were trying to be tough when you really weren't."

"Well, I was," Sara admitted on a small laugh. "I always feel a little like an impostor in this uniform. And with a brawl like that night at Happy's… I don't know what I would have done if somebody had argued with me. Some of the guys I work with would have waded right in and enjoyed the free-for-all. Not me. And I didn't want to pull the trigger on that shot-gun, either."

She turned in the saddle and looked at him from behind her mirrored sunglasses. "It's harder around here, I think, than it would be in a city, because all these guys know me. They remember when I was too tall, too gangly, and tripping over my own feet all the time. They remember when I forgot my lines in the junior play, and when Chuck Mangan made me cry by pulling my braids. It's kind of hard to be tough around that."

"You did a pretty good job of it," Gideon said with a smile. "None of those guys gave you a hard time, did they? If you ask me, they've got a lot of respect for you, and it would never occur to them to challenge you."

"Except you." Tipping her head, she looked at him over

the tops of her glasses. "Your exact words, as I recall, were 'Who made you afraid to be a woman?'"

Gideon winced. "I deserved a pop in the nose for that."

"I considered it." Clucking softly, she heeled her gelding, urging him up a steep, rocky slope. "I didn't know I was so transparent."

"I think it was more wishful thinking than transparency on your part."

She tossed him a glance over her shoulder. "What do you mean?"

"Mouse darlin', from the instant I heard your voice my hormones started howling. It was kind of a crisis for me, in a way, because it had been a long, long time since I'd felt that hot that fast, and it kind of made me uneasy. So there I was, my insides getting stroked into a frenzy by your voice—thinking of black satin sheets, if you want to know the truth—and the person who was causing all that uproar was waving a shotgun, wearing a badge and talking as tough as Saturday night wrestling."

"Ouch."

"Ouch was exactly how it felt. I'd never been into dominance, you know? Especially from the submissive end. And all of a sudden I was panting for this tough... Ahh, forget it. This subject is a loaded gun, and I'm going to shoot myself in the foot if I keep on."

Sara almost told him that he was doing just fine and not to worry. Hearing again that he'd been turned on by her at their very first meeting gave her a thrill like none she had ever imagined. After a decade of believing herself to be a failure as a woman, it was music to her ears to hear someone say that he didn't think she was.

She tossed him another look over her shoulder. "Does this mean I can tie you up with my black silk stockings?"

For a split second Gideon simply stared at her in disbelief; then his laugh rang out, bringing a new kind of light to the sun-bathed woods. "Anytime, Mouse," he assured her. "And bring your .45."

* * *

Their humor didn't last long, however. It had served to distract Sara for a little while, but inevitably her thoughts turned to Joey. They moved as swiftly as they could over the rugged terrain, but fast wasn't fast enough. Farther down the mountain, the search parties would already have set out, looking for any evidence of what had happened.

Sara could have told Nate to hold off, and he might actually have done it, but she wasn't quite ready to risk Joey's life on a single roll of the die. If Gideon's vision had been wrong, it could cost Joey his life.

But she didn't think he was wrong. She was here because this man had turned to her with certainty and told her that he had seen Joey. Because he had known of the blasted tree. Because in her heart she recognized the power in the beliefs of her grandfather and his friend. Because she had felt the power in Gideon.

It was beyond rational explanation, but matters of the heart and soul always were. *See with your heart,* her grandfather had always said. She was doing that right now, following her heart on one of the wildest gambles she had ever taken.

When the terrain leveled out a little, Gideon astonished her by reaching over and covering her hand with his. "I missed you, Mouse," he said.

"I missed you, too," she admitted, and felt a prickle of tears in her eyes. Eventually he would leave, but for now...for now, she was following her heart.

The blasted tree rose in the center of a clearing. It rose straight and true to the height of a man, and there, from a blackened, twisted spot, suddenly split into two perfect trunks which, after curving slightly away from each other, rose just as straight and true as the original. High above, twin crowns stirred gently in the morning breeze.

Gideon could easily see why Chester considered this a place of power. There was an unearthliness to the clearing, a sense of something different, that he had felt in only a couple of places in his entire life. It made the back of his neck prickle. All morning he'd been trying not to think of his vision of this place and what it meant that he had seen it in his mind before he had seen it with his eyes. Now he didn't want to think about the power he felt here, as if the strength of the earth below their feet were somehow magnified and broadcast here.

"I don't see Joey," Sara said, her voice tight. She, too, felt the power of the clearing, and it reminded her of the hush in an empty church.

"He's around." Gideon was even more sure of it now that he had actually come to the place he had seen in his vision. If *that* could happen, then Joey was here.

Slowly he rode around the edge of the clearing, gradually becoming aware of the sound of rushing water over the rustle of the wind in the pines.

"There's running water here?"

Sara pointed. "Over there, just the other side of those trees."

Guided by instinct, Gideon dismounted, and Sara followed suit. They tethered their mounts and then walked into the trees.

"It's maybe twenty yards," Sara said, reaching back into her memory. "There's a deep gorge...."

They emerged from the trees onto the edge of the gorge with almost startling suddenness. Gideon took one look at the rushing water thirty feet below and his vertigo hit him right in the face.

Spinning, splintering blue sky...

"Gideon!" Sara grabbed his arm and shook him. "Gideon!"

He drew a long, deep breath and opened his eyes. He was facing the gorge, facing the demons that haunted him.

"Are you all right?"

He turned, looking into her concerned face. "Yeah. Just got dizzy for a second."

"Let's get you away from here."

But he shook his head and looked across the gorge. "Is there any way to get over to the other side?" Something was compelling him, pushing him, just the same as something had compelled him to climb the mountain in his vision last night. Something was...guiding him.

"The easiest way is to go north from the ranch house and

avoid the worst of the gorge altogether. This is the same creek that feeds into the glade where we picnicked."

He nodded, beginning to see it in his mind. "They brought him up the other side, then. He's over there, Sara."

She stared up at him, opening her mouth to ask how he knew. Then she thought better of it. There was no explaining how anybody knew something like this. "It'll take hours to go back down and come back up the other side," she said tightly. "Hours. Joey..."

Gideon turned, looking up the gorge, then down. There had to be a way. Then he saw the felled tree, maybe eight inches in diameter, that lay across the deepest point a hundred yards farther up. "I'll cross up there."

Sara followed his gaze and drew a sharp breath. "Gideon, no! You can't! Your vertigo—"

"My vertigo can go hang," he said roughly. "That boy is over there, Sara. If I can't get over there to help him, then I deserve to fall."

Her hand shot out and clutched his arm until her nails dug into him through the thick wool of his shirt. "I'll cross. I don't get dizzy...."

"And I used to do this eight hours a day, babe. I have a better chance of doing it in one piece than you do." Bending, he astonished her with a hot, wet, almost savage kiss.

"But maybe he isn't—"

"He is." There was no doubt in him. He had the feeling that this was a moment of destiny, then dismissed the notion as nothing short of absolute lunacy. Too much time with Chester and Zeke, he told himself. Those two old Indians were turning him into a mystic. Just what he needed, another crazy quirk in his mind.

Sara climbed the rugged slope beside the gorge right behind him. She had insisted he wait until she retrieved the knapsack with the blankets and first-aid kit from the saddlebags, and now he carried it slung over one shoulder, taking the climb as easily as a mountain goat while she stumbled behind. It was not the first time she had noticed how surely he moved, leaving nothing to chance. But if a man were going to walk narrow beams nine hundred feet above the ground, he undoubtedly had to assess each step before he took it and stay perfectly balanced as he moved. For her part, she slipped a couple of times, but he was always there to help her up, or to catch her with his good arm.

Finally they stood at the point where the fallen tree made a narrow bridge over the deepest part of the gorge. The drop at this point was thirty-five or forty feet, and the cleft was narrow, almost straight-sided. Gideon kicked at the fallen tree, testing whether it would roll, and found that it had been there long enough to have settled fairly well. A scan along its length told him it was not yet visibly rotted anywhere. As good as he could ask for, under the circumstances.

"Oh, my God," Sara whispered suddenly. "Gideon... Gideon, I see him! There's Joey!"

He turned and looked where she pointed. The opposite side of the gorge was a foot or two lower than where they now stood, and at first all he could see were the low-growing shrubs and grasses that took root in any sunny crack in the ground. But then he saw the dark shape beneath one of the trees, a huddled bundle of denim and leather.

"I see him. I'm going over."

With Sara's help, he ditched his cowboy boots. They were meant for riding, not footwork, and their slippery soles and high heels would be a definite danger in what he was about to do. The he slung the knapsack over his good shoulder and put his bare foot on the end of the log.

The world seemed to shift as if from an earthquake. For a wild, terrifying instant he felt as if he was swaying back and forth on a falling swing, as if he would tumble end over end with the sky splintering above him. Cold sweat beaded his brow, his stomach heaved.

"Gideon...Gideon, don't. Let me."

He turned his head and looked straight into Sara's frightened brown eyes. "I'll do it," he said. Because if he didn't do this now, he would never be a whole man again. Because he couldn't let Sara take the risk.

He stepped up onto the log, every instinct screaming at him not to do it. Then, with his eyes straight ahead, he stepped out over the gorge. Arms out, making minor adjustments for the weight of the cast and with all the grace he had learned over the years at the top of the world's tallest buildings, he walked the length of the tree.

Twice his balance suffered as his mind deceived him, trying to convince him that he was falling. Twice he caught himself with instinctive ease. If Sara said anything, her words were drowned by the rushing cataract of the water below.

And then he was over. For an instant the whole world seemed to spin and he thought his knees would buckle. Almost as soon as the weakness assailed him, however, it vanished in a flood tide of rediscovered confidence and strength. He'd done it. He'd faced the demon and won. He gave himself a moment, a mere moment, to savor his victory, then hurried over to the huddled heap that was Joey.

Kneeling, he touched the boy's shoulder. "Joey? Joey, do you hear me?"

Joey groaned and shifted a little. His face was swollen and bloodied, and it appeared that his nose had been broken. It was then that Gideon saw he had been chained to the tree.

"Sonofabitch!" he muttered. Dropping the knapsack, he rose and cupped his hands to his mouth. "Sara! He's alive, but he's chained here. I'm going to have to try to break the chain."

She waved, signaling her understanding. Then he saw her lift her hand to key the radio mike that was attached to her collar. He hoped her transmission would reach the base station.

They'd chained him here. Gideon thought about that as he hunted up a heavy rock to use as a hammer. Chained him here to die of exposure, or to make dinner for one of the bears in the area. Damn! He couldn't believe that kind of mind. Couldn't even finish their own dirty work.

He found a good-size rock, maybe ten or twelve pounds, that he could hold in his one good hand and swing down against a length of the chain. Then he hunted up another rock, a flat one this time, to place beneath the chain.

For a man accustomed to swinging a sixteen-pound hammer as a normal part of his daily activity, smashing the chain was relatively easy. Fewer than a dozen blows weakened the link enough to shatter it.

The sound roused Joey to a kind of foggy awareness. He was a little hypothermic, dehydrated, tired. Maybe bleeding internally. It was impossible for Gideon to tell. He was just grateful that the boy surfaced to a semiconscious state.

"Joey? Joey, I'm going to have to tie your wrists together so I can carry you over my shoulders. Joey?"

"'Kay."

He had to be content with that. First he wrapped the boy mummy-style from his armpits to his ankles in the wool blanket that was in the knapsack and tied him into it with a length of rope. The wrapping would serve the double purpose of warming him up and keeping him still while they crossed the gorge. Then he took a roll of gauze bandage and bound Joey's wrists together.

He slung the boy over his shoulder, one of his arms over Gideon's good shoulder, the other arm under Gideon's other shoulder. With his hands bound, there was no way Joey could slip away from him.

"Now, don't move, Joey. Just keep still for a few minutes." Only a faint groan answered him. Gideon scooped up the knapsack and started over the gorge. Sara stood on the far side, hand pressed to her mouth as she watched.

Joey jerked once, on the way across, and Gideon did a quick little tap dance as he regained his balance. He managed to give Sara a grin as he steadied himself and finished the crossing.

"Piece of cake," he told Sara when he stepped off the log on the other side. "Piece of cake. Let's get this boy down the mountain."

Chapter 13

Gideon stood quietly in the far corner of the hospital room while Sheriff Nathan Tate questioned Joey. Sara stood near the bed, her hands tightly clasped as she listened. Zeke occupied the room's one chair.

Joey looked a lot worse for wear, Gideon thought. His face was so swollen and bruised, it was a wonder he could even talk. His nose was broken—evidently the cause of the spattered blood Gideon had found—and one eye was so blackened he couldn't even open it. Other than bruises, however, he had suffered no real damage.

The story he told wasn't very edifying. He'd been angry and hurt because no one would believe that he hadn't stolen the car. He had, he admitted, wanted to get even somehow. On a school field trip to the atmospheric research center at Boulder, he had run into a couple of guys who convinced him that he could make a lot of money by selling drugs.

"I wasn't thinking too good," he told the sheriff now, his voice muffled by all the swelling. "I was drunk."

Sara gasped. Gideon instinctively moved to her side and took her hand, squeezing it reassuringly.

"You were drunk on a school field trip," Nate repeated evenly. It was not a question, but the statement of a man who had just heard an unpalatable fact.

"Yeah. Me and a couple other guys."

Nate rolled his eyes. "God have mercy. Where were your chaperones? No, never mind. Just get on with this story. I'll deal with the school later. So you thought you could sell drugs?"

"Only when I was drunk. They said I could take the stuff and pay them their share after I sold it. Later I got scared shi— you know."

"I know," the sheriff agreed. "I take it you didn't give the drugs back?"

"No. I was already on the bus home. I didn't know what to do about it. Finally, I buried the stuff. I figured they'd never find me, you know? I didn't give them my real name, and I never said I was from here. Somebody else must have told them."

"Must have," Nate agreed. "For the moment, I won't ask why the hell you didn't tell your sister or me."

"Because you didn't believe me about the car! None of you! None of you except Gideon!"

"Shh," Sara said, stepping to the bed and taking Joey's hand in both of hers. "Hush, Joey. We're listening now. I promise." Oh, yes, she was listening, and she wanted to gather him into her arms and tell him it would be all right, but she couldn't do that anymore. Nobody could promise this mess would be all right.

"When Sara told me Grandfather had been attacked," Joey continued finally in answer to Nate's prompting, "I was afraid it was them, but I didn't see how it could be. Anyway, I started getting real cooperative so you'd let me out of jail. I figured if I was home, and it *was* them, they'd come for me, not Sara or Grandfather."

Nate nodded, and Gideon felt a strong surge of respect for

the boy. He hadn't turned tail but had come home to face the problem in order to protect his family. It was the decision of an adult, not a child.

"Then Gideon got hurt," Joey said. "I knew then for sure it was them. It *had* to be. Nobody else would keep coming back. That's when I decided to go out and work on the fence alone. I figured they'd know I was home by then and would come looking for me. I kind of hoped they'd take the dope and leave me alone." He fell silent.

"So they found you," Nate pressed.

"Yeah. They beat me up a little, even when I told them I'd give them the drugs. I took them to where I'd buried the stuff and dug it up. I thought that was it, but they came back yesterday morning. They beat me up some more and left me chained to the tree. I guess they had second thoughts that I might tell somebody, so they decided to get rid of me."

There was more, but Gideon stepped outside into the hallway and went hunting for a coffee machine. He had plenty of his own baggage to deal with, he thought, starting with a brother he had just found, and ending with a vision he understood all too well. And that didn't even take Sara into account.

It was kind of an unsteady feeling for a man whose balance had always been perfect, he realized. He had always known where he stood on things, had always identified himself in certain ways. For years he had been Gideon Ironheart, ironworker, tough man. Cherokee half-breed who was ready and willing to make an issue of it. Yeah, he'd always seen himself clearly, and if he'd had to draw a picture, it would have been of him standing alone on a beam at nine hundred feet, steady, sure and untouched.

What a farce. Grimacing at his own foolishness, he dropped change into the coffee machine and then headed back toward the room with a cup of burned-smelling brew.

Coming from the other direction along the corridor was Micah Parish. Micah looked tired, and a layer of mud still covered his boots and splattered his uniform.

"Joey?" Micah asked.

"He's okay. We found him a couple of hours ago."

"I heard he was missing, and somebody said he'd been brought here, but nobody knew for certain what had happened."

"He's okay, Micah. Beat up, bruised, but okay. Sara and Nate are with him right now. You found that missing camper?"

"Yeah. Grizzly got her. She was in pretty bad shape when we got to her, and she'll probably need a lifetime's worth of plastic surgery." He stared past Gideon for a moment, seeing something in his mind, then shrugged it off. "You're looking ragged yourself, man."

Gideon smiled crookedly. "It was a long night for everyone."

"Faith said I was to ask you and Sara to come to dinner Saturday. Think you can make it?"

"I can't speak for Sara, but I'll be there." Gideon hesitated. "Guess I have a niece I need to visit."

Micah, who seldom smiled, smiled then. "You sure do. And you and I have a lot of missed ground to cover."

Gideon looked straight into Micah's eyes, eyes so very like their grandfather's, and saw an acceptance there that warmed him. "In case nobody ever told you, you're the spitting image of our grandfather."

Micah gave a small chuckle. "Knew it had to be somebody, and it sure as hell wasn't Dad."

Together they strolled down the hallway to Joey's room, arriving there just as the door opened and Sara, Zeke and Nate came out. Nate collared Micah immediately, drawing him aside for a low-voiced conversation.

"Ready?" Gideon asked Sara. She nodded, looking up at him with bruised eyes. "Okay," he said. "Just let me say goodbye to Joey."

The boy was staring up at the ceiling when Gideon entered the room, and he managed a crooked smile when he saw the older man. "I was stupid, huh?"

"Yep." Gideon shook his head as he looked down at the boy. "I doubt it's the first time a guy your age has done something stupid, though. Seems like I've done a dumb thing or two, even just last week. Did the sheriff say what he's going to do?''

"He said he hasn't seen any drugs, and he figures finishing out my probation on the car is enough. He made me promise I'd testify if they catch the guys who beat me up, though.'' Joey half shrugged, wincing as a bruise protested. "He also said he can yank my chain hard anytime I get out of line, so maybe it's time I straightened up.''

"How do you feel about that?''

"Like it's time I straightened up. Gideon?''

"Yeah?''

"Are you going to stick around?''

Impulsively, Gideon touched the kid's shoulder. "You bet, Joe. And this summer we'll go do the Sun Dance together.''

"You mean that?''

"I mean that. Now get some rest.'' He turned to leave and found that Sara was standing right behind him. Judging by that funny shine in her eyes, she'd been listening to every word.

Gideon hesitated, nearly overwhelmed by an urge to scoop her up and hug her to death, but then he eased by her and left her to say whatever she needed to Joey in privacy. They had to talk, he thought, but not here.

"So when are you going to do the sweat and the vision quest?'' Zeke asked as they neared the ranch.

The three of them were crowded into the cab of Gideon's truck, Sara in the middle.

"You just don't quit, do you?'' Gideon remarked.

"It's important, boy.''

"I'm still trying to absorb what happened last night.''

"And I keep telling you to stop thinking with your brain. You don't need to *absorb* anything. Your heart understands what happened.''

It seemed to, Gideon admitted to himself, but he wasn't in any mood to give Zeke the satisfaction of his agreement. Nor was he in any mood to discuss sweats and visions. He had more important things on his mind.

"Leave him alone, Grandfather," Sara said. "Gideon will do what's best for him in his own time and in his own way."

When, Gideon wondered, was the last time someone had defended him? Not caring what Zeke might think, he reached out and squeezed Sara's thigh. "You got that straight, Mouse." From the corner of his eye, he saw her blush. "We'll talk about it tomorrow, Zeke," he added as they jolted up the last few feet of rutted driveway and into the yard. "Tomorrow. Sara needs her sleep."

When he had parked the truck, he climbed out and reached back in for Sara, scorning the cast on his arm and the sling he'd long since abandoned. He ignored Zeke as if he had vanished, and turned with his woman in his arms and headed for the bunkhouse.

"Gideon…"

"Hush, Mouse. I'm a man in need."

She looped her arms around his neck and pressed her cheek to his. "In need of what?" Her question held a shiver that seemed to touch his nerve endings with fire.

"Of you," he said huskily as he climbed the steps. "I know you're tired. We'll just sleep, but, God, I need to hold you."

Sara's throat clogged with tears as her own yearning for this man filled her, making her ache with a longing so strong it hurt. "Oh, Gideon," she whispered brokenly. "Oh, Gideon."

He set her on her feet beside the bed and began to remove all the "tough" layers of her rumpled uniform. The tough side of this lady delighted him, but right now, in ways he couldn't begin to describe, he needed the soft, gentle side of her. The Mouse who had come to mean so much.

He threw her gun belt onto the dresser and pulled her shirt over her head without unbuttoning it. "We can wash up later, after we sleep," he said. He probably smelled like horse and sweat, but he didn't care. Sara smelled a little horsey, too, from their ride earlier, but he hardly noticed it compared to the sweet, warm fragrance of woman that emanated from her.

"God, you smell sweet," he told her hoarsely. "You smell like heaven."

He got her naked beneath the quilts, and moments later he joined her, taking care not to bang her with his cast. He tucked her soft bottom against his loins, wrapped his arm around her waist and dropped a kiss on her ear.

And suddenly, for the first time in his entire life, everything felt absolutely *right*.

The digital clock on the dresser said it was just after midnight. Moonlight poured through a crack in the curtains, a slender beam of silver that found its way to Sara's shoulder. Gideon lifted his head and kissed that silvered spot.

"Mmm..." Sara stirred and twisted onto her back. "Gideon..." It was little more than a sigh. Reaching up sleepily, she looped her arm around his neck and pulled him closer. "Love me...."

The sleepy, husky request electrified him. Every nerve in his body woke to sizzling life. Love her? Yes. Absolutely.

She didn't want foreplay. When his hands began to wander, she caught them and tugged him closer. "Now," she whispered in his ear. "Like this...."

With her still warm and cuddly from sleep. Feeling soft and dreamy as if all the hard edges were gone from life. He sank into her slowly, oh, so easily, until he was buried completely in her welcoming warmth. There was no urgency in him, or in her, but rather a gentle, tender heat. He slipped his arms beneath her shoulders and pressed his face into her neck and began to rock them both like babies in a cradle. Soft. Warm. Easy. And oh, so good.

Together they climbed the pinnacle slowly, almost lazily, and when they tumbled over the top it was in a deep, satisfying haze of golden warmth.

"Zeke's going to come looking for me with a shotgun."

Sara laughed softly and grabbed a handful of Gideon's long,

silky hair. Dawn's light was easing its way around the curtains now, a fragile, pink glow. "Not likely. His view of these things is decidedly unconventional." She tugged gently on his hair and for her efforts received a gentle kiss.

"I need to feed you," he said. "When was the last time we ate?"

Sara shrugged a smooth, naked shoulder. "Who cares?"

"I thought so. Too damn long. And the chores.... Damn, I clean forgot them last night. Zeke—"

"Zeke handled them," Sara said. "The same way he handled them before you arrived. Gideon, are you trying to get away from me?"

He froze just as he was bending to nibble her shoulder. Trying to get away from her? Was that what she thought? Was that how he sounded? But the truth was, he was scared she wanted to get away from him, and he was trying to sound as if he didn't care.

Slowly he lifted his head and looked straight into her eyes. The vulnerability in those soft, warm depths made him ache. She had asked the difficult question and now was awaiting his judgment. Sara Yates, who had never wanted to be a fool again, had just stepped out onto a limb and handed him a saw.

"Sara Jane Yates," he said, his voice cracking with unaccustomed feeling, "I don't ever want to get away from you."

Her breath caught, and her eyes filled. "Ever?" she repeated brokenly.

"Ever. Do you...want to get away from me?"

"Never."

Never. That one whispered word was the answer to a lifetime of prayers he hadn't even known he was making. "Hug me, Sara. God, just hug me and hold me...forever."

Two weeks later, surrounded by Gideon's relatives from Oklahoma, his new relatives in Wyoming, and by Sara's friends and neighbors, they faced each other across twenty feet of meadow up behind the ranch house. Aromas of roasting meat rose from below, where Jeff Cumberland was supervising the barbecue.

Sara still wore the white peasant blouse and prairie skirt in which she had married Gideon that morning at Good Shepherd Church. Gideon, too, wore white. White denim, white shirt, and a white head band to hold back his hair. Sara held a blanket and an ear of corn. Gideon held a blanket and a string of jerky.

Then Sara and Gideon walked toward each other, slowly, one step at a time, marking the solemnity of what they were doing. This morning they had made solemn vows. This afternoon they made an equally solemn gesture in the old Cherokee way.

When they stood only a step apart, Gideon handed her his blanket. Sara folded his blanket and hers together, then handed him the corn. He handed her the jerky.

Chester stepped forward and shook a gourd rattle. "The blankets are joined," he announced, and cheers filled the meadow.

"I love you, Mouse," Gideon said huskily, so full of the feeling he thought he would burst. In finding Sara, he had found himself, and now he was embarking on the adventure of a lifetime.

"I love you, too," she murmured back, her eyes shining with joy and wonder.

"Good," said Zeke, throwing one arm around each of them. "Now we'll have new life and laughter around here."

Gideon glanced at him and grinned. "You better believe it, old man."

"Lots of great grandchildren," Zeke continued cheerfully. "All that an old man could ask for...except one thing."

Gideon turned and looked down at the old man. "Not now," he said.

"You really need to do the vision quest, boy. *Before* you do the Sun Dance."

Gideon sighed. "*First* I need to do a honeymoon."

"When you get back, then."

"Yes, damn it, when we get back!"

Sara's laugh suddenly pealed out gaily, and Gideon looked at her. "He did it, Gideon. He did it!"

"Did what?"

"Got you to agree. When we get back, you said."

Suddenly Gideon was laughing, too. "I always knew he was going to get his way. He's an irresistible force."

"Like you," Sara said, leaning close as the whole world seemed to recede. "Like love."

Gideon hauled her into his arms and hugged her until she squeaked. "Thank God for that, Mouse. Thank God."

* * * * * *

SILHOUETTE® *Desire*®

Do you want…

Dangerously handsome heroes

Evocative, everlasting love stories

Sizzling and tantalizing sensuality

Incredibly sexy miniseries like **MAN OF THE MONTH**

Red-hot romance

Enticing entertainment that can't be beat!

You'll find all of this, and much *more* each and every month in **SILHOUETTE DESIRE**. Don't miss these unforgettable love stories by some of romance's hottest authors. Silhouette Desire—where your fantasies will always come true....

DES-GEN

If you've got the time...
We've got the
INTIMATE MOMENTS

Passion. Suspense. Desire. Drama. Enter a world
that's larger than life, where men and women
overcome life's greatest odds for the ultimate prize:
love. Nonstop excitement is closer than you
think...in Silhouette Intimate Moments!

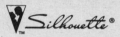

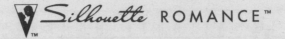

Silhouette ROMANCE™

What's a single dad to do when he needs a wife by next Thursday?

Who's a confirmed bachelor to call when he finds a baby on his doorstep?

How does a plain Jane in love with her gorgeous boss get him to notice her?

From classic love stories to romantic comedies to emotional heart tuggers, **Silhouette Romance** offers six irresistible novels every month by some of your favorite authors! Such as…beloved bestsellers **Diana Palmer, Annette Broadrick, Suzanne Carey, Elizabeth August** and **Marie Ferrarella,** to name just a few—and some sure to become favorites!

Fabulous Fathers…Bundles of Joy…Miniseries… Months of blushing brides and convenient weddings… Holiday celebrations… You'll find all this and much more in **Silhouette Romance**—always emotional, always enjoyable, always about love!